Fork Always

THE SHORE

Leif Garbisch

ISBN: 0615664520
ISBN 13: 9780615664521

Iron heart, I run as if knowing
Why as if knowing
What I am doing
Ever within I head outside
In wind, the winter, and the sun
Breathing air and forging I run
Truth the magnet
That I am

He enters this world like a new thought. This is how creation must've begun. No words, no fanfare, only arrival in time. Has he come because of the death of the girl? Is he here to whisk the young woman to the heavens or, even better, to magically return her to life on earth? And is the man really a man? I'm just asking. It all depends on how you look at things. To me, from my preliminary investigations, he might be a man, but as likely a woman, a spiritual presence, or a breath of fresh air in an unfortunate situation. It's not so important, the profile. He's difficult to see, but easy on the mind. And to this end, into this imaginary room, its one window blown wide with six o'clock light, the sunlaced curtains drawn left and right, comes a man bearing water – I'll stick with that description. He's soft as the spill of evening out of day, untroubling as darkness to a bat.

What's he want here? He watches over the place like dusk. Maybe he hopes to reestablish what's been lost and bring it back to life – if that's even possible. And who is he, really? He's a likeness, a friend, he's somehow familiar – a tree's brown bark, fruit on its branches, a light blue shirt with rip and wrinkles, a ripe peach sky, sweet to the eye. He's the long steeped day now stopping by now stooping down now staying along side.

Still too ambiguous, isn't it? The picture is all over the map. I can't pin down the man. I give no details about the dead girl, either. And I don't explain why the room is not an actual room but imagined. It's as if we're all still figuring it out. And while we learn, the man fills the place with a sense of wonder large as the ocean and with a scope of freedom beyond the reach of stars.

He fills this room now with the end of day, settling here in his diaphanous clothes that reveal the inner workings of light.

He's easy on his feet, too, like some deer stepping through the darkening hour. Put an ear to his quiet, if you want. Listen as he nears the young woman's body. It's getting serious now. He's a drop of water on the tip of a leaf. The droplet glints in the sun, holding the light for a moment, a moment more. He's not quite ready to speak, not yet but soon: Five fifty-one, twenty-two seconds and counting.

The walls are vague and mutable in this room. The furniture is imaginatively placed – a bed, a lamp, one table, and curtains. The room looks real enough. Who am I to judge? If there's a bed here, there's a bed. If a lamp, a lamp. While outside the room, the light of evening plays. Earth spreads unavoidable. And the last day of September slowly turns, unnoticing, by.

September. Earth.

Say a person dies at the edge of the woods. Say she dies while looking at the windblown trees against the sky. Say she had other plans. Could she really just release her hold on this world without a fight? Would she allow herself to be drawn off by uninvited spirits? Could she quietly and without resistance blend with the soil like soulless matter? I can't speak for her, so it seems I've come to ask, to find some answers. There are things this evening I'm beginning to see: grasses, sticks, small blue stones, and a squirrel in the shadow of the sunflowers there. No need to coax the sublime out of the ordinary. It comes with the territory.

And, look, there's someone new, too. It's a boy nearby, as though prompted by an imagination. It's not my imagination. Maybe the boy has got something to say about the drop-by man who kneels beside the young woman, waiting for just the right moment to tell her she has died at the edge of these woods. After being struck by a falling limb this very minute, the young woman is dead. But what does she know about her new way of life? It's a shocking feeling for sure. A blow to the head. A rotten limb. No more time on earth. The end of days. The residues only of loving touches. It can't be true. She's not even twenty.

Let's look at things from her perspective, even if for the moment she's lost her way and sees herself as an accidental old woman in the sadness of her room. It seems very likely that there's also a man inside this place, but she's not interested in him just yet. Possible, too, that there's a boy outdoors on his bike, if she would remember and lift her eyes.

The woman here is alive, lying upon her bed, suffering an unhappy life. She thinks this is her last bit of room. She's got wrinkles and spotty skin. Breathing is difficult. Her eyes are heavy. She's seen her life come this far and has nothing further to say. But I do. She's not old. I'm telling you she's young. This woman is young and a man has come to her room and he resembles the evening. There's a window in the room and a world out the window that if we're lucky we'll get to. There is light coming through. It's good to see.

And what about that boy? Out in the evening, no urgency to him, he spins on his bike. He's noticed through the window, briefly followed. What the hell's he doing, the woman thinks as she looks. He's well known to the rurals, and loved by his sister. A cellist they say, he can be heard playing into the night: Bach preludes, Schumann fantasy pieces. He plays his music the way the security light on the north side of Captain D's barn plays its bulb. That light never shuts off, it seems, like this boy who spins and spins on his bike, the cello he's carried with him placed carefully in its case to the side, protected.

This same boy was hanging once with a group by *Alvins Outboard And Deli*, and it was M who asked him how much he spins – no, how much he practices. Practice what? the boy asked, as if he didn't know. That tuba thing you play, said M. Oh, maybe three hours. So like a half hour each day, M said, calculating. More like two or three hours each day, our boy said. And one of the girls, probably B, let out a breath like you've got to be kidding. Like when dyou have time to just, you know, whatever? Chill? Do nothing? Sleep? Eat? It was just a small gasp. Still, there's always something great released in every sound. That's what the boy's sister says – that everything in the world has a spirit released by its expression. Everyone, too.

But if there is no expression, what spirit then? What if something hovers just out of the reach of sound? What then? If there's nothing to hear, what does this boy know of the quiet, unspeaking man who comes to the room, bringing with him a handful of water?

Hey, bub. On the bike. Buckaroo. What dyou know?

You can ask all you want. He won't answer. The brother rides through the stillness of the room, wheeling as if to rouse it. Nebulous himself, as if he too is imagined, hazily remembered to life.

People call him John, quoting the Bible. He is verse thirteen, or thirteen years old, and they say he increases, crosses the hours, leans into the world more healthy as he turns. Talk about heart. Dr. Payn could give you literature from medical journals, but who has the time, just get to the point: John keeps getting stronger. His mother might send him to public school next year with M and B and them. Or maybe to the city, or to that school for young performing artists up in Wisconsin. There's lots of thought that needs to go into the decision, though sometimes, as his sister once said, too much thought breeds inaction. Though, did she really say "breeds"? Doesn't seem like a word she'd use. She made the statement some weeks ago, then left in such a hurry, and nobody asked her if those were the exact words. So, it remains a question to this hour.

Still John. Back to John. Spinning John: Junny Pelagios, fearless as the sea, sent to play, to bear witness to the evening, one sneaker untied, holes in both knees, nowhere to go but back and forth. He hasn't yet kissed a girl, outside his mother. Wondered, though. Thought about it. Watched their lips move. Especially Jess. Jess got him thinking, made him move his quiet self a little closer to listen in. He's seen Jess's lips just waiting, waiting to kiss that flute. She sat with the instrument poised once, saw him. John-a-gold, red faced, watching her. Waiting and waiting for the right moment to play, to engage, to... He missed it. Missed the chance. And it's like his sister told him, he's a good-looking guy for a brother. Like his sister said, he'd be the man if he put down his instrument, picked up clues, and livered himself to action. Did she really say "livered?"

She says lots of things to him that usually he notes. And even when she doesn't speak, it all sounds, whatever the sounds, like music anyway. Voices, wheelings, wind through the leaves. But John's as unsteady as a memory, now. Biking blue, the blurring sun alongside. Legs must be tired. He's left his cello on the ground, like I said, as he cuts a tight curve upon a world that doesn't feel pain and doesn't slow his pleasure. And where his feet scrape the ground, clouds of dust arise. And where his face catches the sun, there's no denying a ton a tone of life that's released to this world.

This boy, like the furniture – bed of earth and stable world – is part of the room, but what does John know of walls or of some man who streams here with the purl of water in his hands? Not much. Road, branches, hissing leaves, that is John's world. In all his verve, in his swerving back and forth, he didn't witness any man. He didn't see some guy enter the picture, as though to John it wasn't part of his experience, his ride. I'm not saying the man never came. Maybe I'm saying that John isn't actually here.

Seems like he's here, though, doesn't it? Why would you doubt your senses? John spins and kicks up golden dust. The spin is real. The dust is real. The gold, the trees, the sky, this world. And then he vanishes. John and his bike and his cello are gone. That is real, too. But the dust of thought, or the thought of the dust remains. A golden dust sifts rapidly through the dry September air and drifts, at least some hint of it, through the open window, following the man into the room, its one window blown wide. The afternoon lake of light. The sunloved curtains, left and right.

Now the quiet young man from earlier, the one who travels light and carries water, he's the one who is most real here. Water sloshes from the cup of his hands and spills upon the ground. How has he carried this water with him? I wish I could tell you. I wish you could hear him. Maybe you can. There's an ocean in his hands, the shore at his feet. Maybe birds, maybe waves. These sounds are the beginning of recognition. And his abundance, too – hear that, if your brain can hear dimensions. It's everything he is, everything he does. Avowing himself up raiser of she.

Ave. Ave, he calls, as he enters the room.
The boy, as I said, is gone. Long gone.
Ah-vay, again.

There's no bike, no boy, no cello, no music, no.

The man's voice doesn't do the trick. Ave doesn't stir, and it seems very likely that something is terribly wrong. So, softly the young man approaches this person lying still, her seemingly aged body and incurable sadness. She is not what she thinks. She thinks she is old and dying. She is not who she sinks. She sinks and is lost. How to break her spell, he wonders, without intervening.

Into the room comes a praiser of she. In the cup of his hands there's a bowl he carries. It's a definite bowl. It is blue ceramic like a small fruit bowl – green apple seawater, orange sun going down, raspberries ripe and ready life. Have one. The clear water within curves up the banks of the bowl, humming slightly so that if you put your ear to the brim you'd discern in the hum a wish like distant surf, the shy hiss of sedge in wind, a voice of many words at once.

The man places the bowl on the bedside, which is a bedside of leaves and sticks and dirt. You see, Ave's not really in some room, but outside. She's not an old woman, but nineteen. And she's no longer alive. Or is she? The man doesn't dispute Ave's sense of her body or her room. Give her a moment. Give her her due. Doesn't matter just yet who she is, but who she wishes to be. Doesn't matter just now where she is, but where she wishes to be. And a seaish smell lifts a scene right out of the woman's body and places it at her feet, in front of her voice. It's like saying: Here's the world you want to be looking at. Here's the world you want to be talking to.

Ave, he calls, whispering the syllables.

Ah-vay, again.

No slosh or splash to the water now, yet the old woman awakes at the thought of an ocean and broad soft sands, gulls circling and the sky achingly bright. What a beautiful world – that. The woman watches the curves of foodfanatical gulls. She sees the shallow prints of her own feet where she stands on the beach. How did she get here? She doesn't wonder. A beautiful world – this. She doesn't see a local woods with broken limbs and an unreachable future. She doesn't see a withered self, a finished self, now.

Like a child, Ave darts up the coast, followed by gulls. She slows without warning and dashes off again, looking for what the tide has brought in – some drift words, a usable language, a voice from the distance that may be her own. It is sayings of life that must be true. This is what she wants. And she runs looking for these words as if they were shells, calcareous fragments or fully formed cockles and whelks. She runs, looking for words to claim, for any shellish substance that she could call her own and speak with her anxious tongue. Running, she searches the sands by eye by ear by rote. Gulls like halos overhead. Gulls like flies buzzing round her. She has no food and waves them off. She has no time to give. Words like shells, like bits of polished glass. Please. Where are you? I can't say. I can't hear. I can't stand the silence any longer.

Why has the sea forsaken her? Ave loves the sea. The sea to whom she has always given the scan of her eyes, the score of her voice, her musings and her magnitude however small. Shells immortal shells, she runs – any fragment, so to speak. Why won't the surf give back from its abundance? Why won't the hiding sands reveal their bounty?

And why again. Ave lies upon her bed, bound to the earth, unable to move, unable to sigh. Why? The sea disappears. Everything gone. And someone who stares at me, she thinks. God, who is he again and again and. The smell is dust is crud is an acrid, slowing light. An old woman now in the quiet, dying room again.

It would confuse anyone who's lately been to visit this woman, how she got old so quick. It would puzzle any recent guest, John for instance, to hear her voice sputter and quake like a tenuous gas powered surrey. John, who came by late afternoon the day before yesterday with his dusty face, his green apple, and music that filled the room. It would surprise John most of all, as for him she is constant – a sister like the tides, an audience like the stars, a certain slant of steadfast light. And though she watched through the window as he spun, though she lifted her head and smiled for him when he came through the door, though she finally accepted his apple, he wondered where her mind lay because it didn't seem to be with him.

He said: What's wrong with you today? And she didn't answer, though she may have thought, You're one to talk, spinning out there like a dust storm, riding all the way here with a cello strapped to your back. What's wrong with *me*? But she said nothing. He sat with his cello and tightened the bow. She could think of nothing wrong. You're so much in love, he said. You're always in love. Love love love. Don't you ever just want to be out and answer to no one? Not have to come home for any reason? Not have to think of anyone anything else? Not have to have to. I'm never gonna be tied. It's not gonna happen. She stared at him. You don't get it, she said. I like who I am.

How long's it been since you've spoken those words, Ave? Years, it seems. Invented decades, even. Since you were young, like a weed young, like a chick a calf a bale of fresh cut grass young. Since you were young and someone beautiful, young and something lively like opinion, something expressive like fire, young and the whole world crossed your skin like hands and your lips were moist and your cheeks were flush and his, some other his, Oh God, God, what was his name? his breath was just barely and – your beautiful blue-eyed one – his eyes sung all sides of you – thighs and mind, your shoulders, breasts, your sandy feet, your soul. Remember that? Remember when you were young, filled by Nico's breath, his shallow breathing? Nico, Nico, yes, Nicolas. You and he and full with, full of easygoing love, in love with him with you with.

Because you are old now, so old and difficult it seems. Decades away from that time. Decades away from any ease of life or lift of love. Decades away and lost, scratching your back on the leafy sheets. There is no shore, you think. There's nowhere to move. Only this: A mysterious failure to be. This inability to live and this inability to die, even. Quiet now, listening for surf in the wellblown trees. Stopped under the evening sky that is no comfort. It is no comfort because you're completely restless. And you're alone, waning with discontent, as though you're in a nursing home waiting to die. As though your death-watch goes on and on, and the bed is a mess and the world stinks and your rough breath struggles and why are you here when you want to be running home?

Why are you stopped still on your back, unseeing what is outside, unspeaking what is in?

What's happened to you, anyway? A limb has struck you. You lost to a limb. Your numbered days have come to an end. How could the wind, how could the world have done this injustice? You'd rather not think. Besides, it may not be true. You might just be tired. You might just be quiet. You might be yourself. Who in this world could assume you're not?

How long since you've moved, Ave? How long since you've spoken? Maybe a day, maybe ten thousand. Look, I've bought the shore back to you, sister. Take a listen to this. The creek, the bay, the ocean, too. I've never known you not to love. Never a day. Not I. And I've been home with you, and I've been out with you. But you are quiet, still. All to save your breath for what? For living or for dying? And no one may answer. No one may say but you.

LAMENTATION

Dying dying, the light
and each person who is
full of life.

Not really all that amazing, is it? Death's been going on since life came out. Can't outstare dying. It'll always win. Still, dying's not the news. The news here's that I've got my words back. They're all in a bucket, and I can pull them one by one and line them up like so.

Look what I've collected off the sands. It's years and years of words. Every word is a thought that first knocked on my door, and I opened the door to let in the thought and offer it language, like coffee or tea. That's when I was real interested in the world. My bucket's full of driftwood and shells, smooth and knotty, chipped and torn, sand dollars, heart urchins, beach glass, all for me. Makes me want to speak again, just seeing them. Of course, I don't know what good I'd say. My life's so getting me down. My impermissible wasn't it miserable life – if I could only know why.

Mark my treasures, though. Something brought me to this place years ago – birth, I suppose. Maybe I wasn't born right here, but it was near. My God, I was possible then. But what was I trying to say? I was hurled to the world by the longing for a good life, and the passion came through my throat so crazy, it was cacophony, a mayhem even.

Ah, I cried to be on earth again. Ah, I cried. A and A and praise, I cried. Again, I cried. Praise. It was a vowel and senseless rattle, the morning of my first day. There wasn't a knowing I, just me, the crier, bundled upon my mother who dozed in the high marsh, and my father who paced and panicked, then ran for help. He was as far from home as any man can be whose mind is on his troubles. And somewhere down the way from us, lay the foamfreaking fastspeaking sea, the springlusty sea with each indifferent wave, one hello goodbye after another hello goodbye after an ad infinitum adios other. While somewhere up, the morning sky stretched loudly, its trumpeting sun with ceaseless east-less work to do. And above all else, there were the disappearing heavens, that otherworld I'd come from, where my forgotten self roosted far from my reach, dark with her overcoat and silent as God.

Even so, wet and green upon the lowlands I began to live. I was born right there in the marsh, where the sanguine grasses flit between the trees and gave themselves to blowing and growing but not to me. Why not to me? Everything happened so fast, and just as fast it all was gone. I only remember each loss. First the going of the sun, that abandoning light. Then the coming of night and every star, distant from me and dispassionate all. No one answered my birth or my bleating. And yet I was so hungry and wanting. I cried to be. That is how I met the world, disappointment at every turn and no sense of belonging.

"Your soliloquy moves me," said the young waterbearer. "It comes from your current mood of separation." Crouching beside the bed, the man studied the wrinkled words and flesh of the woman. "I'd have you note, however, that you've always belonged. The stars were with you at your birth. The shimmering marsh grass and the clear blue sky, all pleased and present, all in attendance upon your body on the morning of your first day. In your beginning was the word that greeted you on earth. It spoke itself in everything. It actually gave you great joy. Slowly you learned to recognize and record the language, and only in the course of your death have you shut down. Only within your great sorrow is the joy of—"

"Excuse me," said Ave. "Do I know you?"

"I'm sorry."

"Sorry. More an attribute than a name, isn't it?"

The young waterbearer did not have time to answer.

"Attendance upon my body! I'm not some queen, Sorry. What a joke."

"It's just—"

"It's not just at all," said Ave. "Nothing here is just. And I'm insulted by your insinuation of my death. Don't you see me a lie before you?"

"A lie?"

"Va. Va. Alive. Why are you so rude to me?"

"I'm sorry," said the waterbearer.

"I know who you are. That doesn't help explain things."

"What I mean is that there's already been a lot of misunderstanding in a small space of time."

"A smallest of minds," repeated Ave, incorrectly. "Another nice thing to say to me."

"Let's start over," said the young man. "I'll be different. I'll know you better by asking."

"Easier said than done."

"I'm game."

"I thought you were Sorry," said Ave. "What fowl are you now? A native prank? Some wild ploy?"

"The thing is, I'd rather hear your words," said the man. "It's why I'm here."

"Did you say words or worth?"

"Words," said the man.

"It's the craziest thing, to burst into my room for words. I could show you the door. I could give you the boot. They good enough words for you?"

"It's a start. What I need are words that approach life with open eyes. What's here in this room is a fabricated image. I'd like to hear what's real."

"Why would you use such a word?" asked Ave.

"Real?"

"No, fabricated. Name something I've made-up."

"The room, for one," said the man. "The walls you've concocted. Your decrepit, crusty age. Your wrinkles and misery."

"Is it the only reason you've come, to insult me?"

"No," said the man.

"Look, Sorry. You can hear, I'm not very hospitable at the moment." Ave hoped that this visitor might take the hint and leave.

"It's okay," said the man.

"Not for me," said Ave.

"I could suggest you do something about it."

"Like offer you the door?" Ave again tried to encourage his exit.

"Not that."

"It was just a thought," said Ave, resignedly. "What is is is."

And silence followed. Stillness filled the room. The sun slid through the folds of sky. Low sun, quiet. Gleam green leaves. There was an uncertain tightness to the air that if it had been, say, a cello string or guitar string, the room would've been a quarter turn from snapping.

"So tell me," began the young man, unbothered by the tension of things. "Where were you born?"

"What kind of suggestion is that?"

"No suggestion. Just a simple question."

"Is this an interrogation?"

"No."

"Why do you care, Sorry, about where I was born?"

"I'm interested."

"It's not interesting."

"I'd still like to know. Was there any water nearby? The Chesapeake, the Hudson Bay, the Adriatic or Tasman Sea? Did the sands sing or were they silent? How about meadows or a soybean field? Anything you remember? The Brazilian Highlands, The Paterlands, where the mountains moan at each passing ship? I'm just wondering: Were you born in old Croatia, new California, upon the fens of Black Tourmaline, or among the assorted slopes and eases of Finas Madriff?"

"Sounds like you've been all over."

"Not really."

"What brings you here, Sorry?"

"You mostly."

"Me? Did you say mimosa?"

"We have something in common," said the young man. "I just can't put my finger on it."

"Well, stop pressing me," said Ave.

"But I'm hoping you can help me trace the trajectory of your life."

"Yeah, it has been a tragic thing, hasn't it."

"Trajectory, I said."

"I'm all over the place," said Ave. "An incomplete disappointment."

"I don't think so," said the man.

"Don't think in your own time. I'm telling the truth here. The tides were modest where I came from. A simple rise and fall, like me. But you're unlikely to know the spot precisely, as it's a fuzzy way I recall the past. I'm so old, you see. My mind is gone. You were right to call it small. Who I'm from is hazy. How I'm form is lame. Is that the coarseness of me you're after?"

The young man gestured for her to go on.

"My mother was a highland breeze at birth."

"The wind?"

"She was softskinned and sang a lot," said Ave. "But the willow switch reddened her in the early years. Not the gentle sun, as should've been the case. Rough treatment made her run, or maybe it was just that she wanted to live with the Gypsies in the woods. She'd visit their nomad camps nightly, studying medicinal herbs with Elena, watching over babies and bears, hennaing her hair and hands, and dissolving into the invisibility of things."

"Was that good for her?" asked the man.

"My mother wanted to be seen," said Ave. "So, it wasn't all good. Soon, she went out on her own. She fought for her self so she wouldn't disappear. Figuring that no one else would help her, she had to do all the work herself."

"Was she able?"

"Who am I to say, but she survived a thousand and one questions about her early life. Do you get the point?"

"Not yet."

"You're slow, Sorry. Opposite of her. She was an acrobat by trade, a star of the night."

"Your mother?"

"That's who we're talking about," said Ave. "These are the facts I've learned. She turned for leaders in their luxurious bedrooms as they sat in their silk drawers and watched, turning on themselves, if you know what I mean. And she turned for the streetdwellers in their hovels and their nakedness. But after one too many propositions, she spun under the guise of a man, as she was afraid the truth of her sex would ruin her body once and for all."

"And you're sure this is your mother?" said the young man.

"Of course I'm not sure. But it's worth a try. My mother was strong as any man, and that I know. She threw herself a mile high, flipped for one and all, landed on her feet, high atop the grassy wold."

"What wold?"

"This world, of course. She sat alone and looked out at the world, forgiving it for all it hadn't given her. Upbeat and smiling no matter. That's how she was. Nothing got her down, not beatings or betrayals, not being struck by a branch, not even gravity. She rolled down the hill with dizzying speed, and stood up wobbly and pleased on the shore with the other deposits. Even lost her life once, so her lyric goes, but resurrected herself on the spot, just like that tune I once heard."

"What tune is that?"

Ave sung:

"Many and many a day I rise.
This life's no burden on me.
I've got my hands right around its neck.
Each time I die I demand: Resurrect!"

"Never heard that one," said the young man.

"It's me all over," said Ave from her bed. "I'll never die by being knocked, not by falling. I'm inundated with motherly endowments. I'm strong."

"And what about your father?"

"What about him?"

"You had one, right?"

Ave thought a moment. She formed her words before speaking.

"My mother was a landsong headstrong acrobat, a runner with life, and my father was a lady wailer. He phased all moony with crazy moods."

"What's a lady wailer?" asked the young man. "Did he howl at the sight of a pretty woman?"

"Is it earwax or are you purposely trying my patience? My good Papa was a woeful, lazy whaler, if ever there was one. He was always looking for new ships, new captains, always falling overboard and being pulled to by the chuckling, oily crew. The slacker slept on deck irregular hours, imaginary times, looking for rest from work. He took no pleasure in killing the moving creatures that had life, but he did take a boot now and then from Captain Daniels. He took splinters from his own back, too, and ate salt spray for breakfast and beaten biscuits for dinner. Blood turned him squeamish, intestines twined in his dreams, whale blubber made him sickish, and he cried at the sight of every death."

"Sounds like your father didn't know what he was getting into."

"So, why'd he keep at it? That's what I'd like to know. Once, as a twinkle-eyed mate told the story, my namby-pamby father was thrown overboard by raging Captain Dan Eel. He just up and chucked him over, as the boat sped ahead at fourteen knots. But as fate would have it my father found his way back – a miracle of God – back to the ship upon a timely whale. The captain was all bug-eyed with the miracle. Here God sent one right whale and a wrong, useless man. Captain Dan Yell gunned the right with my father aboard, but the whale was Pop's savior and did not sink. She remained by the ship till my father was taken back. The captain stormed to the galley, spitting curses to blacken the air, while my father held to his native smile and his whalebone knife that he carved himself. The world is a wonderful sight, a warm-blooded sight, a leviathan of wonder, he said to whoever. But no one was listening, not even the rats. Then with the oil of the kill,

Pop lighted his lamp, because the stars were too weak to see by. He honored the beast with lamplit words, some poem probably in the style of Melville. Or, as my father preferred to say, he honed his words by the light of the whale. Rammed by waves, my father read his poets and philosophers in lush and rocking light, and when he got home he kept on rocking wherever he stood, rising sinking, up and down, feeling the everpresent sea in his body."

"Do you share that with your father?" asked the young man.

"We share some cadence for the rise and fall. He gave me words and how to use them. Whereas my mother gave me the strength to say."

"How was it they met?"

"You sure want to know a lot about my parents."

"If it's not too much trouble."

"It is what it is," said Ave, thinking. "They met at port. Where else? That's it. The light was draining, and nefarious sights took hold of their eyes."

"Nefarious?"

"Don't mean to shock you," said Ave. "But it's a wicked world, a lascivious seductive place sometimes. All the erotic interests. Yet for Mops and Pops there was real love in the air, don't you think? Well, you might call it love. Or you might call it fate."

"What do you call it?"

"I call it luck," said Ave. "They walked toward each other, both looking out to sea, when low and behold they struck, kaplunking off the quay."

"Sounds romantic," said the young man.

"It was late evening and the moon was rising. They surfaced in the oily water, flailing their arms like drowning kids, kicking and screaming till they remembered they could swim and free-styled their way to shore."

"Lucky they remembered."

"Like I said, lucky for me, I guess," said Ave. "It was sultry that evening. Moonlight melted over the harbor, and their bodies were hot. They stood, dripping on the grass, barefoot, longing for one another, listening to the wild, rattling world all around: Voices cracked from all directions in drunken tones and highballed pitches.

There were urges to dance to the penny pippin pearls of the God rot world, to life to life the low down high game, to body mechanics, to the soft bosom and the blush to see, round after round for everybody, to drink to dance and to sing, to the soul's embodiment, its root in matter better ever yet. Lie with me on the soft mat grass. I'm juiced I'm juicing I'm just for you. There were literally hundreds of lines, most of them bad. It was loud, it was lewd all around them as they walked to somewhere better, among the trees and flowers. For my parents it was the first taste of love. They burned for each other till their clothes were dry, were singed, were almost ash, ready to disintegrate. They walked to a private place, kissing here and there as people do. They discovered just how long they could wait, which wasn't long at all, and soon enough their clothes were gone, burned clean off. They merged, naked, on the dark soft moss near the ivy, hearing nothing of that outer, other world. No more than breathing, lick, and kiss. No more than their own collision and fusion, their first courting impetus, coitus uninterruptus."

"I'm surprised you know such details," said the young man. "And that you're comfortable saying them."

"It boggles my mind to think, but such is how life gets its start on earth," said Ave. "A moment in the shadows. Two half cells that come together. It may be all there is to me."

"Sex?"

"What's wrong with sex?"

"I didn't know you were so interested."

"Well, I am," said Ave. "It was that meeting got my matter started. How else would I be here, talking to you? I clicked into place, and come spring nine months later I was born."

"That was quick. What'd they call you when you were born?"

"Ungrateful, but it wasn't my fault. There wasn't much kindness in my house. I'd have been grateful for a heavier load of loving. I'd have been grateful for a lighter load of siblings. I have five brothers and seven sisters, or four and three or two and none. What difference does it make? Did I ever meet them? Did we play music together or quote movies or books? Did I ever know their names?"

"Did you?" asked the young man.

"Did I what?"

"Get to know your brothers? Do you remember their names?"

"What does it matter now?" said Ave. "What does anything matter now?"

These words silenced things for a while, though who knows how long a while it was. It seemed like hours to an insider, but it was almost no time at all to the trees and the setting sun outside.

"You're a funny ghost," said Ave, upon finding her words again. "I don't mean that you make me laugh. You're just strange, and I can't figure you out. But I'm okay with you and your questions. I'm glad that you're out there and not in me. I'm glad you are not I. I mean it. It gives the world some hope. Don't I deserve some recognition for suggesting that the world outside me might be better than the world that's in?"

"You're such a knot of sadness," said the young man.

"You don't know what it was like to be me growing up."

"Do you?"

"Not really, but I can imagine. I watched other girls with their mothers, hand in hand, their hair full of shine and their faces all rosy like they had on make-up. I saw smiling pips with their pops, learning to shoot cans with rifles and to toss stones in the creek. I wanted to shine and rise and learn. I wanted to travel like a stone to one perfect splash. Instead, I woke like a bug in my sun-starved room, sitting in dust, in darkness, alone. Who was I? Left to myself. Unwanted."

"Are you sure about that?"

"I told you before that I'm not sure of anything," said Ave. "Just, I wish I hadn't been me."

"Who else could you have been?"

"Someone. I don't know her name. Somebody more vibrant and happy. Maybe I'm in her shadow as I speak. Do you know someone who casts a shadow?"

"Well, I —"

"I was a very sensitive girl, you might say melancholic, always lounging on the language of my own death, like Hannah."

"Hannah?"

"Don't confuse me with your questions. What I'm telling you is true. Why else would I say it? I should be praised that I didn't give up. I didn't slit my wrist and drain away or jump from a bridge when the river called. I pushed on. I struggled through. I limped to this age. And here I am, in my regretful way. And why shouldn't I be? How can I be happy with how things have gone? I come to the end with absolutely nothing. Even so, you press me for something to satisfy your needs. You don't get that what you're asking for is ungiveable, ungettable. You ask for the life of me that's beyond the truth. Who are you anyway to ask me things?"

"No, not so," said the young man.

"You are Nonatso? Is that Japanese or what?"

"It's a deserted landscape you paint. There's something you've lost sight of that makes it that way. Do you know what I mean?"

Ave lay cold, almost weightless in her bed, her spotted flesh, and her old fragile hands unmoving.

"I see you in the dark, is what I see," said the man. "But who through the fields made her way this morning, and who now makes her way like the sun going down, like the stars coming up?"

"Who?" said Ave, almost shouting it. "That's what I asked you. Who?"

Ave lay on her back on a bed of the earth, staring, not seeing. Who. The evening sky was somewhere out there, squirrels busy gathering nuts. The questions, the answers. All of this. Who.

"Nonatso?"

"I'm here."

"What about me?" asked Ave.

"You're here, too," said the young man. "But you're certainly not yourself at the moment."

"What moment is it?" asked Ave.

"Just after you've died," said the young man."

"You're making that up."

"Why would I do that?"

"To make me feel worse."

"Does it?"

"No," said Ave. "But I forgive you."

"Do you want to feel worse?"

"I forgive you for being inconsiderate," said Ave. "It's because you're young. You've got the world and your entire life in front of you. I bet you don't care about others."

"I care."

"So tell me – no more ruse and no being rude. What's your real name?"

"There're so many," said the young man.

"I only need one."

"Then consider Samot Fog. There was this girl once who wrote a story for her brother. Do you remember it?"

"Why would I?"

"Well, in it, she named someone Samot Fog. I don't know why, but I sort of like the name – a spiritual glow to it, I think. But, don't get me wrong, I'm no apparition."

"Too bad, I'm fond of Parisians. What is it again?"

"Samot Fog."

"Samot. Like the fish?"

"A variation on the word. Born of my parents up river, I have traveled downstream ever since."

"A likely story. I have met the smell of you before, in the bogs and fens, by the city gates, in the ports and harbors, kneeling in the streets in your own stale urine. At best you are like the shore you mentioned, the carcass of some icky thing brought in by the tide. At worst, like the devil, come to take my soul. You can't have it, wicked sand man.

"Did you hear me, Samot? I said **No**. Laugh all you like, harass me with your hovering and hopping nearby. I'm not going to feed you anything."

"You're thinking of gulls," said Samot. "Do you remember how you fed the seagulls stale bread on those hot afternoons? They'd call their friends. Soon it was a party on the shore."

"How do you know what I did?"

"The waves lapped relentlessly and the graywhite gulls sang lovesongs to you."

"Rave white girls handed love thongs to you."

"You're mistaking my words."

"You're the one walking on the shore with enthusiastic little missy, taking her to the marshweeds and doing whatever. You think I don't know what goes on with lust junkies like you. Erotic ideas. Fantasy feasts. Blooming joys. Men thinking women, thinking always of taking another and another till they've known them all. It's skin and boners. Watching her disrobe, a slip of the hand and all of it is offer. I'm yours, she says. Entering the room naked, her breasts appointed to you, her legs to wrap you with. And you all honor. Honor, honor. You offer your honor, then off her again. Endless sex and body contagious. The little heart tattooed on the small of her back. It's all this titillating love that sticks to my mind like a jingle.

"Sampson? Salmon? God, where are you?"

Ave lay in wait, obsessed with love.

"You're so young, is all," she said to the air. "Starry eyed. Weak willed. Think you've got control. But you don't know what the world'll throw at you. I wish I could guide you. I wish I could warn you."

Ave lay in her bed, longing for connections.

"You're stubborn, Mr. Flog. Beating me till I'm black and blue. Seems you're not moving from my bedside till you get the better of me. How annoying. What do you suggest I do?"

"Not protest so much," said Samot.

"Just give into you, little fish?"

"I don't see it so negatively."

"Of course you wouldn't," said Ave. "You have nothing to lose."

"But I do," insisted Samot Fog.

❖

"In the sunlight you're beautiful," said Samot.

"And in the dark?"

"There's something about you that glows."

"I'm not pregnant, if that's what you mean," said Ave. "Haven't slept with a man since... Well, it's been decades, I'm sure."

"Something shines through you," said Samot. "I'd like to hear how it works."

"You're asking too much," said Ave.

"What am I asking? I could just watch you unfold like a story."

"So old and boring?"

"I didn't say that."

"Time holds me in his fist," said Ave. "It clenches my life and squeezes my blood to bitter stillness. What could I say that wouldn't end like this, only more so? How depressing that would be."

"I know there's more to you than bitters," said Samot. "More to know. Mortar, Mortimer, morsels. If I could hear."

"You're so demanding," said Ave. "Like a father after my best. Did you say we are related? Are you one of my grandkids grown up? A doctor, even? Did I have some kid who had some kid who's a doctor now? I don't remember anything. You're a pretty good doc, though. When was the last time I had such range of motion with language? Must have been fifty seventy years ago. I remember when I was nineteen and had a boyfriend named something. Are you nineteen yet, Mr. Doctor Frog? I bet you are. You've got to be at least. Young, with everything in front. The whole world. It's a miracle you found me. Like when my father came in on his whale. Only a smaller miracle, as I'm not much of a claim."

The thought silenced her.

"I notice you didn't dispute that." The old woman Ave looked young Samot Fog in the eye as he hovered over her bed like some lofty bird, a drift of cloud, one soft color on the ceiling of her room. "My last visitor was none like me, more like a nun. She was dressed in black, had lots of hair all loose upon her head with wisps upon her face. She spoke on and on about death. Sister Hannah. She was artfully sad, I think. She knew people who had died, crashed a few funerals. She even saw ghosts. She went off and on about death. Off and on. Death sure brings people awfully down, don't you think. Or maybe it was something else like her hair that weighed on her. She was someone I liked to see and listen to. I think of her as a good friend, someone I loved like a sister."

"Hannah?"

"That's a better question. Yes," remembered Ave. "Then there was that Appleseed lad. He's always popping in, isn't he? He's curious about death, too, and God and the sound of owls at night. Sometimes, if a person is old like me and about to die, people say under their breath, Maybe she's close to God, because sure as hell she's far from this world. So they think I'm onto something big."

"Are you?" asked Samot."

"Am I what?"

"Onto something big."

"Emptiness, I suppose," said Ave. "I can't stand what I'm missing. All the years during which I grew old, and no one did I share them with. I can't stand the sense of not having any more. It's not just flowers and soup and the wind on my skin, but lots of things, his eyes and hands and the sure sound of his voice."

"Who?"

"How can I say him," said Ave. "The small of my life is largely he."

"Nicolas?"

"Don't bring him out," said Ave. "It was so long ago. Once there were flowers, there was wind, you know what I mean, lying on his chest when I was a kid, him touching my leg, hand on my leg, tasting me with his eyes, music and movies and plans and plays and just trying to be – do you know what I mean – be a decent good person, a part of the world, a... Course, with the sister she wanted to capture my soul for God, but I told her God wouldn't want such a catch as me. Do you believe in God? Do you? Do you, young man? Angels and heavenly hosts? Raphael? Magdalene? Madonna? Holy nights and a light beyond the daylight that you can't see with your eyes? Stuff like that. How do you see if it's not with your eyes? How do you know God's there if He's not right there with you, listening to your life unfold? Now, wait a minute, Mr. Frog. You're not God, are you? Of course, you're not. What am I saying? Do you believe in faith, though? Do you believe in hope? It's love that makes you larger, because the more you love, the more you appear in the world, like budding leaves in springtime, millions at once, and birds in the morning, scores and scores. I remember a morning once. Brother Oscar was there. Do you remember Brother Oscar? Coming up the path. Kicking at the door. His arms full of wood. I opened the door and he smiled. Wooden you like ana-log? he said to me, like some salesman. I'll sell you analogy. I'll sell you anagram: *Oscar is a light. So is a chat girl.* Pretty cheap, right? His voice pressed me the way I used to press beeswax between my fingers and thumb. And there was the backwards way he scrambled an egg right in the shell, how he fried another sunnyside up and made it into a sandwich with horseradish and tomato and— What am I saying? What are you making me say? Stop it!"

"You're free," said Samot. "I like your voice."

This brought a smile to Ave's dry lips.

"It's nice of you to say that. You mean it, too, don't you? You're a decent youth for these times, and don't think I don't know what goes on out there. I like you, too. Are you my grandchild by any stroke of luck?"

"No," said Samot.

"And you're not the ghost of someone I've wronged?"

"No," he said.

"Are you with hospice?"

"Not hospice."

"Just some do-gooder?"

"Well...I..."

"I thought so," said Ave. "Then bring me some water. I thirst."

The young water bearer brought water to her lips. He laid a hand on her forehead and let it soothe her for several minutes, feeling her wrinkles and the structure of her skull. Her body felt real to his touch. It was truly well conceived, an accurate representation of age. What a task it would be to relieve her of the life she'd invented. What a task to get her back to her proper time and death, to orchestrate her recovery, to uncover another world of truth.

"When I was much younger I sat behind gravestones and listened. I wasn't so morbid as you think, only did it on the brightest days. I liked the idea of the living and the dead, but also the feel of stone and the buzz of insects.

"One day a boy and his father came to the graveyard. I hid from their sight, watching as the boy jumped from the gravestones, flying to his father's arms. The father caught his boy and looked about sheepishly. He must have thought it improper to play in a graveyard. So they stopped the game for a bit and read the markers: A sea captain, Captain Daniel Briggs, died at sea. His dog, Pelagios, beside him. There was H Mitchell, died in her sleep. And T Agee, eighty-seven years old, resting in peace. See you in the morning, it said on his stone. The Dalton twins, inseparable in life and death. An old woman named Gwendolyn off by herself beneath a lone cedar tree. There was Nickel and Handel and Britta and them, no dates for their deaths. And there was a man, his wife, their two boys and their daughter. They were buried together. She, the daughter, died young. Nineteen, if you did the math. The rest of the family lived much longer, well into old age. The father in the graveyard paused reflectively with each name of the family: Effie and Critter, Ottar the pendragon, the pensive boy Junn, and the penultimate girl whose name was so worn there was only an E. It was sad, he thought, that there was only an E to her. It was sadder still that the daughter had died so quick and young, at the threshold of the world, before anything was done.

"Come on. Come on.

"The little boy just wanted to jump. He tugged at his father. He climbed the gravestones. Again. Again. Daddy, watch me. The father was too permissive. He looked sheepishly around him, then toward the church. Was the priest wagging his finger through the window? Was God shaking His head? Maybe all the dead enjoyed the game. You can't be serious all the time. Got to have fun with life. So, the man stood near his boy. He held out his hands so that when his son leapt he'd catch him quick so the boy wouldn't fly too far and crack his head on some disapproving granite.

"Perhaps there was a life, back in time. I made my way, only the world made it insufferable. I stepped and strove. I took my leaps, only there were no hands to catch me. I fell hard, and that's my story. Isn't it enough to ask, Did you do your best? And for me to respond, I did the best with what person I was given. What fault is it of mine if I was a faulty one to begin with? My claim is clam, not even a little I. And now I'm shut tight, certainly no pearl. A softness of being. Well shelled for protection. If there's muscle in my word, I don't know what it is. Do you?"

The room was quiet. Was there anyone besides her?

"It's so quiet here," said old Ave in her bed. "Like suddenly I don't exist.   Samot?"

"Yes."

"Do I exist?"

"Decipher yourself," said Samot. "Pick up the thread. Make your way out."

"Decide for myself! You sound like my father. Just tell me yes or no."

His silence annoyed her.

"You're not going to tell me, are you? It's cruel not to answer an old woman despaired."

His silence hurt her.

"Well, you're nothing to me. And I'm not listening to you any more. I'm shutting you out of my will."

His silence grieved her.

"Where are you, Sam Frog?" she continued. "You can't just go dumb. Can't leave me cold. I'm old, unholy. Undaring. Cannot much move. You know I cannot stand. You know I need help. You know how sad I am. Have you no empathy, no compassion, no love!"

Ave lay on her bed in her room in the evening world. A leaf fell on her shoulder, blew off.

"I can't see you anywhere, but I can tell you this: You'll not get away with it. You're going to listen to what I've got to say. I've got plenty to say and most of it bad, because that's how it is, but it's me."

And Ave heard nothing, not the time, 5:51, on the broken watch, inches from her ear, not the ceiling spread with evening or the last September light. She heard nothing at all, and it's strange, because she was listening closely. Had the world gone silent? Had everything abandoned her: Samot and all, her mind and memories, the joy of light? There was not a creaky floorboard alive in her room. Not one whispering branch loose in the world. And as much as she wanted to hear it, Ave couldn't make out the call to dinner from out of the past: *Come in, come in, who needs to feed her soul.* A poetical mother calls Avocetta Isolde in from the shore. The girl is gazing at the...listening to the...absorbing the world without distraction. The mother calls her, but Ave is so focused on the things at hand, she doesn't hear. The mother moves closer, calling her daughter's name. Ave. Ah-vay. She sees her girl, stooped in the mud, observing snails and worms. But her calling is useless. Did it ever get through? How is it possible that Ave heard nothing?

And, if for no other reason than to defy the silence that welled in the room and in her heart, to deny her soul this immovable quiet, Ave spoke up for herself. The old woman spoke, not for

Samot but for herself. She spoke to lay claim to her life, as no one else would. But why would no one else do it? Why, if she wanted things different, did she have to do the work herself? Why not someone else for once? Why not someone else reach out and do the work for her this once? A friend? An angel? A body of love? Why not love do something for her? Why not God for once? Just once in her life. Someone, someone. Take her hold her as much as was needed, lug her from misery and

Kindle
her
so
u
l

PROLOGUE IN SPIRIT

Yes, I will be born. Tomorrow morning. It's almost here. To the world goes the song. And I see my time to come.

I see, too, in pictures that precede me, that I'll grow old and die one day. The images speak for themselves. It's nothing to be upset about. I listen to my destiny rattle on as if it's her joyous mission to be unstoppable. Talk about wordy. My rehearsings now are mere phrases compared to her tome. I've learned a lot about my future life on earth, how I'll burst from this invisible place and hurl myself to solid ground. I'll be young, my hair will be long, and it'll be my job to clean the toilets and feed the dog. I'll happily draw my home in great ungrateful circles. I'll stumble, stutter, blaze now and then like a candle, converse like a human when I find the words, flirt if I want, wax and wane

e
s
i

and flicker and snuff, and then r   as smoke, eddy and curl. And like smoke again I will fade into the background to blend with the clouds. I'll grow old and crusty, my skin will be spotty. The bones of my body will turn brittle. The hair of me'll go gray. Muscles will deteriorate and thinking will run off with the lawn boy. Memory will be all I'll own, all I'll know, and even that will prove difficult.

What's the matter? I'll ask myself. To which I'll answer that matter cannot endure and that each human life falls apart. But where's the spirit within, I'll ask again. Dispirit is all, I'll answer back. I'll be empty and sad, like a weird starless sky on a clear country night. So be light, be wing, be lift, I'll say. And, yes. Why not do it? Don't just let things happen to you, I'll say. Be self-reliant, even at death. You can do anything that you can imagine.

Thus in my ending I'll become a bird. Seagull over water's edge. Snow goose in the sky. Redwing above the marsh. In my final thoughts I'll be a moment on the rise. Once a soft sweet baby, once a swagger gal, once a woman hard as crust, become at last a soaring gull. Ascending, lifting, circling uncircling. It takes my breath away, just picturing it. A bird to end me with, to take away my being and disappear. I see it coming. Laughing. Eee and eeeing. Taking me into night, into death, intuition.

All I'm saying is. Given birth, death is inevitable on earth. There's no escaping it, no matter the bird I witness up ahead, no matter the games I might one day play to delay the final note of me. There's definite language that I hear within: I'll be old when time tightens round me, when it pinches my blood and strangles my pipe. Many years of me will have fallen and most of them will lie rotting on the ground. The end will approach, and no more might I add. Trapped and waiting, achy back, wrinkled brow. A pity I, pitiable and unable to stand. Drips of sweat will skitter down my face. Snakes will pass my naked encrusted thicknailed feet. Flies will buzz their business at my ears. By and by they'll alight on my eyelids. It's true. And I'll try to see their black feet through the thin flaps of skin. And I will listen closely. And I'll try to understand. Yet, being blind and deaf to meaning, I will find none.

Trust me, this is no intention. No invention, either. It is what I am to become. I will die one day, and nothing will stop me. Nothing will get in the way of my undoing. So I am written:

Birth first
unsparkling sequence – day after day
holding out an open heart
posing, closing, loveless
then – life-undoing death
Last bird.

❖

I follow the thought. Tomorrow morning I'll merge with the body that's prepared. I'll be of some weight some worth some clay with possibility taking shape. A whirlwind disguised as a child, I'll emerge as a growing human girl. I'll crawl cross floorboards to the fire, stand with the burning logos burning word burning log o the tree branch snapping at my ears, and I'll spit with the spitting sound of the split and spark, walk forward out of the house, head to the treetipping rise, the wild wheeling limbs out there, mount the green hill unladylike, spread myself disheveled, and sigh at how I'm sure to fall.

Sovereign and young, I'll take the lead. Sovereign and young, my gist will be potential. Thigh I'll smack with my left hand. And off I'll grow. Strut the living smitten situation. Cuss and love and sex and flies, unfurl my self across the sky, charge my wayward down the street, eye to eye with whoever I meet, pausing at each corner long enough to catch my breath to carry on, and never look back. One day I. Never to look back to this. I just won't have the sense to do it. I'll be an earth girl, a work of the world. I'll never look back to my timelessness here, to this sea-legging speech before my arrival on the shore.

Yet here I am now, balanced near birth. The gist of creation works my words. It's one world and a life I'm waiting for. One day soon, the good earth willing. Warm spring willing. One more sun until the birth day tomorrow. I'll experience it soon. I'll taste the living earth better than I taste it from here.

From here. Where is this, anyway? What is it – here? Here is no salt, no pepper, and no sweet smelling air. Here is no matter. No first-hand feel of language on a tongue, no tiny bug feet on the skin of an actual arm – the living learning bite and swearing situation, none. Here is more of spirit, less of spunk, more life to sing about, less bees to sting about. It is worlds within worlds without so many words. Here an alphabet is all so ether, yes sir no sir all so eee sir. Gulls amid mind, their colors gestures only. Their tones more interwoven, less a wall of sound. Winging it widely, soaring it high. Here is fleeting faces forever involving and never meeting them separately, eye to eye.

It's a picture here, no place at all. But the embrace of something solid awakes within me. I call it home. Here is no home with which to know life growing. Here is the plan, the potential, but nowhere to build. Give me place, place me home, in gravity's reach, within reach of my grave. I am reeling out, ready for the sky to open and the light to lay itself upon me. Warm world without, holds me but how? With what hands? In what house of brick or wood? What color my mother's eyes? And what resolution my philosophizing father? What?

Yes, up psyching self. Time is aligning. Movement's affirming. Down with impatience. Feel it, heat. Heartbeat.
The celebration
is about
to begin.
The penultimate dawn is here. This day. Morning like a lion. All around, there is so much to know and to do, as if the all is God and the door is open and the call comes into me: Get up. Meet what's come to see you off. Lie no more in amorphous hope and bodydreaming only. Move with the thought of a turning planet. Look to the world that begins to stir thee. Practice hearing. Practice eyes. Practice tasting. Rise, you learning newborn you eager girlchild you lusting woman you aged flesh all wrapped in one. You I to be – be ready. Rise.

❖

The call begins in warmth this morning. Life is abundant here. One full day before I'm born. Is this all for me?

I see new and shapely things with my welcoming soul. Blades of grass drive their shafts upwards in green greetings. I hear hellos and other playful speech – bright talk of the blueblue sky and hard tones of tree and stone. I hear the morning glory all glorious song, and the lion of each dandelion everyellowhere. The music whelms over me with its beauty, floods me with its praise, washes till I am clean of my own interpretations and prepared, at last, to listen. Does anyone of the earth know this talk, these words released from a single voice and scattered over life? These are truths I will be born with and truths I may come to know, but what will I do if I lose sight of them?

I know something of the world already. I know worry that all this will be fogged upon my arrival, and I will fan out upon the earth silent as a wake, unable to say what I understand now, what I follow, what I move with and what for. What if I don't open to the sky that opens me? What if I don't ever again hear this here sound? What if I can't say what I have to say?

It's a chance I'm willing to take, as I go out to sea. I'm charged with ideas and urged by unseen hands into becoming. It's a chance I take to arrive on earth, to roll ashore, to kick my legs, to touch and go, and face to face to support myself against all else. It's a chance I take that is no chance, that has created itself, that says: *Dissolve – you must go forth. Make waves, spread wake, give shape to this love you carry, this need to be born.* And I, at sea, give way to you.

❖

Celebrate now O spirit.
As always before a birth
The heavens and earth
Jig and jibe. Celebrate now
Until the sky aligns
And the moon amounts
To Virgo.

By tomorrow dawn your head will be crowning. The earth is near. The rim of world you wonder at it widely. The hint of wind you hear the seaocean. See the ocean roll to shore and splash with light upon the marsh. Hum of voices. Spring in song. Home of all who are born and will be born. Grasses you're to be laid in, loose green rhythms, greeting lines. Salt meadow soft meadow swaddling hay. Soft April patens. The effort of every word to welcome you. The hand of every fading star to uphold your days. You cannot wait.

Heat penetrates your stillness and you wish to funnel your way through. It's a crowd, it's a party, it is so much going on that it's difficult to know what to say. Words mesmerize your soul with many possible plots. How will it play out? How will you play out? Sound so fluid you sail upon – a body of water, a universe of tones. Not far to go. There's a shower of life giving now to you. There are games and celebrations, frenzied feastings. There are greetings green and blue, salads salsas salutations all

<pre>
                a
        d   r
        n   o
                u
</pre>

"Hello. How've you been? Good good. Wheeling karma? Keeping warm? Good good. Glad to hear it. Been down the shore yet? But why do I ask? Looks like you're just heading that way. Came myself to *The Mow*. **Enosh** – that's what they call it back home. Seen the juncus along the way. They tickle me the way they talk salty about things. Every juncus has its day and plenty of biting green words, if you know what I mean."

"The grasses..."

"Softer grasses are gossipers. They spill what they've heard without a moment's thought. And them other spiky reeds is vicious stuff. Their cutlass tattlings bring on worry. Worry if you do, worry if you don't. No way out of worry. I'd like I would to get through one day without a fretful thought. That's not much to ask, is it? Course, there's no sense wasting my breath. What is is is."

"Do you..."

"Worry? Course I do. You've got to listen to worry, bend the way the breeze bends you. No way out of worry. You've got to be polite and civil to it. Sall in how you ride the waves. Don't let frustration tempt the tempest out of you. Tonly makes the swells more surly. What I'm telling you is, all of time's a trip and there's a purpose to its ticks. I've smashed enough words together to knowhat I'm saying. I've takenough small and fragile vessels through the nightliest storms and here I am to tell it safe and sound."

"But..."

"Why do I tell you of difficult things? Last minute laying it on the line, I spose. Things go easier if you know they're not easy."

"It's not exactly..."

"What you want to hear. No. But it's good advice to any beginner, and an adventurer at that. I give a glimpse of reality. Fun damental thoughts. Hi ho. Good luck."

The speaker gestures as he leaves. You wave good-bye, and like water with wind your soul is ripples. You make your way toward the crowd the shifters the bodies of life – but stop when a snake stops you. Boys and girls are everywhere, poking the mother.

"Leave her alone," a sweet voice implores. "You're so cruel."

Happy faces plead to play on.

"She's got a family among the rocks. She doesn't want it, all your goading. It's shameful."

But there's no stopping the soldiers whose orders are to wonder and prod at every curiosity.

"We're aweful, we know." They say it together, bright as a unison. "We're sorry that this is our joy. But look at it this way, the way she moves. Zing zing. Look at her go. Zang zang. Where's she now?"

You veer from the spectacle. You stoop to the earth and, your sight suddenly on serving life, speak with the spring shoots.

"What'll it be?" you ask the young growth.

"Sun inside and out. Good air. Pure water. Earth well cared for. No genetic manipulations, please."

"How will you grow strong?"

"With the warmest thought we know."

"What's the warmest? What's the thought?"

"We don't know it by name."

"Does anyone among this crowd know?" you ask.

"You do. You do."

Not true, you think. You don't know anything by name. You get up and shake the idea like hair from your face. You don't know much beyond this celebratory mood. You can't even tell the difference between left and right, up and down, this and that. A host of others pass and repass, faces shadow themselves with hats or hands, eyes squint against the untamable power of light. The games people play are hard and fair. And the music, filling the blue sky like a storm, intensifies with the sun. You float over to the concessions for a drink of lemonade.

"Hello, my friend."

"Drink, please," you say.

So the tender takes a long drink, placing the glass soundlessly down.

"Saw a drunk man once cut a lemon in two," he begins with a grin. "He pierced the rim with two small holes, tied a piece of twine in an ample loop, and wore the half on his head as a hat. What a perfectly funny thing to do. Hence the good name, Lemonhead. Later, I heard, he did it with an eggshell. It is near enough to a miracle when a thing comes perfectly funny, or perfectly beautiful, or perfectly sad. Like once there was a man with Lyme disease. His daughter came to me. She said, my daddy's got limes. I said you bring him on over right now. She did, and we made some of the most delicious limeade."

You smile with the picture of the mad lemon hatter, the perfect egghead, the pitcher of limeade to cure a citrus man.

"Hear the onrush as I pour a drink for you now," says the tender. "Who makes the sound of it, lass?"

"You?"

"No I don't. I make my own sound, not it."

"Who then?" you ask.

"It's its own blood, I tell you. Own self."

"This is blood?" you say, holding the lemonade.

"Ah."

"Ah?"

"Delicious self. It makes its own sound and flavor," says the tender. "Blood is the self put into a cup, into a form to hold it, put into motion. It rushes to and from the heart like a circular stream, a great river, the ocean of you. It's a vital organ, lass."

"Blood?"

"Heart. The heart is the organ, the holy music, the universe that serves you, that you serve."

"How?"

"Has a life all its own is how and lends itself to you in time. All the organs do. Lung for living in and out. Liver for learning lessons. Stomach and bowels for digesting the world, both good and bad. And heart is for heat, for warmth to hold and share."

"Yes," you say unknowingly.

"Who makes your heart, lass?"

"Do you?"

"No, I am a tender not a creator. Tell me, lass: Are you all strong there, then? In your heart?"

"I am strong enough. Thank you."

"Thank you, good lass. But you might lose sight of that strength."

"How do you know about my might?"

"That's what I'm all about, my friend. Knowing. And so are you."

"I suppose," you say, vaguely.

"Well, take something, give something," says the lemonade tender.

"I will."

But you don't. You give nothing to the tender. Walk off with your drink, and by the time you get around to sipping it, it's warm.

How everything happens so fast here. The heat is on you like a pent-up thought. Dancers spin by on the one side, singers note you from the other. And by the blink of you they are far afield, near the flowers, dressed in silks and weaves. They are like clouds overtop the distant islands – white, graywhite, wispy. Clouds aloft, a drifting audience, veiling unveiling, sailing unsailing. You return for a cooler lemonade, and it's all sold out.

"I'm sorry," says the tender. "But don't be disappointed. It isn't so unfortunate. I met a woman once who was so disappointed by the sketch of her life that she hemmed and hawed for more detail and more color and more this and more that and she missed being born. Now there's an unfortunate life if ever there was one. The artist missed her very creation. And then there was the young mother, died giving birth, never saw her child. Oh, it was sad. But she was so distraught she forced herself back to life before she was ready. Some things take time. Blind at birth she was. Her eyes were full of woe. So, if it's the cool tang of lemonade that you must have, you might be disappointed. But it isn't the end of all life, now is it, if you don't get what you want. If you fret it too much, if you're disappointed to the core of you, you'll close the very eyes you need to see with. And with eyes closed, you'll miss the one birth this day is about."

"Birth? Where?"

"All is life from luminous thought, a child from life, and earth to grow upon. Speak of the life, you who are behind words. Speak of the living, of all changing matters. Speak of the child, she in the hay of the greengrowing marsh. A lay of the marsh, a child for the future, a song for the present, a girl undisturbed in the warm morning sun.

How came this marshling
From God's love
To acres of mud and green
From the mystery to the cove
From unseen to seen?

But don't let me steal the show. The storyteller tells it best."

"What story?" you wonder. "Where?"

"In the saltmeadow hay, of course," says the tender, pointing to the distance. "There are two already gathered at the spot. Beautiful mother to be and a fairfaced fisher of a youth, a fatherish sort, his own mother's favorite son. Athletic is his shape, not overly muscular however. She is firm of thigh and thought. Step over. Step up. Circle round and listen to the master taler. He'll sow your spirit upon the earth, into the warm muck earth. He'll liven your mood with hearty words. He'll liven your body with the air of his words. Tingling your blood, he'll empower you to move on your own accord, a separate being brought to life. All praise."

❖

"Any moment now," begins the teller, "there will be, give praise, something of a birth."

"What thing of a birth?" questions the woman listener. "Don't you mean – A CHILD, give healthy praise, IS BORN?"

"Shh," shushes the teller. "Let me tell it as I see it. The birth will be of a child, but she hasn't arrived yet. My story as it starts is about what comes, give praise, before. Now, before the blessed event, there stood a man and woman, the likes of you two." The teller smiles and fixes his eyes first upon the young man, then the young woman. "They were poor, independent folk living a coastal, secluded life."

"I'd rather not be associated by your words with such flotsam," says the horizon-eyeing man. "As I am rich and my company plenty, there is no compare."

"Rich in seadeep aspirations and the flounder and bluefins of your imaginary nettings. But I'm talking the truths of earth, not the fantasies of mind. I'm talking the physical ways, the world of mice and Mendelssohn."

"Who?"

"Nevermind. A pun my honor, I jest am tossing you to see how you bounce. No more fooling. I promise."

"I tell you," says the man. "I have an assortment of peers and friends. I've got a fine rig, hooks, oars, and motors. Everyone near, every person as far as the woods knows my name. I am well endowed."

"You sound cocksure of yourself," says the storyteller. "But my words are the line to follow, and in my tale the folk are wanting, hard-working souls who don't party much and never interrupt. So, if the pair of you two don't get better grips on your tongues, I'll leave off my narrative and we'll all be the worse for the forsaken journey."

The two keep quiet and the story goes on:

"The man was handsome as honey bread, a young one with schemes and plans. He would bound this way like a happy pup and spring that way like a panther. But he couldn't keep one thought for long. He could take a net and dip for days at sea for the sake of the catch and the adventure. He could travel to the wooded highland and pile logs onto flatbeds, hauling all afternoon till sweat drenched his linen and his legs ached mighty. He could focus on the antlers of a buck for half an hour without blinking. He could hold his drawn bow steady for ten minutes or more as the buck approached, but he could not hold a single thought or the softness of a face for more than the count of three.

And as for the woman whose face was soft as pea blossoms, she was no wimpy chick at her sturdy man's side, but plenty able. She was strong pretty to look at, a force of her own. Free fresh flirtless fierce. Her shirts she kept clean by washing with saltwater. Her spirits she renewed at sun-up each day. And, true, she was much in the way of substance as well, for she was both heavy with child, and stuffed with burden over her man's roving mind.

What's on it? she'd often ask him, hoping to know, to clear her head of distrust.

Garnet? he'd repeat, mishearing her question, pausing for an inappropriate amount of time. It's a rock, he'd explain and say nothing more.

She'd stare at him suspicious of this misunderstanding and his curious pause. And she had good cause to be concerned, as her husband had percolations. He had a plan. And he took his wife out walking one afternoon when the air was still and the sky vivid colors. They went together to the saltmarsh hay. The mudflats were in view because the tide was low. The mudflats were golden because the evening spoke upon them. The ocean was close enough that you could smell its salt and, if you put your ear to the air, there it was – a humble yet expansive voice. The sun in the west, at the time we're talking – you could see it dip slowly into the horizon. Going, going. Almost gone.

The man stopped walking and turned to his wife.

How is it we're caught like this? he asked, looking past her face into the distance.

Like what?

Knots in the netting. Nets in the hold.

How so? she asked.

How so do you see that wild-o stallion? He pointed to a horse in the distance.

Yes, she said.

I'm going to catch it, to ride it away from here.

Away? When so?

Sooooo... he began, stretching the word, longing past his wife into the distance.

So, what? she asked.

I've got this for you, said her husband. The man untied a cloth sack from his waist. And it's a nice soft ground if you've got to fall to your knees. I've tested it. Then holding out the sack, he listed its contents: There's some money in it. My gold-hilted knife, how I'll miss her. A charm against the summer drought and one against Jack Frost, both writ by my grandmother and employed by me. Some cord and such in case of a bind. A chunk of bread, fist of cheese, an incredible amount of stuff if you think about it. And vodka in a horn. The best. I'm reckless and restless. Rely on myself most, you know. Wind makes a sail billow, a boom jibe. It changes a man's course similarlike. It was fine of me to be with you when I was. I won't be sorry when I die.

This was the most he'd ever said to her. It made her happy to hear his loose words, so pleased in fact she missed the cutting edge. But when she saw her husband cast the sack and turn, tearing toward the wild stallion, her heart sank and she called from the depths, What is it, Pella? Come back. Come back. The baby. What are you doing? Where are you leaving to?

And when he didn't even turn, she called again, more loudly. Come back, Pella. Our child. Our life. Our home. And when he showed no interest in her provincial words, she shouted: A jug of beer and a lifelong bed. Scut along the cheek of me, taste my inner thigh. What the fuck's going on? Flesh better than any mistress and drink aplenty every night. Friends and meat and family treasures. Come back.

And when he didn't even stumble for a drink or return for her flesh but stayed his course, she knew he was gone and called: The devil have you, then, and your handsome face. Your look will be a curse. Do you think I ever liked sharing a pillow? You never had much participation in you. You think I'd've stayed with you forever? I'd've run off first if not for my conscience. Consideration for the baby. Our child, she shouted. I'm fucking honorable. I'm... Our child, she shouted.

And she threatened to strike him down, if ever she saw him near enough. Strike him down fast. Repay him for her every tear, of which there had been many. She spit on the marsh and sank to her knees weeping not so much for the loss of a love but more for being left alone. And now the sun, too, even the sun was leaving her to fend for herself, hiding itself completely behind the earth so as not to be involved. The gulls heard her crying, the hawks and longlegged egrets. The crabs in the estuaries, the fish flopping at sea, the whales and the porpoises all got wind of the abandonment, all got an earful of her sadness. Still, the young woman would have accused all these creatures of indifference, for where were they when she needed them most? Not at her side, nor in her sight.

The woman, heavy on earth, pregnant and angry, looked at the sky. The clouds were rich with color. They hung saturated with hope. And it came as a feeling of sympathy, as if maybe the world was with her. But it was shortlived company, as the colors drained, leaving shapes that hovered near the horizon gray and nondescript.

The woman did not get up, did not go home. She was at a loss for words, and it was a muted world as night approached. And far out, dividing the earth from the heavens – the horizon itself. A line along the curve lay of it. A fading line, dissolving day of it. She, a young pregnant woman, rocking life among the hay of it. As a gentle wind moved the marsh, pushing grasses, shifting thoughts, and making room for something else even more remarkable than what had just occurred. It all was happening so fast. What could she do? Where could she go? There was nowhere to be but here."

So, the story ends, searching the sky and the marsh for clues of what will come next.

The sun, well below the horizon, will take many hours to rise. Night is on the palette now. And the woman who'd been listening to the story, the young pregnant woman sits alone on the grasses. Everything has come to this. Is it really true that her husband has abandoned her? How could anyone do such a thing?

The woman slumps in the saltmash hay, listening to the lament of such a life, which is her life and her lament. She thinks of rising, of going home, but she cannot move. She cannot budge against the weight of what is on her mind. And hours pass, darkness crawls upon her face and arms like biting insects. She cannot brush against the fate of it. She cannot clean her mind or body.

Then with her burden come the first pains of labor. Cruel and bitter punishment! The herb woman had said it would not happen for three weeks. She had put her hand on this soonmother's belly and said, *Three weeks. Not a day less. And don't let your mind play games with you. Do you hear me? Are you listening? Go for a walk. Talk to the stars.* And that was only yesterday, when the herb woman spoke. At least, that's what the pregnant woman thinks.

Now, our woman scans the dark marsh, her hand on a gold-hilted knife. She is here giving birth unless she moves, unless she walks. She cannot think well, nor rise to the task of sheltering herself. She might as well just stay. Might as well take the knife and kill it quick before it even breathes. It is her first clear thought after so long within a fog. Might the idea motivate this young woman? The first thought falls upon her in her momentary weakness. Where does the thought fall from, it is so unnerving? And is her weakness strong enough to support the deed?

The woman kneels, clenching her teeth. Hours pass as minutes when there is no pain. Minutes as hours as the pain comes and goes. What is time when there is only oneself and a knife and the all-luring night? Midnight creeps up from behind. One a.m. comes and goes. Two, three. Where has she been, her body in increments? Four in the morning, quarter past. How quietly each hour comes upon her like eyes first, then ideas antlike, roachlike, cobwebs, dust, a scummy film of sweat. She thinks now of hiding, but there is nowhere to hide, thinks of killing, but who first to die. It is easy to kill, not so to die. Thinks of living, but that is crazy. It is crazy to live sometimes, crazy to put up with so much pain, crazy to do a thing you might regret.

O, what is there to do? She grits her teeth. Or what to do but this? Hand on the blade, clutching it so tight it melts in her palm, melts and she looks up at last. The nightblessed stars are hid behind wisps of clouds. She clutches only air and yells to the stars. Come out come out wherever you are. I want to make my case to you. And the stars hear her plea and come with the change of wind. Those clouds were only lacing. They clear away.

Upon seeing the stars, the woman drops all thought of killing. The thought falls in the tangle of grass and is quickly lost. She does not reach for it. Why would she? It is the last thing on her mind. Was it even ever there? There is only pain and being out with the stars and the presence of life. She hardly knows her name anymore, or her husband's name, or that the wind is blowing gently now to clear the sky and clear the air and dry her face of wetness. She hardly knows what is happening to her or that the dawn is nearing. Morning is a river whose mouth opens and light pours forth. She sees the sky lighten but does not know why.

Squatting in the high meadow of marsh, the woman leans against the south wind, which dries her sweat, which puts its arms on her shoulders like a shawl, which has said nothing to her throughout the roughest hours of the night. Hours hours hard as rock. Garnet garnet, fire and blood. Shit. Such pain. When will it end? Her body against the world, her weakening mind. If only she could let go and fly. But she holds tight as she can to the earth and flares wide with such urges she cannot believe. There is a face in her mind. A first horizon. A spring time. A person with. A breath of. She pushes at once two three. At once two three. And pushes twice as hard. Twice as hard she screams. And all of heaven haven is on her. One two. Squatting in the marsh, the dry soft grasses, the sun just coming, she feels the flood of giving, the food of blood and half of life draining from her body and all of love moving in. The crown the shoulders the sweet release. The rush of happiness, swarm of light. She gives birth in seconds. At once, is done. All that remains is...

Quickly she collapses, ready to...
Notnow.
Her body like some droopy flower, thirsty for...
Notnow.

Her hands needing to feel and see. All that remains is to hold her baby, to welcome it in her eyes.

The wilted mother drops a hand to the crown, the head of hair, the chest, and the tiny heart of her baby girl. A girl, she notes. A little girl. She's warm and soft. There's nothing in the world so soft and living. Yes, there is something, and here she is. Breath for the world, then into the body it goes, and back to the world. Yes, there is breathing. What more does this mother need to know? This living moment. This moment together, alive. What more can anyone ask for?

The new mother pulls her baby girl to her chest, wrapping her with her shirt and sweater. Her exhausted body releases itself to the stars above her, which are morning stars now hidden behind the rosy fingers and first bluing of the sky. With her child on her chest, the mother sleeps. Heart to heart, the heat of each other, the hope of life. What more could anyone wish for at the start?

All about the living. It's all about the life. No energy for dying. No. Not now. Now will be well. No possibility of dying now. But when? Sweet blood. Swift blood. No one will die. No one extinguish. No one will quit being till never. Till never forever – not till all the winds stop and the stars no longer shine and the birds no longer sing and the earth no longer earth has up and gone. And not even then, as we'll follow the earth wherever she goes and live with her transformations, with her new winds and stars and whatever the birds, and not die to this life or ever be done. And all will be well. All will be well forever, for good.

Night dissolving, new breath of light. Everything is eyes for this. Everything is hands for holding. The morning girl. The wonder of. The moving blood. The small breeze gently on and off the creek. Her cheek. Her perfect skin. This day. Begins

ONE

April, she was born. Stars gone early on, larva of day – the dawn.

She was very different back then, unformed and soft. She had to get used to the earth from scratch. There was a first time for everything. Her face welcomed the sun, but she was unable to speak a word of it. The wind tickled her feet, birds sang at her ears, an ant crawled on her arm – each experience was new. And where was I while she was at home? Hidden under some rock? Tucked between the clouds? Out in space, among the stars? There she was, obvious to see on earth, while I had no talent for the world just then. She and I had nothing to do with each other. Not I at first. I hung back, waiting till she was older to join her.

Nevertheless, I kept close watch on that newborn as I bided my time. She was born on the ninth day of the fourth month, the fourth moon of the year. She was born on the hay, soft and clean – a simple salty baby. And her parents – did anyone see them step to the scene at the shore that morning and announce in one proud voice: **Behold. A show of delight. Our magical physical child?**

There was no show. No audience, either. Her parents ran like watercolors. They breezed away like quick goodbyes. They were out of there so fast, the newborn girl seemed, at first, alone.

I think her parents must have been the sea and sky. The sea swept in with all its verve, then slipped away. The sky hung low at the beginning of day before lifting, becoming aloof again. Her parents were like gods, swooping to the earth, and then returning to their distances. It was a bit sad, really. Anyone who saw that tiny child lying in the grasses, anyone would have looked to the mother sea and father sky, saying: Why aren't you holding her? Why aren't you loving her? Why have you backed off?

Breathing the greening world, the newborn child slowly learned her place. The spiritual world diminished in her ears like notes after bowing, and in her soul like a splash of water evaporating in the sun. Her cradle was the marsh, high and dry, above the tide, below the line of trees. And if it seems sad to you that there were no parents, just give it time. A proper mother and father are nearer than you think.

One day, a clear day, a child was born. Her Firstmother Sea and Firstfather Sky set her down on the shore. They probably loved conceiving her, romping at the horizon and mixing their different natures. It must have been fun coming together for the sake of this infant, though maybe they'd hoped for a bit more get-up-and-go out of their girl and that's why they withdrew so quick.

The baby just lay there, among the grasses of the marsh. She was like a drift of wood or some plastic bottled brought by the tide. All that remained of Mother Sea was some glisten and some salt. And after Father Sky took his hand from his daughter, when he backed away to miles of forgetfulness, the child opened her eyes and they were blue.

What did this girl know of her lineage? To think that her mother was the singing sea somewhere, and her father the far spreading sky – impossible. She really had nothing to say.

And when she inhaled, the girl filled with wishing for a more stable family, for faces and voices, a breast for milk, and a knitted hat for her head. And when she exhaled, she lay ready for anything. Then warmth swarmed upon her, swaddling like a blanket. You are not alone, said the warmth, and it relieved the girl some. And as dawn climbed the sky, the fingers of light soon pressed this newborn and called for a name.

Who are you, girl? You, on the ground. You're new here.

The child did not answer, and the light proceeded to strengthen and to name the things it touched. There were grasses where the newborn lay – spartina patens. There was a tree to her side – a budding sassafras. The bird on its branch was a singing redwing. The world nearby was solid and sound. Not bad, for a beginning.

Soon there was a special gleam upon the water, and a few far floats of clouds. Words rose, rolled everywhere. Wave after wave, the ripe rapping world was waking. The world spoke, filled with light. It spread and gave forth a present sense where many conversations moved at once. It was hard for the girl to know where to listen.

The sun itself broke from behind the low clouds. Screams of gulls cascaded down. And the redwing from the nearby tree flapped past. What was the girl but a place for this world to meet her? What was she but a thought brought to earth by heaven?

A place? you say. A thought? Alive, more like it. A miraculous story, maybe, out there in the marsh, but also quite ordinary and human. It was nothing far-fetched. And supporting this newborn, beneath her small weight, rested her flesh and blood mother, which just goes to show that all true things eventually make themselves known.

Where did she come from, this woman? It's likely she'd always been there, don't you think. There was the girl's mother, some gulls, the sun, and that redwing. It was a bright new world. And nothing of the world frightened the child. Even as the sun spoke loudly up the eastern sky, the girl was not afraid. The rays of the sun were strong, but the words did not intimidate our child.

"Welcome to the world," said the sun that morning. "Don't bother getting up. It's a lot to take in. But believe me, you will live long and belong. You'll lean to the left. You'll rise to your rights.

You'll make your own light for the world to see. And one day you will reach your rear

your ears

your dreams."

The gulls in their arcs laughed at such silly language. They screamed and flapped across the face of the sky. Or was it the girl's mother who made these sounds? The woman whispered to assure her child, and it was no distance to that voice, as though the mother's voice was the girl's own voice. Some might say it was the remains of the sea upon the marsh that was speaking, but most would agree it was the growing truth of her flesh and blood mother that now warmed the girl, language so loving and comforting it pressed like hands. The touch of her mother came through loud and clear, and the girl knew it and was happy.

So she was born on an April morning. Life proclaimed itself again on earth, tucked in a small body. And does life sing more shallow every day like an evaporating pond? Or does it fill each moment to overflowing, and the banks of one's self must rise to keep up? Which way does life run, in or out?

The spellbound infant hardly moved. She took no food, and voices descended upon her as she lay. The marsh spoke, waterbirds, the grit of sand, and the lap of the creek – their stories were loosely worded and difficult to grasp. The unpeopled kingdoms of the world did not feel fret or concern, only magnanimous love.

And what can be made of so prized a being as love? No one is willing to tangle much with the word. Its power is unpronounceable, says the wind in passing. Its space is far ranging, says the sun. Its tone is swells and swirlings, says the water. Its sway is this way and that, say the lanky grasses. Its voice budding and blossom both, say the flowers. It is endlessly particular and forever expanding.

"Forget about it," said a turtle, crawling over ground. "Not my job to describe it."

"What won't you describe?"

"Love. Isn't that what we're talking about?"

"Won't you at least give it a shot?"

"Electrical shock?"

"Not shock. I say, won't you at least talk about love? You're a natural."

"An actual what?" said the turtle.

"They say you're fond of your own foundation."

"I suppose you're right. A pond may be the foundation of love. I truly love water, and I care for words. Don't get me wrong, but I even caress them sometimes."

"Like poetry?"

"Trees do me no good, no matter Poplar or Palm, Birch or Baobab. They are out of my reach."

"But poetry?"

"The chicken? What good is poultry to a turtle? The sludge of their mass manure washes from fields and ruins my waters with phosphorus and algae blooms. The way they're raised arouses much consternation in the coop of the mind."

"What about fire?"

"What about flies? All the flies around the chicken coop? Or did you say friars? You didn't say fryers, did you?"

"Not chickens, not flies, not friars or fryers, but fire. Fi-re. FI-RE!"

"No need to get all heated up," said the turtle. "Just ask and you shall relieve me."

"Do you love fire?"

"I do," said the turtle. "See how easy life can be when you ask the right questions? I enjoy the spell of it, the spill of warmth on a cold night. Wood smell and all. The elementals come to play in the flames like it's the sea. They flit and frolic. They dance hither thither. I enjoy the games and flames, matters not that I am slow."

"Is the warmth of fire love?"

"A warm tub of fire sludge? Is there such a thing? Your mind's a muddle and your tongue a tangle. Get it sordid out."

"Word deranging turtle. Let me at it again."

"Add it quickly," said the turtle. "Get to the sum."

"Warmth from fire, elementals at play, the beautiful light. Is the answer to everything love?"

"Who's telling?" said the turtle.

"I was hoping you."

"Not I," said the turtle. "Don't you see that yet? My ploy is mere avoidance of mean answers."

"Why mean?"

"Aren't you looking for something more than average? Something great?"

"Yes."

"Then don't look for meaning from my words," said the turtle. "Though words give me joie de fever, I can tell you nothing you wish to know. Ask that fellow if you want the bright word. He's more lucid with his tongue. More looser, loopier, luminous too. Belongs to the agency. He's your means."

"That fellow? But which?"

"Ask better but where," said the turtle. "You look completely in the wrong place always. He's got the will of a whip, quick as sibbling bicker and sudden as a weed."

The turtle moseyed off and the other voice went on:

"Fellow, fellow, come out for me. They say you have a sparkling mind. Show yourself in your entire. Fire, light, lantern, ho..."

"Looking for me, are you?"

"I suppose," said the seeker. "Is that all there is of you?

"I'm burning bright beside you, aren't I?"

"Not really. You're awful quiet for being so close. You look put out."

"I'm obscure is all."

"Obscure Saul. Is that your real name?"

"William the Wisp's my name. Professional flirter and evader of questions via my quick witted answers."

"What are you up to?"

"About here on you," said William, raising his hand half way. "If I'm feeling sprightly tall, that is."

"Are you sprightly now?"

"Settling down for the day," said William softly. "Watching myself go out."

"Don't go. Please, stay."

"Come from the marsh, I do," explained William. "Nighttime I'll play again. I'm so tired now. That's all I know, though much more could I say, but only if you ask."

"Why are we here?" asked the seeker.

"Following the child," said William.

"Is she a child to follow?"

"A child of Allah?"

"You hear like the turtle."

"I'm here as myself," said William. "But it's true, I do like the turtle. We all like the turtle, here. She's a sister to everyone."

"What I asked was this: Is the child a she to consider?"

"No sheep but very considerate for a girl so young. I've not yet heard a complaint, neither from nor about her."

"Is she the answer, then?"

"To what?" puzzled the Wisp.

"To the question of love."

"Love is hardly the question to ask. But how."

"How what?"

"How long will she live?" said William.

"Why? Is there some doubt about her endurance?"

"Doubtless," said William.

"Doubtless what?"

"Doubtlessly something will come down," said William. "Story has it she will live a long life, but that is not my tale to tell. I know the otherwise. I have visited the end of time, which comes at the close of September in nineteen years. I have witnessed the wind and what it does to loosen branches from trees. I've seen what is and what's to befall. Each new life has its look and each new look enlightens us. Still, sometimes the truth is too personal to blurt. I'd rather keep quiet."

"What do you know?" asked the seeker. "Could you at least whisper it?"

"I could, but not to just anyone."

"To me?" asked the seeker.

"Or not to be," completed William the Wisp.

He went to the baby asleep on her mother and said... said low...whispered it, really. It was too muted a sound to comprehend from a distance. Will then kissed the girl and skedaddled.

"What did you say to her?" asked the seeker. "Why does no one tell me anything?"

William was nowhere to answer. He was in fact gone, and into his place settled a bird. The morning redwing returned from a brief excursion to sit on a limb of the sassafras tree. She came back to the shore to deliver her message. Her message was words, more words, but would they be direct this time?

"Your father is on his way," spoke the bird, as if to the child. "That's as clear as it gets. I saw it from above. He comes with help – a doctor of no particular stature. Oh, he looks in touch and struts okay, I suppose, not that I really care for the touch of a doctor or his strut. I don't care for his cursed cures, either. I get my medicine from the life I'm born with and its connection to a more spirited world.

"Less medicine, more life: That's my motto. Long as I'm permitted to live and not be poisoned, I'll do alright. You humans are not so well equipped as I to simply live. Little do I care for the human lot. Yes, they say if we birds were more like you, we'd know such things as the structure of our wings and the physics of flight, but then what a mess it would be. It'd be hell to fly because we could never just *fly*, not without thinking how it works and if we're generating enough lift and whether we're considering the square of the drag over the route matrix. We would know the more and live the less. We'd have more human attributes and less heavenly ones. What a sick and suffering thought. A caged idea – and it's stuck inside me now. Shit. Why am I the one who has to know this stuff? I'm surely going to die someday, stiff from matter-of-fact thinking. I and you alike, dear child. Away, away with all thinking that dwells on and on without getting you anywhere.

Wash your wings of the dirt. Find freedom in the flow and flight, the up and Tao. Save yourself and fly.

"O new and opaque child. Friendship is the birds above, not for the birds but of them. Living lifting of the birds. Spirit is a bird on wing. Listen up. Look up. Be fey. Be free of knowing. Else you will falter."

Off went the redwing to sing and play on the sturdy grasses of the marsh.

And the newborn girl listened to it all, even in sleep. She took in these conversations that happened around her. Her face sometimes lifted in near smile, sometimes fell in near frown. And what's so odd about that? Is it too much to suppose this child might be interested? Too much to suppose she might be responsive to the life streaming in and out of her like seawater through a sponge?

"Too early to say for sure." These were the doctor's words, a bit too audible for the father's anxious mind.

They'd come from the west, just as the messenger bird had said they would. And now the doctor stood with one hand pressed against the sassafras, his feet crossed. The father kneeled at the side of his wife and child.

"But I seen em born worsen this, and come out with all their hairs in place and able to recount their letters and numbers just fine as 60 gauge stockings. Fact, I recall Celti's girl born years back in vicious snow. Weren't able to see to her for seven days. And to think, that girl's mother, Celti, hell, she didn't have sense whatso to get the hair off her own face. But look at the little lass now. Pretty as a plumbob and twice as bright."

"Evie, she's worried," whispered the father, getting up and gesturing for the doctor to consider his language. "Can't you be a little more soothing?"

"Soothe doesn't move me, son, and don't matter much to the wee un, neither. She can't make out my words, not a wit of em, nohow. A bit of that breast wouldn't hurt the lass, though. Stiffen her up. And that's what we're about, now, isn tit?"

The doctor was very pleased with the configuration of his speech, and the father thought he should agree, but he couldn't get in the words.

"Life always works herself out, son," said the doctor. "I remember Henrik Baabi, down to his last straw. Nothing I could do. Shook my head and washed my hands of it all. Too bad, I told him. But you can't live forever. And Henrik got right angry with me, swore at my upbringing, at my giving up ways. He swore under his breath and over it and through. A one-man uprising. A curse chorus, I called him. God Damn you Doc, I'll show you. I'll fucking well make it. And so he did. So he did. You see, I left it up to him, and he wanted to live. Now, let's get on back and I'll have a proper run-through. Got me a craving for a cappuccino, something warm up my innards."

The doctor unhooked himself from the tree and began walking away, out of the marsh, followed by the hunched father with child in his arms and his wife on his back, arms wrapped around his neck, plus his own sack hitched to his belt.

"Yes, down to every biting flee, son. I'm a might fond of life. Always it puts a sparkle in my eye, ever since I was a child. And now that I'm within sight of my formidable years, every new un who comes along brings me to joy and a feeling of satisfied."

The doctor turned, saw the staggering father.

"Let me help you with that, son."

The doctor unhitched the sack from the father's belt, swung it over his shoulder and continued across the mow to the dirt road that led to town. After a while, when the houses started appearing, so did the early risers, some at their doors, others in the fields.

"Payon Payon, what are you doing out at this time? Never seen you up this early before."

"Birthing, my boy. Healing and birthing. It's my right."

"Who you birthing?"

"Jason's boy's lassie's child."

"Topher's married?"

"I don't say he is. I don't say he's not."

"Christo, the jargonot?"

"Why d'you callim that?" asked Payon.

"Ever heard him talk. It's a mystery what he's saying."

"Go on, son. Back to your dreaming. Your words make me crave good sense. 'Sides, I've got work to attend to. They're on my heels, so let me get on."

And the doctor continued down the road, well ahead of his charge, till he came to a fork and took the left prong whereupon he went further till he came to a bridge and stopped in the middle to toss a coin for the luck of it. A boy and his sister came out from under the bridge where they'd slept in hiding from their father.

"Payon, that you tossing coins?"

"I'm the one," said the doctor. "Who is it 'dressing me? What deity? The river god or the muddess of the bank?"

"Friday's the day it is, Doc," said the boy. "Don't know nothing bout no muddy dress."

"It's us, Payon," said the girl. "Right before your very eyes."

Down he looked and saw the children. He gave them a twitch of his head.

"Toss one them coins to us," said the boy. "We're run ragged with hunger."

"Come now, children. You've been more hungry than this, I'm sure."

"Father is angry again. Jurgie broke the spigot and let the water spill."

"Why, that's a shame, children. But I don't have the time or the energy to discuss your problems. Can't you see my charge?"

"We druther see your change," said the girl.

"You'll likely see my boot if you don't stop your racketeering ways."

"Please, sir."

He threw the children a coin from Christopher's sack.

"Any more, sir?"

But seeing inside a most beautiful knife and a bottle of spirits, he shut the sack up tight and put it on his shoulder.

"Don't you ever tellit others that I don't care."

"Who you making healing of today, Payon?" asked the girl.

"They're coming right along. Old Jason's son, swift-footed Chris Cross, with his what's her name that leaf-trembling most luscious wife, and their child newly come to this world and nameless in herself. Now get on and quit bothering a busy body."

But it was the doctor who got on, till he came to his house, where he took off his boots and threw them aside and warmed the water, waiting by the kettle till it let go a whistle. The children, too, waited on the bridge. The boy knew Christopher from the stories told of him fishing at sea, and he knew his beautiful wife Evita known as Sophie from the sweet of her brown eyes down. He'd seen her change her dress once. He was hidden behind a bush. Oh, it was breathstoppingly momentous. She like a goddess had a wise length of hair that covered her to her knees almost. But no matter how long her hair, he waited till she moved it, which she never did, and still he waited, and still she never moved it. And then she did, but not enough. And just so, now, he waited with his sister to see what he might see. But Sophie, Christopher, and their noname child never showed.

"Must be they're a real god and goddess," said the boy.

"More it that old Payon's lost his skill at conveying," said the girl.

It was not so much a loss of skill as it was a loss of patients. This is how it took place: Take the road back a ways and you come to Motherwort Leontine, the old herbalist. She had just awakened and plodded to her window to mind the rosy fingers of dawn when she saw Payon go past.

"That old twister," she said. "What wickedness does he work this early in the day?"

And when she saw swift-footed Christep bearing a child, and his trembling wife riding along on a horse, that horse being Christopher himself, Mother Leontine was beside herself with curative thoughts and a mind full of tinctures. She rushed out to the family and guided them to her house before Payon might turn to check his wake.

"Lean on me, child," she said to Sophie, helping her through the door. "When was the little one born? Just now? On the water?"

"Excuse me, Ms Lion, for not knowing all. I've got a hint of it inside me. I'm just so tired, it all seems like rumor."

"Of course, my child. Why do I make you speak?"

"I think she was looking forward to life," said Sophie. "So she came to shore. Isn't she beautiful?"

"She is," said Leontine. "More than I can say." Motherwort turned to Christopher and added, "Has that pretender Payon played his part in this?"

"He's done nothing for us," said the father with distant eyes.

"Then he's done his best," said Leontine. "The hand of Providence is the preferred midwife. Now, let me do what I can for you."

Father and mother rested in the cozy room as the herbalist bustled about, shuffling things. Sunlight streamed through the window. The baby slept in her mother's arms.

"I have a slosh of milk in the pail yet, for our new mother. Fennel and goat's rue, I think are best. I'll ready a bath with comfrey as well. And my new father, some hops for you. And for you..." Motherwort Leontine gazed at the newborn, "For you I'll..."

The girl opened her eyes.

"Do you recognize me, child?"

The old herbalist reached for the baby, lifting her gently from the mother, rocking the tiny bundle in her old sweet way.

"Things change, don't they." Motherwort's eyes rested on the child. "Things stay the same." Her mind soared upon the sky, sailed some private sea, caught on a snag.

"What is it, Mothertine?" asked Chris.

Leontine stood quiet a while, settling into the child's eyes as if into heaven itself.

"Nothing," she said after the spell. "A certain look I see now and again in a child."

"Good or bad?" asked Christopher.

"Nothing in a child is bad, therefore all looks good to me."

"But what does the look portend?" persisted Christo father, full of concern.

"The port end the starboard end, what difference is it to love?" And she continued, but to the child alone. "Now what would my poor departed Galen have thought of you? He'd a been taken, I'm for sure. He'd a carried you in his warm good hands to your most proper place. I've got hands, too. I know where you belong."

She carried the child back to her mother and led mother and daughter to her own bed.

"Feed her, Sophie. Rest well. Shall I make it darker?"

"Please."

"You'll have a bath later. Does your mother know?"

"Know?"

"Your mother and I, it used to be we.... Why isn't she with you?"

"She's followed my father," said Sophie

"Across the way? But when? I did love your mother so."

"It was six months back. October."

"How am I not part of this life any longer?" said Motherwort Leontine more to herself. Then to Christopher, who had followed them to the bedroom, she said, "And your father, where is he?"

"At sea, no doubt. And my mother is deciding where to spend the night."

"Home is no good?"

"Home's never been good enough for her."

"You're at peace with the odyssey, I note. At the very least there is adventure in each path. I'll double the hops and make your wife some raspberry tea. Do you have the placenta?"

Christopher and the old woman left the darkened room.

"It's in my sack," said the man.

"Where is your sack?"

"I don't know that I know," he said.

"We'll find that we find it later," said Wort Leontine. "Now you must rest swell. I'll bring you some drink and food outside in the sun. The sun is good. The three of you are in for an adventure of your own, as I am witness to the premonition. I hear a child is quite a task."

Leontine and Christopher were soon outside the tiny house. They stood with the insects and the piles of wood. They stood with their backs to the open window of the room where Sophie slept with the child. The sun shot lances from behind the trunk of a tree, and as Motherwort spoke her rusty frame staggered in the light.

"The sun widens my eyes this morning."

"Don't you mean the daughter?" said Christopher.

"I mean that it is a gift, and looking is my way of giving thanks."

Leontine stood for several minutes staring at the invisible world revealed, then continued in an advising tone, speaking as if the entire family sat before her:

"To each of us, there is a way. Be patient and do not run off, dear father. Have a progressive heart not increasing bile, dear mother. Time and space are yours, dear child. Take place on earth as you are spun."

She paused a moment, and Christopher, not knowing what to say, stared into the distance where he would be left alone, not asked to respond.

"Life without time and space is nothing to compare," the herbalist went on. "With each birth I see the big picture of **LIFE**. It is bold and goes on beyond my ability to see. A child is rooted to ages past, growing stem and leaves and bud. A child has roots and potential flower. But who among us is able to bloom with utter freedom that she may speak of God without having her own petals altered by the name? Who may speak of God without her own colors changed? Who may speak of God and not lose herself?"

There was no answer. Leontine went on:

"Why not each one of us? Study the eyes of a child. See the wish settle into a body. It is God's wish for life on earth. A big, bold picture of life on earth. At the heart of the picture is the wish, which moves all matter. And at the heart of the wish is love, which compels the soul. Where did I come from? Where am I going? Every soul is here to bud and become and to know more than it did before."

Motherwort Leontine drifted in the wake of her words.

"Any children, yourself, Wort Leontine?" asked the burly Chris, trying to bring her back to shore, to language he could follow.

"No, I've never had them," she said, released from her self-imposed spell. "I've always been too old and barren, but mostly too alone."

"Yes," said the young father. And that was the end of his sentence. But not the finish of its route.

Yes.

Yes.

Yes.

To the child half asleep just inside the window. Yes. To her bundle to her ear to her Yes to her soul. She took the word from her father, and in her mother's arms she absorbed the Yes. Opened her eyes briefly and lit upon her mother's sleeping face. Yes. Who had said it? Yes. Who spoke to her now?

Some otherworld inside the child spoke. The child understood the gesture that compelled her to leave the arms of her mother. Yes. To leave. To come. But her mother's arms were walls. They were warm. It was a warm house within. Those arms were just so strong and soft and firm and... They kept the girl from flying off. But still, the otherworld beyond her mother and beyond the light said, Yes. Said, Come. Compelled her. Gestured for her to leave. But still those arms – the complementary weave, tight and supportive and yes, right here. But... O that otherworld again. All so.

You will grow, said the invisible world. No doubt you will grow. But, now, come. Just for a moment. It's not so far. It's not the greening world who calls you, not the sunstruck place where you are, but somewhere closer to your heart where the growth of all plants and the light of the sun got their start. And you. Where you received your start as well. Yes. Come along. It's a party, a part of you always. We miss you so. Just for a moment. Before you forget us and think only of the earth: mud and puddles, ice-cream and stuff. One small lick look laugh yes again. Please.

And why not? It was an easy passage. A rainbow bridge and an undulate run. Winging it over the fields, the folds, and then the melting in. It was an easy passage. It was easy for the girl to go away, and while being away to also be inseparable from the earth and the arms of her mother. It was easy to be two places at once. The life, the love was everywhere. All she was. Was everywhere, too.

Slither black of a one trick snake – the bellyrubber, her lowly trace upon the ground. Remember the snake, the one who was prodded and poked? What a smooth arc, her line. This was the same beautiful creature as happened before the child was born. Dancing leaves and windblown hats. Abundant people from the skies like stars. Sun so warm her feet were burning and every organ pulsed deeply for a chance to breathe. Apples and lemonade, red round cupfuls, spring popping punch. It was a vibrant daylong exhilaration with no time to think it through and no reason to deny its joy. Not one cloud took control of the party. Life floated along, Fun Damental *– a ship on the crimson and the crimson on the sea and the sea on the earth and the earth in space and space – say it with zeal – it was pure unadulterated levity. No keel running aground. No grinding, grimace, no cry. No doubt at all in the face of such confidence. All joy of being. And the chance to be alive somewhere. Joy of wanting to live again on earth. Again on earth. Yes. On earth.*

Yes.

Self contained, the child slowed. She caught upon the confident word. Came back to be in the room with her mother:

Yes.

The newborn lay in her mother's arms. Round about the garden goes the hugging wall. One step two steps you will never fall. There was a gift of time surrounding the child. There was her mother's soft flesh. And gravity's tireless support – all making this home. Her mother might let go at any moment and the child would not float off. She was delivered from one world into another – from strength into arms, from love into hands. She had entered a world where separation is the growing story and touch the voice that slowly tells it.

Slowly the girl would know that she is separate. When she touches something else, when she says **What**, she would begin to know. What words would awaken as the child grows? And would those words enliven connections or deaden the world? It is a mystery how things will turn out. Mystery is born at the same time as the child. A mystery in the hands of her sleeping mother.

Her father sat on the front stoop, drinking. His eyes were heavy and occasionally shut as he stared toward the sun where the bright of it lanced through the lowest branches. Ease up – it was only a small amount of drink. Don't judge. An early drop, but nothing to make him drunk or even wobbly. Sure, thoughts buffeted Christopher, and the new life frazzled his nerves. The sun caught the father's cheek as his head tilted forward, and then it let go so his head would be free to rest against the house. Ahead so free in life. To lean against the house. Face in the shadow. And quiet as can be.

The small cottage was silent, sleepy, and motionless. The wise old herbalist had left without a word to collect dandelion roots and leaves. Some geranium, if possible. A few briny rhizomes from the budding marsh. Mud and clay for binding. She had gone, too, for water for a bath. She would draw the cold liquid from a well on her way home, quietly pump it by hand, bucket after bucket, and lug the weight. No complaints. No words from her other than footfalls and slosh.

So who spoke if everyone remained quiet? There was one voice inside many voices, arms around the tiny baby. What voice sounded as birdsong every now and then, as insect hum and shifting bodies? What voice spun winds, sprung of the world? What were these words that jumped red and engulfed blue, that honed as heat and then coo cool cooled? What wetnesses were they and what dry? The words were everywhere. There was no end to the curiosity. And who among the curious heard the leading word that reigned over all in the flux of sound? Was it they or we? Was it she or I who sensed the thrill of life that led the way? As the world ringed round the sun, spurring wind and weather, spinning night and day.

TWO

Step up. Attend. Take a load off. Here are bare pine benches at my door for bums and toads to sit upon. Sip on water, slurp if you like. You've heard it already of the birth, how small the babe was, how ready to be reeled in. But it's still the early days of the newborn girl. Don't curse her yet. There's lots of story left to tell. Here are pretzels, nuts. Sit and listen to the fairy fine nature of early on life, as she winnows and grows toward her gravestone gate concurrent with my crusty feet. In sonorous might. With fragrant sea.

Synonymous I? Vagrant me?

Stop making fun and listen.

Once, when times were teachers, there arose a mountain from which to see the earth better. And were you a resident of those times and perched on that mountain, able to survey the situation below, that learnable world would have struck you at once as the slow formation of a thought. Looking down at the earth, you'd have seen a vague collection of shapes and colors in a mistbound soup.

Only in the course of your persistent gazing would great tracts of land have separated from the fluidity of the place and forms emerge that you could know. Only in patient time would those forms have taken familiar shapes, their lines becoming recognizable as rivers winding their ways, cutting through the solid ground and coursing to the great sea. And only as things became clear, would you have been able to zoom-in to the trunks and limbs and lacelike twigs upon the face of the earth, and at last to see the distinction of barbs of a feather lying upon the mud, the tracks of worms within that mud, and the mark of some running fox – away.

Human trails, too, would have appeared. And they did appear. And so they were seen. There were footprints on the shore, leading to a man. The man walked fast, aggressively. He strode with purpose and carried a small bundle of a child, strands of the baby's hair glistening in the sun. And what a beautiful sun it was this morning, but there wasn't much time to enjoy it. The man had business, and another line of prints pressed after him. This was the mother, running to catch her husband and child. She paused now and then in the difficult sand, holding out her hands, palms up to support the sky, beckoning him to stop. But he wouldn't stop, even though her fingers radiated like rays of the sun as she reached for her child.

This is that same family we first met in early April. It was a May morning now. The man walked briskly with his sacrificial lamb. The girl was just a month old, and her father carried her gently. Her thick hair lay dark to begin with, but it would change, it would lighten in time. Her eyes were skyblue like those of her father, and she had a milk plump body taking on materia earth.

The man stopped. The 7:00 a.m. sun tried in vain to warm his heart. He planted himself beside a boat at the edge of the bay and waited for his wife. She came and the man placed the child into her hands. The mother, Ev Sophie, believed for a moment that she'd caught the fallen heavens. Alas, the man would not let his wife hold the girl unguarded. He kept a hand on the infant and quickly snatched her away when he saw his wife's weak mind. The mother's thoughts rose from her heart toward her tongue, but they caught in her throat like a lump of bread. She looked at her child, thinking: I gave birth to that girl. Thinking: Sad are the things that are not held, that slip from fingers as a loving God slips from the. From. The mind. Thinking: No I cannot I will not I **NO**.

Ev Sophie pushed against her husband who held her back with his bulk. He placed the child into the hand-hewn log boat that jounced with the small waves that jumped at the shore.

"Husband. Monster!"

"Monster! You are stupid. I am man."

"How so?"

"How not so? Are you not my woman?"

"Wife, yes. Mother, too. Just as you're a father. I struggle to understand you. You are stone to me. You are impenetrable."

"Think less, suffer none," said the man.

"What else is there to do but understand?"

"Do as I do," said her husband. "Reflect God's commands. Thus my soul stirs me to action."

"So I've heard, like daily lashes on my back. Only now the pain is real. Only, now the pain I know is wrong. I've reflected upon it, and I know. Do you not see? This pain floods me greater than the light that swarms the day. It is unkind, unkingly. It's an unwise thing to do."

"It is no unthing as you so rant. No malevolence of me or He, the kind and wise, the most king of all."

"It is this magical mind I fear in you. You are bewitched."

"Bewitched. I'm the very opposite. I am free to live life just as it is truly spoken. Stop switching me with your bewitching verse. Stand back. Take comfort in commandment. I will cut the line."

Ev Sophie held her husband's arm gently and pressed her words.

"You are loyal to one thought alone, the thought that will lose us our child. How can you say it is true?"

"Woman, how can I say you are true if you doubt me? That is the larger trouble today."

"I only doubt that sending our child off, alone, in that boat, is the right thing to do."

"Quit your quibbling and listen well or I will break you as waves break the watersphere, as sun breaks the atmosphere, as God breaks me."

"God," shouted the mother. "Who is your god? Is he mine as well?"

"He is. And as I prayed to our God that our child would live, He offered her existence at a simple price. A deal was struck."

"It was not my deal," said Ev Sophie.

"Must you be part of everything?"

"Raising our child is my decision. It is ours," said Sophie.

"Stupid woman. We do not decide about life. Only God decides. He told me: *I will give her life.* He said it to my ear. To my ear. Our child. He spoke, saying: *I will give the child life, if you will but sacrifice her to Me.* Do you wish for her to live?"

"I—"

"It was the voice of the All, the Mighty, our God, atmosphere, sun, the length of time, the fire bond. Why do you make me repeat this again? And I spoke back, not to the air, but to the voice. I said: To Thee? I asked it. To Thee? as though I had the right to question. And a third time then, To Thee? Yes, said He. Said God. The strong syllable – Yes. Does not that word mean anything to you? Because my mind heard it shining and robust – a commandment. What dull numbing does your mind hear? Would you carry with you a limp and lifeless carcass rather than the infinite trust in God?"

"What trust?"

"Patience, Lord," said Christopher skyward. "Trust is the river Miles, the North Shore, the sea itself. Trust is the flow. It is the heading toward, the not against. From before all time, trust is eternal, internal, unpronounced, in all layers of life. Accept what must be, because it is decided. Why do you protest at the last moment like some headstrong weakling? Break upon God's will, go not strong against it. Hold out your arms in offering. Know that you have no say."

"Did we not bring forth our child out of our flesh our time our loving?"

"Did not God?"

"Did we not accept the child unto ourselves through my labor and our commitment?"

"Did not God?"

"Can we not be the foster bearers before this God?"

"Can not **you** accept **His** will, our God?"

"Did we not show our own will as we conceived and birthed her? Why must God possess our child who was born on earth and whose health is of earthly reflect?"

"Reflect on this: Her health is of Divine light," corrected her husband. "Be pleased you are chosen, not so proud of yourself that you can pit your simple words in opposition to that light."

"Have we no say in the manifestation of our delight?"

The woman gripped tight her husband's left arm.

"None but thanks to say," said the mighty son of Jason, son of lascivious Sireen, stripping away his arm. "The greening fields and the fishful waters are our blessing." Standing knee-deep in the bay, he removed a knife from his belt and showed it to the world. "Say thanks to the spring. Show appreciation to what grows. Grieve not for what leaves us. Respect the dead."

"I see the life," said the mother.

"You see nothing but yourself. Favor God with all your heart and be reminded of what he has given us: Ottar our firstborn son already at our table. Ottar remains who will honor us with his continued strength. Summer will soon be with us, the fruits of all living will ripen well. Be happy with the life you are given."

"I am given life. And Ottar yes. But this is our child, too?"

"You are tiresome. When will you listen?"

"I always listen," said Sophie.

"But you do not hear. The green comes on. The delight. Look about you like a child yourself. And whatever God's will, whatever words He wishes, such is His mind. Hear it. Learn it. Say it out."

"Have we no minds of our own?" she asked.

Christopher bowed his head, tired of her waywardness.

"None but to mind the mellifluous word of God that wends our way," replied Christopher from his bow. "The *Yes* that strikes my ears at least. Mine, at least, if not yours through your stubborn wax."

The child in her boat let out a small peep.

"What of that bird, that voice that strikes the ear?" said Ev Sophie. "Have we no thoughts of our own that demand we protect her life? Can you not think it possible that what you heard of God was not mellifluousness but rather laughing words set to fool you?"

"God does not play games," said cross Christopher.

"Have we no thinking of our own on matters of life?" pleaded Sophie.

"You go on and on, and it is already decided. Think less of yourself and you will less be fooled. Man is slow to understand life and insufficient in his language. God is a quick and ravenous God."

"My heart is hungry, too," said Ev Sophie.

"All hearts are God's. All hunger is God's," said the word-weary father. "No less our child simply because she came from your womb. I've had enough. Now go. Stand back."

Christopher pushed his wife away. He looked at his knife, loved the sharp gleam, and cut loose the small boat with one slash of his blade. Then he shoved the hull hard and stood watching the curious current spin the bobbin tight before casting it out the bay and straight to sea. Solemnly, he gazed at the diminishing vessel, the seaworthy wavecutter. His wife buried her face in her hapless hands. How fast the boat made its way, as though on wings, as if on spirited water.

Christopher the Enchantable, trod off, unmoved. He looked ahead, straight as the tall pines he approached, never once glancing toward his wayward wife or seaward daughter. His duty done, God's will be done. Good Christopher would land in heaven no matter the number of daughters he let go. Good Christopher would always live by authority. He would not author his life. Good Christopher would not fall far from the fixed stars that gave him power and ample aloofness.

And Ev Sophie, she clawed at the water to retrieve her child and threw her arms to the heavens in hopeless pursuit of justice.

None, of course, was given, and she fell to weeping on the spot. Her tear-stricken face swelled and flooded with salty torrents, wave after wave from her unfathoming eyes. It would not stop. She had no power, no depth, and no height. The sky, it was indifferent. Blue insurmountable blue. One distant, unspeaking sky, doused in light.

❖

Think what you will of magical things, the child in the boat was fairy blessed and sturdy as a tall tale. Still, it's likely she would have died if the sun hadn't harbored beside to comfort her and take on her care.

Truth is, the child was unlucky with parents but fortunate with the elements. The warmth of day raised her, fed her soul, and blanketed her each crisp night. Days passed without regret. The light came forth and subsided. And the whole sky she suckled for years just floating. She suckled the sun, the stars, Venus, the moon. She suckled the rain clouds, the gray clouds, the cumulus and the nimbus. There was plenty of food, plenty of drink. And as the air carried her onward, it left upon her brow such a gentle breath that the growing girl smiled as though she was kissed by God.

Kissed – she learned to feel the word. By God – she sensed the life unfolding. Waters lapped at the hull near her ears and soothed her. They bound her boat to the surface of the sea and bore her countless fish, as she grew able to eat them. The fish jumped from the waves and flopped at her bare feet. They spoke the language of martyrs and cooked themselves in the oven sun, pretty much feeding themselves right into her body.

And why not? What's the problem with this story? It's not so difficult to accept, is it? Isn't every life one thing after another, some things miraculous, others malevolent, and most things falling somewhere inbetween? Isn't each person one unfurling fact, with maybe a little fiction thrown in now and then? Had death starved this child in the boat or swallowed her at sea, what would we have learned but that humans are fragile and death is one mean, hard fellow? Whereas I say rather that humans are durable, and it is life, as we each eventually learn – life that is sufficient menace, more tutored in grievous offerings and in difficulties than is death. Death just comes by at the end and gets all the credit for causing distress. I say that life has the bigger hand in it. But that's just me.

No doubt this young girl afloat was blessed so she could live out her life. She was hoisted by deities and fed by sea favors. But as time drifted past, as her body and mind took form, she lived more apart from that sacred world. A person growing up in this world today can't survive on divinity alone. And our child became a child of the earth, separate and sure. Heavenly touched at first, her substance grew distinct as her life went on. Sure, the warmth of sun, the air and water, sustained her with their continued stance. Yet all the while, it was a distinguishing self that was taking hold, the solidification of a most earthly girl.

Though the workings of this change were gradual, the consciousness came overnight. Our heroine rose one day to her feet, unsteady as she stood, and was struck by the world outside her. She wondered over the edge of her boat at so much wavery, boring sameness. And as the wind pushed her on, the hope of something firmer gave her pause to think. She said in her heart, *Sure is the place for me.* I think she meant *Shore.* The girl needed something solid, a real world. She needed somewhere to get out and run.

Call it years, if you will, her time in the vessel. The girl in time came knocking on the shore. It was morning, a quarter past seven. The boat beached itself after such a voyage as would have made Magellan, Erickson, and Odysseus proud. The sun eased from the underworld again and climbed the sky to shower sweet light. Land ho – sand soil flowers flotsam and shit. The waters of her infancy were a far wake away. The waters, having done delivered the loot, now fanned back to God. What was the word? The feeling? The kiss? Some far off memory, a now fading voice. But then there came another.

"Wake up, my child," said mother earth, soothingly. "You've wound your way against great odds. Been birthed to parents both weak and foolish. Been chosen and cast out. Been set adrift on unconscious waves. Abandoned to life itself. You've been bobbed, sunburned, and blessed. Do you know it? And still but a child. A fabulous girl, hair bleached blond, eyes sky blue. How old are you now? Do you know? How long since you were let loose?"

The child could not answer, not aloud, as her conversations had never traveled beyond her interior world.

"I know what it's like, my precious," said the earth. "There are times in the year when I keep to myself, lots of thoughts all deep within. But I'm of no concern here. It's you who is needful. I'll find you a proper place, a home. There's got to be some good fisherfolk with a spare room nearby."

The earth set her mind to thinking.

"How about Lox Strider the bass catcher with his sun-loving wife, Suzette? There'll be eggs every morning and hikes outdoors in the afternoon. And at bedtime, there'll be bright, warm hugs. Won't it be nice to be inundated with love? Or, of course, there's Ester Goodenup and her harpoon man Barclay. He loves the stars and she sings the rhymes: *Dorry Florry fieldmouse, living by the stream. A B C D E F G.* Oldtimey voices, the both of them. They're Luddites when it comes to the progressing world. Legend has it, Barclay, once swallowed by a Sperm whale, was held in the coffin for nearly two days. Exciting stuff. He lived, but lost his love of the sea, his skin bleached white by the acid. The man'll never cast a hook again, but he and his woman will make a fine net for the likes of you. They're good, decent folk. What do you say? The sweaters Ester knits are always delicious colors, and the stories Clay tells spellbind your mind. But you're not responding. Should I take that as a No to both sets of parents? Well, there are others, child. The world is full. Some rope maker or baker of bread, then? Warm loaves every morning, knots to count. There are bankers for your money or lawyers for your rights. Teachers, champions, singers, and scholars. Geologists, ecologists, filmmakers, and poets – I've a soft spot in my heart for anyone who creates. Or, if you'd rather, I could set you up as the child of some initiate, a wise old soul with a passion for beginnings. You have any preferences? I'll fix it for certain, given time, I will."

Why would I want any fixings like that? thought the child, standing in her tightrimmed boat, the gunnels pinching her thighs, her head growing rapidly, five...six...over seven years high. This boat is too small, she thought. And she turned away. The early May morning on her brow. A need to stretch.

"Who needs it more?" asked the earth. "Me or you?"

Me, the girl almost ventured.

"Stretch out, then," said the earth. "Reach, for I am bountiful. Yearn, for I am good. Hope, for I am upholding. Walk, for I am daylight. Speak, for I am all ears."

But the girl kept her voice locked in her throat, not wanting to share.

"I'd say you were seven," said the good earth. "Am I right? Come out of that boat. I won't bite. There are trees and grasses and dirt and stuff."

The girl stepped from the seven-year vessel, shed it like a first tooth. Go on fairies, take it back, she thought. And when the girl looked behind, her boat was gone. She knew at once where she stood. She stood on the shore, and the shore was firm. She knew that she'd have to walk now. Run, if she chose. I'm here, she churned inside. I do what I want. I do what I can. I do what I do.

"I," said the friendly earth. "Is that someone new?"

I stand if I say so, said the girl to herself as though she were figuring it. Alone. She looked around her. Alone. She shivered as if she was cold.

"None of that, my child. Don't go being afraid." The earth bent her way with the limb of a nearby tree. She touched the girl on her shoulder. Ah, the girl was like the earth. She was matter of fact, a clump of dirt, quivering leaves in the morning light. She was good. The earth touched the child and immediately knew her like a daughter. "What do you mean, alone? What about the sun and the green world I lay out for you everywhere? What about the soil underfoot? And what about my friendship? Is there no part of myself in you? Do you stand there and ignore me?"

The girl said nothing to the claim of partnership or to the accusation of ignorance. It was one long moment without a voice. The trees on the bank held their tongues. The grasses hushed their swish and song. The blue flag flowers stilled their flutters. Even the ants set aside their work and waited.

I – the girl struggled with the word, but could not get it out of her mouth.

"Something caught in your teeth?" joked the earth. "What do you call it? A brillig, a tove? Some little twillig will be the pick to get it out."

The girl found a twig and scratched at the ground, thinking of names and naming things.

"Where were you born?" asked the peaceable earth.

The girl had no idea, so it was difficult to say. The sea was in her mind, but its sound was so beautiful, she couldn't get it out. She studied the scrawl she made in the mud.

"To what parents?" the earth persisted. "Perhaps I know them already. Let me give it a try. Your Pop is handsome, isn't he? A youth of some bulk. Just tell me if I'm wrong. His name is Christo or Topher and he has scrapes and calluses on his hands, plus a very stubborn mind. And, if I'm not mistaken, your alluring mother, Ev Sophie, wears lots of gypsy black. She's got Moldavian eyes and black brows and a face that screams for attention. She's a strong beauty, carved from the curve of my graceful arm. Am I right? Of course, I am. But where are they now?"

The girl didn't know where, nor was she certain if her parents were those two. If only she had an accurate memory, then the girl would have known for sure where her family was and who.

"I'm onto you, aren't I?" said the earth. "But if you can't tell me where, do you at least know when you were brought forth? Or was it second or third?"

I was brought first, she did not say.

"No brothers, my child? Oscar Noonboy and the new babe, Johnick the Suite? Just you? You by yourself, nothing else to it?

You, here, sitting on my soil, barefooted and dirty with nothing to say?"

"Do you always got to talk so much?" sputtered the girl, looking up at the trees. The words flew like startled birds. "Can't you leave me a loam?"

"I can't leave you alone. I love you."

"I don't got to listen to you if I don't want to," said the girl.

"So young and plucky like an ungrammatical chick. We could work together on your form if you'd lend a hand."

"My hands aren't library books. I don't want to share."

"This doesn't sound like you." The earth was sad. "If it's a presentiment of who you'll be, what a rotten gift."

The earth was stern, but the little one held her own and cast down her eyes to strike the earth low.

"Nothing you can do will hurt me, my child. Why not take a trip inland, away from this shore. Come to a high place and look down. You can feast upon strawberries and ripe apricots. Listen to the coyotes exercise their voices. Hang out with the huckleberries. Watch the onions grow wild and free. It's all sweet poetry to my ears."

The girl moved from the shore, far from the water. It was almost eight o'clock, the sun still rising. The earth followed her upland, speaking constantly.

"Hey sweet pea. My little periwinkle. How do you like it here? Lots of trees, hills you can look down."

"Are you ever going to stop talking?" asked the girl.

"Oh, I don't see that happening," said the earth. In fact, I'd like to say a few words to help you through the rest of the day."

The girl sighed. The earth ignored it.

"In the morning, people, usually, are their most optimistic. Though, sometimes, they can be a bit grumpy."

"I'm not grumpy," said the girl.

"Morning is all about brightening," said the earth. "High noon you start getting hot, and in the afternoon the bees really hum. You drink the day, run in circles, fall hard, and get back up. Cool evening, the colors slow, and the sun dilates through the thick atmosphere. So long sweet sun. Where are you off to now, you wonder? But just before the bauble sets, you stretch your shadow to the edge of the world. Light plays a fanfare at the horizon, introducing an amazing show of colors. Nice, isn't it? But no sooner said then dull. Things turn gray, then black with stars. Nothing wrong with stars, in fact before you go to sleep you give them a look out your window. Leo the lion, the Big Dipper, too. You put your things away, toss your shirt and pants in the dirty pile, try to remember something...something you did...something. You lie down to sleep in the dark good night.

"But you don't sleep just yet, do you. You lie awake listening, wanting to play. The mice in their meetings, the bats in their flights, the foxes on the sly all come alive at night. So why not you? Homer's up, and he's just a pup. Come Homer. Jump. You call him to your bed, but he'd rather stay downstairs. Sun gone down, moon coming up. Homer's like the sun, he down. You're like the moon. You're up in bed, staring at the dark window, listening to the bark of trees and the bang of stars. It's an interesting world, if you think about it. And all the crows, too. Suddenly, the crows come down with their dark robes and black lace wings. You meet the crowd, the crows, I mean, and they move you to sleep. Their blacks are soft and their backs are warm. Their wings are sufficient to carry you off. You bask in their deepness. You sleep with wings under you, my child. Sleep.

You sleep.

"You grow into the night, becoming a giant. Your head is up among the stars and your feet are long forgotten. Who cares about feet when you can fly? Who cares about the earth when you're atop the universe? Footings in me are the last thing on your mind. It's just how it goes. Every child loses sight of the earth when she falls asleep at night, you no less than the others.

"So, there you are, high and mighty. Sleep, my nodding ragwort. It's a sweet good night. Sleep my lassitude lass etude, melodious sleep. But I'm still here. I listen as you breathe. I see what dreams you dream and what dreams you don't. I am with you throughout the night, no matter that the spirit of you shies away from me, carried by crows, by causes unknown. And soon we will meet again. Daybreak, you will return. I look forward to it, my child. You will wake once more. A new and cheerful day. And I'll be here again. I'll be everywhere. Every minute of me will tick fresh ticks, and I don't mean those awful arachnids that suck your blood like vampires. I mean good times."

The lulling voice of the earth slunk off, done with the day and donning the night. The child lay fast asleep on the barren high-ground. She sat hunched in sleep, exhausted from the wearying words of too much earth at once. And she saw the spreading darkness, feathers of the crows, eyeless crows. She saw the ominous crows, black and bleak, voiceless and cold. Why did they make no noise for her? Where were their caws, their cackles, their eyes and lifting wings?

The child lay empty in this darkest place, far from the shore. She lay unsettled in an emptiest place, as if something had deserted her. What was it that left her alone in this dark? The earth, the sun, colors of the world, mother father family life. She wished for a pup, a Homer to pat. She wished to hear a friendly yelp, and something more.

A familiar
Home
A singing
Mother
A playful
Father
A happy
Ness

Oh, well. This young girl was alone. That's how she felt. And in her dream she pounded the ground she lay upon, fist by fist, day after day till blood tricked from her palms and the dirt sipped it thirstily.

And out of the earth where her blood had flowed was birthed a horrible demon who took the girl home and smacked her about the head when she forgot to wash his plate after eating, or when she was slow with his cup of cool water.

Why did you forget such a thing? I need to know why. I need to know now. Tell me why. Tell me now. Why. Now. Tell me. Tell me.

Such was the first bad dream the young girl had, and often it was repeated. The thing about it, maybe it wasn't a dream at all but a disappointing life. Because when the girl awoke, yes, it was a new day, though it all felt sadly the same, tight and binding, as her dream. And what was wrong now? What wrong now? She had overslept again.

THREE

Here we are again. Things look different, don't they? I'm not quite sure what to make of this girl I'm telling, even though she's me. That must sound strange. I'm just being honest. When I come for good, when I enter the story for real, this girl will evaporate and I'll be much more at home with the person I'm telling. Until then, it is what it is. There's probably some lemonade in the fridge if you want, but I think the pretzels have gone stale. Don't eat them.

Story has it, the child soon walked about like someone's daughter. Word is, he wasn't very nice. Our girl was growing, but she still sputtered when she spoke. Don't we all, sometimes. She breathed the same old argon rich air as everyone. She was afraid of the dark. She liked some things and hated others. Typical for a girl her age. She was a phlegmatic sort who was made to work till her back ached out and she couldn't feel her hunger. She thought little, said less, sniffed at the June flowers and saw what she could of the world around. Yet, the feel of things, which should have been full of awe and wonder, was an awful feeling for our young heroine. It was all business and burden and very little childhood. That was rough. I can sympathize. Some get it so troubling tough. Others don't. I don't know why. She was one of the some who got it bad. Let me see if I can recall.

Once, in a place as much like here as anywhere, there came a stunning day. Cloudless. Clear. Morning. Hunger. More hunger. None could resist the call: **Rise. Welcome. Smell the distant fields, the food in the colorful valley, and the flood of intoxicating odors – pine and moss and the ferns in their unfurling. Stand. Greet. Conquer. All.**

The June sun rose over the leafy world and stole gently upon the eyes of a halfsleeping girl. Springtime turned overnight to summer, and the blue-eyed child lifted her head, turned her eyes slantwise upon the sky.

Ack, sun! Waking was such painful news to this child. Even the gentle nudging of the sun was sting. The man sitting beside his girl saw those round and far-roving eyes. They reminded him of his sameyed wife, whose eyes though brown not blue had such similar roundness and the seductive look of places far away.

Oh, that scamming enchantress, his Evita Sophie the gypsy wench, unfaithful slut, the smut of her flesh, her wretched winching ways. Tighter. Tighter yet. The vamp. Belle elfin sort sans merci. How he might grab her and remold her body, if he only could. Hold her. O, down. Down. He choked on the stinking reminder of her air. The hate in his life was for the whole of her being. He thought only how this woman, his abandoning wife, had iced his heart with her coldness and fired his soul into unforgiving. Cooked and crazed, it was a red raging soul. Things still burned in him, bludgeoned him, wound his flesh tight, clenched and clinched him, pinned him high and mighty. Vengeance – the gentlest thought that moved him now. He simply had to punish her for his lost face and humbled pride. He had to find her, bring her back. He had to relieve his anger, to beat the fire that blazed inside him, to put back time, to start again, control all life, to demand consistency, insist on one truth, to—

"Rise girl," his voice slammed, his right hand rousing his daughter roughly. "You sleep too long and the morning is half over. Why don't you wake at the crackest dawn?"

"What time..." began the girl in her sleepy voice. The trees were bright beside her, smelled green and sufficiently summer, even though the season had just begun. It was a delicious smell, and there were bountiful colors in the meadows beyond.

"What..."

He would not answer, he was so wrought with flame. But she dared to touch his side with her finger, dared because she might burn and a small burn would get her moving. It was the only reason she had to touch him. She'd felt it on her flesh before, felt her insides burning with his spurn. And now, she felt his red emotions again when she touched him. He spun and glared upon this sunken sprite.

"What is it?" he bellowed.

"Wh-what..."

"Spit it out."

"What food is there?" she stumbled.

He looked at the sun cleaving through the trees – just after eight by the light of things. A smile shifted across his face.

"Sun. Sun is the food of the day," he exclaimed. "Because you have waked so late."

"What about you?" she bravely questioned.

"Me? Good of you to be concerned. I've had my fill."

The girl stood and shook herself free of her long sleep.

"Are we going down?" she asked.

Still looking at the sun, eyes squinting, he crisply spoke:

"We're going forward, you donkey, not down. I've told you."

"When do we stop?"

"I've told you."

"I'm tired of walking. I'm tired of—."

"Whiner, whiner, pants on fire. Are you deaf?"

"No."

"Who would know it," said the unrhyming man. "I've told you all. And still you wag your tongue with questions. Everything is what I've said. You're just like your mother. Why don't you listen?" Her father adjusted his gaze from the far off sun to the somewhat nearer harbor with boats. "Clamp your mouth. Pack your stuff. Eat your crust. Let's go."

Her father tossed a tear of rye bread, and the child ate it and drank her stale water. Her disagreeable hair hung upon her face.

"Clean your face. I see only snakes. What captain will want such an ugly crew as you?"

"Snakes!"

The girl backed off. Her father headed east from the hilltop down to the port, disregarding his daughter's alarm. She came running after him, wiping the snakes from her forehead, wiping her mouth with her arm.

"Why do we have to go on a boat?"

"Are you as stupid as your words?"

"No."

"Stupid as you are dirty?"

"No."

"Stupid as what, then?"

"I'm not stupid," braved the lass.

The father stopped.

"And yet you remain with me in my black shadow. Ha," he burst. "I'd say that's stupid. Stupid is as stupid does. And stupid is all you can do."

She did not understand him, but the tone, as usual was unpleasant. They stood among the heavy grasses, the clover and greens that graced the hillside.

"Where's your rhyme and reason?" asked the father. "It's your same question everyday. Why why why?"

"You never answer me."

"Then why do you persist if you get nowhere with your quest?"

They continued and after a while the girl asked:

"Where is Mama? You mumble about her always."

"I don't mumble."

"I hear you in my sleep."

"You don't hear anything."

"Why won't she come back?" asked the girl.

Her father spit.

"Are we going to rescue her?" asked the girl.

Her father was silent.

"In my dream you were looking for the motherland. Is that where we're going? Does she have her own place?"

Her father stared at his daughter as they walked. He stopped, bent beside her, and took the girl roughly by the shoulders.

"What dream?"

"I—"

"I am not fond of dreams. Their mystery frightens me."

"It was nothing."

"Every nothing is something," the father roared.

"It was you, aboard a ship. You sailed off with lots of men."

"My crew? My throng?"

"I don't know their names," said the girl. "You beat the sky and the boat bounced the waves."

"You see, your dream is wrong. Waves do the bouncing."

"There was a big word – MOTHERLAND – in white letters on the water. Other words, too."

"What else was written?"

"O this is odd. O this is us."

"O what is odd? O what is us? Your dream is stupid."

"And your name, too."

"My name? Good."

"No, it said Christopher."

"I know my own name," said her father.

"And laughter," remembered the girl. "You heard it. I heard it, too. Laughter at you. You spun to me, thinking I was behind all the laughter. Your face was a blade, flashing silver. The sun was a yellow volcano. The sunlight jumped on the waves. I saw the jumpy sparkles. I saw the sun explode. It swallowed you whole. It burned a hole right where you stood. And you were gone. That's all. Nothing more. The sun disappearing you, and the ocean squinting where the ship went through."

"You are wrong. Most everything you say is wrong. The sun does not swallow and oceans don't squint. Neither am I burned by the sun. I am like the sun. I am of the sun," said her father. "See the sun in me. See me shine and flare and feast on fodder of the day. I am strong and will not be made weak by anyone. Do you hear?"

"In my dream, the sun got brighter and then you were gone," challenged the child. "I watched from the shore. I saw it happen."

"And I say you are stupid if you give mind to your dreams. They are nothing but child's play. You'll not be left on shore but coming with me. And why? Because I say it. Because there is no choice for you. You are my charge. I am decided to put all matters to rest so my soul may be at peace. Your fate is enslaved to me. You follow my lead like wet follows rain. Were my mother or father, God rest their pitiful souls, alive, so be it you'd not have remained with them. Oh, they would have wanted you, so you might clean the stalls and sweep the floors, so you could've been their grunt and grime, to grind you sharp. Hard labor for a child is something good. Mending the sails. Difficult work for a mere half-empty glass like you. Toting tools. Terrible work for a girl the likes of you, the way you whimper all the time, complaining at the slightest ache and pain. They would have insisted you stay with them, to lighten their load and toughen your soul. They would have bartered for you, but no. You are with me till the end. Me, your father. I'm the one to put all matters to rest. You are part of the matter. You are so much like your mother, you changeling child. You must learn a proper faith in absolute truth, not capricious fiction. Do not expect to escape your fate with me."

He stared down the hillside. The girl saw her father's storm that blustered about his steel-eyed face. His grip was iron and firm, constricting her blood, her flow. Her heart worked hard to unleash herself. She felt such pulse on this quiet morning. It beat throughout her body. And the winds on this warm day rolled in from the south.

"When we reach the port," said her father on the level, "you'll secure a ship for us."

"What's secure?"

"Get, you imbecile."

"How me?"

"How not! I'm told there's a captain who takes a liking to young girls. Let him touch you till I come. I'll not be long. Besides, they will have heard of me. I've got a reputation. There's a list of great captains. I'm on that list. They'll want me upon their wimp vessel. That is all you need to know. Am I being clear?"

The girl felt his fingers squeeze even tighter. The pain in her arm increased to the brink of all she could take. Her mind dulled and the man's lips flinched into an odd smile that showed how powerless he truly was. He released and continued walking, but his terrible grip lingered with the child, leaving an impression on her skin and suffocation in her heart. He checked his belt for his knife, and his pocket for the gold coins. The blade was his utmost concern.

Every night as they had journeyed to this place, she had watched, intending to sleep, but the sound of scraping metal distilled her. She was all ears and eyes – listening, watching as he took the switchblade from his belt and sharpened it. Even had he not used it during the day, he honed the blade at night, and then tuned it upon a leather strap he carried. Stinging metal, tone of blade. Sound enough to disturb the dead.

He struck her, too, with that leather when she fell on the trickiest rocks or forgot to carry him water pronto. She hated that strap. Hated its sound. Leather on her shoulder just as the morning birds were singing. What an awful discord. Then the whole world became still, quiet, except for her eyes that welled with fury. In her thoughts she flung that strap to the weeds, but it always snagged on a troublesome bramble, dangling just enough off the ground for her father to see it. There. Calling him with its pitiful quaking voice. Don't forget me. Look this way, my good hand, my man. Look over here. Don't forget me. And in her mind he always reached for it. Ah, my friend. I've got you.

"Water." The possessed man called to his daughter as they walked. The girl's own thoughts dissolved like salt in boiling liquid. She fetched her father his fill.

"This is hot," he yelped, throwing most of it on her face. "And tastes like sweat." He spit. "Have you dripped in my cup? Did you not dip from that stream were we slept last night? Did you not bury the horn to keep the water cool?"

She stared at the ground.

"You didn't..." she began.

"Go back," he said in level words.

She stood.

"Go back," he barked to the treetops.

"But we're on our way."

"Do I not have eyes in my head? I know what we're doing. Did I not say that I wanted drink? I wasn't speaking to myself. Is there something still unclear to you? I want the cool water from that stream. Now go."

"Will you..."

"Do you think I will stand still for you? It will teach you to listen, to do as I say. You will run, and you will come running down the hillside into town for me. You will do whatever I say. Running as always for your father and your precious jewel."

He dangled a necklace and his daughter was hypnotized. What could she do but return to the stream? There were berries near the steam. She would run. It was not far. What else could she do? She had no mind for options. Besides, he carried her jewel, the metalwork, the work of the old gypsy. Dark eyed gypsy, late night gift. The girl could almost see her again, that hunching woman. The old woman's face was wrinkled in the moonlight. It aligned with the stars.

She was kind, remembered the girl. She had deep eyes, dark like her own mother's, or so she'd been told. There was easiness about the gypsy's voice and pleasure in the old woman's hand upon her back. It was just the right weight. And was she a gypsy, really? And was it true the girl's mother was a gypsy, really? Everyone always told her stories. Was it true that the old woman was her grandmother? Maybe so. She was a heavenly woman who made necklaces out of stars.

Her father coughed. He spit and dangled the gift. Why did he carry the chain that had been forged for her alone? Forged from stars for...

❖

The old woman had made it, and it smelled like garlic, like fennel, precious spice, a gift. The gypsy fingered the metalwork and it singed her hand it contained so much love. At least, that's what she said. What was the necklace made of? The girl wanted to have the wonderful thing. It shone. It was streaming light. What was it, really? She wanted it so.

And the gypsy woman showed the child the gleam of the jewelry and touched her with its brightness. It smelled like heated fat, like basil, like flowers, like the night full of stars.

Look at all the stars, she thought.

It was a clear night where the girl and the old woman sat. The child knew the heavens nearby, and every thing and every smell came because of those close and perfect stars. The two sat in front of the fire and stared. The smell of burning wood, cooking meat. Sizzle and spit. Cough and spitting flames. Look up. The turning stars.

"See. The mark of God," said the woman, holding out her hand, showing where the necklace had scorched her. "Mark of God. Heavenly G."

And didn't it hurt?

"No, it doesn't hurt," said the woman.

"Why did God..." the child began. The last word meant nothing to her. What was God to her?

"It's for you, my Periwinkle."

"But God... Why did..." the girl repeated in curiosity.

"The chain and sweetest love, my Periwinkle. Look at the mark, chickadee."

The child saw the burn upon the old woman's palm. It curved like a serpent. It crossed and recrossed itself in perfect form. The gypsy held out the metal.

"Someday the soul will be strong enough to hold life without the burn."

"What?" asked the girl, distracted. She longed for the chain, the wonderful thing.

"Take it, and do not let it out of your sight. Keep it yourself."

"What?"

"Take it," the old woman repeated, her hand extended. "It is nothing more than a symbol, like a word that says my love. You carry the life. And your journey with life is what matters most.

Live sure with the gift. There can be no doubt that we all are blessed. Okay now."

The girl stared at the finely wrought necklace and smiled at its iridescent beauty. This was something she could love. A rainbow after clapping storm. A friend who is happy to be with you.

"It is only the beginning," said the woman. "An object. A gift. It's not the truth itself, but a reminder."

The child, immovable, looked upon the necklace, and the old woman coiled it into her hand. Soon the girl asked in the quietest voice:

"Do you know where my mother is? Are you my... grandmother?"

The woman did not hear the whispers. Her ears were old and senseworn.

Grandmother. That was the last word of the conversation. Night full of stars. The old woman looked upon the sky in the privacy of her mind, alone, unapproachable, fingering the studded dome. No more talking. The fire near their feet burned slow. And as the dark woman pointed to star after star, her throat, observed the girl, fluttered as if the woman were singing.

How could she leave her father? He spat on the ground. He held the wrought jewel and smiled to let her know he was her master. How could she leave him? He pocketed the jewel and relieved himself to make mud of the dusty ground. He gave much of himself that burned in her but none of it singed like love. Off she ran for his water, fast for his drink, knowing she would return and he would be neither grateful nor different.

And the old woman had said God when she showed her hand, but what of it? What was in her palm, really? A birthmark, scrapes, a scar? God was a large word in the girl's ear. It was nothing that could fit in an old woman's palm. Straps fit in palms. Knives were perfect. Berries. Berry stains. Did God have something to do with knives and fire, scratchy thorns, and being hungry all the time? Did God have anything to do with the green earth and water and fruit ready for the picking? The earth around gave more trouble than answers, like rocks and roots for tripping on.

The girl continued running. She too might spit sometimes. Onto the ground. Right into the stream. She relieved herself by squatting. The ground would become wet, become mud. It wasn't a golden arc, though. No glistening stream. What did she see of herself? Not much. But no – what did she see? What? There had to be something.

She might some days wonder about being a robber girl, stealing food, clothes, paper for making things, whatberry colors for painting with. And she might even cry, but why? And how to cry, to make the tears work for her but not make her feel worthless? How to do more than just get up and go, to the steam for water, to the earth for early summer berries, get going get down get back to her father, back to the walking, her tired legs and dirty hands, get up each morning and go, get this get that, fetch like a dog? Not even a good dog. Not a dog people loved. She might just die someday like the birds her father stoned, die someday like the rabbits he broke with his bare hands, wrenched with his bare hands, their limp bodies lifeless, die someday like a plant a bug a drop of drying water on a sunny stone – dead. But how to keep going – how, if she couldn't? She was helplessly lonely. She would have to live long and full to get over that feeling. She would have to livelong and great like an eagle, an osprey, a floating gull so high on sky.

The girl dipped water now. Cool. It was cool. She continued fast, did not stop. The world around her, upon her flesh, touched her lightly. Warmly the world caressed like a mother. Maybe a mother. Who knows if she really had a mother? Who knows if she and her mother shared similar eyes? Who knows how a mother might touch? Who knows if it would feel good like the world sometimes? How could the girl know anything about her own time on earth if she felt no connection? Her feet dragged along, unconnected even with the ground. To begin with, the ground was distant, the world was far, and the eyes of her mother and the love of her father, far farther than she could bear. Yet, she would not lose sight of her gift.

Such were the half conscious thoughts that welled and danced rings round the girl, dancing concentrically from where she ran, out to some other body, to where she was growing. Her arms swung as she ran. She knew very little of her current body and nothing of any other body. How could there be another body? The girl knew nothing of her growing, either. She knew only the physical water in the horn and running faster faster to her father.

Her father was a long way off. He dripped sweat as he walked down the road, which was a road not in service any more. As he neared the port city, the sun crept up the morning, drying all the dew from the fieldgrass. Anger, as usual, overwhelmed the man. What was keeping his daughter? She was always making trouble. Nothing was ever easy with her.

He turned, hearing her approach.

"It's about time," he said. He noticed her blood.

"What story is that?" he asked. Was this concern?

"A scrape on some thorns," said the girl.

"And where are my berries, you selfserving tyke?"

He got out his leather and swung it. Stung the air with whip and snap.

"Here," she whimpered, pulling from her large pocket a wrap of wild strawberries.

He wolfed down the lot.

"Never hold out on me," he commanded. "Nothing evades my knowing. I am..."

She did not hear what followed as she was gazing at her father's shadowless form. The sun lumbered midway up the eastern sky, cutting at the child's torso.

"Where's your shadow?" asked the daughter.

He looked behind but was not alarmed. There stood the powerful man in full light of morning, casting no shade.

"It is as I said to you before, and now my whimpet you perceive – I am as the sun itself. No room for a shadow to encumber me."

The girl looked again, and her father's shadow returned. It struck the ground with a thud, lying dark green at his back.

"Move on," barked the man. "What ails you, donkey?"

The girl led her father to the city docks. She heard him, at her back, dragging his shadow down the road and cursing. It was a rough, dirt road, pebbly in her eyes, burnt ochre on the soles of her feet. Soon the panoramic view of the port was interrupted by particular buildings and, all at once, people everywhere. It's sort of exciting, thought the girl, seeing the commotion on the pier. What were these people doing, and where had they all come from so quick?

It was a wonderful earth in her face and at her feet. It was a warm southerly breeze on the side of her face, if only she could have enjoyed it. But there was very little enjoyment for the girl in her life, outside of seeing her father asleep. Still, she was young. There was the chance for improvement. Why couldn't she have her childhood back? This was the proper time to befriend the dirt and play with colors, to entertain the sky with her wishes and the water with her games, to stand upon this June stone or pluck that June flower, to taste crab cakes and taffy and to smell each spice of the cooking June world.

Her father shoved the girl's left shoulder – the loafer, the day-dreamer. She stumbled on. And father and daughter made their final descent from hills.

The a.m. harbor cast a royal blue welcome. It brimmed with watermen and pitching masts. The girl now ran ahead, into the breeze. She left her father far behind as she sprinted to the docks that swarmed with workers. How long it had been since she'd known such a crowd. What was all this work about? The fishermen and sailors looked at her oddly, her hair like a shewolf, disheveled and knotty. Naively, she smiled, feeling at home here. There were briny odors and oily smells. There were rays of sunlight on her bow, her brow, her—

"Hello, small one," tapped a tiny bright man.

His tap was just enough to stop the girl's thought.

"Who are you, child?" Again he tapped on her shoulder as the child stood staring at the workboats, the ships, the trawlers and sloops in the harbor. She jerked his way. "Don't be alarmed."

She said nothing.

"Where's your mother, child?"

"I don't..."

"I'm sorry," said the man, his bearded face bursting with sunlight. "I forgot. You don't know. But what about your father? You know him all too well, don't you? Is he a good man or a cad?"

She would not answer, because the words confused her.

"Or should I call him cod? I smell a fish in your wake."

She said nothing to the sunny little man. Why was he asking her questions? She wasn't inclined to discuss her life with strangers.

"Cat got your tongue, my little periwinkle?"

"Periwinkle?" said the girl, happy with the word.

"That's the tune. I notice softness about your inside, no matter the hardness going round. And true, I'm not at all hard myself. Not unkind, good periwinkle."

The child thought this over.

"However, little children running free are sure to be caught by ones who are nasty. Officers of the law. Loyalists of the lock and key. Laborers of the docks. Some deal with children roughly. They are rogues and ruffians. Some bite off their ears and call them bad names. Those ones are stooges of the devil himself. But you're too quick for those dimwits. Besides, I'll not allow anything bad to happen. But, I'm talking too much, aren't I?"

"A little."

"Just listen to these quick words and take them to heart. There is a house, far from this village, at the corner of a field, high hills behind, a weeping willow with no business being there. The calling of the woods is what you'll hear there, pine maple hemlock wind. A couple who has no girl lives in that house. Two boys are all they've got. How sad for them to be so girlless. They are demanding, but honest. They eat Sunday breakfasts as a family, but sometimes things feel a bit gloomy inside. I've heard they want a periwinkle lass to brighten their ways."

The man noticed the girl's confused expression.

"It's simple, my child. I'm a dreaming man, a man with visions. All good children need a home. I'm fostering your well-being out of my dream."

"What dream?"

"In the beginning the dream was you waking up. You weren't very happy, and it made me sad. And at the end, you went to live far inland. Don't ask me how, but I think things went well after that. I'll offer you a map if you need directions. What do you think of the plan?"

"What plan?" asked the girl.

"Of escape, good child. And a different life. Now speak quick of your father. I know he's coming."

The girl turned up her eyes. After a spell she spoke.

"I have dreams, too," she said. "Just last night..."

A hand clasped the sloping shoulders of the sun-drenched man.

"What is this waffle I sink my claws into?" The voice clapped loud. The fingers clenched tighter. "You're talking to my charge, grandpa." The girl's father cast the old man aside and looked toward the ships of the harbor like an eager child among chocolates.

"Enough of your sprinting," he said to his daughter. He held her in place with his iron hand. Then he turned to the wimpish man with the sunny gray whiskers that roughed up his face. Laughter spilled from our father's throat.

"You're still here? Why? I thought you'd've run off like a mouse."

"To serve you, if I June."

"If you June?"

"The very month. Just after if I May. It's summertime. A beautiful tune."

"Enough prattle. Tell me, old mouse. I need a ship for the Balkans."

"A ship for a bald man?"

"The Balkans."

"For you, bulk man?"

"Not bald man, not bulk man. The Balkans, you deaf drone."

"Ah, Balkans. Yes. I do no work, have no sting, and cannot hear well. Therefore, I offer you my seed of knowing."

"What seed, you little irritant? I swear I'll make you cry, if I don't hear better language from your lips."

"Enough of balling, more can do," said the old man. "I know of such a vessel as will carry you homeland. Motherland, actually."

The word stopped the father, as he thought of his daughter's dream.

"Where?" he asked.

"In my head, of course, where knowledge is stored for use by the brain."

"Of what good course is your knowing, if it leads only to idiocy?"

The burly father smiled at his cleverness.

"Now tell me which ship it is and where, old man."

"The witch is the Ocenchantress you must travel if you're to be made aware."

"Aware of what, pointless fellow?"

"Where you're going – that's my point."

"I wish to know where a certain ship lies," said the father more to himself. "I want a simple answer to a pointed question. Why am I met with this comedy?"

"Your ship will never lie, my bulky bruin. But will sail a true course."

"Enough of wit and more of where," yawned the father.

"To the Balkans."

"Where is it?" said the father, his voice rising.

"I've never been, but am told it's a good ways off. There's a dilemma, however, and that's the sea. The sea is both the way and in the way. Without the sea, you'd make it there by foot."

"Where is the ship I need, little man." The beast spoke calmly. "If I'm played with any more, you'll make it somewhere by my foot, and it won't be good."

He began to kick the old man.

"Please, kind sire. It is in the harbor, no doubt, where all ships lounge – ringing riggings, righting wrongs, heaping hulls with precious cargo. Captain Eidon Posset is your man."

"Eidon what?"

"I don't know the name you wear, but you put on tyranny well enough."

"You are but a dwiggart and a swill."

"An odd combination of words."

The father took the man by the neck.

"Which ship, my simpleton, or need I find the answer in your blood?"

"G-G-Good soldier. Good god." The old man pointed emphatically to a classic ship. "G-Goes by the name, P-P-Pseidon."

The father released the little man and smiled.

"Captain Eidon of Poseidon. Is he the one who likes the girls?"

"Aye, he is. He's fond of all humans."

"Then he's a fool," said the father, and to his daughter he commanded, "Take this gold, girl, and secure us passage. The poop for me. I have roughed the seas enough and will not stand below. The break of waves is my home. For you, the steerage is the order. Now run. Show flash to me, show flesh to the captain. And refer to me by name. I am known far and wide."

The girl carried the gold to where the good Poseidon harbored. The two men watched her run.

"She's a fast one, sire," said the little man. "Nothing will poop her out. Steering toward the age of eight or nine, si?"

The father remained silent.

"Too much of a question? Or is it the Spanish accent that confused you? Perhaps the counting is too severe?"

"I am not interested in you, ancient wreck."

"You insult me with your uninterest. I am a beggar after every scrap of knowledge."

"Then beg apart from me, as I have no information to satisfy your hunger."

"You word yourself terribly well, but no word of heritage?"

"What word of heritage?" asked the father.

"Just one. A simple number. I wondered it myself in the beginning of this joust. Is she just eight or past it? Is such it her age that suffers you no end?"

"You are such it I suffer, clown," said the father. "Will this it ever end?"

The two remained silent for a while, the old man nudging close and Father Christopher brushing him away as if he were a fly. At last the girl ran up, a rescuing sight, announcing her findings as she flew.

"The parson I talked to," she huffed.

"What parson?" demanded her father.

"Godspeed."

"That's no name."

"Said they've been waiting a month for you to come. Why are we so late?"

"Did I not say I was well known," said her father.

"Another said have your seal eggs ready. What is a seal egg?"

"Sea legs, you swill," corrected her father. "Now, tell me what."

"What?"

"When?"

"When what?"

"How much time till we depart?" he shouted.

"They cast off with the bell of a very soon hour."

"There's beauty in that bell," said the old man.

"This day!" Christopher exclaimed, ignoring his nemesis. "All is good. My timing perfect. Fate has made this happen."

"Not fate," said the tiny man. "Dreams more like it. Captain Eidon is superstitious. His dreams lead the way for him."

"This captain is a simpleton. I'm wary of dreams. Is there no other vessel?"

"They are waiting for you," said his daughter. "With a commode and a hutch."

"Commodious cabin, no doubt for hatching your ideas," corrected the tiny man.

The child reached into her father's pocket. He grabbed her wrist, and time and all things froze.

"The gold," she said with calm. "Captain Ion came to me. He'd take none and I pushed it three times. Three. I called you Captain Christopher. He stared at me like I was an angel. He knew the name because he found it in his sleep. Asked if you were of Marsweed? Yes, I said. Is his father Jason, he asked? Yes, but dead, I said. Tall and stout? he asked. Like an oak, I said."

"An oaf?" asked the old and wiry man.

"Then he yelled."

"Yelled?" questioned the old man.

"Yelped like a puppy," corrected the girl. "He said, By God it is given. Said something about assuming you."

"Amusing you, no doubt she means," the old seaweed nodded. "Captain's got plenty of fine stories to tell about whales and winds."

"And others got like flees all jumpy and glad," said the girl. "They were gladdest that you chose their sloop."

"Gladys?"

"Whatever the word. They were happy," said the girl.

"Sloop!" her father bellowed. "She's no sloop. Count her masts. Take note of the rigging. Her ropes will sing like a hundred harps at sea. Why am I surrounded by imbeciles and blight?"

"Be light with your daughter," came the little man to the rescue. "She's sloppy with words, but let her have her say. She's only a wee tadpole. Be happy you are Christopher atop the world, honored with a commodious situation. A roustabout man such as yourself, a bright and lively fellow, so be it. A rigmarole. You will raise the morale of all you meet. You're well known far afield for your lip and labors. Hallelujah! Praise the lord!

"My name is known this side of the mountainous world." The recognition had stroked his ego. "I am not surprised."

He released his grip, and the child pulled back her clenched hand.

"It seems you are even more famous than lightning or thunder," said the little man with the ample gray whiskers. "Perhaps if we all had your headwinds, then wherein truth we are mortals, we might instead be called gods."

"Speaking of headwinds, take my things to the ship," commanded the father to his daughter. "I need a drink to toast my luck. Wait for me aboard. This town is no place for a pip like you."

"Heigh ho then, merrily we go," said the old man to the master. "Follow me to the drinking hole to nip a plug o gypsy brew."

The father grabbed the man and squeezed him breathless.

"Never utter that word in my presence."

"I resolve never. To mention the. Unmentionable again," gasped the little fellow. "Only remind me which word it was."

"Gypsy," said Christopher, releasing his Herculean hold.

"Never heard of such a sea as The Jip. But to The Tip Sea am I headed if you will take me to the water's edge."

"I'll take you, old drunkard. And pour you a grape sea glass of it myself. As for me, the rip sea rules my raging soul, and a trip this good day I'll take upon it. How long I've waited for revenge. I've journeyed from farthest shore to the mountains and over, foot by foot by never forgiving. *Forget not, forgive not* – it is my powerful motto. The year is not yet over. She'll not escape her fate, which is the fact of me. Godly I'm guided by one line of thought."

"What gilded line of thought do you go by?"

"Fate, small grandfa. Fate is in my hands. I have a faithless wife and her devil of a daughter, a blade and a merciless will, no more."

And off they went, the meek and the mighty, for a belly o brew before sailing.

❖

The sun dutifully arced across the sky. Bright heavens, up there. Blue waters, hello. June colors of the land, farewell. The ship cast off and sailed steadily out the harbor.

Captain Eidon Posset stood at his helm. All hands sprang to his clapping orders. The sky rang with his words as the men hoisted the mallowwhite sail and tugged on the rawhide halyards, tightening the sheets. Hard to. Lay on. A beam wind came upon the starboard crisp. Ho, the work was rugged tough. The men were gusts of labor and lusty one and all, kissing the wind, the naked spray, as if it were a woman. And, because the wind was not enough, Captain Eidon blew like a gale. The canvases caught the air, and the strong ship made her way, slicing the waves as swiftly as food cuts through hunger.

Father Christopher stood on the poop, looking back. It was good to be aboard and sailing. The port wove into the shore and our man Chris could see few remaining details of it. He noted a point of land that beckoned with two figures and a bit of metallic gleam laughing to his face. What detail was this that caught his eye? Christopher stood entranced.

"She's nowhere below," came the voice of a midshipman.

"Look again," Chris said, not turning. "You know this ship, if you know anything in life. Find her hiding place. She's there."

"I looked three times."

"Shoot the nearest star then and find her where she's at. There's always a fourth."

The midshipman, his lips never meeting, returned to the interior of the ship, and Christopher continued his backward stare.

"Excuse me, sir," said a young cabin boy.

Christopher spun at the needly voice.

"What... Who the prick are you?"

"I ... I..." he stuttered, all a grin.

"Spit it out, Grinwell?" said the father, burning.

"I am assigned you."

"An ass beside me. What of it? I have my totegirl. Go on. Tend another hive, drone."

"As you wish, sir. But by another's wish I'm instructed."

"What swish are you talking about? Speak English."

"Yes. Well, I've come to say..."

"No more," boomed the father. "I've had my fill of words."

"Have an eyeful with this glass, then. See her on the shore, among the bobbing gulls and simple grasses." The boy was pointing. "Sure enough, I thought you knew. But Captain Eidon sai...d..."

Christopher wrenched the hand scope away, cutting the boy's word in two. There on the shore, with the wimpish slopeshoulder drunkard, he saw his daughter. She swung something in her hand, left right left right, like a pendulum. The greenery of late morning marsh. The June hills in the distance. And the boat cut on. Commotion on deck. Away, away. Suddenly Christopher recalled his daughter's dream.

"Turn her about."

"Turn her about?"

"The boat, you clucker."

"I'm sorry, sir."

"I am Captain Christopher of Marsweed."

"I'm sorry, sir. Even were you Odysseus himself I could do nothing."

"I say, turn her for my girl. I mean to retrieve her."

"Captain Eidon bellows the orders, sir. Besides, he knows of your girl on the shore. We're heading to the southern hemisphere. It's winter there. Day by day we'll be getting colder."

"The South. But no!"

"There are no two ways about it," said the boy.

"I was promised passage to Europe."

"It's a shame you were mispromised."

"Speak again, miscreant, that I may hear something more to my liking."

"Cookie crumbles. Just desserts," said the boy. "The wind is picking up."

"I'll pick you, lightweight. Toss you to the wake."

"Sir, I will return when your mood is less risky."

Christopher feeling the need to toss something, tossed the scope into the waves and howled at the slipping shore. He even thought of diving, but knew he could not swim.

"You cannot swim, sir?" said the cabin boy. "That's a shame."

"How do you know my thoughts, swine?"

"A lucky guess, I suppose. And sir, there is one more thing."

The boy pulled a paper from his pocket and read.

"Your daughter has her chin."

"Her chin? What are you reading that makes you sound like an idiot?"

"A note."

"More of a not to my ears. What anatomical drunkard wrote it?"

"A man less my size and weight, much older."

Christopher snatched the paper.

Her chain, he read. Not chin. He reached for his pocket. The metal was gone.

"Where is it, pincher?"

"It?"

"The chain."

"Ah, is that the word. I saw no A. I swear I saw no A."

"Give me the piece."

"There is little peace at sea, sir. But I tell you, your girl she has her peace on shore. Orders were to read you this news. I'm sure it must make you happy."

"The chain. She's stolen it from me."

"I'm sorry to hear that. Is it important, sir?"

The father reached for the spyglass, forgetting the waves had already swallowed it.

"The glass was a gift from the Captain," said the cabin boy. "He meant to see you hold it."

"Common thieves and drunkards." Christopher's words slashed the air. "Fools surround me. I will not be done."

"No, sir. I believe you, sir. You are very smart."

"I've been abandoned. I've been wronged. Where is the captain?"

"On the Q-D."

"The what?"

"It's jargon, sir. But he will not permit a visit till he's in the mood. Perhaps the morrow or some week by and by. I hope you have clothes for colder weather, sir."

"I've been cheated of my wares," roared the father. "I will not let a week go by. My marrow boils injustice this moment."

"It's a long voyage ahead, sir. Only time will tell. Have you heard of doldrums? There's a chance we might meet them. I hope I won't be flogged. I've heard you can whistle gently into the calm to bring on the wind. I'd rather that, sir, than a beating."

Whereupon the cabin boy turned, and when Christopher turned to find him, the boy had disappeared. The ship, too, adjusted its course and sped on. It crossed into lower latitudes, taking on wind and leaving a wake. Sometimes there were fish the man saw. Sometimes a solitary seabird.

"May God refuse your existence," said father Christopher to the horizon where the shore and his child once stood. Then he elaborated on his curse: "You will live thinking the world is good, only to learn how wrong you are. You will suffer and decompose in your wrongness. You will hope for an answer until your hope runs dry and all that remains is your questioning soul. Then the question will vanish, and then your soul. There will be nothing left. Good luck, my child, in the life you have chosen." And he spit like some venomous snake into the waves, and the waves laughed wildly at his mistake.

"Well, lookit here. Under the boughs." It was old man Agee, coming upon his young friend in the clearing. She stood overlooking the wide creek below. "What brings you out so early in the day?"

"I..."

The girl was startled and didn't know what to say.

"Cat got your tongue, little periwinkle?"

"No." She stuck it out. "What about you?" the young girl challenged.

Old man Agee stuck out his tongue, too.

"I'm a wanderer, by trade," he said. "Out looking for songs. Do you know any tunes?"

"No."

"What's the matter?" asked the man, sensing some wrong.

The girl said nothing, but there's always something in nothing.

"Are you sure? Looks like you need lifting."

"What's lifting?" asked the girl.

"Well, the sun is for one," said Mr. Agee.

"I like the sun," said the girl.

"And what about strawberries?"

She nodded.

"What about fish?"

"I don't like fish."

"No fish?"

"No," said the girl.

"Tell me what the problem is," said Mr. Agee. "So I can help."

The girl stared at the marsh and the creek below. "I wish I was somewhere else than home. You know, on some adventure."

"The ocean, is it?" The old man stared at the imagination. "Help me to see it as you do."

The girl grew excited.

"Well, a man goes off on a boat. But his daughter and this like wizard are standing on the shore."

"Are you sure he's a wizard?"

"Well, he knows things, I guess."

"What else?" asked Mr. Agee.

"It's no sloop that he's on. But it's a real old ship. See all the masts. The sails are white. There's wind and freedom. It's a stiff beam wind."

"Beam wind? That's a funny thing to say."

"And freedom," reminded the girl.

"Freedom is a big word," said the man.

"Big as God?"

"What do you know of God?"

"I've heard people talking," said the girl. "I was under the table and nobody knew. I stayed there and heard everything."

"You little spy."

"I was with my dog, Homer," said the girl.

"I know Homer," said Mr. Agee.

"We both were quiet under the table. They were talking about God and stuff."

"God is in every dog," said Mr. Agee. "And freedom is as big as God."

"Oh."

"Open a pathway through the slow sad sail,
Throw wide to the wind the gates of the wandering boat..."

"What boat is that?" asked the girl.

"Bit of a poem by Thomas," said Mr. Agee.

And they stood, looking together at the imaginary sea.

"But what was it about the man on the boat?" remembered Mr. Agee. "Why'd he leave his daughter on the shore?"

"She left him, because she was mad."

"And why was she mad?"

"Because he's never happy."

"He's never happy?"

"Well, not today. He's like a storm."

"But the skies are blue," said Mr. Agee, looking.

"I know."

"What's her name?" asked the old man whose beard held crumbs of bread and smelled of fields ripe with hay. He laid his hand upon the child's shoulder.

"Whose name?"

"The ship your father's on."

"Who said he was my father?"

"I thought you did," said Mr. Agee. "But maybe not. My mistake."

"It's Poseidon," said the girl.

"That's the spirit," said the diminutive fellow. "That's the name of an old friend of mine from way back in mythical times.

You know some myths don't you. I've seen the books in your house."

"Yes," said the girl.

"Well, may all leviathans beware that ship."

"Why would the violins beware it?" asked the girl.

"Poseidon did not care for music, not the way you and I do. He had a mighty temper and took it out on violins."

"Why did you like Poseidon, then?"

"It was a long time ago," said Mr. Agee. "But a ship named after him is good. A ship is a good thing. May a far off shore accept her bow and sprit."

"Why spit?"

"To clear your mouth of saliva," said the old man, and he spit on the ground to show how it was done.

"My mother, I mean the mother, is in another land," said the girl. "That's the problem. Maybe she's a prisoner or something. And he's gone to bring her back."

"He's a hero, then. You must be proud."

The girl looked through the trees into the marshy muddy creek below.

"But he's angry about it."

Mr. Agee waited. The girl went on.

"Would you be proud of a father who makes you walk for months and months and beats you when you bring him stale water and calls your mother terrible names and tries to steal your magical necklace?"

"Those are awful things," said Mr. Agee. "Is it part of the story?"

"Who knows what's going to happen next," said the girl.

"It's difficult to say," said Mr. Agee. "But I'll walk you home and we'll see."

"I can't go home," said the girl.

"Of course you can. You have a good home. I've been there many times."

"I don't want to live alone," said the girl.

"Of course not."

"I don't want God to refuse my existence."

"Where did that come from? Under the table?"

"I don't know. But I don't want to die."

"Who would?"

"I've decided to live a long time."

"Long and full, I hope," said the man.

"And no one's going to steal this."

The girl held out the simple chain for the man to witness.

"Ah, the magic necklace."

He fingered the metal and returned it to the girl's soft palm. He knew what a good imagination she had. He would take her home, just to be sure everything was okay.

"We all have a bend of bad blood within our veins now and then. A twist of turmoil, I like to say."

"What's term oil?"

"It's a real mess, like your room, I bet. Complete confusion. Who knows what's going on?"

"Oh," said the girl. She thought of her room, which had lots of paper on the floor.

"But, the main thing is, it's easy to clean up the mess. All I see is a beautiful morning, more concerned with living than with dying.

And every wave of the way
And gale I tackle...
Spins its morning praise...

No point in moping and mumbling. If you stand around too long, all the June bugs find you and start sharing their bites. Look there."

The old man brushed a tiny bitum from the girl's arm.

"The nasty little taster." He paused, observed. "How fast you are growing."

"I am?"

"Do you help your mother at home?"

"Sometimes."

"What about now?"

"I'm going to stay up here."

"All day?"

"I don't know. Can you show me how to fly, Mr. Agee?"

"That I can. I've taught others, you know."

"I know."

"So where to?" asked the old man.

"I don't know."

"That's not a good place. What about home?"

"Not now. It's too much shouting."

"I see. You can't always run away from troubles, though. Storms pass over and the sky always clears. You'll see it is different by ten o'clock."

"What happens at ten?"

"Not just ten. It's every hour. Every hour is different. In every hour there's room for change."

These words meant nothing to the girl.

"I bet your father feels bad," said Mr. Agee.

The girl listened.

"He sees that he was wrong," said the man. "He always does. He's a soft man at heart. Like an oyster. Do you like oysters?"

"Yuck."

"How about a bit of fresh bread?"

"Okay," said the girl.

"Don't be making up bad tales about people without letting them speak for themselves. It's not right."

The man held out a chunk of bread that looked familiar and good.

"Your own pretty mother baked it for me."

"I helped her," said the girl.

"That's why it's delicious."

The bearded man fumbled in a pouch for something else. Where was it? Oh, well.

"Smell that piney smell. This is our bosky land. Get a whiff of your comforter who hides in the scent of things."

"I think it stinks," said the girl.

"Who is that talking, no one I know?"

"It's me," said the girl.

"Only me."

"Who else do you want?"

"Want? Why, I had some bitter batter once," began Mr. Agee. "I was sour for days and days. Then butter made all the bad things slip away."

"That's stupid," said the girl.

"Maybe, but it worked for me. Someday you'll find what works for you. Until then, I want you to go easy on things. Don't hold them and fight with them and make up terrible tales. Let them in, let them go, move on."

"I don't really like butter," said the girl.

"It's not so much about butter. Here you are and here is God," said the man, pointing to two spots on the ground. "You are a growing girl and you're not too far separated from the mark of God. Hold open your mind to the mark of God. All you have to do is be open, not closed. Do you hear what I'm saying?"

"Open, not closed."

"Make sure you put the comma in the right place," said Mr. Agee.

But what did that mean?

"Now, let's go back down the hill with vim and vigor."

"Who are they?" asked the girl.

"Where've you been hiding, child? I know you and your father play with words. Doesn't he make you laugh?"

"He's funny sometimes."

The girl smiled at something inside her.

"That's the spirit. I knew you had it in you."

"What?"

"Happiness. It's a good thing to have. As for me, I've got to get back so I can shave it off.

"Happiness?"

"No. This God-awful beard."

"Why?"

"It itches something terrible. But before we go, let's have one more look."

The cloudless blue sky filled every space that was not taken up with limb or leaf. The marsh below rippled like water. The creek beyond sparkled with sunlight. And the far off horizon whispered, *Where are you coming from? Where are you going?* The ocean, yes. And some distant shore. The girl turned. There was no more ship and no more story. And side by side with the perfectly placed old man she made her way home.

FOUR

It came to pass the girl went out of one day and into another, out of another and into the next. She ate and grew, ate more, grew thinner. She stored her worth so it remained unknown to everyone, including herself. These are just things I witnessed.

As for her looks, she was much like any one else her age, no differences such as scales or feathers or exoskeleton, though she made up such stories. Fill a young person with imagination, and she'll never go hungry, or so they say. And as for her home, she lived far from the water. She'd have you think otherwise if she could. She can't. I do her thinking now. So distant from the shore was her home, the woodland animals had no words in their vocabularies such as tide or brine, whitecaps or gulls. So removed from the shore was the girl, it took all she had in her to conjure a wave lapping on a beach or water slapping at the side of a drifting boat.

Springtime summer autumn, she stood, winter – it was any-time she could get away by herself and imagine a life along some shore. Mucking in the mud. Messing about with seaweed and shells. Rowing a boat. Oh, it was a dream of hers: sculling oars, soaring hawk, and saltmarsh cooking in the sun. But there was nothing of it where she lived. Smells where she lived were stale and stagnant. It was so much land and trees, puddles and trickles down the window when it rained. Only one tiny stream out back, offering hope when it wasn't dried up.

A rivulet cut through the woods, and often the girl stepped in its flow, fingering her precious necklace as she looked for fish. And all the while she rubbed and looked, an incantation rang inside her: *Three two one, albatross and sun. A wave away an ebb a flow, the shore birds cry and tide doth pull. Be mine abalone, barnacle.*

Doth, yuck! What stupid language. The girl hated words that weren't contemporary. But if she was lucky and the necklace had been well buffed, in a day or two a picture of the saltmarsh and watery world would appear before her. It might be a boat run aground on the sand. It might be the sun playing tricks on the waves. If the girl was real lucky she'd be rewarded with gulls afloat on the sky. These imaginations would swoop through her mind, dropping oysters upon her hard inner noggin. Crack – what a feast.

But it was only games, wasn't it. And it wasn't long before our girl grew beyond them. As she awaited a change of scenes, reality emerged daily in ever-greater detail. Her body rounded corners and her legs and arms grew long. Her figure blossomed like the many wildflowers in July.

What more of this girl do you want? Part of me thinks we should stop right here, while her body looks good and the days are bright and warm. Why persist with growing older and all the trouble it brings? There is no escaping trouble. It comes fast. If trouble is what you want, I'll go on. But here's a good spot to exit, if you wish. So, as joy slugged her way, bitters raced more often. Pokeweed, nettle, thistle – those were her true calling. And always this failure of her soul to step up, take charge, assert itself. I've got to nail these truths upon her. It's not pity or resentment that does the nailing but honest to God reflection. That's all I'm saying.

And, while I'm at it, let me unweave some fibs. Like, where'd she come up with the idea of being marshborn? Was it from reading? Was it from the woodland birds she fed in the palm of her hand? Perhaps the little twitters spoke to her of other lands. But I'm telling it to you straight when I say her home, from the beginning, lay deep in the woods, far from any shore. And where'd she pluck that necklace from? By gift, by Heavenly G, bicycling round, by birthright, out of some gypsy infatuation? I think she stole it is what I think. Unless it was from that county carnival, a winner every time. She may've won it there for popping three balloons.

My point: if we're going to continue, we've got to know what's real. And what's real is a common girl in a common place, stuck in the middle earth, the middle land, in the middle of nowhere with hens all about. Maybe that's what adolescence is like. You invent yourself as some great thing, but you're really just so down to earth.

Mad crowd cluckers caught our girl by the ear each morning. She shook them loose and watched even hummingbirds, those glorious birds, hold still by the flowers. She saw her fathermother as a tedious couplet. Truth is she feared neither knife nor leather strap, but became bored by the pecking lack of content in her life.

And she carried herself alone, away from the doldrums of family life when she could. All of them were sluggards. There was one oafish older brother, another sickly younger one, a smallminded barrelbodied father and sweaty earthsucking Godbarking maw. Not her preferred lot, but how could she resist them. True enough, she tried. She gave herself an adventurous name. She was made of less earthy stuff than they. Or else she was just a dreamer. What a weed was her life anyway, deep rooted and tough. She longed for more sweetness in her soul, like a Rilke poem she read in a magazine, like a painting by Chagall she saw in a book. It's all such a wasteland I see and reveal. Gather for yourselves what I cast – the real, hardlife words that undermine the spirit.

Ho hum July. Sunday home. Tombstone house. Everybody dead to the world at nine in the morning. There was no blood about the place. No inspiration. Nothingness. A quiet death. Just leave it.

Aenea the peerless. She was thirteen and some. And it came to pass the Holy Spirit flit about unknown in her home and eventually all tuckered out fell to sleep in the corner. Aenea was awake, gulping the sterile air. Her face pressed to the widowpane, she'd been up since just before six.

A ruckus in the room next door now rattled her senses. Morning to you, my pretty dumpling. It was her parent's room where the rumpus was. Why din well. Brouhaha. O wake, good mother, good father, good God.

Aenea moved from the window. She stood with her ear to the wall, listening to the squeaking bed on the other side. She heard the breathing and squeals and slaps from that room. What the fuck? How could they stay in there till nine in the morning? All the other animals were up and about, but not those two: her hay-bed father and cavernous mother – the stud's whinnying mate. Her father was bearded and brawn. Her mother had rolls of flesh, and there was sweat always sweat dripping from her.

The fire burning in their room was not from wood but from rubbing flesh. Aenea pinned her ear. She heard every word, every breath, every bite of meat and each smack o the logs like the crackling simulation of fire. Creak of the floorboards. Someone's moving, she thought. Aeneas listened to the room and heard the picture: her father romping on the floor, her mother bending over bedding, sweat beading down her fatty back and breasts. She was a mammoth mother. Talked of nothing but food and God and blessings on the home and bed. She was half buried in all her hair and valleys. It made Aenea sick to think. And she could not stop such thoughts as were naked, as were her parents. She pressed her palms to her eyes, but still she could see.

Usually, the girl guarded against her father waking. He always woke with the sun when it poured through the window to stroke the west wood wall. But today he was lounging. This Sunday both her parents were still in bed, and her father whispered dirt and swept between thick Evie's legs. It was enough to make Aenea sick. She removed her ear and listened out her window instead, where the light spoke loud, breaking through the glass with summer gladness. Out there she saw it – oafish, slow. Not the light she wanted.

Outside stood Ottar. He moved with some sunsloshy dish to feed his cat. Always had that dish each morning, selfsame stride from left to right. He was even more constant than their father, more constant than the sun and stars. How boring. And in her room again, near where Aenea stood, sat meek Junneth deep in bed and book, his head tilted to the page and the moist omen of his open mouth.

Speak, sluggish one, thought Aenea. Look this way, you frail mite, she wanted to say. What ghosts and stories are entering and leaving the orifice today? she wondered. What a loafish lot was Ottar. What a diminutive wreck this little berry Juniper. And these were her family. These. Nothing better. No one else. These and these, just these again.

Oh, please, they could not belong to her. How could she and they be of one blood? They stung her with despair and stunk up the acres of land about the square log house. She could smell the stench in the room, the reek through the walls. Some odd salt smell mixed with mildew and stale air, unwashed flesh, body oil, and bacon fat.

Christopher, the woodcutter. He never washed and would on every day but Sunday rise with the light and praise be to God make his son work, his daughter work. Come, girl, he would call. I need a hauler, a hailer, a nailer. Whatever.

"An altar for what?" she asked

"Don't change my words."

"A whaler, what sea?"

Then he would scowl upon her. Raise his hand. Had no sense of proper humor, her father.

"Here pussy pussy."

She heard Ottar call his cat to the milk. Ottar carefully set the dish as though placing it upon a landmine so no milk would spill. Every drop was needed to feed the cat. The cat, too, was fat. Oaf brother Ottar was there to make sure that nothing changed.

Aenea heard a thump from the other side of the wall. Heavy handed breathing. Maw falling to the flog, a log upon the crispeaking hearth. Squeals and shushings. July heat. What of it? Aenea pressed her ear to butter hear. Couldn't keep her mind off the fat. Melting, melting with the fire the other side. Get out the wax to polish the world with. O rubbing bodies. Offensive friction. What can you do when everything's laid bare and none of it will ever shine?

Aenea heard the tiny grunts that were endless bliss. She heard the clicking of her younger brother Junny, reading in his bed. And Big Ottar bustling in the kitchen for what? All of it so boringly predictably unwanted. She had to pee. Aeneas went to the bathroom and returned, somewhat less. Every movement brought her down. Every noise took her by the throat, making it difficult to breathe. It was little sense to her. And her eye picked up the sudden shout of southmoving sun. A slant of heat crossed the sill. It angled toward her feet, where she witnessed this one-sided slice of light.

And speaking of amplitude and the unjust nature of things, why did her parents get a big room of their own when all the siblings had to clot together? It wasn't fair. They were only two. And why did all these people have to bother her so? Why couldn't she have a room of her own, an attic room away from the dullards. All of life is injustice. Ice and just cold air creeping through the floorboards every winter. Suffocation for no reason and ants in summer. Ants in lines. Ants in formation. Crawling ants on everything. Ice and ants and O.

Isolde, was Aenea's middle name. Isolde and Tristram fell hopelessly in love. But Aenea was not in love, and she was no king's daughter, either. Why not? At least she liked the I of her middle name. That was cool. She liked the water part of Aenea, too. But why wouldn't the windows open? Who painted them fixed? What stupidstupid person would make it so the windows wouldn't open in summer? That's all she really wanted to know.

Too much like a Trojan boy was her given name Aenea. She knew it, but what did it matter. There was a man Aeneas in some Roman poet's writing. Anchovy was the prince's mortal father. Venus was his mother, born of the sea, like Aenea herself, like I so I, she wanted to believe. Aenea, the sound of her name was like some great adventure. It was full of mastery and determination. She who was steadfast, stood by her name, and day-by-day she wandered with it. And lo she was bold and would make her way and would do great things and would—

"Come pussy pussy."

The sunlight sliced in the window, slashed across the jam, innocently breaking the room with its beam. The ritual of the light turned Aenea's romping parents to laughter. Hold – the lateness quickly spunem spitem wokem up. Her father took the day by the horns and shook it loudly. Lazybones, lazybones. Where're all the lazybones? The floor in her parent's room was soundly stomped upon, as Christopher put on his boots and laced them. All flesh was stowed and the day was upreaching.

Ah, Godly the summer trees – green towers pointing to the heavens. Fear not this world in all its indifference. Fear not the work it takes to make it here. Fear only the singe of fiery sun if you laze about like a slug on the road. Arise. And the crisp of her name came anon:

"Annie. Up. No lazing about on God's day."

Her father pounded on the wall. His tolling was the same each day. How did he know which fist to use? It was always the same, she could tell. The right, put to the wall, just above the shoulder. Left holding his pants till Evie brought him his suspenders.

"Out of your sleep nest. There's work to be about."

"Tis Sunday, Chris," whispered Ev Sophie.

"There's been half the morning to spend with heaven. It's time for the earth to have its due."

Her father gave his wife a playful slap to the rump and laughed loud from his barrel. Her mother left their room and made grease in her kitchen. Every Sunday morning it was smoke and fat, a veritable feast. How did she know to cook with just the right amount of salt and vinegar? Where was her book? Where were the recipes?

The pine table was soon set with butter, bread, meat, and milk. Ev's sloppy face was ample shiny. The late morning sun slid across her oily skin. Glorious day upon us. First begotten feast of day. The warm meat muffins. The bright wind waffles.

The fried egg upstarts. Hear the outdoors hymning. God in His heaven. The earth in mirth agog. Agog.

"What are you looking at?" said the mother to Aenea Iso, her staring daughter. "Help me with the dishing. Look sharp."

Aenea went to the basin and soaped her hands. The family sat, waiting. The slimy bar of soap slipped to the floor, under a stool. Oh, the annoyance of life.

"Don't just stand there. Pick it up."

The soap was covered with dust and cat hairs.

"Come on," barked Ottar. "I'm hungry."

She picked up the soap and helped her mother carry the grub to the table for grace.

"Grace."

Heads bowed. Slick tongued Father began:

"Praise God, the sun and seasons four. Summer warmth, good food of course. Praise all light, all dark of night. The sky and seas and forests."

And Mother ended:

"Let good burning be within \ to sear away all vice and sin."

Ottar sneezed. He wiped his nose with his sleeve.

Slovenly rag.

"Bless you," said the maw to her ravenous crow. The chickens were pecking out the door.

"Dirty birds," said Christopherus fatherus.

"Enough. They are food," said Maw.

Ottar manhandled a club of bread and stuffed it in his wide mouth. His insatiable appetite continued unabated, and soon this firstborn brother had swallowed half the food of the morning feast.

"Take it easy, bub," said the father, smiling behind his whiskers. "I've never seen a boy so hungry as you."

"I'm growing."

"No less than Junneth nor Annie."

"Aenea, thank you very much," said Annie.

"Enough nonsense with names," said her mother. "Your father is making a point."

"They're skin and bones. I'm meat and muscle," said Ottar.

"So I see." He slapped his son hard on the shoulder. "Then you can be the one builds me my barn."

"Come October, I'll have it done. Hew the logs and join each timber. I'm a master builder like Glen."

"He took up teaching," said his Pop.

"David, then."

"The timberframe genius," agreed his father.

"Bulky be my name," said Ottar.

"So be it." His father laughed heartily.

The family ate and drank so to fill their mortal insides. The blue-eyed daughter watched the clouds roll in. It was gray in the wake of a beautiful sunrise ship. It was awful.

"After brunching, Annie, take the tractor and wagon up the hill. You know the place. I've got my logs to haul back to the mill."

"Mule."

"Mill, I said. Get the wax out of your ears."

"She's weak is all," said Ottar.

"Hush," said the mother. "Remember your brother."

"Remember your brother and call him by name," said their father. "There's nothing so weak as a periwinkle."

"A what?"

"A dog whelk that wimps from door to door," said Ottar smiling.

"Dog whelks have ridges and grooves round the opening of their shells," corrected Junneth. "A shrub of the Apocynaceae family, the common dogbane, might be confusing you. Or vinca, of the same family and not at all weak. It's periwinkle, like the snail. I'm reading about it now."

"Enough with your jawing," said his mother. "How will the lord ever heal your body if all you do is read books?"

Aenea pushed from the table but did not rise. Junneth was about to speak of ghosts. She saw his mouth hanging open, saw the words forming in his throat.

"We've got a ghost again. In the house," he said. "A woman who is worried."

"Warty?" said the father. "Maybe she's a witch." He laughed.

"I saw her," said Junneth. "She came to me for help."

"Tell her to read the Bible every night," said his mother with a mouthful. "I'll leave it on the table. The Good Book always brings good news."

"She had a necklace of tiny dead birds and a bag of millet seed," said Junneth. "She called herself Birdy."

"Birdy was she?" smiled his father.

"How come Junjun's the only one to see such sights?" wondered Ottar. "I've got my eyes on."

"The boy's sensitive to the other side," said Maw Evie. "He's got a duty to lead them to the Lord."

"Swagger die if that don't make sense," said Chris the chopperus. "Lead them on. There's work to be about even on a Sunday."

Aenea rose from her chair.

"Brush your hair," said her mother. "I've never seen such a mess as you to dishonor the Lord of his work in this world. Have you no shame?"

She took a brush through her hair, giving the room the rip of untangling. Quietly, the air received each stroke, the chewing mouths, and the hush of all voices.

"Reverend be by later, I suspect," she heard her mother say.

"Why so?"

"See about absence in church."

"Abstinence, you say?"

"Our not being there."

"And what will you tell him?"

"The truth," said Maw Evie.

"Always best to be honest with the lord's henchmen," said Christopher.

More chewing.

"What's going with Gunther?" she heard Ottar ask.

"Wants a pen."'

"For his pigs?"

"Man's a simpleton. He's got some of the best cropland around and it's nothing but fields of junk grass and pigs mucking about."

Outside, the sun mounted the sky. The conversation no longer entered Aenea's mind. She stood at the window. The ground was dry and hard. There'd been no rain for weeks. She laced her shoes and took her pack. She carried a chunk of bread and a canteen, heard the kitchen say something about sausage, as out the door into the warm morning air she went. Stood smelling the heat rise from the ground as the sunlight settled on her. Ottar charged passed.

"Out of my way, wild spargas."

She pushed back.

"You're too skinny to clink with me, weaklink."

Ottar shoved Aenea to the ground and he laughed till she wanted to punch him. Gallantly then, in contrast to his belligerence, he lifted her from the ground and brushed the back of her shirt with gulping hands. Ottar enjoyed his strength and chivalry both. The squire the screw eye the knight to be, empty loop for a head. He spied the chain around her neck. Where did it come from? Hell, it'd be nice to have and sell, he thought. The gold of it glinted. It glinted once more. Then the sun was covered for good by clouds.

Somehow Ottar smelled of sand, of salt. Aenea let him flood her face. Foam and spray formed his being. He was a popple sea. Surly waves rose. They crested and broke. There was a westerly wind from somewhere. It was a whispery seawind, warm and wet upon her. Then off Ottar strode to the mill, spitting in the dust. She saw the spittle form a mud ball on the earth. And the sensation of ocean ended. Amen.

Aenea stood, nowhere to go, not knowing her own thoughts, not trusting her perceptions. Then took her father's handsaw, not his tractor, and slowly diminished up the hill to cut a maple limb for the music of it, to sing with the saw, to look for periwinkles climbing from the waves – O she was a wild one – and maybe stumble upon God on a Sunday near ten. God. Out on his day. On his day out. God. And that is *the word with the wool on it*, or so they say who've had enough story and just want to stop. But who says such a thing, and where do they say it? Who's ever heard an expression like that? It must be in some place far from here, far from where Aenea walked, far as a million footsteps even, far as some unimaginable life. It's hard to imagine a life so real. Away. From here. Away.

FIVE

She watched, disheartened, as the clouds move in to suffocate the morning. It was difficult to breathe, to see very far. She noticed the half-hidden sun disappear, saw the sky congest with gray. Humid air hung like a curtain, obscuring the world. The molecules sung in delirious circles, demented with their expectation of a storm. She struggled home, sweating through the thick of it.

Love makes you do some very weird things. The young woman emerged from the trees, walking on the pathless hill. She hurried down the steep terrain and stumbled toward her house. She was coming from a party, still in her mask. Who was she, really? She could've been a Carthage queen, a dogcatcher, or a young farmer with her loose button shirt and heavy shoes. Had the party been one of those masquerades, some costume ball? Is this something we should really believe, not the bit about staggering home from the party, but the part about the disguise? Why not? Love, as they say, can turn a girl crazy, make her someone else. The wind quickened and gusted. It tilted the world.

The young woman stood a moment, entranced by the sky. It looked to her like a charcoal drawing. Any minute now, she thought. It was coming. Ten in the morning. The middle of August. Then the window opened and rain pelted through. The young woman was able to distinguish the first drops of the storm as they struck the leaves and wet her arms. The large drops slapped her face and remarked again and again upon the ground near her feet. Small pellets of hail followed, melting on earth. Then rain again. It came down in sheets. Running water. Puddles, rivers – holy shit.

So, here we are again, the same girl as before, only no longer such a small glow. She was stubborn and thin, with widening pupils and blue iris eyes. Her exhilarating skin hid under her loose clothes, and the swell of her breasts she kept secret. I'm not saying she was anything special. I'm just saying, she was young and fresh and on her way home.

Haven't I told you the making of her often? Haven't I told you how she woke one morning in some marsh with redwing blackbirds and the sun shining near six o'clock? I've probably worded you numb already. All her growing and solitudious ways. I told how her learning was done in her head and casual body, how once she spat into the wind and it landed on her shoe, how another time she scratched her name on her desk and suffered endless sanding to remove it, how a few years back, she was fourteen at the time, and her teacher, Ms Bertoli, grabbed her by the shoulders and lay into her simply because the girl wouldn't talk. *Speak up, you mute swan, you blob giraffe*, Ms B blurted. *I'm up to here trying to know what's going on inside that head of yours.* But that story might not be entirely accurate.

Who wishes to meditate on all that past and muddled stuff, anyway? I'm done with it. No more. Rain in the August morning, clearing in the afternoon. That's where we are today. It's a rude guide who takes you where you've already been. Let's move forward.

So, the young woman walked in the driving rain, looking for protection. Just the other day, she'd written a poem:

Call of earth
the living edges
of each leaf and limb
in wild buffet, feast
of green, free
fare for everyone.

Come swallow
come finch, come
dragon fly

She was seventeen and a half, scanning the place. Over there.
There. She saw a rustic building, some hunter's shack tucked in
the woods. She ran to take shelter.

The young woman stood in the doorless doorway of the shack.
There were no windows inside, no furniture, only branches and
stones at the threshold. She faced the deeper dark. The silence of
the walls, her garbled mind. Entered then onto the earthen floor,
and as her eyes adjusted she saw the scribed wood scratched
with words, etched with pithy sayings of love and endurance:

Roses red
Violets blue
Long and hard I
Grow for you

That was just stupid. She read the names, the people who'd
been there. It was like some bathroom stall. *Trev and Raychel. Heats
forever.* Probably meant *Hearts. JesmynJoss Unseparable Luv.* There
was even a name she may've known: Tony. Tony and Lailah Sims.
She once kissed Tony. But who is Lailah, she wondered? Kistim.
Kissed him. Kissed Tony? He was part of some play, wasn't he?
That story of Queen Dido and the founder of Rome. Romeo,
Romeo, wherefore art thou? It wasn't Tony she cared about, but
– should I say his name?

Let me pause for a minute and say right out: She never did
like Tony much. Her body ached for someone else five years
older, visiting for the summer. If I could paint you a picture, I
would. Roots and branches. Starry nights with gentle breeze. She
saw him cleaning out paintbrushes with a hose. He would be at
the party. Tristan and Iseult. PhilemonBaucis. Always together,
always entwined. I'm talking the color of thunder, cool of the
mind, and the Nick of time. I wish I could tell it better, but none
of that has anything to do with

This tool shed. This hunter's shack is where she honed herself in a difficult world. Sometimes the world pleased her and she wrote poetry about it. Days were easy as a carefree mind, radiant as a face in secret love. There was palpable goodness as of her thigh against the loose and scratchy trousers, and names of things, names in her mind, so many words for a world she loved. And then, all that was lost.

I wish there was not this lingering sense of loss. It makes my words seem desolate and incomplete. And damn the thought that insists on me telling it. Who the hell put this thought inside me that I must tell her unfulfilled life? I'd much rather die without the indignity of this tale, though I feel even more hopeless in that prayer.

This I see: The young woman slumped on the dry ground toward the rear of the room, her chin resting in her hands, face sopping and round, the twitch of her fingers and flush of her cheeks, her eyes flooded with the falling world, the cascade of the whole outside, the gray late morning raining down. The morning relinquished its enlightening approach to the heavy storm clouds, till it reached an equilibrium between coming and going, between having and not.

The sky existed just inches away, it seemed. The heavens spilled rain and the wind wailed like a beast. Ho, the liquored youth shivered wet. Must have still been drunk, don't you think? She closed her eyes. Opened and closed them in restless exhaustion. Wanting only to love and be loved by him. While I...

I live in my bed for death alone. I'm dry and still and don't know what I want. Yet, I'm asked to wonder. Who is she really? What's on her mind? As if I might have some understanding, as if I could bring it out.

Anabel bit her lip and held like a statue that August morning. Her body shivered imperceptibly, wholly wet. Into her mind, a million thoughts came and went without leaving a mark, which made her feel restless and yearning for things she didn't have. She burned like crazy in her head, but her face shone with the cool statement of the moon, almost glowing against the dark backdrop of the abandoned shack where she squatted.

Maybe she bit her lip slightly for Tommy Troy, thinking his shoulders and handsome hardness, his strong possibility of adventure. Tommy was with her several nights ago. She'd eyed him then, her cotton dress see-through and her knack for shape and seduction showing. This was her skill, to make love her custom and spare no one, to wage war till the haughty were brought low before her.

"Anabel?"

"My sister, Anna. Is that who you mean?"

"What?"

"Aeneas, who do you want?"

"I'm speaking to you," said Tommy.

"Dido I go by," she said.

"Who?"

"It doesn't matter. Your ship is damaged. You are here. Come closer."

"Anabel, I'm bound."

"You cannot move, then?"

"I can move."

"To me."

"I'm leaving you."

"With your fleet?"

"By car, by foot, does it matter? It's just...

"Just?"

"You know how it is," said Tommy.

"Who is it, then?"

"It's... It's not about that," said Tommy.

"Ah, the glorious ship, Lailah Lavinia."

"I hate it when girls do that."

"Aren't you afraid of rumors?" asked Anabel.

"I'm not afraid of anything. I'm just telling you because, you know, it's the thing to do. So, I'm going to leave now."

"Lailah, then.

"What?"

"Leave, then," said Anabel. "Set out in quest of her beak, her worm adorned breast, her apple filling."

"What's your problem? Just forget it, Anna."

"Don't call me that."

"This is stupid," said Tommy. "What do you want me to say?"

"Say, you stand before me like a wall. No chance of getting through."

"I'm not a damn wall. And I'm not fucking suckered by you either. I can walk away."

"Walk then."

"I am."

And he did.

"What a wimp."

"Why?" he said, turning.

"I want to be devoured."

"Eaten?"

"Known."

"Known?"

"KNOWN," she yelled, but it was all just invention and echo inside her head.

Anabel shut her eyes quick, losing Tommy Troy to the waves. She didn't even like him. She was a blind girl, a glad girl, sitting in the dark shelter in the woods, dripping wet. Her head rang like some August cricket, a loose cicada, angry bees. What inside her made her skirl like constant insects? Her head was like the cavern of a bell. Some cave.

Anabel alone, she scooted back and leaned against the farthest wall, maybe twelve feet from the opening. She felt the rough wall through her shirt. It wasn't a very good costume she wore. How had she fooled them at the drinking party? Maybe she hadn't. It had been such a crowded house. She had disguised herself as one of the masses, and walked right through the front door so not to stand out. All the evening spent, far into the night, early into dawn. She'd stayed and drank. She'd played games. She'd sung and flipped through books. Hey hold this a minute, someone asked her. He gave her a bucket of ice, the iridescent colors melting, and every minute burning up. Red blush berries, tulips and bodies, people practicing together on the sofa, like lovers. Where could she put the bucket of ice? She took it to the kitchen. She put it down near the flowers. She could do anything if she just thought it through. She could live any life she liked.

No one heard her coming, no one saw her leave. They were all still sleeping. And no one had recognized her, either, not the nice woman, Hannah, who stood like a statue for the men to admire, not the guy from the grocery, not the girl from the P.O., not the handsome stranger by the stairs, the one who was so kind to her, the one whose name kept challenging her mind. Oh, who was he when he stood beside her? She couldn't even think. Who was he when he walked away and returned more beautiful in the moonlight? What was his nickel voice, his nice language? A penny, a penny, five cents for your thoughts. Oh, well, he said. I have to leave now, he said. I've got to work early in the morning. What do you do? she asked. I'm painting a house, he said. I saw you cleaning out your brushes, she told him. You did? Yes, she said. Did he not want to go off with her? Did he not notice her breasts hidden beneath her clothes? Did he even know her name? And then she stood alone, and the room turned dull. As the guys crowded and patted Tommy Troy on the back for his victories in baseball, his conquests in life.

Anabel leaned against the back wall of the hunting shack, game as a wild goose, skittish as a peacock. She'd fooled them all, hadn't she? Hand on her own breast – it was her own hand as well. She had no desire to break the pact with celibacy there, with them, that crowd. Especially not after Nicolas left. And fuck them all, she steamed to the air. Damn myself, she muttered. Not Nicolas. I mean, Yes him. Anabel Allabloom thought, or tried to think of a line of music, a song, some poem to help her express her love. Ack. Who the hell am I, unable?

The room ran circles around her. She cringed beneath the clouds that dumped upon her thinking, as though the roof of the shelter wasn't even there. She scooched to another corner and watched the rain slant across the entrance. What a sorry sodden world.

Anabel sat clutching her knees. She shivered a bit. Her face was wet and smooth as onion. She was hardly even drunk. She took off her disguise right there in the room. Who'd have thought she was a girl underneath? Her breasts wrapped tight in a sport's bra, her hair chopped short, her baseball cap. She peeled her shirt, undid the bra. Sat airing out, the rough wood of the wall upon her back, the soft fingers of light tightening her nipples. And then there was the necklace she was wearing – that too. The rain-softened light gave the metal a faint gleam. Light fell on her skin as if her skin was switchgrass, mimosa leaves, dandelion seed, clover petals, pea blossoms, and as if the light itself was felted hand puppets, flies fleece fingers, tiny black ants, a very slight shove. Anabel awaited Dionysus, Adonis, someone. No one came. It should've been someone. She put on her shirt again, leaving it unbuttoned so it hung like half-opened curtains. **Hell. I am body**, she said to the room. **Body is a home of me like no other. This is where I act. This is where I work. This is the what of me, not the how. I move.**

Those were bold words for someone mired in her imagination. But she didn't move much – that was the thing. A dog barked in the distance, and this is what Anabel did, she thought about the bark and made it a story. She saw a good-looking guy making his way to her through the glut of weather. Dogs in the distance barked because the man walked past their farm. They barked when he crossed the pasture. They barked when he crossed the beans. He was making his way to her, and that is mostly why they barked. To let her know. But Anabel, caved in, was unable to do much about it. She tried to think, to play. The barking stopped and started again. Stopped and again picked up. How slow he was in getting there. With the surge of wind, Anabel swallowed hard.

Out there. Some guy was on his way. He himself was full of storm, and his feet were caked with mud and dung. What a mess. But who cares. First a golden retriever disclosed the man's movement. Then it was a terrier, followed by the yelps of three or four black labs. The quiet young man was nearly spooked into running. He splashed on faster.

❖

Who's moving past our house? Molly Jargo, the farmer's wife, looks out the kitchen window. She peers into the rain. An errant fox. A doggone wolf. Some clumsy coyote. A delinquent thief.

"Curt. Curt. Look up from your fixing. The dogs are all afrenzy. See who's out there setting off this ruckus."

"O Christ," he says. "It's raining out."

"Our chickens, Curt. My prize melons."

"There aint nothing wrong."

"No harm in checking, either."

"Can't you see I'm—"

"Can't you just go?" commands his wife.

Stopping his work, Curt grumbles off to investigate. His wife's every fear must be researched. Curt goes out, looks around. He sees nothing but the backs and beaks of chickens in their coop and the waddle of a few mudloving ducks. There's the blurred line of trees in the distance where the hills begin, and the blobs of the black cows in the field. Some plucky goose, no doubt, he thinks, whose gander was upgot. A flip raccoon who ran past and repast. That was the fuel for the bark, says Curt to himself.

"Christ, Molly," he exclaims upon returning. "I'm tired of chicken out evry durgurn burk."

"What is a burk?" asks Molly mending.

"The rain is all it is," says drippy Curt to his beloved.

"You're sure of it?"

"Sure as milking brings up butterfat. Cream, my crop, I'm confitive."

"Confident and positive?"

"Thoroughly convinced throughout. Those dogs always flip at the least thunderclap."

"Well, thanks for chicken. I mean, checking."

She pulls the yarn from its skein. He leaves for the barn with pliers sticking out of his back pocket. The farm pups no longer howl. Good enough, thinks Molly, and settles back to her knitting, lowering her eyes on Curt, listening to the downpour, thinking how he'd not know where to find them – the pliers – and knowing he'd come back to scrounge for the tool. Ha. Hopeless. He.

Leave those two, thought Anabel in her windowless room, safe from the rain. It's not about them. It's the guy: He steps this way cross Curt Jargos' beans. Why's he out on a day like this? Is he going to stop or will he walk right past like I'm none of his business.

Anabel was unable to say for sure what he would do. She thought of herself as the maid of the farm, like in one of those painting, but not like a garden statue, like someone who seeks her own fortune, maybe a farm of her own or a studio in the city, a family some day, probably a dog. What will this man have to offer me? she wondered. I'll show him my greasy hair and no sweetness and cast him off like a dried up beetle that I find in my lap, him and his loose talk that only wants to drink me between the legs. I'm the tap of both me and my body. I'll let him fill with looking and fling him like a stick. My days will be better off without him. But what if he overtakes me first. I've got to be ready. He's strong, like some Lancelot. Maybe he works out at the gym. Not me. I'm stronger by preparation not by lifting things and putting them down. His limbs have muscles stretched and strong, but mine have a mind to move me somewhere. My meat is figuring things for myself. His is hot beautiful flesh. Those creative hands. And eyes that are feathers brushing my neck, the skin of my shoulder, half touching, half leaving me free. I'll have my way and lead his hands where I want them to be. I'll— Shh, he comes.

Anabel listened closely, but he wasn't there yet, so she imagined it further: We'll look at each other and be good company. Ask questions about where we each grew. I'll describe the nearest town in detail, and he'll say something about Auckland and Madrid and how the sun comes and goes differently different seasons. You're so full of it, I'll say, not knowing what it is, but wanting to tease it out of him. We'll dissolve each other's artifice till we're sitting there as real as possible, happy to be quiet for a moment. Then for another moment. And after sitting quiet for that second moment, I might as well ask him a few leading questions, such as about traveling by himself and how many girls he manages and how he takes them and how he leaves them behind like obsolete words. What's an obsolete word? Telephone booth. Pocket watch. That's four words, he'll say. Just answer my question, skor dung, I'll say. And he'll turn upon me, angry, his soul burning to say something from deep inside. His eyes will be fire over me. Two shouting stars. He'll tell me that he is who he is and how he is and where he is going is his own damn business. He'll tell me I can come if I can coexist, and I'll spit on the ground, the sizzle of my spit on the August hot ground, and I'll say, I always coexist. Do you? I'll ask. There's absolutely no other way to be, he'll say. And I'll love him for his look and for his mystery and for his passionate response, and I'll take him down like the chattel he is while no one watches and he is paralyzed with fright by my charge and by my firmness both. Stunned by my aggression, too. The living blood is who I am. I am blood and gust. I'm singing naked like wind that moves branches, and you so want to see.

Anabel did not move. She studied the entrance of the cave. Rain and sweeping trees. The hour creeping on eleven. She knew she should be getting up. She knew she should get— Shh. He's come:

"What are you doing out there?" she calls as he passes the doorway.

"Doing?" He stops and looks in at her.

"Where are you going?" she asks.

"Seeking," he says. He's very concise. Verb, subject, object all at once.

"To see what king?" she asks. "To meet or to conquer him?"

"Just seeking. No king."

She gestures for him to come inside, and he does to get away from the storm and the dogs.

"The girls will ridicule you for the shortness of your answers."

"I'm to the point," he says, shaking off the rain.

"Is that what you'll tell them?" she asks.

"I do not care for those girls."

"Don't care for those? What care do you mean that you don't? You don't want the girls? Or won't see to their needs? Which is it?"

He says nothing. She does:

"Come on. Tell me what's in your heart."

"I can't express it."

"Are you a simpleton?"

"I know what I need to know."

"Are you able bodied?"

"People've said I'm reckless."

"Oh, you'll be wrecked, don't worry. But you'll keep going. You'll never stop."

"I've stopped here," he says.

"Lucky for me, but not for long. I'm luckless in love just like you."

"I have a trick or two to play," he says.

His soft, sculpted chest pillows her cheek, just imagining it through his shirt. She takes a moment to take off that shirt. She's nuzzled against him, and the more she imagines it, the more she buries herself into his skin. Her hair is between his fingers. He rubs her forehead. Her body is light.

"Maybe we should stop this," he says.

"Why?" she asks. "Don't you like my hair?"

"I do, but tell me why you cut it."

"Tell me why you care what I do."

"Tell me why you chop me down just because I wonder about you."

"Tell me why you won't lift me out of my mess and save me."

"Is that what this is about?" he asks.

"I don't know," she says. "There's more to things than we think."

"All I have is one line," he says.

"What line?"

"Uninvited, I go where I will, alone."

"That's my line," she says. "You stole it from me."

"I said it first."

"But it's mine," she says

"First to speak, rules the day. All others weep at their delay."

"Are you saying I'm like all the others?"

He is silent. He didn't mean that.

"Then we will fight for the right," she tells him. And they tumble. Over and over on the dark earth floor. The sun is nowhere near, rain spills down. There is the sound of something ripping, but they won't stop to fix it until they're done. Their bruised and baking bodies bleed. Spirit moves their happy blood. They fill they flow they fly they

And still Anabel was not ready to move. She tried to remember where she was last night. She tried to remember all she'd drunk. Maybe it was nothing. She really didn't like to drink too much. Maybe she wasn't even there. But how could she not have been there? How could she be only here? She had to get here from somewhere, and it might as well have been from there. It was no good to be here from nowhere. There was no happiness here from nowhere. It was empty here if there was nothing else but this, and the rain kept falling, and the wind wouldn't stop. Why didn't it just stop? She couldn't say.

Anabel could not move. She could not say. She shouldered the darkness on either side, bearing the weight of heaven above and

the wetness of the world without. Hell, those dogs just kept yap-
ping their heads off through the steady rain. And why were they
barking? Was someone really out there?

The answer approached in whispery steps. Anabel looked
up. The shower quieted, the wind went weak for a moment, and
there stood a man before her, hovering like some god. Adonis.
Dionysus. Someone she knew. Tall dark silhouette at the entrance
of the cave. She felt his presence, but could do nothing about it.

"Who are you?" she asked.

"Who am I not?" he answered.

"Lots of people. Do you want a list? You're not the president.
You're not Albert Einstein. You're not Michelangelo."

"How do you know?"

"There's no marble dust on you. There's no paint on your shirt."

"You're very observant for someone so tired."

"Where'd you come from?" she asked him.

"Same as you."

"You were at the party? I don't remember."

"It doesn't matter," said the man. "I'm here now."

"Seems like it," she said.

"What do you mean by that?"

"I might be dreaming," she said. "Or fantasizing."

"Maybe," said the man. "Do you want me to go?"

"Not really."

"What do you want?"

"I can't think of anything," she said.

"Do you mean you're unsure or unable?"

"I'm just blank inside," she told him. "Like one of those cards
you buy but there're no words when you open it. You open it and
it's blank."

"Ah," said the man, as if that was a good response to her
being blank inside.

"Why do you keep looking at me?" she asked.

"I guess I'm hoping you'll put a message down."

"I don't have anything to say."

"I understand that, but you've got such a good imagination.
Can't you make up something?

Rain's coming down. It's stormy weather.
I sure hope you're feeling better."

"Are you sick?" she asked.

"No," he said.

"Well, I've got nothing for you."

He nodded. In his hand he held an apple. It was dripping red.

"What's with that?" she asked.

"It's a heart."

"No it's not. It's an apple."

"What apple bleeds like this?" said the man. The apple dripped beads of dew into a blue bowl.

"What's the bowl for?"

"Concoctions," said the man. "What do you want?"

She stared at the blue crucible that bubbled red inside. Blood. Heat. Heart. Sun. Storm. Lust. Love.

"Tell me something you need," said the man.

She knew what it was. She just couldn't say.

"There's got to be something," he persisted.

"It's difficult to know for sure," she said. "But I think I let things slip away."

"Okay."

"It's not okay. I need it to stop. I want to love so it's real. That's all. No stories, no playing, no masquerade any more. I want. To love. So it's real."

And the man felt bad, for how could he help with that? Could he give her a brand new puppy, a reverence for water, a generosity toward life, a floating leaf, one bead of dew that looks like a jewel, a boat of her own to take her places, a good night's sleep to bring her back, to bring her here just like before – only better? What could he do?

He touched her shoulder and she realized she had not buttoned her shirt. She quickly pulled away and drew the flaps together, buttoned them. The place where he had touched her shirt was dry now. The whole shirt was dry. Her body now dry. His hand was like a few ounces of sun.

"I didn't burn you, did I?"

"No," she said.

"Are you any better now?"

"I'm okay," she said. "I just wish this was over."

"The storm?"

"Whatever. To not be sad any more, like I'm missing out on things."

"You want to love so it's real," said the man. "What if I can't help you?"

"Then what good are you?" she said.

"That's pretty rough treatment. It doesn't sound like you."

The man was right. Anabel felt bad.

"Sorry. It's just... I think I'm going to be sick."

She closed her eyes.

"I think you should go," she said, opening her eyes, staring at the ground, feeling suddenly nauseous.

He nodded. He finished the concoction he was making in the blue bowl. He didn't give it to Anabel but drank it himself, the sow, the grouse, the spirited silhouette. Would the medicine have helped her? But he was gone, just as she had asked. And what was the point of him anyway? What was the point of anything?

A chilly breeze landed on Anabel's face and buttoned front. And in the man's place was a simple girl, who could easily have been Anabel's younger self, though she could've also been some girl from town or the farmer's niece. She stood in the doorway with a lump in her throat that looked like a bird. A swallow or finch. A finch or wren. A wren or redwing. A redwing blackbird it was, sure as the raindrops that splattered on the rocks and ferns outside.

"Who are you?" asked Anabel.

But the girl kept her mouth shut. She was afraid of her bravery, so timid and strong, willing and unable at once.

"Who are you?"

The girl opened her mouth and out flew the blackbird, past the oval of her lips. It took off like an escaping prisoner, flit like a bat, fleet as a ship upon some frictionless sea.

That's freedom for you, thought Anabel, watching the bird tear from the room into the world and gone. That's how I should get going, just happy to be out.

Anabel watched from her place on the floor as the birdgirl, too, dissolved in the rain. A trickle of water from the doorway ran toward her feet, across the dirt floor. And Anabel's own life, her Goddamned stuck life, became mud. She was deserted again, as if it were the only possible feeling to have. And the only companion before her was wetness on the floor. And the only thing to do was to stay here until.

Water of the world, surround. Wind, roar down. Why was she so quiet with people when perhaps she could have said much more? She never did know quite what to say. But it wasn't her fault. Why was she hollow and sad when perhaps she could have grown full and happy had she only done more, moved more, seen more, been more, taken better care? She sat in the middle of the room, unsupported, unwashed by the rain, watching it trickle and puddle slow. She was unable to conquer the world just yet. Mostly, this inability wasn't like her, only now it was. She sat ongoing but how ongoing, just here in this catatonic inwardness with the world taking place around her. Sat ongoing but going where, her blue eyes welling and the tears and the dirt dripping down her round seraphim face, and she cried and cried and cried and cried and cried and cried and cried and cried and cried and cried and cried
       and
         cried

SIX

Whir and sudden sorrow fill me. God of melancholy lures me. September looms portending, and flames leap at my name – hoping to devour. The season brings me dissonance.

A
nd
she
remains
unaffected.
Round is her face,
small her disturbance.
She's glad voice today, feels
no pain, knows of nothing wrong.
She moves side to side across the empty road. She reels in the muted light, sliding left then right, hair growing out. She knows there is someone to think her. There's magneticness. There's connection. She knows her skin is certain to be learned over and over by his touch. For sure she knows, she's liked and to be loved. So I say,

how could
she
be
I

Things change on the fly for the young. One day you're down, the next day up. One day you're thankless, the next appreciative. I wish I were harmonious again, energetic like that young woman. Look at her unmistakable giddy, her unmissable up. She moves like it's what's she's built to do. It's good to watch her walk upon the earth, off the road, easing past the cows in her freedom. Seems like she's happy is what it is. She's someone who rhymes with me, reminds me with. I just don't how she could be I.

Can anyone help me understand the picture of that young woman I was? She walks with confidence, sweet legged like some horse, some smooth cruising mare. How easy things are for her. Why, you'd think I'd be different. You'd think, seeing her, that I'd light up in my mind, reflecting on good times. But that's not how it is. I'm full of darkness, holding on until I die. We're two very different people, one now one then, here and there, and it's I who has won out, unfortunately. I have the floor, the voice.

Whatever I do to evoke it, my life remains mired. I cannot gain any sense of success or shake the feeling of ultimate failure. I see the various ages follow upon one another: birth to infancy, lost years on imaginary travels, arriving as a girl among the chickens and flatness, nothing to inspire me, and then lulling myself up in years, staggering into that hunter's shelter. It's difficult to remember accurately. It's even more difficult to understand how I got through. But I see it now. It's easy to see that young woman I was, looking deceptively good as she cuts through the fields. Nineteen years old. The end of September.

Sometimes I see the various shapes of myself. They flow to me on the current and I pluck them like leaves, wilted and wet. And where do the shapes come from? Up river, I guess. Where in all the changes is the person who remains unseen but standing, as if she's beside the current, watching what's left of it, seeing the river itself run dry in the late summer light?

Though my words do not set out to convey despair, they seem to arrive at the place easily. It must be who I am, don't you think? I'm a death-moth beating against some hopeful light, my wings singed and labored out, my consciousness burnt from the brunt of me. O, give up, stupid woman. Close your mouth. Stop the show. Nothing good comes from these pictures. That babe young woman walking in the world seems so optimistic and bright. I wish I could tell her, *Nothing good comes of your life.* I wish I could call out to her, tell her to stop, turn her around, and make her do something different. But I can't. She goes on. Nothing useful may be had of this story if I can't. And I can't. All I can do is see what happens. I'm doomed to suffer all I see.

What would become if she were to escape and go on to live a separate life? What if this happy person I see were to separate from who I am and go on to live a life of her own? Go to the city or another shore, go on with thoughts I can only imagine and with people I will never meet? What if her life were to have its own mark – footprints in the sand signifying movement, etchings on a wall signifying love? Who would she be now if she were able to keep away from me? There's some serious thinking to do on those lines.

As long as I can remember there has been this sense about September, always the same sadness when the month digs in. But this is not a quality I can explain. Is it summer ending? Simply that? The omnipresent feeling of leaving one thing for another, leaving home for school, leaving fun and games for monotony and work, leaving summer love behind and embarking to the cool, anonymous world. The earth changes with the month, cooling in the North, putting the days to rest and pulling out its most beautiful colors. Colors, yes. Leaves begin to find their hues, letting go of the common green. That's also September's doing. For some it's a time of coming out, for others a time to fade and be gone. Ah, the joyous oranges and lusty reds of the maples and sassafras. The light filled yellows of the ash and willow oak. The silvery, whispery remains of the beech. Yes, I see. And the muddy browns of me.

September brings the feeling that I'm wedged between the rocks, unable to change directions. What happened to me to make me stop changing and growing? I'm such a wreck. I look upon the scene from my distance. And do you see what I see? The radiant girl, that lusty young looker who pits her existence against mine. I think I like her. And do you see what else I see? Do you see what's coming?

Just past that image of my youthful self, a ghostly scene paces through the woods. It's a funeral procession. I don't know why. It stiffens the landscape and tightens me till I can do no more than stare. I see the solemn faces proceed among the trees. What does this have to do with anything?

Death frightens me. It always has. The shifting feet as the crowd makes its way from the eleven o'clock hour toward the noontime elegy, connecting their thoughts to the same young person, to some young person. Not the same one as me, not to that happy young woman, I hope. Those dirgers have to be walking for some other person, don't you think? As for our girl, what's she doing walking through that field at this time of day? Is she taking a short cut to work? Is she a member of the procession who's forgotten where to meet? Is it to join the others that she is headed, dodging cow shit and sucking deeply on air, to intersect that funeral bunch? But why then does she seem so happy and refreshed? Why wouldn't she be somber and showing some respect for the dead? Maybe it is her best friend who has died. Maybe some old classmate. I cannot remember anyone particular dying, that I as a young woman might've had to hustle across the fields on a warm, windy day. I can't remember a thing about that scene except I'm seeing it over and over. I see a smile on her face and no aching in her heart. It's a bit confusing, wouldn't you agree.

I've been commissioned to speak and am trying to come to terms with my life, that day, and those heavy-eyed trompers who make as a spectral background. I can't stand to see their anguish. I don't want to know the purloined soul who they pursue. What an imperfect passing must be playing on their minds. Such lost potential. And to prove the imperfection someone stumbles. I'm seeing it for the thousandth time. Some man, he stumbles.

It's a recurring stream of this memorial walk. I never see it differently – the same one stumbles. Always him. His face is that of someone's father. I know him. I've seen him often. His hair is light and full of wind. Yet, he is nameless in my mind. A memory and a stumble and yes the constant wind playing the tree leaves vivace, and then the slow, graceful notes of those mourners as they walk towards the woods. There is a sarabande by Bach, I remember. There is a requiem by Mozart, I can hear. There is a cello piece by Faure that seeps through the air, filling all space. Where does the music come from? I haven't figured that one out. And though I am not a member of the procession, the atmosphere engrosses me. Air at my ear a prayer, and all I am is listens.

Forgive me my ramble. I should remain focused on the work at hand, the person in progress and not the death. She, to be exact. I will take up her story, which leads to me.

I'll say it again – the securest thing about her. It is being alive, it is trail blazing particular hours and making out with the earth and seasons, month by month, mouth to mouth rejuvenant. It is the butterflies that dance about her when the wind dies down. And certainly she can be a monarch, too. Sovereign in herself, no doubt.

Pay attention close to her as a self is revealed. I've said it before – that self is I. She is burgeoning I. She's a wild one, too, with an independent spirit. Don't give in to demise no matter the mournful suggestion in your ear. Rather, see the metal of her form, the necklace swinging to and fro, the molting of her iron life and the scoria of the past. I'm sad to say she will just end here. And words refuse to defeat her image. And words strain to define her presence. And words will keep her company – growing old toward me.

Avocetta Anabel Aenea, loose on the wind. She leapt like a mare over the fence and galloped through the field, stopping only now and then to take in her freedom. She had come to this moment after nineteen springs and more than two hundred and fifty moons. Best of all is autumn, she thought. It's an awesome way to season things.

Usually she kept her thoughts inside her, but every so often she spoke up. Sometimes she spoke to herself, sometimes to the world around her. Once she had to respond to her father who, in explaining the captain descending upon his daughter's soul, had said:

> It's true – Your captain builds bridges.
> And.
> Watch out – He comes with a sledge.

"Did you say sled?"
"Sledge," said her father.
"Why would my captain have a sledge?"
"To keep you honest."
"But I'm the captain of my soul," she said. "I don't want a sledge. And I don't want to be kept."

Avocetta slowed, remembering this conversation as she walked alone, leaving the road and cutting through the field. She looked at the hills and sky, the custard colored clouds mid morning. She heard wind yelping like a pup.

> Hey. Hey. Hey.
> How you smell
> sweet walker
> just a sniff a
> shake away.

Avocetta saw the distant dog staring at her. Then he trotted off toward someone else. She saw that someone else, too. He carried a white Spackle bucket. Jesse's dog, she recognized. Nice pup. Good dog. Reminded her of her very good dog, Homer, five years dead. She turned away.

> And what about us? Look
> for God's sake look at how
> the light strikes the trees. Seasonal
> weather we're having, isn't
> it? Bright windy. Hey.
> Hello – You still with us? Pay
> attention here. Give us your awe.
> Forget that dog. Watch
> your step. The cow cakes
> are messy stuff. Do not
> be deceived by their
> sweet smell, my
> love.

Some of it lip and some of it love. Avocetta enjoyed it all. The gusts of wind took on Van Goghic whirls, and the fringe of grasses was tasseled light. She walked through the pasture. Hello, Jazz. Hey, Justina. There were other cows she recognized, too. But she was just a visitor to the field this late morning, not an apprentice to the farm. Avo Cettie was off work for the day. She was free and inexhaustible, looking for nothing particular.

The eleventh hour light praised softly through the clouds. A steady wind gusted from the southwest. Avocetta walked at a brisk pace, the muscles of her bare thighs flinching with each step. She had in mind a picture of a man, several miles back by now, who owned his own car and tore after life the way the sunlight tears for earth each day. He was her kind person, the kind with a mind like a sail full of wind, even during calm. He spoke so effortlessly, too. Not like her. It was Orpheus singing. She wanted to be like that. It was the breeze that loves the branches, when he spoke. It was whatever loves the leaves while passing, always passion, and she felt it on her skin as well as in her mind. God aglory. Salutatory. There was so much joy in being young and in moving and in effortless love.

And was there truth to his thirst for her, too? Why doubt it? Was his name not Michelangelo Rubens? Was it not Nicolas Chagall? Something like that. Was his hair light brown, his eyes deep blue? Yes. Did he look to the same places she looked, see the similar stars at night, the same geese flying south, the same shadows, yes, at four in the afternoon on the white picket fence near the pigs?

Avocetta blinked at the sky, awaiting confirmation. She listened to the ground under each step, longing for a clue from the underworld. There were many things, always would be things, hidden from her. Worms, bones, grubs, fossils, other people's thoughts. Nothing wrong with being private, but was love a private thing? she wondered. Was love something hidden or was it out there, always? It had to be something of a treasure, she thought. If she dug into love, what would it be? Would she even find it? Would she always find him?

It was a very untelling world that answered all her thoughts. Avocetta heard the wind, which blew her off balance. She listened as far as the leaves on the trees at the edge of the woods a half a mile off. Those leaves were getting ready to turn yellow and scarlet. She could almost make out the change of key, the character of each tree.

A green leaf fell, a hint of orange on its edge. Avocetta headed that way. There were no restrictions. A squirrel leapt from tree to tree, so easy. And the hills trembled high with anticipation, and the wood-edge would receive her, she heard.

Who's coming?
She's coming.
Apple hymn?
A hummingbird?
Avo's who.
Her human hue.
Her hum and
Ahh…
Her
Hmm…

The land conspired to bring out her improbable voice. The place talked about her – her mouth, her lips and eyes, the swing of her arms and make of her hands. Each tree coveted the rub of those hands against its bark, and its alone. And every leaf trembled for a look from her eyes, a taste from her tongue, and even a sacrificial pluck. No problem.

Or was it she who coveted the loving touch of the world? Or of someone? It was good to be out, but to be with Nicolas's was better. His shy hand wanting her, upon her bark, beneath her shirt, on her breasts, salubriously within her like skeletal support, like muscles and robust emotion, sea motion, waves waves washing waves, crashing, sizzling on her shore.

Avocetta was in love. The equation for her was *I + World + Time = Possibilities*. Love was no problem. It was a risk she was willing to take. Her heart was not cautious. She had watched Nicolas go in the pre-dawn morning. The room was full of his paintings, the smell of wet canvas. There were ideas everywhere. There were dirty dishes. Maybe she should've gone with him, but she didn't. What would she do on her day off? She pressed her fingers on the glass. How satisfying and terrible at once when he shut the door and she watched from the window, through the mudspeckled panes, and waited for him to turn, and he did turn, and then she saw him get into his car and disappear among the cedar trees and birches. And his vanishing had made him all the more alive in her.

The equation was simple. Love is a doorway facing both people. Equal. There is separation. There is the passage between. And maybe he and she would move toward each other. Maybe they were even made for one another, as the eye is made for light. Maybe they were each made to know the other, the way the soil knows a seed, even more as the plant itself lifts from the earth to the sun. They were entwined somehow in a most human way – his body and hers, his walking and hers, his leaving and turning back then turning to go, and hers. And though he went to a place she would not follow, and though she walked to many places he did not go, they shared this earth like a loaf of bread. So, why would she even question the sky concerning his love? Or await a clue from the ground? There was no doubt, and the only question: As she went out, how far would she go?

❖

Avocetta made it to the wood-edge near noon. A scurry of squirrels again, and leaves that pealed with laughter against the wind. The world was made of movement, stillness, voices, and thought.

She stood the moment, then made a first step into the woods. Her bare leg scratched a thorny branch, which brought a trickle of blood. She dabbed it with her finger and looked for a different way in. There, just up ahead lay a fallen tree, and it was surprising to see that on the trunk sat a girl, maybe six. Curious, really. What else to do but go over to her.

"Hey," said Avocetta as she approached the child.

"Hey."

"I didn't see you at first."

"I'm not six," said the girl. "I'm seven and a half."

"Who said you were six?"

"You did."

Avocetta thought about this.

"If I did, it was a mistake."

"That's okay," said the child. "I'm not upset. My mother says that I am a mistake."

"I bet she didn't say that. That would be mean."

"What did she say, then?" asked the girl.

"Probably, Everyone makes mistakes. Or, Learn from your mistakes. My mother still says that to me."

"Yeah. I guess that's it."

Avocetta didn't know what to add. Then she said:

"You live around here?"

"Depends what you mean," said the girl.

Avocetta was stumped by this response, so she said,

"I'm not six either. I'm nineteen and a half. We share a half."

The girl stared at Avocetta.

"What's it mean?" she asked.

"What?"

"Your name."

"It's a sea bird, Avocet. What's your name?"

"Ave," said the girl.

"I like that," said Avocetta.

"Me too."

"When's your birthday, Ave?" asked Cettie.

"April."

"You see. I'm April, too."

"Ninth."

"Curiouser and curiouser."

"My brother is a quoter," said the girl on the fallen tree. Cettie nodded.

"Are you here for the death or the lament?" asked the child.

"What do you mean?"

"A death is when someone's no longer living. A lament is..."

"I know the words."

"Which one, then?"

"It's nothing like that. I'm just out walking. Did someone die?"

"This evening. But they're coming first."

"Who?"

"All the sad people. First they come, then she dies this evening. When it's backwards you see what happens after, first."

"You watch too much TV," said Avocetta.

"My mother doesn't let me watch any TV."

"I never watched much either," said Cettie. This conversation was tripping her up.

The girl stood. She bumped lightly against Cettie's side. Avocetta looked away from the woods, across the field and saw the procession marching her way through the autumn flowers, past a fox in the shadows. She's right, she wanted to say but held her tongue. The fox looked up at the line of mourners.

"Why do you change your name?" asked the girl.

"Change it? What do you mean?"

"Nobody's going to know who you really are. Don't you like your name?"

"I like it," said Avocetta. "A sea bird, remember."

"Mine means *Hail*. My mother says it means *Live*, but I think it means *Good-bye*."

Avocetta thought of ice pellets hailing from the clouds. She really should get going, she wanted to say. But what about the girl? Neither of them spoke for a moment. Then the child raised her eyes to the shorebird.

"Do you like goldenrod?" she asked. "I do."

"I like it, too."

"What else do you like?"

Avocetta thought about this. I like Nico, she thought. The smell of wet oil paint. Cerulean blue. I like singing alone, she said to herself. When nobody else can hear. I can bring it. Acapella. Kalevela. The Grand Canyon. I like rivers, lay lines, green grapes, the sun, light on water, light on leaves, light on most everything, just to be here in the light. And Keats for his beauty or truth, but mostly because Mama read him when I was young, and Ahab because I read him to Papa, all those watery words. And Carroll for his wit, I guess, Issa for his response to life, Emily, HD, Rilke's poems. But they don't sound the same in German. His sonnets and elegies most. And Homer, she thought. What a good dog she was. Life charge. Charmed life. Changing seasons. The fall. The rise. Nicholas Artistic Farmhand He. His tousled hair. The shy sea inside him. I. Dido for her passion. Aeneas maybe. Used to be more. Hannah, Pierce, Dove, Finch. And Oscar and Junn for a thousand things I'm sure. A thousand natural wonders. Bugs, butterflies, sliced apples, you name it. And the edge of anyplace, for sure. Mostly that. Each edge. An arm, a woods, a leaf, a face. The edge. And shore the shore yes shore.

"What else?"

Avocetta thought of gypsies, geese, the black of night, the deep of a cave, the dark of a room, the sound of a cello, a guitar, lightening and thunder. Nicholas harvesting from the field or paining at his easel. The touch of his brushes upon the canvas, a shovel full of dirt, strokes of color, the smell of manure of pigments of onions. The lure of other lands. The lore. A million things to do in life. Listen and see. Taste and touch. Chords and clouds and cancerous growths on trees.

"Yuck. What else do you like?"

Cettie thought of sleeping and waking early to run. Nicholas's hand under her skirt, moving on her thigh, moving across her body, his autumn red and sleepless eyes. September and wind, trees moving against the sky. Trees moving, jet exhaust drifting, shifting clouds and hailing heavens.

"I didn't know Evan was sick," said the girl.

"Who said anything about Evan?"

"I heard you say ailing Evan."

Cettie had not said that.

"There's so much to like," she told the girl. "What about you?"

Young Ave leaned against Avocetta, pressing into her side as if to live there, to be her child, her blood, the marrow of her bones. She wanted to be a tree growing in her eyes, her ears. She wanted to be the beat of her heart.

"Are you cold?"

"They're still coming, aren't they?"

Avocetta didn't remember who she was talking about.

"They're going to start talking soon," said the girl. "They'll talk as they go by. It's not anything I like to listen to."

"Who?"

Avocetta had forgotten about the mourners heading her way.

"Who?" she repeated, more to herself.

The girl burrowed deeper. So deep, in fact. Avocetta's hand rested upon the fallen tree, where she sat, now, alone.

"There's nothing to be afraid of," said Avocetta aloud. Nobody with her. Though, maybe there was.

Something new had entered the world, some thought, some earthly device. It was not a feeling Avocetta liked. It confined and restricted. It tried to limit her life.

Startled by the snap of twigs and the crunch of the ground, Avocetta looked up. The treetops, as before, in their tireless dance. The sky was alive. And someone approached her with his words.

His voice was familiar, but perhaps only because of Nicholas at the edge of her mind. Avocetta wanted to think of Nicholas, to bring him in, just for a moment. She heard his rolling voice, a marble on a rug, barely perceptible inside her. At the door, heading out before the sun.

See you tonight, he said.

When?

Eight, seven. Maybe six, he said. The end of five.

She had smiled at his words that decreased their time apart. The end of five. What was that?

See you, she said.

But Avocetta did not see Nicolas when she looked up from her seat on the tree trunk. She saw the mourner who stood near. He'd come to the fallen tree at the edge of the woods. It was as if everything was different now. Just by bringing his sadness into the equation, her life took on some troublesome feeling.

"I have come back, this far," said the middle-aged man, his hand on Cettie's shoulder where she sat on the log. It was as if she was a post or limb he used for support. His eyes were swollen and his red face foreshadowed the autumn maple leaves. He rested his hand on Avocetta, saying nothing for a while, and neither was she compelled to speak. His hand slipped, falling limply to his side. This she watched. It was slow, intent watching, as if some cinematographer had zoomed in to study the hand. It was such a minor thing, really. His long fingers formed crescents, the tips grazing the jeans of his leg. For a moment he was still and the woods smelled of sesame oil, of diesel, of autumn wind. The other mourners, so etheric they blended with the world, took on the shapes of trees – maple, pine, larch, and oak. The man dropped to the ground like a leaf. The wind could easily have blown him away.

Avocetta knelt beside him. Cettie hardly noticed the child inside her any longer. She took the man's hand so to keep him in place. This man must be the little girl's father, she thought. That child was most likely a ghost. Yes, she must be dead, Avocetta decided. And, yes, it was something in the man's eyes that was family. His face was a handsome one, wrought by the sea and horizon, sculpted by wind and salt spray. What was the matter? It felt to Avocetta that she should say something, but she didn't.

"I wish you could hear me," said the man. "If you..." He took leaf mulch in his hand and ground it to dust. "I was at sea when you died. I wasn't far. I'm not a bad person, really – a distant father sometimes, but I learn best when I'm away."

"What did you learn?" she asked him.

"I had a pen and pad in my hand, and I noted the clouds and the ruckus to the starboard south. The gale played with my boat as if it was a cork. And to the portside – I turned to see a great sperm whale off my bow. Look how the waters burst with life. See the impulses in everything. I jotted this down. *Being in excess wells up in my heart.* Do you like it?

"Yes."

"It's Rilke who wrote it. I felt so empowered. I had to say more. It's how I make myself happen. The waters swelled abundantly with wind and creature, with the spirit of God. And out of that abundance, I wrote. I felt the spray of the sea and watched as the great berg lumbered, as it loomed like a warship to accost my tiny boat. Then, unprovoked, the whale sprung at my hull as though I'd just killed her offspring. There was no reason for the attack. I braced to absorb the assault. I'll be destroyed, I thought. So, what do you think happened?"

"I don't know," said Avocetta.

"I threw my pencil at the whale's eye. It didn't stop her, and she cracked my hull. I jolted side to side with the shift of things. Everything went topsy-turvy. I lost hold of my boat and fell into the ocean. It's like when you were young and we went out in the storm and the wind blew us crazy and we got soaking wet. Remember?"

"Maybe."

"But this was different. I was out alone. I cracked my head against something. And all went dark as though I'd died. I thought I had died, which made me question. Does Death exist? I remember wondering. I'd never felt his presence before. Is Death a man? I don't really know. I cracked my head and sank into darkness. There was less and less light, as if my days were draining and my living was over and I couldn't go home to my house any more. I couldn't go back to the people I love. But it didn't happen to me, did it? It was not my head that was cracked. I'm sorry it was not. I'm so very sorry it had to be you. I just don't understand why."

Avocetta held his hand. She didn't know, either.

"It was you. I didn't hear you cry out or fall limp. I didn't hear the final minutes of you trickling out, tick by tick by. And then, at once, I did. The sound of a light going off, and loss. It was all awake in me, and I came as quickly as I could."

"I know. I'm sure you did." Avocetta wanted to reassure him.

"I came running, looking for you, looking for my girl. Trees and broken limbs and trash. Shit, fucking shit, what kind of father was I? Crumpled refuse everywhere, even in the uninhabited woods. Remember that old hunter's shack?"

"I do. I think. I must. So, is she your child?" asked Cettie, picturing the little girl whose name she couldn't remember, thinking this man must be speaking of her. How sad it all was.

The father rocked back and forth, unable to hear, his hands now empty of the crumbled leaves. Wind tore through his hair. It crossed his face and rocked him. Avocetta felt his grip tighten upon her hand.

"What's the matter?" she asked. "What is it? What?"

The sailor man sat on the mulchy earth, waves rocking him, wind splashing over, and hair spilling into his eyes. Avocetta's hand was no longer part of his grip, so she withdrew it and watched him hold his place in the world and gracefully rise. The father stood, a hardwood among the conifers. What was he, a stately oak, sappy maple, beech or birch? Tall and slender, he made his way back to the other mourners. Then they all slipped quietly into the woods.

❖

It had likely been brought on by something she'd eaten, or the jasmine tea she'd drunk for breakfast. Avocetta looked for a clue, something of either the girl or the man who had pressed her. There wasn't any evidence, not a single snapped twig or the merest indent upon the nearby earth. Though perhaps, she thought – but it may only have been wishful thinking – perhaps there was a slight warmth in her palm.

Avocetta clenched her fist. She opened her hand again. What was it except her blood? That little girl, the father, the sadness – what was it all? Just blood? Blood running wild, in her veins in her palm in her brain? Food breaking down and messing with her mind? Jasmine tea or the cold mushroom soup for breakfast? Oh, well. It's over now. It's a fascinating world. There's always something going on, always something that makes you think.

Avocetta dabbed at the blood on her leg as she probed the woods for hints of the haunts. Squirrels sat eying her, providing only their momentary stillness. She scrutinized the trees just to make sure there wasn't something clandestine going on. The branches moved without any secrets. They bore no guilt. Cettie looked for some invisible weight that might cause those trees to suffer and maybe to crack. Everything seemed normal. And each leaf held its edges against the world, longing again for the joy of her seeing, for the lightness of her being. It really was a welcoming world that awaited her. It really was her joy that sated things, that mated with things and brought them to life. There was no doubt that Avocetta was a young, living person. And though to her, her mind may have seemed small, like the flecks of white asters at the edge of the woods, it was in truth growing larger and burning to sing.

She stood for a moment, looking back, fixing all she saw somewhere inside her. Noontime filled the panorama of this place, down to every nook and crevice. The sky was a smooth blue sky, and the Avocet released her question marks and any gloom of the world or downhearted words and eased into the woods without a scratch.

SEVEN

High noon
hook of sky
look for me.

I've heard it all – the story of the young woman who went out for the day. She walked through the fields to the woods, went up the hill in joy, blablabla, in poetic control of her outlook and destiny and then something happened to change things, but it's all sort of mysterious and – well, yeah. Whatever. I'm not being mean to her. It's just, where's it all going? We all know it's leading to her last breath, that's where. It's heading to my wrinkled old self, as she lies frail and forgotten in her hospice room, dying in some bed where a guy like a fog hovers over, demanding her life.

Well, I'm not that old biddy any more. She'll have to wait till I get there. I understand I cannot avoid my fate, but I don't want someone else leading me to it like a memoir. I'm right here, ready to live my own life. And since October is a time for leaving and for change, let's change things up. That child character is finished. We're done with her story. The old one is unreliable. We'll get to her later. I am come.

High noon. High time for resolve.

I will take over from here till the sun goes down. I I I, the master of my soul formation, all information being nearest to me. Let my old flesh hold tight to her linen and fold it between her stiff fingers. Let her suffer her withering skin till I get there along my path. I'm not being cruel, only what can she really know about who I am, lying there in bed, imagining? What can she know with a sick heart as her modus operandi and death her next move for sure? She's a worrywart anyway, weighted down by the end of life. That future is not I. I am present, always.

My name is Ave Isolde Anabel Ocetta. I admit that most of the rattling so far has been an honest attempt by that dying biddy. There's a hint of truth, if you hold the words up and turn them in the sun just right, so the angle of incidence equals the angle of accident. Some of the stuff happened, just as she said from her deathbed. For instance – I was born. Though, I hardly knew it at the time. How sweet it was, I'm sure, prickly soft amid that marsh with saltbreath all about me. Nice. And, okay, let's say there was a mother like water, and a father of air. Why not? I'll give her that creation. And sure, I probably grew upon unsteady ground, bound to my body like a boat. I learned to walk, to talk, to taste, to see, to listen and think. I may've even taken in a few moments of love in my youth. Delicious.

I admit, as well, I had feelings of disconnection and moods of solitude. Who doesn't? Sure, ill thoughts came my way, and a sturdy joy, too, I suppose. I'm not disparaging all of her story. But a memory of moods does not paint a true picture. Analysis from some remote and crusty mind hardly seems likely to be accurate. My portrait must rather show that the nebulous whatever about me is the brushstroke of I, each step of the way.

So it's decided. I'm the one to tell myself while moving in the midst of it. Who would put up with being told in retrospective words when the real thing asserts itself, stands erect, shouts *But here I am? Let me speak.*

Gull on the go, I'm here to play my role and wing my way and live my life and meet with whatever demise awaits me. That's how it should be for everyone. People have to do their living for themselves. Or else it will be done for them and done for them improper, leaving them powerless. For the truest life, a person's got to be as near to herself as possible, speaking as one. So let it be with Ave.

I'm not telling stories. I headed into the woods, up the hill. After some time, I descended upon a path I'd never seen before. The straight way was lost, so I took what curved. I descended unquestioningly. Everything spiraled. I knew somewhere inside that I'd never make it back to where things were familiar. I'd never get home, even though a curve by degrees becomes a circle. Though that's on one plane, isn't it? The world was different now. Things weren't what they used to be, or, suddenly I'd become a stranger. But not once did I wonder what had happened to guide me away from my old life. Not once did I question what went wrong. I just kept walking the way of my feet.

Funny thing is, I thought I'd be away just a while. I thought I'd return to my old place in time, marry that tall one who made dogs bark, painted in oils, and left dirty dishes in the kitchen sink. I thought I'd hike every coast, go to some college, pilgrimage to Mt Fuji, have a couple children, write poems, spin yarns, marsh grass, sun light, night fall. You know. But a short time passed, then some time greater, and finally so much time it must have been many years. I was unavoidably different by then, even though I'd remained on the same unaccomplishing path. And that path just curved and curved, going round things, things that I never took up, and never went though. I suppose, in retrospect, I should've gone through some of those things, but I didn't.

There were times, of course, that the path emerged in a field where there were no obstacles. There was nothing but space and time. But even when there was nothing, my mind kept harping on things. I did not see clearly, and my feet moved without thinking, going slower and slower. Fast growing vines snapped at my ankles, and, truth is, I was coming to a standstill. I guess life didn't satisfy me as I thought it should. And if I ever wanted to share something from my heart, as I must have, as I'm sure I did want, there was barely anything to sing inside, let alone anyone to sing it to.

Then one day something happened. There was this terrific storm. I heard the crescendos of thunder descending the heavens as I sat in the backseat of some blue car that wasn't even mine. I waited out the worst of the storm as hailstones plunked the roof and rain blurred the windows. Then, as if to assert myself, I stepped from the car into the terrible bluster. I'd known wind before, but nothing like this. I was picked up and blown away like a plastic bag, a piece of trash. I passed through hill towns, over mountains and woodlands. I was blown near the coast and I couldn't even get down to touch the sand. There were cities I came to where people walked in isolation, studying cell phones and streetlights and bus routes but never noticing me. I said nothing. And I'm proud of myself because I kept on going without taking rejection personally. I reached out to no one for support. I asked nothing of anyone as I was blown. But the odd thing about it, through all this incredible passage, there was something about me that remained in place. There was stillness, maybe a stuckness, about me as I was blown. I was a powerless recipient as if I was some book in someone else's hands and he rifled the pages, and those pages were my days going by as I waited in his hands for it all to stop. And where did all those days come from, and where did they go? I don't know. And what was I left with but the sense of a missed story. What had I missed? Could I get it back? Couldn't I just be myself and not be so done?

Enough! There came the day I'd had enough. I slammed my hand upon the ground. It was an October day, not much different from today. I'd stopped for a moment to rest just outside some know-nothing backwater place. I lay on the windswept earth at the edge of the village. Maybe I'd close my eyes for a minute or two, I thought. Then this bird this raven this crow descended out of nowhere right onto my chest as though I was a piece of bread, some food. But instead of pecking it sat, splitting open its breast and bleeding warm blood like so many words upon my body. I saw this as a sign, but it made little sense to me. I lay there and took it, feeling the flow of blood. It reminded me how I used to feel sunlight inch onto my skin when the sun came out from behind the clouds on a cool autumn day. Nice.

Who had sent this creature to discover me so wordless and tired? The bird had come from the trees, most likely, because there followed a few orange leaves in descent. But what kind of bird was it? I mean, besides a crow. Was it a spirit bird? Was it some woman disguised as a bird? Was it some guy I'd known from years back, spilling his heart onto me like I cared? It said nothing, the big crow, besides its blood. What do you want? I asked. Nothing he said. I'm not food, I said. Nothing he said. Who are you, blackbill? Silence was the answer. Right, I'm not so stupid as that. I know who you are. I know what you're after.

Here's the thing I've learned living in the world: When you think yourself insignificant, when you're feeling down, there's always something comes along to exploit that weakness. If you're not somewhere strong in yourself, you're a target, and it's open season on your soul. Shit. This crow, this dirty robber, was like some devil attracted to my wounded soul. God, you'd think it would be different. You'd think an angel would come, but that's not how things work, is it? Your life is up to you. There's no protection, no deterrent but you.

The crow was a scavenger. But not of me. So, I clenched my fists and would not relinquish the bread of my being. Still his blood dripped on me, down my stomach, right between my legs, my inner thighs. His sharp talons dug into my flesh to make me hurt all over. Have pity, have pity, have pity on—

NO.

Not I. I wouldn't play that role. I stood and brushed the hair from my face. Straight as any human, self-reliant as any beast. Sovereign, I stood.

Standing makes all the difference, sometimes. I could see better, for one, just getting up on my feet. I could make life my own. I could go into town and learn my way. I could fight. I would not roll over, close my eyes, and be voiceless. And standing, there I was, my typical self again. No bird. No one to talk with except the one who I am. My mind was still a mess. My legs were scratched from thorns and bramble, but I felt no pain anymore.

Thus, I came one afternoon to the far side of the hill.

But in truth, had there ever been anything other than this side? I can't say I remember it much. There were stories, I think, of a graduate girl, a farm apprentice with benefits and housing by some field, sunflowers drooping, seasonal goldenrod, pigs cows and goats. There were stories of a friend with a blue car of his own and a chest to lay my head upon, stories of a loose haired guy who liked to paint and play with other people's colors. Nook or Mick, some greenwater brackish hick. Who knows? It wasn't relevant any more. Besides, stories aren't real, are they? Maybe there had been a young guy and maybe he'd been fine. And maybe he'd lost interest in my body. The scum. If it's not one body it's another, that's how most men work. Maybe he'd flown off in search of other fodder. The cur. The curd. Things had turned sour. And maybe I was better off without him. That's one way of looking at things. I'm not saying it's good.

My new life was full of friends such as D D, Shamus, St Joak, and Norine, who taught me to steal. I decided to be like a hurricane and do the blowing myself. I don't mean it like that. I would keep with whatever crowd and be whatever I chose, and the hell with what was chosen for me. If I decided to work, I'd work. If I decided to crash, I'd crash. If I decided to wake at noon, so be it.

Somewhat, it went okay, as much as does any plan. I had a place in the town, just over the laundry. My room was empty except for the hum of the refrigerator and one small clock with a minute hand and whole numbers. The hum and that hand were my only music. The clock ticked sweetly, which put me to sleep.

One day, which was no different from the rest, I woke with the clock's three hands near twelve. I heard it at my ear, and then there came that steady hum in the background. No human voices where I was, only mechanical. The noon sun, hiding at the window's edge, moved a bit to the right and shone through, crossing the sill, which held my collection of bones. It was good to see the sun. I stirred and felt its light lying near my arm, on the white sheet. The sun pressed shyly upon my bed, as if saying, *Do you mind if I'm here?* No, O sun. Bring on your bright language, I thought. Delicious. Bring your touch. Your hold. Your inside warmth. Your you.

I lay naked, half out of the sheet, just out of reach of the sun. And there were its rays, like fingers, I thought. My yellow one. Such willfulness you give me just looking at you. You fill me with your warm good looks. My attention shifted to the small dry bones that I'd put on the windowsill a few days before. Those bones of some bird seemed more body than ever in the flood of light. I could see the bird flying. I could feel the strong hands of the sun near me. I would not be changed by the sun, but seen more true. I thought of the world in light of the sun. I thought how everything is beautiful to me. I thought how the light doesn't show anything that isn't there. I inched my hand closer, nearly touching the light, almost loving it, and being loved. I wanted to do as much for the sun as it did for me. I slid my body closer, opened my hands, my heart, my legs, to become full of light, my thighs with shards of sun, my skin, my...

Oh, how dirty I felt that noon hour. Using the world for my own pleasure. But venial, yes? I stood and quickly dressed. Was there pardon in the air? I felt so ashamed. I'm not disgraced, am I? I asked with worry. I'm sorry, I said to the sun, to the day, to anyone listening. I'm sorry for everything, for this lack of accomplishment, and this waste of time. Though who was I talking to, really? How stupid was I to think anyone would care what I did or what I didn't do. There had to be a better way to spend my time than to lie about and apologize.

A letter way, yes. I wanted some real male, sorry for the pun. The post office at that time was still conducting business, I think. Snail mail wasn't a thing of the past quite yet, and I was expecting a letter any day. Is there time, I wondered, before the window closes?

Half past noon, I walked into town. I took to the sunny side of the street for the company. There were no hard feelings on the part of the sun. Neither of us had done anything wrong. It was a blue day, no clouds. Guys studied me as I walked, like some boardgame or playbook. Older men looked me up and down. I could feel their eyes appraising my body, like I was someone built for their approval. But I'm made to prove my own points, not to satisfy all of theirs. It's not that others don't make good points, some of them do. It's just everyone's sort of alone in this world, and you've got no one but yourself to defend your place on earth. I am my master my minion, too. Pilot and crew. Captain, mate. I'm here for a reason.

I knocked my way down the road and righted it toward the P.O. When I got there, Hannah whistled at me from across the way. She shook her bag, and thousands of feathers all tangled inside rubbed together. It was seagull goose blackbird swan, all at once. The feathers made a minor sound I was sure to hear much later in life when I had more time to think. I gave Hannah the nod. She said words, which came at me backwards and I was confused. It was lyrics I couldn't make out. I smiled in Bb and pointed to the sign above the post office door. Hannah was a friend from way back, not one of my new crowd. I made a mental note to make time to visit her, but a car roared by to break us, and the mental note together with Hannah were lost. Sometimes things are musical. Sometimes just weird. The door of the office was glass. I'd been looking at a reflection the whole time, which explains things, I think. I pulled the door, pushed my way in.

Nice lady Shiloh, what a sad story, stood guard behind her countertop, stamps in her drawers like a toe line employee. I'd gotten there in time, before her break at one.

"Hey sweetie," she said.

"Hey," I said back.

"Ava," she began, always saying it wrong. It's not Ava but Ave. Not like I cared.

"Yes."

"I know it's wrong but—"

"Nothing's wrong," I said.

"My mother was Ava," Shiloh continued. "It's a simple mistake. I don't mean nothing by it. Did I ever tell you how she played the piano at night?"

Yes, she had.

"Night after night," she re-told me anyway. "I recall it clearly like I'm living there. I'm telling you, I can put myself right in that room, plop myself in a chair, and listen to Mama play Mozart and Chopin. I didn't care for Chopin. And Beethoven. Moonlight sonata. Ever heard that?"

"Think so."

"The piano was a real shiny black. I could see myself in it. Yamaha, I think."

"I thought they made motorcycles."

"You're right. Maybe it was something else."

"No. I'm sure it was Yamaha," I said.

"Not a night went by without some scales and tunes," recalled Shiloh. "You come in here, and I think her name when I see you. It's a thing I can't shake."

"I don't mind what you call me," I told her.

Shiloh looked at the clock and sighed.

"Ten minutes till lunch."

"Close early."

"I could get into trouble."

"Aren't you the boss?"

"It's only ten minutes. You've got a registered letter. Letters are becoming extinct, like the tigers of Africa."

"I think it's more Asia," I said.

"Let me go see," said Shiloh.

She always looked after me, like I was her daughter, though she had her own two children, roses she called them.

Pierce and Lempi – not the two roses – came into the post office. They laughed it up in a corner like it was a pub. Pierce quickly worked to seal some package to send. Something for his mommy – dirty laundry, perhaps. Lempi looked over the want-eds. He noticed me in the room. Gave me the nod.

"Kinda looks like you," he said, looking first at me, then jerking his head toward the oldtime wanted posters. Who wants either of them, I thought. I turned to Shio. "What is it?" I asked her as she came back to the counter.

"It's from your father. You have to sign."

I signed the green slip.

"Your Pa, huh," said Lempi.

Pa Huh. You're pathetic. And he was. But this was impossible. My Papaya. O pen. And see.

Lempi looked at me like I was insane. I hadn't said a thing to deserve it.

"Go back to your police work," I told him.

"The ink's still wet," said Shiloh.

"That's delivery for you," I said.

Lempi swaggered up behind, poised like a proclamation.

"Suzi," he said, cause he always called me that. "You and me should go down south. You interested?"

I sighed.

"Got some business with Rodman," he said.

"Rodman's a has been."

"He's got some stake in the matter, don't you think."

"None of his meat sways me," I told Lem. "In fact, I'm sure he's rather pointless."

Lempi's mind whirled to recover from this small defeat.

"Shine smart in that dress," he said from the blue.

"Praise school," I said. "Praise my education."

"I was thinking," he began, but Shiloh shut him off.

"Do your thinking where you've got a mind, Lem. The woman's got business wit me." She actually said *wit*, and it was wry humor to my ear. So I laughed, and Shy motioned me behind the counter, put her big **Closed For Lunch** sign in clear view. Lempi stood looking like a wanted. Pierce hung back with his package in hand and a big buffoon expression on his face because he was seconds late to send it off.

"Give me a break," he said. He didn't bang the walls, just held the box and his dumbness. Shiloh took pity.

"Give it here," she said.

Pierce took care of his business, Lem at his side, nothing but the looking eyes of him, which was all he ever was about. Lem's eyes were his most muscular part, bulging from use. Just the other day I saw him toting twenty pumpkins with the slightest glance, and he was barely breathing hard. Hell, he was no prospect to enter my life. There was no dart, no depth, no daring to him. I hung my disgust on him with a sneer, but he and his little friend Pierce were long gone to their truck, to their lurching out, spinning dust, to their lunching on sandwich meats, wheeling off.

"You with me now?" said Shio. This time her language was proper.

"Not really."

"If I had half your looks, I'd be worried about even them boys."

"Life's easy," I said. "No sense to worry."

"Life's a blur to me, too much of it is sorting."

"Sordid?" I asked. Had I heard her right?

"When Billy chunks a plate at my head, it's sordid enough."

"When?"

"Last night." She showed me the gash under her hair.

"Why'd he do that?"

"It's what I do gets to him."

"What'd you do?" I asked.

"Didn't have to do anything really but ask him about the cellar. Meant did he clean it like he said he would. He's got his workshop down there, but it's where the kids like to play. Course he heard his life when I asked him about the cellar, and everything came crashing. Shit, fucking bitch, he said, all loud and in my face. I hate the cussing most. Course, he was drunk. You know how it is."

"Not really."

"You get what's yours."

"Bruises?" I said.

"He's a good father, I guess. Sometimes he makes things."

"Gentle soul," I said.

"I won't complain."

"You never complain," I said.

We stood in silence in the back. Shiloh was maybe ten, twelve years older. She never ate lunch long as I'd known her. What was she doing taking a break with me?

"It's your old man," she said, fingering the envelope.

"Right. The letter."

"I'll read it to you, if you want."

"Are you my attorney?"

"To save your eyes," she explained.

"Why, you've got the optic nerve," I said. "But I spose it's mostly nosy of you."

We stood again, picture of silence.

"Well," I said. "Where is it?"

She handed me the letter, but I didn't reach out.

"Go ahead," I told her. "I've got nothing to hide. Be like at bedtime. Make your voice low like Papaya always did."

"You want me to read your letter?"

"Not to yourself. Out loud."

Shiloh smiled.

"You tickle me, A."

I thought of A, the key of A minor as she opened the envelope. A melancholic mood. She seemed to enjoy the words.

"A little louder, please." I could barely hear a thing she was reading.

"Sorry, Ave." It was the first time she ever said my name right. Surprised, I looked around expecting to see someone else, but it was only me and her, or she and I, the grammagician correcting what I thought. Grand magician. I smiled, thinking on magic and the subtleties of words. The room was warm florescent air. October was cool and fresh outside.

Shiloh read with the loveliest voice, rising and falling, and I hate the word lovely, but it's what describes the sound coming from her throat. The cloudless midpoint of the day, a poem by Dickinson. She inscribed the simple noon in sunny voice.

I moved to the shade of the words and waited for something beautiful to overtake me, like a car with a handsome driver, or a white picket fence in low sun with autumn weeds poking through, near the pigs. But I didn't get what I wanted. The language I heard reminded me of loss, of missing things, of grief. I wanted something different. I wanted someone real, real hands holding me, giving me gifts like red and green apples, like orange maple leaves, like true encouragement of life ahead. Why was this letter sent to me? It was a holy and difficult thought. It was the phantom shape of sounds. Who spoke in my ears, my mind? Was it Shiloh or my father, was it me alone or was it someone else, some jokester, some prankster, some mindmessing fiend?

Dear Ave:

I'm on the shore, facing the wind. There's no let up. There are birds passing by and others in the marsh who see where I stand. I'm not like Mama. She knows the source of joy. And you know me. I must possess joy. Control it. I toss words like sticks and watch them drift away on the tide, out to sea. Let there be salve in what I have to say.

Staring across the water, I'm on the shore. You could walk here in your sleep if you wanted. Remember once long ago when it was just you and I, ten years back, halfway through your life. It seems like some painting in my mind – a static, two-dimensional time. You and I stood here, right at the keystone of this cove, as if it were the top of an arch. You were happy then. You listened to my stories. You weren't missing from this world. I didn't have to look hard for you.

I ought to carry a picture of you. A photograph. That's what I should do, but I've never been much for carrying things other than worries. Maybe I've got a picture hidden, one from birth in my memory, or one from when you were seven and it was those fables I told about crows and camels and turtledoves, and the myth of Pegasus. You wouldn't let me stop. Or when you were eleven and you wanted to go down river on a homebuilt raft of plywood nailed to logs, off to see the world and find your fortune.

I can see that girl about you, spilling from your head and heart all that you wanted. You wanted to move, you wanted to know, you wanted to visit shorelines and cities, other countries, planets and galaxies, the edge of the universe, climb Mt Fuji, see the Sahara – all the places you could go. I've got that picture pretty well etched inside, but nothing to take from my pocket and look at now. I can't really see your seven-year-old face, eleven-year-old face, your nineteen-year-old face. Nothing but my tenuous thinking on the shore.

You always wanted to travel, my shorebird. Boats excited you, migrating geese. Countries made you want to look them up in the encyclopedia. The sea that watered the world's ancient roots made you wonder what things were like back then. Ancient times, Persia Rome China. You steeped your imagination like tea and drank. You dove into the world, cup in hand. And I saw it. I loved that about you. Don't think I'm blind as I let on. Don't think I can't know you where your heart is. Please don't recall the mud and malfunction of me. I can remind myself of those enough. The muck and stuckness in myself I see. I see where I lack courage – it's an old story. I see where I lack commune – it's a true tale. I see to the horizon, but what I miss is up close. What I miss is togetherness, the real us, like when we once stood on this beach and it was wave and warm wind, the gulls looping on air, and you, my beautiful daughter.

I'm trying to get somewhere simple. The shore sings around me in the October light. It is acres of blue up there. The sun overhead. There's the everpresent water at my face. Words and rhythms, shapes and sounds are what I know. **Being in excess wells up in my heart**. *It's all very certain to me. Yes, Ave, I'm lost. I am silent in places I should be better able to say. I look for you, unfinding. Again, I look. Left and right. Neither here nor home do I ever find exactly what I want to say.*

I know I know – I'm one to speak of being home, of having my feet solidly on the ground. The hypocrisy of my volume outweighs the words ten tomes. I've always been off, away in body and mind even if not in my heart. I know what I'm like, and I'm not much for changing my style, am I. Who really is? Style sticks to me like burrs. And it's not that I don't need to change. I do. If I could only look at things each new hour and become what it takes to see them.

But what prompts this active perception? It's too easy to be lazy and not pick off the burrs. Laziness is me all over. Doors have gently appeared in my life, which I've never gone through. I'm stuck in myself. Planets may transit, Uranus may be in opposition, epiphany may come, wind may call me to sail, but if I don't go with the flow, I'm the same old impediment – me.

When then? Well, if I'm lucky, there comes a different route, a more aggressive approach. It comes when my guard is down and time is over-ripe with frustration toward me. So Goddamn frustrated with my sluggishness. What to do with such a clod? That's the thing. So, a door claps me in the face with it's opening, and suddenly I've got nowhere else to be but through. My life forces the issue. It stuns me with opportunity. It fills me with dread and laughs at my fret. It floods me with fear and offers no support. And I may go through at this moment or drown.

So it was, Ave – last night, a few hours before dawn. I lay upon my boat. You know the one. I bobbed in the ocean, gazing at the night-tending sky from the deck of Melancholic Drift, *thinking upon the changes at hand. Life has always been about looking for change, but I haven't been present enough to notice any difference, let alone the life. I lay on my back, lit by stars and phosphorescent foam. The wee rocking moon rose from the ocean and hooked my eye with its crooked smile. If I had cried out,* What's it all mean? *no one would've answered. Watery sounds wove among the lights at sea. I was comfortable there in the bob and weave, closing my eyes now and then to the stars and moon and water. Nothing much happened. Cool winds blew. They carried the world to me as a fabric laid over my body. I felt the world conform to me, but still it made no sense. I had no real separation. Quiet as always, I lay and received what was offered, the dark night and the hypnotizing stars. My body was warm and the air delicious.*

Then, at once, I heard a tempest surround me. Winds from everywhere beat at my body. They caught me where I lay. They stood and shook me. If winds were emotions, they were fed-up and annoyed. They picked me by the shirttail. They cursed and shoved. I took it as I take everything, without much of a fight. And so I was heaved like laundry, flung overboard. I was tossed from my casual place in the course of this world. Hands did it, I'm certain. Providence, that good being. My boat pitched and wailed, struggling to return to my side. She swung her boom, dropped anchor, barked and bounded like a faithful dog, but to no avail. Briefly, I saw my tiny ship reach out to me and then drain into the night, calling out with attenuating clanks of her rigging and smacks of her hull upon the water. The smile of the moon lay just above her sail, and I floated in the ocean with no support.

Luckily, I float well for a difficult man. No panic at first. Head back, I kept my cool, my eyes on the heavens as if waiting for help. The odd thing about it, I floated in a hub of calm. The winds had left me alone in the middle, while just beyond this inner circle the desperate sea clamored for my life. I was a morsel to the raging waters, no great meal, but the ocean seemed to want me more than anything. Still, I floated in my preferred calm. But I knew I couldn't float forever. I didn't know where I was, though I knew it was deep and I had no boat. I was doomed to drown in this eye, and damn it the stars just twinkling with glee, laughing at me, and damn that moon with its stubborn smirk, making its way higher by degrees.

Perhaps you can imagine the isolation I suffered as I approached inevitable death. I struggled against the gravity of such a calm bed of sea, and with so much energy and life nearby, wanting me like the smell of marshes, or coffee with cream. What was that life out there? Did I even know it? It was everything, really. Sophie, my children, the world I live in, what I live for. Why wasn't I out there with it? But I couldn't take hold and I couldn't draw near, there was nothing to do, nothing to have, nothing to cling to, nothing.

Perhaps you can imagine the feelings I found during those intense minutes of my life. Everyone is led by his feelings. Homelessness was the welling pang, and I was present nowhere. What life had it been — to never take hold?

But I'm telling you, Ave, I did not sink. And I believe it to have been more fortunate that I faced death with despair and vast disappointment than that I was saved. I can only guess how I did it. I don't recall anything happening, but I found myself ashore, alive, at the water's edge not far from here. That's what I really want to tell you. I never lost my life. Impossible. A person can never lose his life. Or hers. Not me or you or anyone ever.

❖

I came to my senses, Ave, just out of the water. I sprawled like seaweed, completely dry. Who knows how long I had lain there before I woke?

There were colors at first, the sense of beauty. I tuned my mind without lifting my head. Shore birds walked nearby, avoiding. Geese above, they didn't seem to care. A few clouds in the sky, but what else was there? God and angels, hope and love – I could sense none of it. But I felt your presence around me, Ave. I heard my girl speak like the colors and the salt and the sun on things. You were trying to talk me out of my sadness, to lift me up. And I had to stand, even though I wanted to curl up and cry.

Noon. Here I stand, close to you and far at once, where the sun smooths my thoughts and the wind serves my words. I am light, again. I am alive. Everything of the earth waits to be touched. Why not share in the creation? Why not you also? You know the place, Ave. You've been to this shore, could get here in your sleep, I think. The timeless, tireless waves keep rolling. The tide takes debris out to sea. There's something on the horizon, but it's moving away.

Do you know what watching the horizon is like? It is your life, it is loss, and no coming back. You are like a cormorant or gull, floating by on the current. I watch you approach from wherever. I watch you up close as you go by. I follow you as far as my eyes can hold you. And suddenly you are gone. I squint to perceive you more. I focus my attention and pull, but I can't bring you back. Out of sight now, good traveler. Out of time. You are the empty horizon. It's a very dear and forlorn feeling: the beauty at once of your being and then you not being here any more, of seeing you just days ago and then not seeing you again, forever

What a word that is to me. Forever means not again or again, no matter how long I look and no matter the depth of my longing. This rips me apart. Who wouldn't cry just looking here? Because the horizon is death. It is the last of you. Forever and ever. And I can take no lasting loss. I can stand no forlorn feeling. I want my real daughter, my Ave.

Then comes a soothing form upon the horizon, from across the blue. It's a sail or whale, some lifting bird. This is not so much happiness as it is learning to see. The form emerges from the ocean without a splash. It's the holiest note I've ever heard. I watch the music alone from the shore.

But I'm not alone, and never will be. To have time and peace of mind and, as that is simply not enough – the togetherness to witness the truth of another in me. To perceive the closeness of life, right here, returning. And the light from my eyes goes out to meet all opportunity, all being, and maybe, once more, you. To accompany life to the shore. To sail alongside. To ride within. To remember to steer, and steer with love. To know.

"No," I shouted

How I was enraged by the gravity of those words lulling me to sleep, putting me to death.

"Get away from me, fucking deceit."

Oh, I was livid at the end of this language, talking as if I had died and then wishing me back like some boat out of the blue or some phoenix rising.

"You've tricked me to listen to this."

I shouted at whoever stood before me. I couldn't see, I was so angry.

"You're not my father. My real father wouldn't write me dead just for the melancholy of it, for some transcendental experience upon the shore. Go back, demon. Back to the Goddamn sea."

I pushed the impostor into the waves, into the tide. Her head hit something. I heard the crash and could almost see the terrible mark on her forehead. Her blue shirt filled with air, bubbling wet. I was vivid language myself now, red and rigid with resolve. I was muscle and might, fiery flesh, fast form. And I ran from the post office, glancing only at the mugs. Lempi was right – there I was, third over, eyelevel. There I was, a criminal. Murderous I. Shiloh lay on the ground. She didn't pick herself up. Why not? Someone shouted my name, I think. Someone called after me, bringing on the cops, I'm sure. I dashed out the glass door and headed far from that place. Sun so sweet it stung my eyes. Sky so pure it grabbed at me wholesome. A danger. Wanted in life. Most wanted. And I never really knew. And I didn't want to know.

EIGHT

I **was held prisoner.** A nightmare.

What happened?

I ran from it all, like some dissenter of life, clawing for a reverse of fortunes, no telling where things led but down, nor knowing better of the failing that I grew, nor speaking fall but falling nonetheless.

Things were that terrible for you?

How don't you know by now! I bruised upon the earth without a place, then lay a moment, then legged it into November, tripping over twigs, small stones, stumbling past the glances of others, like rods each look, like roots their glares. It was so much I rushed passed, swept round, racing the winds and never pausing once to be pinned for my terribleness or blamed for my impotency, even though it was true.

What was true?

The no salt only part person about me, the word unheard and unseen colors of me, the deeds indeed misdeeds, plus my slim have-dones and all the stuff I would never get to do. Trembling, I moved and trusted no one to help. Kept to myself and hid out in the dark under bridges and in the damp under leaves. Then I holed up at last in a dilapidated barn. I was swallowed by the shadows, among the farmer's cats. Wind blew through the cracks. It was awful. I was hungry and cold and the world closed in like suffocation from all sides, and nowhere I looked could I find peace or much sense of...

Go on. Of...

And then, I was found. Found out by the winds and the others who came in. I couldn't keep running forever, could I? They found me in that barn, where I'd paused to catch my breath between places. They moved on quiet feet, first poking behind the barn where the ducks hung out anonymous and the rats had made their wagers against my freedom. I heard them coming. Then I saw their faces in the bright outside. They smelled me, they knew me, I was their game. They were satisfied to have tracked me down, and I didn't even attempt to flee.

Were they the law?

What law! I sat with knees drawn up to my chest, the back of my head against the splintered wood of the barn. And as I sat, my eyes upon my captors, I knew it had to have been the barnyard cats who turned on me. Somehow I knew it was the felines turned me in. I don't know why. I thought they'd been my friends, those tabbies. And to reason it out that they were the ones who brought me down, that was something rotten, because I love all animals so. Maybe they were tired of my rummaging through their fur, stroking their whiskers, stealing their sense of independence with my presence. Maybe they wanted me to move on. Who can blame them? Who can blame anyone? And who can blame me for things that happened bad? Am I the one to serve all sentences? Do I have to be the scapegoat of life's misadventures? Am I the one to be sent down for what violent misdeeds no one ever even bothered to explain? Sent down, hauled down hell to the underbelly darkness, starkestness of soul, starving to know the reason.

Wasn't it autumn?

Not season, reason. I was caught by the injustice of life. I was welded to a lie.

Wedded?

You heard me the first time. I couldn't resist the force that pulled at me. It was hands unkindly killing.

Unkindly? What do you mean?

I was held in place against my will, forced to submit to the wishes of others. Am I so unforgivable? It was torture.

What specific torture?

The prison itself with its death-sentence of words I had to listen to. There were farewell letters hanging on the walls. And the walls were walls I was made to build from scratch.

What made you do such a thing?

I had to do something to protect myself from the vicious attacks. I was teased with the smell of burning matches that gave me hope of light. I was tormented by cool tricks of water from some faucet I couldn't get to. I was beaten senseless by dark to keep my rhythms off. And I was stifled by so much airlessness that I had nothing to breathe but madness, and nothing literally nothing to eat, no soup, no bread, no water, not even vinegar.

So you built walls to make things worse?

How could they get worse? I was not a person God considered, let alone the guards. I was purposely avoided, and every request remained unanswered.

By?

I cannot remember by and by exactly.

Requests such as?

Wanting things.

Things such as?

What a person wants.

Such as?

Are you writing this down?

No.

Things such as the sweet-talk of breeze through the dry grasses. Or the brow of the woods far off, and then moving up close to see the trees with most their leaves gone. Tidbits of the earth, you know. And a guy who comes by with paint on his sleeves. People without judgments. Parents, brothers, a girlfriend, say, who brings cider in a glass gallon jug and stays after dinner to brush your hair. And pumpkins. Just pumpkins. Pumpkins yellowing in the field. Where bobwhites. Where mallards. Where wild turkeys grow.

Game birds?

Whatever. It was the sense of home to me. But I had no part in it anymore. I'd been spirited away with one quick sweep. Do you know what it's like to be removed, imprisoned for no reason?

You had no lawyer, no recourse?

What law had I broken? Did I dishonor my parents or betray my country? Did I squash too many bugs? Did I steal the bread from a starving child and pass the day without a word of thanks? You know, you make things up just so you might make sense. You picture things in your mind's eye, the light on the water or a tractor in a field. You try to seize the sun, to see what's yours, just because maybe then you'll know what's wrong. And does it help? I don't think so. I had all the time in the world just sitting there. Nothing got clearer but relentless unapproachable anger. And the walls grew taller, keeping me from the real world.

You were building those walls.

I didn't want to do any of it. I wanted to speak up, but how could anyone hear?

What did you want to say?

I couldn't utter a word. I was so exhausted. But I wanted. I wanted to get it out of me what was in and burning hell.

How hell?

Are you really so dense? Hello, hello. I tried to get out. Hello, I'm here. Listen to me. Hear me. I wanted to break free. But my voice was trapped even worse than I. A tiny reminder was all I needed. The squeak of a mouse or a shard of mirror to let me know things were normal. I used to always have a pencil in my pocket. I needed something to write my defense. Seems all I had to write with was an unwieldy mind.

Weedy?

Seedy, more like it. I was a criminal, wasn't I? No one trusted me. I was a crazy girl, unrecoverable, not worth the time. I was forgettable, mostly. Life would go on without me. Life always goes on without us prisoners. No one came to my cell. No one came to hold me in his arms. It's like I wasn't there any more. But I was there, and real. I am real.

Real, you say.

I sat for the loneliest while and waited. It was like I was in my grave. I must've done the worst thing in the world to be so deserted. I waited for the twilight to come and go, for night to begin and end. I waited for the dawn. There's analogy in the dawn.

An analogy with what?

With waking fresh, of course. The sun comes each morning in freedom. But the only way I was getting out was if I dug. So I dug the ground around me till my hands bled and blood mixed with the dirt. The place was pretty dark where I was held, except one brickswidth slit for light high in the wall. I guess I put that window there.

You say you built it all yourself?

You know I did. Stop asking me that.

You could have done it differently.

All things are equal in retrospect, but at the time you do the one thing you can. Maybe you shut yourself in. Maybe you try to dig yourself out. Maybe you re-invent yourself so you can lose things again, only differently. In the end, nothing really matters except that it's over. I looked up at that window. So much grease.

Geese?

How is it that when you are wrong, you are actually right, but if I say something, if I want to say *grief*, I get it wrong?

What about the geese?

They had business down south. One day I saw them migrating past the opening high up the wall. It was about one o'clock by the look out there. Dark birds against the blue, a cluster of them like grapes.

I take it you were hungry.

Their honking flight made me think about the earth, that I could bare it only by closing my eyes. In my mind, I became the geese. I thought if given the chance I could carry my own language.

What language is that?

A two-faced one, like those geese. I saw right through them, wishing to soothe me with their grace of God: *Beautifully, beautifully, do the work of love. Do not worry. Do not fight it. Go gently, gently into death.* Hell – I only became more wanting by seeing them. Less instinctive. More burning. I would not give in to death, no matter what hole I was in, nor what walls around me I had built.

Wanting of what?

You keep asking me that.

I like to hear what you say. It's poetic.

You're funny, you know. Maybe that's what I wanted, something funny like a Butterfinger bar dropped on the ground, or when three fish walk into a pub as a joke, but none of them drink. I wanted to ride a bike across country and take time with the rocks in the Grand Canyon. I wanted to run my eyes over skies and my ears through rainfall and put my voice into someone who would listen and would love me and bring me a present and it wasn't even my birthday. But I had no voice, and the only weather was darkness. The nearest someone was my own desolation. Still, I wanted things more. Little Foxy out of the heather, running towards the woods. Oak and cherry trees, swamp cypress, silver beeches whose winter leaves remain on the branches to sing a papery song. I can almost hear it now. Ruffled hair, a hand upon me, driving rain, driving roads, driving crazy fast. The gabled end of buildings, the gulpable glow of apples and pears. But I was...

You were...

Do you work for some magazine? Is this for some story you're writing?

No. I'm just wondering: Did someone come to visit you in your prison cell?

No one did.

How are you so sure?

I was there. I should know.

Maybe you're forgetting?

Okay, there was someone. There was the warden, I think. So what. What could a warden do but lock me tighter and taunt me with the key.

Did you speak to him?

He was all business and I had lost my voice.

You were unwilling.

I was invisible.

You were undeniable.

I was infinitely busted.

You were Ave.

I screamed. I cried, but nobody heard me. No one believed I was alive. So I took out a stick from somewhere to write with.

November, one o'clock p.m.

Dear _____,

Emily Dickinson wrote: *Each Life Converges to some Center / Expressed – or still.* My center is inexpressibly dark, the day outside expresses light. This is how things are for me: My ankles are bound together. They are joined to a long leash so that I cannot move easily except to crawl about and scratch at the floor and walls. I'm not naked, but might as well be. The rags I have to wear are threadbare and wasting away. There are no colors or songs. I call this inferno. Every minute is infinite, and each next minute is infinite more.

From above, far up the wall, slants one blade of light that pierces my heart each day. The light keeps its distance. Its angle tells me the time and month. The incline speaks to me from a distance, because it is afraid of me. And with good reason. I would fight it for the life it has.

What I see now from that light is that it's one o'clock on some November day, the year of unlord unknown. Out there, out the window in the wall, it is always sunny, even at night. How can it be always sun outside when I know there must be clouds and rain, when I know full well that the earth turns away from the star for twelvish hours at a stretch? How can it be that there is this blade of sunlight that assumes each hour of the day and torments me like flies buzzing around my head? Nevermind – it's not worth thinking. It's only stupid light and nothing I can reach.

I'm just sitting here, hugging my knees. And what I see now is a man. He comes my way, walking where the beam of light falls. He's not coming down the light like some angel, he's just in it. He must have entered my cell while I was busy thinking. He is probably the warden. I can tell by his fine clothes. Wouldn't everyone like to be him? A man who, like a seducer, strikes you with the softness of his step and the confidence in his sway. Strikes you and strikes you, until you succumb.

He's Medusa, I look away. I will not even glance at his face. But the person takes my chin gently in his hand and forces me. He forces me to deal with him. He forces me to decay in his grip. I resist this oblivion, but he is strong. In strength he is my master, by his force and lead. He tilts my head to the shaft of light, bends me till he laughs out. The light creeps near my body, approaching my stomach. Lunch, he says. And I wonder who is meant to do the eating, the light or I. He eases up, and something kisses me on the cheek. When I am alone again, I'll wipe it off autonomous, but as for now, I am his complaisant minion. This warden is serious. He wishes a rhyme. Roses are flowers are wilting / stars.

Some verse, he says, stroking my hair, reminding me of writing I used to do and how he is sure I still have it in me. He touches my face the way my mother used to touch it when she brushed away my hair with her fingers or the way my father would roll his hand gently where my cheek was coolest. They'd sit with me for any length of time, tease my tangles, praise my flesh with the gentlest touches, or just wait me out. I remember my mother's singsong voice, her beauty and harmonious mind. I remember the heat of my father's hand and my coolness that mingled with his attempts at fatherly love. I was a girl once who was at home. With the warden it is the same this instant. I do not hesitate to try some poetry:

> Iron man and sunful singer
> Master guardian mist and dirge
> In this mansion of unhappiness
> You are architect of life on earth.

Come, he says. I'm not so powerful as that.

He releases his hand from me and strokes his chin like some great thinker.

How about a sonnet? he says.

I say these lines:

> Entire me I cannot do full well
> Nor sing of things, nor budding words to be
> With you here standing, lording and this hell
> For without life, there is no poetry.

It's not a complete sonnet, he says. Do you have any free verse inside you? I love free verse. Transtromer, Cummings, Millay, how about Stevens. I like that one about ice-cream. What about Kinnell or Levertov or Brooks? Something inspirational and loose.

Why not, I think. The sooner I do it, the sooner he'll leave.

> November in the after
> noon my God
> there is no one
> thing to see
> in this dark
> great home
> less room I am
> alone and my
> love dreams
> of stuff

He nods for the longest time. I imagine he's putting in punctuation and joining the words to understand it better.

I call him he, but I'm beginning to wonder. The voice of the person is thin as gauze. It's like wet, smooth soap. The voice is quick and evasive. Once spoken, it soon becomes lost on the floor, having slipped from my mind as though it is base, as though I fear thinking the voice so much I have to let it go.

Do you think yourself unthoughtful? he asks, prodding at my fear. Do you live life unlearning? Have you ever visited that nature preserve off county route seven?

Why answer such stupid questions? I am prevented from clear thought. I'm detained from life. Do you mean the wildlife sanctuary off Blackwater Road? I cast my eyes upon the floor, at his feet where he stands in the shaft of light. The ground is alive with roaches and ants.

Do you ever think to yourself that you've lived good and plenty? says this tormentor. I don't mean the candy, but that you've had a gay life. And now it's time to move on. That death is just another friendly face.

I'm not gay, I think, but am silent against such presumption.

You're hearing me wrong, says the warden. I simply mean happy. Haven't you lived long enough to place the world in its proper sequence, to align yourself with the sure next thing?

Still, I say nothing.

I only wonder about the smoothest thing you know. Skin is one. Light is, too.

I don't know about that texture, I say.

Then perhaps neither do you know about the text or texture of yourself, rough or smooth, imagined or true.

This is an unusual interrogation, I think. I simply repeat what I said earlier:

Entire me I cannot do full well.

And he says all stumbly like it's a date: So's it a crime, am I too clumsy to hope to hold to ward to wish, maybe even to um ask you out? Of yourself, I mean. He fumbles with his words, which is odd because of his eminence. I mean, continues the warden, to what end does a free person live, let alone you, ragged, bare breasted, self-contained, and raw.

I pulled together the threads of my shirt to cover myself.

No matter to me. No need to be modest. I could not care less about your breasts, except that they seem to burden you. I suppose it makes me wonder, but what it makes me wonder I won't further trouble you with, except to say you are imprisoning yourself by the way you look at things. It isn't me.

Me? I ask, and I feel so small to repeat his word as a question.

Yes, he says, unaffected by my size. Didn't your mother ever sing to you when you were young?

I don't remember it. At least I don't know or can't think or hear it or... What did you ask?

About your mother. My own mother sang to me, says the warden. Her voice was like an angel oiling my ear. The sweetness of her song was warm oil to loosen the wax of the world, how that world sometimes entered me and hardened, imprisoning me with its grip. Though some might say it is each of us, not the world, who makes things difficult. We contrive a world that fits our senses. We concoct false scenes because we're afraid. Maybe it's we who need to loosen our souls – oil them, so to speak, work them with our touch, make our soul accepting and discerning of what comes its way. Did your mother do anything like that with her voice? Was it a tender voice that worked for you? Did she help to loosen whatever it may have been that held you in place, and then at night help ease you to sleep? If she is anything like mine, I'm sure she did. Yours is an angel, no doubt. I have no mother other than an angel, myself. No father other than absolute support, the one who puts his large hands under me and lifts me when I'm down. Once, yes, I was saddened by the absence and the callousness of my father. Once, yes, I had to be sure on my own. Once, I loosened my hope upon the face of the earth, and it was good and I loved everything and was loved, and then I watched it all disappear like the evening sun for the very last time. Now, I must admit, it is less sadness that I feel, more truth from every angle. I have lost nothing. I hold it more by acclimating my soul and accommodating a much greater sense of the world. And the more I hold, the more I can give back to love. What do you say to that?

I say nothing.

He stares from the shadows of my cell, as the beam of light moves past him, across my belly, toward two.

Give me some indication of your hope, he says. Something to let me see what would be inside you if you had not lost it.

I oblige him his request:

> Murmurous life, a stranger I am – mo
> mentous seas and time run ashore—
> give gleams upon water, grant endless bare branches
> sing out the winter, the afternoon sun
> and leave me not leave me don't leave me undone

I hear you, he says. Now, I'll give a verse back. I learned it many years ago when I was a girl.

A girl! A girl, I think. You, I think. A girl!

Does it surprise you?

There it is, the truth of my warden. I knew it. I knew it, I think. She speaks, and her voice is just how I imagine it:

Come out come out
Wherever you are

.

And she's gone.
Into the shadow, out of sight.

No sound to her going. Again, I'm alone.

The darkness at my feet terrifies me. The blade of light angles through the window in the wall. It is long after one, nearing two. I want only to go out and see the day. I want only to see the afternoon and how it reaches in all directions, to see the stark beauty of the season and an unconstricted sky. Is that so much to ask?

I want to revisit old haunts and come again to the edge of the woods, and then to leave the woods alive, to return to the faces of others, to the gables of houses, the converging lines of the road, and to doors. Is that so much to ask?

I want no more than to leave this darkness and this breathless air. To be forgiven whatever I've done. And to live again. To have my crimes be put aside that I might step out and run not away but towards, with purpose and, as the warden said, love. It's not so bad what I want, is it? It's not such a terrible thing to wish for. To be free on the earth and grow like grass in and toward and for the sun.

Sincerely,

No. Of course it's not, my sweet peep osprey. You're my little fisher. You've nothing else to do but grow.

It's an easy voice on me, like that of my mother, soft as milk-weed seed. I gulp at that voice. I sweep my eyes for it. I wait for its waft again and all its gentle worth.

If you want to get to know something, don't be afraid to ask. Exercise yourself. Run up against things, no matter how difficult they seem. You can figure it out, I know.

Rub? Is that what you said?

Rub if it helps you. Run, walk, see. Do what you've got to do to move on.

Where?

There are lots of places, she says. So many ways to go.

Give me one to begin with, Mama.

I can do that for you, my periwinkle.

And I wait for what she has to say. I wait some more. For a moment, I think she's given up on me.

Meet me by the saltmarsh at two, she says.

Those were the last words spoken in my prison cell. There was no sound of her going. I lay alone.

But there was a spark now and then in the room, like some key, which may've been the glint left by my mother's words. I was like a child again and everything was possible. Nothing was ever locked when I was a kid, not the bathroom door, not the car or the closet. The windows had no curtains and the world outside went on without walls. So, in my cell, I looked to see if there was any possibility there, as well. And there was. Just like that. Or, I thought it had to be true. What could keep hope from living here? I said. The world is full of possibilities every step of the way. So, where's the door? I wondered. There had to be a door in that prison room. My chains melted away, and I got up to find it. I stood, I looked, I moved toward freedom, as if escape was just a matter of doing it. And so it happened. And so it was.

A breath and another
upon the dark place.
Exhalation, inhalation
exhalation, me. *Out* is
that I wish to go, and *in*
is that I wish to be.

NINE

It was past two already. There was no marsh I could see, no salt I could taste in the air. For a hundred miles, centuries in all directions, the only water I knew were frozen puddles, dripping faucets, and toilet bowls.

You hope for a particular kind of life, maybe you even ask for it by name, but that is not always the life you receive. I'd gotten out of one prison and run into the next. I was landlocked where I lived. I was walled in by a strange house, in which I felt I was a stranger myself.

It was hot inside that house, and dry from the wood-burning stove. The fire sucked the moisture and oxygen from the air. Sometimes, if the door to the stove was left open, an ember would pop onto the wood floor. You had to tend the fire constantly and keep an eye on things. But what was there to do other than tend? I tended to all mundane things. I was envious of others who had exciting lives in the city or foreign countries. Even in town would've been better. Likely, too, there were some lucky souls living the life I wanted by the shore. I was envious of those ones the most.

Hot and dry, I sat by the woodstove drinking black coffee. Do you know what it's like to be weighted with stasis, seeing nothing new day after day? The clock, the table, the over-ripe bananas, the same coffee maker. It was as if Dante for some unknown reason had put me there in that kitchen, in the ninth circle of hell. The woodstove itself made it over 80 degrees inside.

Dante. Why'd you do this to me? I asked.

Nothing. Where was the answer I asked for? The entire world lay hushed. It offered no sign and very little hope of creation, other than dust bunnies built right there on my floor. Then, as if it wasn't enough, all the bunnies bred more and more rabbits till the house was a mess.

I sat in my kitchen, looking out the window at the farm and the chicken house and the field of corn stalks cut off at the knees. A few geese waddled through, looking for grain. I had the nagging feeling there was something I was meant to do. Had I planned to meet someone? Seems to me, for all my efforts, I'd gotten nowhere. In fact, it was likely I'd misplaced a few years along the way. I'd probably lost them and they'd never turn up again. Seems, too, there was some matter for apology tied to that loss. Was it something I was sorry for, or had the world itself done me some injustice?

Round and round the house, I heard the children playing games. Lentil stew simmered in the crock-pot and shirts hung drying, strung inside from post to post. The song of the fridge went on again off again, on again off. My god, it was pathetic, all the domesticity. The compost bucket needed emptying. A load of dirty dishes in the sink.

But there was one window in my kitchen that looked upon a much more satisfying sight. It was through that window that I saw the white-toothed mountains of the Rockies. And when I flipped the window, I saw Mt Fuji. I saw the Euphrates River. I saw County Kerry in Ireland. I saw the Alps. And the nicest flip of all was when I came to some marsh in the evening light. It was a long look out the water with the sun hanging low, not a ripple or a sound. Pretty sweet.

I returned the calendar to December and hung it back on the wall by the telephone. Sure did look cold in that Rocky landscape, with crisp blue skies and glossy snow peaks. The picture only served to tighten my mind. And the tighter it got, the more I wished to leave my little home with its dormant interior and those soprano voices like it was a playground outside. What's with the singing chicks? I wondered. What was all the commotion? Really, I never had heard so many children in one house before. And I thought: If they are mine, I'd like to know it now, before the clock strikes three and my coffee turns cold, and then some second grade teacher calls for a conference. Any number of things might happen at once, and would I be ready?

I listened more closely. Yes, they were my kids. There were three voices I could distinguish – one was almost tenor, two was out of tune, and three was high as heaven, small as a flake of snow. The children ran about like chickens, pecking at the frozen ground. A girl, two boys. A gull, two burros. A man passed by the window. Good looking, I don't dispute it, hair whipping at his face, gloves on his large hands, paint on his sleeve. Farmer, landlubber, carpenter – what was he? He waved like he knew me, smiled and gestured up the road, holding himself firm so the wind wouldn't carry him away. Sure, I nodded. Whatever. Seems he was a husband, my husband, a father, the father. Who knew? And those kids, ours as well. Why not? I was under a lot of stress. I was too busy with myself to be sure. Lucky for me, the man was taking the children with him wherever he pointed. I didn't have time to think about family. I had been away, and had just returned. What was it that the calendar said – December? Saturday? Sunday? I didn't know the date.

It's not my fault if I was lax on a few details like what color chickens and how old were the kids. It's not my fault if I didn't remember the day or the nit picky particulars of everything: the name of the street I lived on, the number of the house, my husband's occupation or his name. The point remains, I was forgetting something I had to do. It was somewhere else I had to be.

Nobody seemed to be thinking about this but me. And I was tired of thinking.

Shame on me for the things I did that I wasn't conscious of. Like marrying someone, for one. Like tending the fire, for two. Like having children, for three. The list could go on. Can you imagine a more complaisant life than one where you're not participating in it? Can you imagine a more boring life than one where you sit in a kitchen, spirit going out of you, coffee growing colder, and there you are, held in place by the mockery of walls, watching a road out the window bisect the world with its pitiful line? Can you imagine the insane sameness of noting the afternoon wind roar upon the fields for the millionth time, or of listening once more to the whistle of air through the window frame? Can you imagine the remarkable wrongness of witnessing over and over the bare trees tossing in their sleep and empty bird feeders cluttering the branches? And all the while, those glossy peaks of December just stood there, calling. What was it? What day, exactly? Some day before Christmas. Some day after all.

How ashamed of myself I was for not living more like a gleaming sword, a storm, a rousing speech. I sat simmering at the kitchen table, pent up and ready to explode. I knew nothing of these people, really. Likely, I didn't even live here. They let me into their home out of kindness. Thank you. It's amazing how a life can be full of unknown people. You can spend all your days among strangers and choose not to be interested or get much involved. So, what was I doing sipping their coffee and pretending I was more than just a passer-by? There was no sense to my being in this house. My legs were stiff from sitting in one place so long, and my back was hunched and sore. It was time I straightened myself out. Time I got moving.

Remember how you did it when you were young, I thought? Never dwelling on the negative, just traveling light.

I jumped to my feet. I didn't tend the fire. I didn't put on a coat. I ran to the door and through it. That's how you've got to go sometimes. Can't mess with Dill and Dally, those dawdling ladies who would have you waste time with gloves and scarves and have you check all the electrical appliances and insist on both a prayer to Saint Christopher and some long drawn-out good-bye. Neither can you wait for that nut Meg to be used up before you buy some Cinnamon. When you need different spice in your life, you need it now. So, knock over the half empty Meg. Spill her out if you have to. Shove out the door and make for the world. Make it your only business to do what you must.

I was out the door in a flash, refueled by the brisk December. The sun up ahead, just after two, reminded me that I'd missed some appointment. Behind me, clouds encroached from the north, defacing the blue with ambiguous gray.

Maybe the sky meant snow. I wasn't prepared. I walked on the road with no winter coat and with sneakers I still held in my hands. I gulped down the road that gobbled each step like a hungry lion. When my feet became sore, I stopped and put on my shoes. Looking back, where was that house? It was nowhere. Those children won't miss me, I thought. Maybe the man with paint on his sleeve will mourn the loss, but what can I do about it? What can I do?

It was good to be out on my own, that's what. I kept walking through town and out the other side. I passed houses on the outskirts, some with Christmas lights already lit, and it wasn't even dark out. The world is full of curious things, and I was thinking on these curious things when I saw her. She wasn't the one I was supposed to meet, but there was something about her that made me stop. I wracked my brain for her name. She stood at her door in the dull gray light, half in her house speaking in tongues, half stepping out. Her dress hung dirty and torn at the hem, top buttons missing. I moved closer. And the closer I moved, the more

I understood her gibberish. And the more I understood it, the more I wanted to be part of the conversation.

"Hello," I called. "Are you talking to me?" I moved within a few feet of the half-housed woman.

"Seven four seven four seven four."

She chanted these numbers. They meant nothing to me. Her fingers tapped on her leg, the leg that stood on the front porch. Tap tap tap. Tap tap tap.

Gwendolyn. Her name popped into my head. I heard it at first somewhere inside me, and then saw it, as if written on air. I must've known her from earlier days. It made me happy to remember, because now the world felt a bit more secure, which is odd to say, as Gwendolyn was acting very bizarre indeed. I watched her a moment, trying to recall her life.

She was even thinner there than I remembered her from before, and she was a stick back then, with one good eye and one blind. She used to drink vodka mixed with M&M's first thing in the morning and vodka with green chilies in the afternoon. I remembered how the kids all called her Gaga-lyn because she acted crazy. But to me she was always Gwendolyn. Gwen for short.

"Ms. Gwen," I tried. "Think it'll snow?"

She looked right through me, saying numbers.

"Seven four seven…"

"It looks like snow to me," I told her.

"Don't matter none, snowpeas or beans," she said.

"No." I began to correct things, but she was onto something else.

"They's all gone out. Certainly is a hot one."

Okay, so maybe she was a bit bonkers, but I pressed on for what I needed to know. Geographical information. The lay of the land. It was her territory, not mine.

"So, Ms. Gwen, why I'm here. Do you know of any marsh nearby? I mean the real thing, not a ditch full of phragmites."

The woman sharpened her expression. She half looked my way, half off, wanting to find the place I was asking for. It was her blind eye that did the seeing of me, while her other eye darted about, looking for the marsh. It's a fact she stood quietly, but I knew by the look of her that she continued to speak inside her head. Funny what you hear sometimes by looking:

"Don't you be going out at night. Nother rule I have is never alone, never at night alone. You hear me. And never swim in no moonlight, either. If there's ever a way to trip and fall, you'll find it, and won't be Gwen be saving you. If there's a marsh Enosh down the road a bit, well so there is. You'll get to it when you do. But he won't be home anytime soon. Don't go looking for a way out of this mess. You hear me? You just listen up good. Don't go swimming late at night."

All that rant. Something struck me, though. Somewhere in her words it came to mind how she'd lost her boy. I remembered it. Gwendolyn killed him herself by accident.

"Y'know that old cat of yours was so lazy wouldn't catch the mice," she said to me as if I was someone else. "Loved that cat. Loved it sick, loved it to death. We don't need no new cat."

"We had a big old cat once, too," I said, remembering it now that she mentioned cats. "I had a dog named Homer. We had to put her down."

"Don't tell me no stories. I'm tired of your stories."

"I'm sorry," I said. And I was. I was sorry for things that happened. I was sorry for not saying the right things.

I nodded. We both stood at the entrance of her house, trying to think of something else. You see, she'd lost her boy backing him over with a tractor. Micky. He was four years old, round little boy, always dirty, shirtless in the spring and summer. Gwendolyn was an early morning drinker, and that's when the tragedy happened. We all have our difficulties, and I don't mean to be hard. But, why the hell was she driving that tractor anyway? Shouldn't they have taken the keys, locked them up. Shouldn't they have done something? Wasn't there some social worker who could've helped? Why wasn't anyone paying attention to her spirits? They say after the funeral, she slept with the first man she saw. I don't blame her. I blame the man. Hers was love sickness. His was unforgivable behavior.

"Now you run in and cook whatever you need from the fridge. I'm'a just stand here on the lookout."

"I don't need any food," I told her.

"Shit, they loved me," said Gwen. "I was they Mama. Don't you mismake me none in your head. Don't go blistering me with your contempt. I was they Mama."

"I know," I nodded.

But why didn't she see where she was going? I don't mean to be mean about it, but where was her brain, besides lost in candied vodka? What was she thinking when the tractor hit her boy? Can you imagine the scream? Your heart just falling out – can you imagine it, like when you're on the water and you drop your keys overboard and they go down into the twenty-foot murk and you know they're lost for good? And why weren't there any angels nearby? What happened to the angels who should've been there to help? Can you put an angel to sleep with thoughtlessness? Can you push away an angel with mindlessness?

Gwen stood against her door, half exposed. Her dress lowly unbuttoned. Still, I couldn't resist the momentum of my own quest.

"I'm sorry about everything, Gwen. I'm just looking for the marsh. Hello. Hello. Do you know the way to the cove?"

"I aint the home you're looking for," she said, the cut so low and her leaning forward so I could see most of her breasts. "No one here you're looking for. Micky aint nobody and Buddy, he's but seven years old and cat even look after his own self, let alone his brother. They both off wandering down where they don't belong. But you've got to love em. That's the onliest truth. Got still to love em, because you're they Mama no matter living or dead. You're they Mama no matter what they do to shake you off. You're always they Mama."

I stood with the woman just long enough to notice the precipice of my own saneness. Didn't want to fall off. Had to move on.

"Bye, Gwen," I said, stepping back. I waved her way, but she didn't see. She stood at her halfway house, blending in and out the door, talking hollow, her eyes on somewhere I wasn't seeing. I wasn't seeing what she was seeing. I wasn't looking how she was looking. Wasn't thinking, wasn't looking, just walking off down the— Oh, damn it all. Damn me, I'm stupid. There's sometimes this terrible feeling that has no words only such a ripping at your heart as happens when... I recalled what it was. I walked from her porch. I paused a ways off, on the road, no cars, no one, just me sunk by the thought. Shit, that's it.

Truth was, Gwendolyn had had another boy, lanky bit older than the young runover, Micky. Barton they called the bigger one. I liked Barton a lot. His eyes were dark and he'd run up to meet you as if you were the very best thing, ask what you were doing, tell you he'd been fishing or swimming or hunting for arrowheads out in the field. Always a smile. And you'd say, Me? Nothing much. And he'd repeat it, like who're you kidding. Always something you're doing, he'd say, dripping with joy like he was happy in the pouring world without an umbrella. Soft light in his eyes, he'd hand you his very best arrowhead to hold. Nice one, you'd say. You can have it, he'd say. I can't take it, you'd tell him. But I'm giving it to you, he'd say. And what a sweet voice for a boy. It was beautiful to hear, cheerful and full of good words, like a little Buddha.

I liked Barton a lot. As I walked away from Gwendolyn's house, I remembered he drowned one night. It was all the word in the morning. He and Anthony Turner went down to the creek, dipping with the moon. Who knew they were there? Moon knew, I guess. Just wanted to be out of the heat. It was hot that summer, a hundred in the shade. Went down to Enosh where people go sometimes. There's a nice marsh to the side of the cove, and a good place to swim with a float someone put out. Was a hot summer night he drowned. He was just a kid. Down at Enosh. He had no father to tell him not to. He had no mother to tell him not to. He didn't listen to her rules. Cars went by his house, going places. The cat lay about while the mice ate crumbs. So much heat, just sitting inside and sweating. Anthony came by. Anthony was older. Come on, let's go.

The whole damn world gets real sticky sometimes. Sometimes, you just need to cool. The two dipped with the moon, but Barton went deeper. He swam out a ways. He couldn't swim back. And that beautiful body of Barton, that seven year boy, his cheerful face so beautiful to see when he came up to you in town, it was fine cheeks and dimples, smile made you unwind, eyes made you think he was someone you could trust with your secrets, that body came face down in a marsh not far from here. If it was annoying to be dead, nobody could hear his complaints. If he was gone from the earth, where did he go? No one could say for sure.

I walked from Gwen's house and remembered the news of Barton's death and felt sort of rotten for having spoken of a marsh to her. And why hadn't I offered a bit of sympathy, a hand to her shoulder, and words such as, *How are you doing? You look good in that dress.* It wasn't like me, I thought, to have spoken so thoughtlessly to her, to my Gwendolyn my Gwen with her flat dish eyes, those cupless saucers.

I spun in my mind for my sister Gwen. My heart tried to wake me, but I didn't go back. A person is permitted flaws, isn't she? She's permitted some missed compassion, I hope. There's a built-in allowance for mistakes in life, right? Or must we each be perfect always? I won't hold my breath for absolute perfection.

I contemplated returning to Gwendolyn to say I'm sorry about the marsh thing and ask her how she was. Two boys dead, and living all alone. It must be hard, I would've said. At least you've got that Russian fellow, Mizik or Ritznik, looking after you like a father, I'd have reminded her, cooking you fish he catches, stocking your freezer. And people like Sophie bringing you bread. Nice of her to bake it fresh. And that young man Oscar. He cleans your kitchen and your toilet. He makes your bed and leaves flowers in a vase on the kitchen table. I would have reminded her all of that.

I should have gone back, said those things to Gwendolyn, offered her some money or a Butterfinger bar, except I didn't have any, should have offered to bring her lentil stew some night, should've said I'd come by and talk about self and soul and angels and such, the way my good friend Hannah talked with me about spiritual things. I should have gone back and asked Gwen to visit my house, my family, my hub and my fine healthy children. She wouldn't've come, but at least I would've done the right thing.

I would've treated her life with dignity. I would've shown that I care. But I didn't do that. I just went on.

Walking on, who knows why or where? All my mistakes made me think of my home, where I'd come from and how I'd left. Had I closed the woodstove door? Had I even closed the front door to the house? A draft through the kitchen would fan that fire well. I worried about an ember getting loose, a fire on the floor. Those old wood floors would go up in flames, the way a young girl bursts into love with the slightest of thoughts. I was worried about the house, everything in it and everything else.

Maybe if I used someone's phone, if I went to the next house I saw, the white one with blue trim, and used the phone of the kind understanding people who lived there and who didn't think I was crazy to be miles from my own house, miles and miles, walking absurdly with no gloves on and wearing no coat and the gray sky waiting to dump snow on the flat of the land, maybe if I did that, then I'd get the answers I needed and things would be okay.

It was certainly flat there, if I'm remembering the terrain correctly. Maybe if I knocked on the door a woman would come my way and survey the situation. She'd look at my sneakers, look at my bare hands, look up to my face, and ask me in, ask me what's wrong. And I'd tell her about Gwen. I'd tell her about death and how a mind can go crazy if left on its own. I'd tell her about my family, my home, the chickens, the kitchen, the woodstove and all. She'd understand everything. Her voice would be so comforting and clear, it'd be no trouble to listen, and each thing she'd say would be something I could do. She'd insist I get warm. She'd insist I have food. She'd insist I call home. I could do all that. I knew I could.

I didn't think twice about it. I knocked on the light blue door, picturing all the while the phone call I'd make: I'd dial my house, 519-5019, easy number to remember, and that good-looking guy with paint on his sleeve would answer. Yes, he'd say, and I would say, Close the door, and he'd say, What door? and I'd say, The front door, of course, the one I left open, and he'd say, I already did, and I'd say, Okay, good, and he would say, Who is this? and I would say, Don't you know? and he'd say, No, and I'd say, It's me, Ave. Ave? Yes, Ave. Don't you remember? Has it been so long? Have you cleared out my room? Because I'm just out walking. God, it's not like I'm dead. I'm just here, somewhere, and I remembered that I forgot. I'm not lost for good, just not there with you. I don't mean to be absent. I'm not calling to say good-bye. I had to call to tell you that I was worried and that I care about you, that I always care. I've never been obvious with things, you know. But I know the people in my life, and I love them all. And I know what I want. I want to live and to learn and to love even more. And he would say, Where are you, anyway? And I would say, In the house of some very nice people, talking on the phone. It's the home of some really understanding folk who let me in. I'm just staring out the window while I'm talking to you. And it looks like snow soon, so I might not be back tonight. Bad weather, you know. Not good for traveling. The wind's quite a problem. I might not be home for a while. Alright? And Nicolas? Yes, he'd say. I love you, I'd tell him. And it's not just my lips and hands but all of me, marrow and more, the largest I can be. It's all my heart. It's my biggest wish. I wish I could work my life with you. Do you hear what I'm saying? Are you listening to me? And I'd wait for his response, but there'd be such silence, it would make me think I'd done it all wrong. So, I'd try again: Tell everyone where I am, I'd say. Paint a good picture of me. Tell me things will be okay. Read books to me at night so I know you're alive and I know I am, too. Give me some kind words, some music to let me sleep well. I don't even know what sleep will be like where I am right now, but I'm here for a while and I feel so alone. And then he would say, How long a while are we talking? And I'd say, I don't know, but I'm working on it. Alright? And he'd say, Alright, I guess. I guess, alright. Then there would be an uncomfortable silence, and we both would hang onto the silence before hanging up.

Anyway, that's what I was going to say on the phone. But when the door swung open, I forgot why I'd even knocked. Just stood there, dumb. It was a beautiful clear-eyed woman, about my age only older. She smiled and took me in. Lucky husband, hers. I didn't see the man. I knew the woman was nice just looking at her. I knew her husband was somewhere not far.

"Where's your husband?"

"He went to town with two of my children."

"Two of."

"I have three. And you?"

"Three, I think. I confuse them with the chickens sometimes."

"It is confusing. They must be young."

"They are."

Suddenly, I remembered what.

"May I use your phone, please?"

"It's by the window," said the mother, pointing.

I followed her finger west, along the wall where the tuba stood, past the clock, getting near three, to the window, snow just starting.

"I've got to gather some wood," said the woman.

A boy came in the room, sixteen, seventeen.

"Ot," she said to him.

"Hot?" I repeated, more to myself.

He looked at me. His bright, sunny face.

"Did you ever go over to Gwen's with the bread?" her mother asked him.

"Yes," he said.

"And the loaf for Mr. Agee?"

"He has it."

"Would you gather the wood, then?" she asked him.

He was looking hard at me, thinking he knew me, thinking to know.

"What?"

"Firewood," she explained.

"My hand, Mama. Remember."

He held up his cast. What had his mother been thinking? She hadn't been.

"Then you can keep... What did you say your name is?"

"Ave," I announced.

"Keep Ave company. She's using the phone."

"Looks like she's just standing around, using the air."

"She came here to use the phone."

"To what end?" Ot asked, looking at me.

"End?"

"Why'd you come way out here to use our phone?"

"Just had to is all," I told him.

"If you use things, they won't like you much," he said. "They won't let you in again. They won't want you to come back. They'll end up hating you. My advice is, don't use anyone. Work together. Take what's given, give back what you can."

The beautiful mother walked away from her son's philosophy. I heard the door open. I heard it click closed. Which came first the click or the close? Maybe they were in sync.

"Your mother's in sync," I said.

"You're in rags."

"She's a nice woman," I said, ignoring his observation. "Really beautiful. Stunning."

"Stunning," repeated Ot. "Where'd you get that word?"

"It's a good word. I like it."

"Good for rhyming with. My mother she's stunning outside, off running and humming in time. But when she gets back, she'll be full of attack. Gunning, and fuming inside."

"That's a stupid poem," I said.

"You started it."

"How did I start it?"

"With your stunning word."

"Brilliant, then," I said.

"Too British," said Ot.

"Stellar," I suggested.

"I know a girl named Stella, if that's who you mean," said the young man. "She's in the twelfth grade and plays with imaginary numbers."

"What are they?"

"The small letter i," said Ot. "The square root of negative one."

"Negative one doesn't have a square root."

"That's why it's imaginary. Do you like to imagine?"

"Yes. I'm also good at math," I said. "I like to solve things."

"Geometric proofs? Desargues' two-triangle theorem?"

"No."

"The case of a negative index? Let $y=x-2$"

"Why so negative?"

"To be or not to be below zero."

"That's how I am with money," I said. "I'm below zero."

"A negative is like a debt," agreed Ot.

"Do numbers die?"

"Debt, I said. Not death."

"Oh."

Ot was studying my body. I could not pick up the phone with his eyes on me.

"Why the skimpy sneakers?"

"I couldn't find my hooves?"

"That's pretty funny," said sunny young Ot.

"Is that your real name?"

"Is what?"

"Ot?"

"It's Oscar."

I thought of Oscar kissing his girlfriend. His groping touch upon her breasts as they sat in the back seat of his parent's car during a date. Would it be quick? Would it be as fulfilling as the bright sun after days and days of cloud? I was obsessed with love. I had to say something to change my mind.

"Who plays the tuba?" I asked.

"Tuba?"

"Who plays?"

"Tuba?"

"I think I've heard this conversation before."

"What tuba?" he asked.

"It's a funny word, you hear it enough. Tuba tuba tuba wha-tuba. What's it to you that tuba taboo?"

"I like your rhythm," said Ot. "But it's called a cello. Hello cello. You can have fun with that word, too, if you want."

"You didn't have to make me feel stupid."

"I'm sorry. I don't always say the right thing," said Ot. "I was just teasing."

"It's alright. You're young."

Oscar went to the instrument and plucked its strings.

"My little brother plays."

Cello, I thought. I should have remembered. How stupid of me. I always forget the important things. How bad to forget, to be no part of these words or these people or this life anymore.

"You look weary," said Ot. "Like a lot is on your mind. Want to lie down?"

"Where?"

"The edge of the woods, under the trees?" he suggested.

"No. Not really."

"I didn't think so," he said. "Where would you lie down, if you could?"

"In my own bed."

His expression didn't change.

"There's a bed in the attic room, if you'd like?"

"Whose bed is it?"

"My little sister's, but she's not home. I assume she won't mind."

"That's quite an assumption," I said. "Like the Virgin Mary being welcomed into heaven. Don't assume anything about someone who is taken from earth and lifted toward heaven. They might not want to go just yet. There are beautiful days to be born upon. There are lots of great days for life on earth. There are other days on which to die. But not today."

"When's a good day to die?"

"Middle of August," I said. "Some hot summer day when the air's full of sun and the smell of every flower you pass reminds you of being young, of being in love and everything is stunning, and it's many many years from now."

"Okay," said Ot.

"Okay," I said.

"You know, heaven is far away in August," said Oscar. "It's where the plants all want to grow, but they can't quite get there. And now, in December, it's heaven on earth because the spiritual world's come close. You don't have to go far. It's warmth and love inside you, if you look."

"That's a nice thought," I said.

"Now's the time to be close to God," said Ot. "If you can just feel the presence."

"You sound like Hannah. She's a friend of mine. How do you know about such things as God and life and you're only... How old are you anyway?"

"I like to know things," said Oscar. And I could have sworn his eyes were on the nipples beneath my loosefitting shirt. Thinking on my olive breasts and living flesh. His thoughts felt like tiny scratches, wisps of hair, shapes of light. So delicate was the touch I could almost be taken to heaven by the joy, the lift, the assumption of it all.

"I mean it. You look tired, sick. Do you have a fever? Mama won't mind if you lie down upstairs. She loves people."

"All people?"

"I've never met a person she didn't like. But she doesn't like them sick."

"Sickos?"

"If you're sick, she's worried for you. Mama don't like no worry in no one."

"Well, you're a nice young man, even if your grammar is bad. Handsome, too. I bet you have a girlfriend. Stella, is that her name?"

He said nothing, leading me away. He actually took me by the hand. What a gentleman he was.

I went upstairs to my attic room. I lay on the perfect bed, taut and cool and soft. My clothes covered me like loose sheets. My feet rested at the end in their sneakers. Everything happened so fast that I couldn't really figure where I was or if this life was my real life. And the snow out the gable window captivated me. The flakes skittered and settled through my mind. They tasted the earth for the very first time. Snow around my body my room my time. Light as a feather, ample weather. A body about me. A body of snow, cool at first, then melting.

Melting over me, like a body. Who was it? Someone I knew, someone I loved. And he had no clothes, his naked skin. He had painterly hands. They were creative, not rough. They sketched my body and settled my mind, smooth as air, gentle as subdued light through the windows. Snow, more snow. The windows were windows that I remembered in my life. And a writing desk, a desk for writing by the window. Snow beyond. Terror inside. But why? It was love. It was sickness. Love is no sickness. Love is not terrible, only terrible to lose. Too beautiful to behold, to wrap with my arms.

Nicolas. Say Nicolas. St. Nicolas. It was near Christmas time. That I remember for sure. I lay in bed, tired, confused, and trying to picture. Every person I knew was linked to me. Every thing I loved was bound to me. It was certainty that we should meet, he and I, upon this bed. To test forbidden numbers, imaginary scenes. To curl like garlic flowers about each other, to smell the bitter breath and taste the changing weather. Oh, I was sick in my heart, this home, my soul. I was sick on my tongue, in my tasting and words. I was sick in my head, my affairs, my room. Was sick with longing, be-longing, and saddened to no end by my limited self.

Sad for a moment, but only a moment. My eyes were closed, and the sun, no matter all the snow, came over me. I lay alone. And my face was suddenly swept of hair. Someone swept it. It was a hand upon me. I smelled the natural perfume of some person I must've known. I felt the rub on my head...my neck...my...my. Reaming eyes, whose look like a ribbon fell loose upon me. Gentle as all snow

      settling

           down.

And I felt relieved of every bad feeling. I felt cured of my fever and drought. And, ah, the love that welled within. And what within me was there to give? Was this a test? I wondered. Was this an offering? It was nothing to be afraid of, and I took and took and took what I could, wanting it to go on forever.

❖

I opened my lids. It was as if I was a child again, in my very own bed, my mother beside.

"Ave. You're awake, my love."

The stasis was shattered. The stillness was stirred and rippled by words. The woman above me, her haunting dark eyes. She tucked the sheet about my shoulders, pulling the blanket over my toes. What happened to my sneakers? Who knows? Then she lay beside me, underneath the blanket. She lay abed a moment beside me, holding my hand as assurance.

"You'll feel better tomorrow," she said. "Papa has a compress for you."

"But Christmas," I said.

"Don't worry about Christmas. Look at the snow come down. Let it take care of you."

"How will the snow take care of me?"

"Just imagine yourself in it."

"But it's cold," I said.

"It's gentle and soft and settles on the earth as love."

"What about the animals. The deer and—"

"They don't mind."

"Will I go blind like Miss Gwendolyn?" I asked. "My eyes are all blurry."

"No."

"Like Helen Keller?"

"No."

"Like who?"

"You won't go blind at all. Your temperature's coming down. Remember, you're the snow. You'll feel much better tomorrow."

I felt the warmth of this woman. Her eyes were on me. I could feel the look as if it was whispering flakes. Then she turned to the window, to watch the snow. Then back again, eyes on me. I felt the lightness of this woman, her cool hand on my chest.

And suddenly I thought... I knew... I... Sometimes you don't have to be told things to know. I bolted upright, quick questions rising. Kicked off the sheets, my mind a mess of light and dark.

Whose bed was I in? Had I abused the kindness of this woman, my mother? Had I confused my brother as lover? Had I really been that bad in my life? Was I so awful a person who couldn't get anything right? And who were these people who haunted me so, taunting my thinking, and messing with my time? Who were these ones who gathered about me to tease me with their terrible love and tempt me with their warm reception? And why was I so weak that I couldn't act on my own? To think my own thoughts. To say what I had to say. To do what I had to do. And be who I had to be. Was I such a fragile human being that I couldn't rise and live rightly? Was I such a terrible human being to deserve all incongruous facts and mind-numbing fate as was given to me? The whole shebang. The life and death. The stun.

TEN

I **jumped** from the bed, picked a few thoughts from the floor, and stuffed some mementos into a plastic bag. I found a pair of winter boots and a coat in the closet, as well. Then, I stood for a moment to look around. How stupid was I not to stay and work things out, but how could I remain, the way I was? I was so muddled in my thinking. I was such an unsettled soul.

Truth is, once I'd been someone who others liked to talk with. I'd been a girl with ideas that people took in and tossed back. We tangled our words in midair, and it was work to get to know each other but more it was time spent living together.

What do people do when they live together?

They tell jokes and stories. They go to the pun theater for a play on words. They eat and drink. They bitch and complain.

And then what do they do?

They stop telling stories. They tell what is the truth for them.

Do the puns stop?

Usually.

Does the complaining stop, too?

That's more difficult.

Once I'd been a young woman worth waiting for even in the middle of the day, just after three when there were other things pressing like homework. I remember those hours, and people like O who wanted to go skating or build a birdfeeder with scrap wood and reeds or play me a sonata on his drumming stones, and J with his cello who wanted to practice in my room, always in my attic room, and Mother in her kerchief and Pa in his cap, or maybe I just wanted to walk in the woods alone, looking for feathers, and tracks of a fox, and angels in the snow.

Once I'd been someone with a good life, too, and it didn't annoy my parents to wait a bit longer till I got home. They were willing to sacrifice for me, even if it was nothing more than their time and even if it was only to listen to what I'd done with my day or to read what I'd written. Some insipid story, I'm sure. Sophomoric verse. I mean, who were these people who did so much and got so little in return? I can't think who, not now. I can't answer my own questions. But I do know that things were different back in the day. Used to be I had a good mind. I had strong will and direction. Then all of a sudden something changed. All of a sudden I couldn't breathe. Everything stopped moving but the wind.

I stood in that room, knowing I had to get on. And there it was again – my necklace. It was a long time since I'd worn the thing. I snatched it from the bedside table and linked the chain around my neck. It tickled down my front like beads of sweat. It was typical of me to feel this, the coldness of the metal, typical droop of me, too, my breasts.

I'm not afraid to say it. We all get older, don't we? And what with all my children – have I mentioned them? Even some husband, I suppose. I'm trying to paint a picture. But who can recount the years? Fifty. Five hundred. I'm trying to get a sense of the passage of my life. But who has time for that? A little after three, the clock said. It was time I ran.

Quietly, I went down the stairs and slipped out the front door. I did not pause to contemplate my ways. I didn't once look back at the tracks I'd made, which were selfish I'm sure. What had I done to make me so afraid of myself that I wouldn't even pause and look behind? Perhaps I needed counseling, consoling, decoding.

But who has the money or time for that? Besides, what person is skilled enough in those arts to deliver the goods?

And how far would I have to go back in time to return to something worth talking about, I wondered? Fourteen years, twenty-eight years, fifty-six years, all the way back to the day I was born? Would I have to reach into another incarnation, where I shot the afternoon sun from the prow of a ship, starving for the touch of another, dying of too much wind and incurable passion? Is that the gist of me, the seed of my being?

Who was I anyway, in a previous life? Was I Ave? Was she somewhere near? Am I always the leading role, no matter what my name? Whoever I've been, am I I, unleashed in time, in the country or on the cobblestone streets? Breadbaker, dressmaker, acrobat act. Poor as sick soil, or wealthy as butter. Did I walk in the mud and ruts in the Dark Ages, rescuing birds like Siddhartha, saving mice like Saint Francis, patching wounds like Silvanus Healer? How far would I have to regress to understand the course, or is it curse, I've taken in life?

Once outside, I ran from that house. I had my old necklace and new boots. I had a decent coat and a bag with some food and stuff. How far would I have to go to know a bit of truth? Back to Pythagoras where I was in harmony with the spheres? Or all the way to Eden where I, as a spirit child, played with the lions and lambs? That far? Why not even farther, beyond the earth and this universe, beyond even time. Maybe if I looked into the wish that started all life, I thought, I'd see my real self revealed. But it just wore me out, all those far off thoughts.

On and on under the heavy gray sky, I ran. I remember reading a story once of a person who was slowly erased, so by the end of the work she was an empty page. I remember hearing a girl once tell me that her life was a mistake according to God. How could it be true that God disapproves of what is becoming? Wasn't it His idea to get things started?

Maybe so, but what did I really know. I saw clouds piling up as I went. It was such an equivalent sky, I felt. There was no inspiration or depth. I saw no masterpiece of Van Gogh with his swirls. I saw no accomplishment to my days. And no angels hovered near to dispute the emptiness. No Elohim, no singing Seraphim were there to teach me or lessen the load. No light broke through the clouds. No whisper came to warm my ear. It was as if everything had left me, as if everyone I'd ever known, so uninterested in my burdens, had unquestionably gone.

I needed a pickup, a lift. Maybe just a bit of luck. I needed to get off my feet and fly. So when I saw the empty car, I didn't hesitate. I spied the keys, hanging from the ignition like tempting grapes. The keys lured me in. The car spoke the perfect lines to me. It was a few seductive words and I was there. I was had. And I stole it.

It was a nice car, too. Four-door with six horses and a radio that caught a signal the minute I turned the key. Call it unconscionable. Call it fate, if you like. Call the car bright silver – neigh, quick. Quicksilver. Neigh, presto. Neigh stallion, mare. Call it vivace. Veni, vidi, vici. Fast vita. Pro vita. Call me to life. I felt good behind the wheel. I felt me again. I felt young again. I would be okay. I would not be voided no matter how deep the void. And I would not be negated no matter how negative the mood.

The engine sounded smooth, and when I pressed the pedal, I was off. Godspeed. I was so far gone, I'd never come back that way.

❖

It was January. New beginning. Resolution. I could be full of optimism and no debt, like a negative number. The car clock read 3:11. I turned the radio off because it was music from the past. The best music is current music, which was that of the falling snow. The flakes hissed on their way to the earth, and I crushed ice crystals as I sped. I had lived long enough to know exactly what I wanted. Fifty-five, fifty-six, if I was a day. I wanted the ocean, the warm weather sea.

It was January. On the whitetop road, snow accumulated inches thick, sticking to my wheels. Tires, alright, tires! What do I know about cars? I do know that sometimes driving can be dangerous. So, maybe I should've gotten off, pulled in at the diner, had some coffee, but my speed was incredibly forward, and no one was on the road. I had it all to myself, except for the snow. There was the company of the flakes at my windshield, settling upon trees and over fields, blurring into the grayness beyond.

And I thought I saw
I heard I thought
a geist, a ghost a

Word inside me was snow alone. Outside, there was the steady whiteness. It was an hypnotic message from which I could not turn away. This calming presence was more than snow, it was someone near who filled my mind, even my car. I liked who she was who came into the car and sat in the passenger's seat as I drove. I looked over, said nothing. I watched her a moment, then back to the road. She could've been me back in time. She had my eyes and the same tangled hair. A sister perhaps, my better self, she was younger in appearance, infinitely more easy on the eyes and sweet as the gentle heat coming through the vents. This was someone I still wanted to be, I thought, as I sped through the snow on the softness of the road.

But what good was this ghost to me? She wouldn't even talk. I looked over again, and then turned away from the subject. I rolled down my window and reached out my arm. I let my arm fly along, riding the wind with my winglike hand, and then catching that wind with my palm, feeling my arm kick back. I blurred my eyes upon the world and joined the rush at my ears in a conscious effort not to think. I followed the legions of flakes and enjoyed each one that landed on my skin. It was tiny pricks and my arm went, numb. My mind went numb. I forgot about the girl, the ghost. I forgot about me. No sailors were out in this storm, no risk-takers I could see. Not one snowplow even. Not a single bird.

Still, it was difficult not to have pictures in my mind. What do birds do in the freezing weather, I wondered? I knew that tree sparrows feast in fields, in marshes, in the cold. And chickadees fluff out their feathers, trapping air. What good would that do against thirty below winds? Other birds shiver to generate heat. A degree an hour they could generate, but at what expense of energy? How sad to think of months of shivering, of terrible shelter, of scant meals that a bird must endure. If I was a bird, a junco say...

If I was a nuthatch, I'd be bold and knock on someone's window. I'd be a raven, maybe. I heard about such a knocking raven once. Or a robin. I once knew a woman who spoke to robins. She took in all birds that came to her window. It could've been a dove descending, breaking the air and breaking her heart, or a wren with a damaged wing, hopping near her window, pleading to come in. If I was a bird, I'd knock on the glass. I'd peck at the front door if I was a chicken. Then I'd go live inside with the company of people. I'd welcome the lifting of the sash, the opening of the door. I'd sit on the arm of a chair and have ambitions and hopes, like that bird in *Stuart Little*. It would be a happy family, interesting folk inside. I'd wait out the worst of weather. I'd look forward to spring.

"Wouldn't it weaken you?"

"What?"

"Being taken in like that."

"No way. I'd be stronger than I am now."

"Handed all your food in a bird bowl, cared for by blankets rather than by instinct."

"It would be nurturing," I said. "The opposite of abandonment."

"Birds aren't people, you know," said my ghost. "They live in the wilds. They survive on their wit and have no woes. They don't need people."

"I didn't say they did need people. I didn't say they couldn't survive on their own. I said, if I was a bird. There's a difference."

"Oh," said the ghost.

I looked over to the empty seat. What was I doing? Must have sounded like a crazy person, driving fast, fighting with myself about birds. The wheels almost lifted from the white of the road so I was flying, flying almost in my silver six-horse car. My flying car. Me flying. Tires, I mean. Tires, not wheels. Word of the world came out from behind the snowy veil, but it was no clearer to me than before.

I heard things that kept me thinking of ghosts and my life. And I did not wish to think of those beings who came after death, but I was unable to resist. What spiritual crop grew out there, waiting to come to anyone who would listen? And what were they after, the ghosts? What were they there for? It was the whiteness that made me listen. It was the unconditional presence. It was this phantom, my spirit, delicately formed, difficult to discern. I could not stop myself from reaching out again and trying.

"Who are you?" I asked.

"Still me," she said, at least I thought it was a she. I had to keep my eyes on the road as she spoke. "It's nurturing to know about the spirit. There is no abandonment when you realize it."

"Realize what?" I asked.

"That matter is meaningless without a spiritual gist, your geist."

"Hissing demons, gnashing their teeth, tearing their flesh, and yelling their heads right off their bodies?"

"That's not me," said my ghost.

I considered the ghost. I considered her words.

"How can I know that you are good?"

"How can you not? I hope I'm more essential to you than some ghoul. More like a geist."

"You keep saying that stupid word," I said.

"I do?"

"Yes."

"At least I'm consistent," said my ghost. "It's difficult to find the right words to explain things. Do you think it's stupid to find the right words that give meaning to yourself?"

"A person could spend her lifetime and come up with no better word than fish or fake."

"Snowflake?"

"Fake," I repeated. "Not flake."

"Do you think you're a fake?" my ghost asked.

"No."

"A fish?"

"No."

"A fast driver?"

"Maybe," I said.

"So, where are you going?" asked my ghost.

"To the shore," I said, and I thought about it a moment and went on. "Hey, if you're so spiritual, you might be able to answer this. Do you think God gets out much? To see the world, you know? Is God ever at the shore with the shorebirds?"

"Why do you ask about God?"

"I'm just trying to get the attention off of me," I said.

"At least you're honest," said my ghost. "You run from everything, don't you?"

"I don't want to talk about it," I said. "Let's just drive and be quiet."

Time went by, more of the earth in passing and none of it clear, more falling snow. I wanted to turn to my ghost, but was afraid.

"What are you thinking?" asked my ghost.

"I'd rather not think right now," I said. "When I think, I stop moving. When I stop moving, I come up empty. When I come up empty, it's all I can think. Circles, circles. I'd rather just drive and come to the shoreline. When I get there, I'll arrive by myself and know it for the first time."

"Someone else is always with you. You can't just abandon her by not thinking."

"Who her?"

"And you can't abandon God either by not thinking."

"Who said anything about God?" I said.

"You brought God up," said my ghost.

"I did?"

"Yes. If a thought descends, are you able to realize it? If God is here, are you able to know?"

"Where here?" I asked. "In the car with me? I was asking about the shore."

"All I'm saying is, if God is inherent in all you see and all you are, do you even know?"

"I know nothing about it," I said. "Look at me. See me driving. I'm only a person here. You're the spiritual one."

I felt the ghost's look fall upon me. I was in her perception, her thought.

"Nice car," said my ghost. "How long have you had it?"

"Look at all this snow," I said, ignoring the question. "It covers everything and makes a new beginning possible."

"You are the snow, then. And you are the wind. You are the driving. You are the road. Who else are you? Where do you come from? Where are you going?"

"I've told you enough," I said. "I've said it already."

"Aren't there more personal things you want to say about yourself? Beautiful details that make you happy?"

"There might be, but I'm just going to drive now. Nothing else."

"Good idea. Those details might turn around and bite you. Avoid anything about yourself that'll only make you weaker."

"I don't need your sarcasm," I said. "I don't know if it's a good idea or not. You're mixing me up. I'd really rather not talk about it."

"Right. I'm with you. Let's put a lid on it. No more talk. It's driving me crazy all this talk. Let's just look at the

THE SHORE

snow

sn   ow   sn

ow   s   no   w

s   n   ow

sno   ws   now

s   nows   no   w

snow snow snow snow snow snow snow snow snow snow snow snow
snow snow snow snow snow snow snow snow snow snow snow snow
snow snow snow snow snow snow snow snow snow snow snow snow

"Have you ever seen it come so fast?"

"Probably," I said. "I don't keep records."

"It gives me a feeling that everything is possible," said my ghost.

"I feel lonely," I said. "Like a desert."

I looked in the car for a bottle of water. It was difficult to search and drive.

"Nothing?" said the ghost.

"Yes. I feel like nothing."

"It's not what I was asking. I was asking if you found anything to drink."

"No," I said.

"I'm sorry."

"That's what the snow says to me," I said. "It says, Nothing. Then it says, Sorry. It covers the earth and severs connections."

"Power goes out in the house," said my ghost.

"Pipes freeze," I remembered.

"Families have to huddle. They read books by candlelight. They tell stories to each other. About the time Uncle Mike came to dinner and brought his banjo. About Oscar in Pakistan building a school. About the time Homer chased the groundhog and actually caught it, ripping it apart."

"That was terrible," I said.

"It's what families do," said my ghost.

"What family do you mean?" I wondered. "What family do you see in this car? You're too much the optometrist."

"Eye doctor?"

"Optimist, I mean. You're too starry eyed. The emotion with the snow is loneliness. It's starting fresh with nothing and no one."

I waited for the ghost to contradict my words.

"Abandoned by my life," I said. "That's what I'm saying. And I'm tired of saying it. I just want to drive."

"So drive."

"I am."

"Every word you say lives within you," said my ghost. "Birthed by its desire to be known, just as you were born with a desire to be alive on the earth. You saw the time and place and loved the world enough to take it on. I remember."

"How do you remember anything?" I said. "You don't have a brain"

"Who needs a brain to remember," said my ghost.

"Well, I have a brain, and I was born in some marshy place with the sun coming on. My mother told me, and I remember it. I grew up happy."

"There you go," said my ghost, as though we'd gotten somewhere.

"What do you mean, there I go? I didn't go anywhere. Everything was taken away. I had no say. If I'd had say, things would not be like this. Things would be different."

"Things are important to you, aren't they? What are those things?"

"Experiences," I said as I drove, looking for the road in the heavy snow. "I like my experiences."

The car went quiet inside. There was an eerie calm. Wind from the window rushed past my ear. The wheels slipped on the road. Let me drive. Let me go. Let me be. Let me...

"Drive, then," said my ghost, breaking the quiet. "But it's dangerous out there. What if you wreck?"

"I'm a good driver."

"Still, I wonder if you've cut yourself off from life too quickly?"

"What's wrong with you? It's not me. It's not me doing the trick. I'm the one who's been abandoned."

I thought about closing the window. Of turning on the radio. Listening to music.

"You know," I continued. "I was in love once. God, how long ago was that? He kept a calendar in the kitchen, and it was always December because he liked the picture of the mountains. I liked some other picture. We fought about it. We were different that way. He won out because I let him win."

"Was winning so important?"

"Of course winning wasn't important. It was all just a game. Things were fun. I liked playing. I liked being in love, even if it was only the beginning. Or maybe *because* it was just the beginning. The feeling lingers without substance. It's fog. It's smoke. It's... There's nothing more I can say about my life. Is that okay with you?"

"I'm only responding to what you dish out."

"Like mac and cheese?" I asked.

"More like bittersweet chocolate," said my ghost.

Wind wind wind, as I drove as I drove. Wheels wheels wheels, on the road on the road.

"Life is tireless," said my ghost. "And it's senseless if you can make no sense of things."

"Your stupid aphorisms don't change anything."

"Antagonism toward life is a step toward knowing the spirit that—"

"This is insane," I said. "Can't you just stop?"

"I'm not the one who needs to stop," said my ghost.

"Of course you are. It's gibberish."

The ghost was quiet, as if offended.

"I'm not offended," said my ghost. "I'm afraid."

"You're afraid!"

"You're driving too fast."

"Don't worry about it," I said. "Nothing can hurt you."

The snow angel was quiet, as if to tell me in all her subtlety that what I'd just said wasn't true, as if to get me to realize that others were in danger, not just myself, as if saying that I was not alone in life no matter how I felt, as if to say—

"What are you saying?" I asked.

"I'm not saying anything," said my ghost. "You are."

Enough. Enough. The hell with all this. I rolled up the window and turned on some tunes to protect me from thought. I sped on the white slick road, wishing my way south and making it so. It had made no sense to me, that language. Too much wind. Too many words. It had hurt my ears. My face was cold and my eyes had frozen. But now, with the window up, in the heat of the car, listening to pop, my eyes quickly melted. I looked out the window, searching the snow, the air, the dove gray sky, for land. I looked for somewhere to rest. I could have drowned in my eyes, there was so much deep looking in them. And I never slowed down. Just rolled on. I loved the earth so much.

Who would want to leave this earth? That's the thing about belief in God. You have to leave the earth if your belief is ever to reach its goal. You have to fly to God when you die, away from world. If you believe in God and Heaven, you'll be happy to leave. I'm glad that I'm uncertain. I'm glad I'm a healthy skeptic. Who wants to leave? Who wants to die when there's so much living yet to do? Who wants to stop when—

❖

Everything screeched to a halt. Whatever it was came out of the gray with no warning. I admit it was my fault, but not my intent. I slammed on the brakes, must have skidded and spun.

After I struck it, the car careened into the ditch, tilted to its side, and stopped. Something flashed before my eyes, not the thing I'd just hit. Maybe it was my life, but it didn't seem to have much significance or depth. Probably it was just the whirling world as I pitched in the car. And my face was lacerated. I like that word. But otherwise, no harm done. There was a tiny cut to my forehead and a trickle of blood. Besides that, there was whatever I'd hit. I must have been doing fifty or more. I'd certainly killed it.

I climbed from my car to investigate. Poor creature. Just look. A deer lay suffering in the snow, its blood leaking onto the perfect white. The snow guzzled the juice of the body. The air sipped the odor and the wind took it west.

I didn't mean to hit you, I said to the deer. I wasn't looking. I didn't see.

Lot of good my words did. The deer lay her head on the snow, lifted it, and lay it back upon the cold pillow. I thought I understood her suffering, but what did I really know? I saw her language with its broken words. I heard some voice inside me, speaking the spirit of her being. For a moment, we were together, deer and I, neither of us sad. I burrowed my attention in the doe. I listened as she lay bleeding. I felt her life fighting to stay and draining, both.

Don't go, I offered in a pitiful attempt at rescue. She could barely hear me, let alone understand my concern. And I saw her life leaving, like mist from the early morning creek or smoke from a smoldering fire. She lifted her head again. The snow sizzled upon her, the snow deepened upon her, the snow covered her thin fur, her eyes. She laid her head forever once more, as I stood so helplessly watching what I'd done. And the whole of her soul, the deerness of life, reached round me, through me, and then dissipated among the falling snow. And that was it. That was all. She was removed from her struggle to live each day, taken from her bones and muscles, from each hair and hoof, dissolved from her body. What was it, this deer-life I was sensing? Where was it headed, what heaven, what place? And why was it I who had done it to her?

I am such a careless sort. Always have been. Speeding when there is no need. Going out in inclement weather, lightning storms, and gales of near hurricane force. I love the speed and vigor of the world. I love the exhilaration of freedom. What was I thinking? I wasn't thinking. I must have been too self-absorbed.

Then, as I looked upon my kill, I knew that I had weakened the mighty force of life by one, and my heart stood still and tears began to well. They slid down my cheek and cooled in the icy air. There I stood, alone and wrong. There I stood, berating myself for my misdeeds in life. And I should have mourned over the creature. I should have laid a hand upon her body. I should better have loved her that instant, and then maybe all would have been forgiven. But I turned away, walked a few steps, and stood alone, my hands stonecold near my sides.

Next it was tender, almost fatherly concern upon my cheek. It was fingers, a gentle hand. The warmth of someone stood beside me. His glove, I felt, was off. I had not heard the truck. Man from his snowplow, guardian forgotten. The scruff on his face was what I noticed first. Then I saw him slip the glove back on his hand.

"That your car in the ditch?"

"Yes."

"You just ran off the road?"

"Hit a deer," I said.

The man looked around.

"You're shaking. Must have done more damage to you than the animal."

"What d'you mean, more?"

"Deer must be alright, run off," he said. "But you're bothered by it. Got a slight cut on your face."

"I killed it. She's alongside the road. My car crashed somewhere. I'm sorry."

"No need to apologize to me. You skidded off the road. We'll get her out."

"Her who?"

"Your car."

"Oh," I thought. My car. I thought he meant the deer.

"What's your name?" the good man asked.

"Ave. But I hit a deer. I saw her in the snow."

"I'll look, Ave. Stay here."

The man walked to his truck and soon returned.

"I've radioed help. Come sit in the truck with me. It's warm."

He helped me up to his vehicle.

"I was heading to the ocean," I told him.

"That's the spirit. Who wouldn't want to go to the beach?"

"I like it when no one's there," I said.

"No crowds. I get you."

"Just the natural place," I said. "The shells and drifts. Water's in my soul."

"You've got a good soul, then," said the plowman.

"I don't know about that. I was waiting for something good to come, then I hit the deer."

"I didn't see any deer," said the man.

"I don't know how I'll get there without a car,"

"Where?"

"The shore."

"Oh," said the man, remembering the shore. "We'll get her out."

"Who?"

"Your car," said the man, but I thought he meant the deer. We arrived at his truck and stood for a minute.

"You ever been?" I asked him.

"The ocean? Sure."

"I could listen to it all day," I said. "Lots to learn. Lots to love."

"All the L-words," said the man. He opened the passenger door for me. I got in. And we sat in his truck and waited. I felt dazed and dumb.

"You from around here?" asked the plowman.

"Not far," I said. "I was born on the saltmarsh."

"It's in your blood, then."

"What?"

"The shore."

"I guess."

He cleared the gathering snow with one sweep of the wiper blades.

"My father had a sailboat," the plowman began. "He was a right good sailor. Wanted to sail around the world. Storms didn't concern him in the least. **IN KNOTS** was the name of his boat. He took me out once, but I got sick from the tilt and bounce. I'm not much for life on the water. But I love the ocean, nonetheless. Sometimes things you love are things you're afraid of most."

"What do you love about it?" I asked.

"You know, I've never thought."

"Well think," I said, and then I felt rude for being so aggressive. He didn't seem to mind.

"The oblivion during calm, I'd say. And the delirium during storm." The plowman paused and went on: "You know how a great body of water toys with your mind and turns you loose? I love that. Also the ocean takes you places and it tends to your soul, if you let it."

"You love the T's of it."

"You might be right. It is an awesome tease."

"Could you drive me there, now?" I asked.

"Oh, I'd like to. Swear it. Like to take off from work, but I've already radioed help. They'd come here and wouldn't find us. It'd anger my boss. He'd curse up a storm. I'd lose my job, and that's an L-word I don't much like."

"I understand. I wasn't really being serious."

"I know," said the man.

"Look," I said. "I'm not crazy, if that's what you think."

"Who's thinking?" he said in earnest. "Do I look like I'm thinking? You're shook up." The man had a firm, chiseled face under his scruff. He was handsome in a fatherly way. Soft eyes. Nice hands. Piles of words and layers of feelings. You could tell there was plenty inside him to say.

"What about the deer?" I asked. "Someone might hit her in the road."

"I didn't see any deer. Must be you bumped her and she ran off."

"Ran off to die."

"Deer are tough," said the plowman. "They don't die easy. Heal themselves of most wounds. Wisdom runs with them that they make use of, only they don't know a thing about it. Most likely, you'll bump into her again some day. You'll have a good laugh about it all."

I opened the door of the truck and got out, holding the door for safety. I looked at the road where my car went off. Saw the hint of tracks through the furious snow. Saw no sign of the dead animal. Got back in the cab, snow in my hair. We sat for a quiet stretch, no cars, and no let up to the world around. On account of the weather, the world pressed close.

"Snow's sure falling," the plowman said with utter obviousness. "Might be I'll just have to take you to town myself. Take you to the hospital. Make sure you're okay."

"No," I said. "That wouldn't be worth it."

Snow accumulated on the windshield, and the plowman turned on his wipers to clear it.

"You know," he said. "Could be it was a ghost."

"What ghost?"

"Lots of cars run into deer this stretch of the road. I've heard that there're thousands of ghosts about. There are stories people will tell. My friend, Captain Pim for one. He saw a ghost, nearly made him piss his pants, excuse me for saying so. He was driving near springtime, a long time ago this was, when he stopped for an eight-point buck. Deer turned to his car, put down his antlers, and walked right through. Now, Pim liked to hunt, and he thought this was the ghost of one of his kills charging a message to him. Frightened him so much, he quit the gun. Took up taking fishing parties. Businessmen came from the city. He'd take them all fishing way out in the ocean."

"Deer ghosts."

"Dear ghosts. Sounds like you're writing a letter. Dear Ghosts: I'm writing to ask what you're made of. I'm writing to find out who you were in life and if I might offer some comfort to you now."

"You're a good man," I said.

"Well, it's nice of you to say so. I'm not much but a plowman in winter and a laborer my whole life, but I like to help if I can. People are everything to me, I don't mind saying so, even if I keep to myself."

"But, you know, I saw her blood on the snow."

"Must have been someone else, years back, hit a deer in the exact same spot. Roads have memories like that, I think. I've seen phantom blood on this road before. Trust me on that."

"I do. You're trustworthy. T words, remember. But I felt a thud."

"Well, I won't speak to that. As I told you, might be you bumped the doe. You skidded on the snow, she ran off to her family. And all's well that end's well, as Shakespeare said. All's right with the world."

"Maybe."

"Aye, we don't want to sit in here and argue about it, now, do we. I've got some water in the back of the truck. For your face. Antiseptic. Your car'll need towing. Too bad for that. Police will be involved. I hate that hassle. Authorities like to stick their noses in everything these days."

The man got out of the truck to get what he needed from the back, what he thought I needed. But what I needed wasn't in his truck. Nowhere near. Besides, it was too difficult for him to secure. So instead of arguing about it in my head, I thought of my car. I thought of the deer. Police, I thought. What a mess. The deer was one mess, the car another. I'd stolen it, hadn't I? I'd turned those tempting keys without proper permission. Oh, the complexity of living. It was difficult enough just to be without also being a mess. Yet, I wanted so little, really. The shore to walk upon. Marsh in the sun. Waves at my feet. And I wasn't getting any closer sitting where I was. And I was too old for doing time. I didn't want to be arrested. Not stopped, either. I wanted to keep going. I'd not let them take me, not alive, not even dead. I'd get what I wanted. I'd be who I was meant to be, I would. Such a simple request is beach. Such an undeniable prayer – a life coming to shore. A place to be.

It came over me all at once, and I bolted from the truck. Never said good-bye. Left the door wide. Ran like. Fire in straw. Melting snow. River to sea. Ran for the woods for hiding. Who'd ever guess me there? No one would. No one. My face stinging with pain, my ears ringing with the shouts of the deersaving snow-shaving voicefading lifeliving man.

ELEVEN

Trees towered above me. I lay on the snowy ground of the woods. What was I doing there at this eleventh hour, late in the afternoon? I never finish anything. If someone had come and spotted me, the way I was hypnotized dumb by the quiet of trees, he'd have thought I was dead.

The dead in the woods lie unknown.
Tree limbs have no need of names. The owls
watch for life, then fly away silent.

Someone would have thought, had he come, that I had hit my head and kicked the bucket. He'd have thought I'd lit my last, leaving my wick dark and cold. If someone had come, his response to my body would have been a whisper to himself as he stood shivering, seeing me lying on the ground, staring through the jumble of treetops to the sky. Is she dead? he would've wondered. She's not moving, except for what the wind does to her shirt and hair.

❖

Of course, I wasn't dead, was I? But what was going on? I was acting a bit strange. How had I gotten there, anyway? It's difficult to explain. I'd just wandered off, like I was on some wilderness survival expedition. I wish I'd packed a Snickers bar in my pack, or a space blanket. A first-aid kit would've been handy. But no. I used to keep a journal. I wish I'd packed that, too. I thought I'd brought something to write on. I looked for it everywhere and couldn't find it. I used to have this blue notebook when I was young, living at home. So much time for writing, then. When I was young, I had time for words, and the words grew into hopes and ideas, full-fledged stories. But as I lay in those woods, the time just seemed to slip away. Less time, little movement, no hope. If things kept as they were going, what would be the point of my life?

I stared at the winter afternoon, but it was no help, only gray. I stared at the trees, the sky. No sun, no warmth came through. Branches crissing and crossing, occasionally moving. It would be a long afternoon, I thought, if this kept up and I did nothing to change things.

Then into me, into my blur gray anguish as if from some sympathetic source, came words. These were not spoken words, not written words, but language nonetheless: Pine and fir boughs. Brown crisp words like twigs and trunks. Lacy words like hemlock greens shoving themselves on the gray air. Foxes, deer, broken limbs, one soaring hawk. Words formed like snow right out of the earth. They grew inside me and it wasn't even spring yet. Words appeared on the face of everything, a sudden language to live for. There was a reason for my being in that wilderness, for sure. I was alive on earth to experience things and to say something in exchange for what I received. And the words formed for me from what I pictured of my earth: stately trunks rising from the melting snow, oak and maple and bare branches that, though still asleep, were beginning to feel the light, their life, like waking from dream and seeing the true world again.

The end of February. Spring was just around the corner. I was lucky to see this, or if it was not luck it was a gift, or if it was not a gift, I'd stolen it the way you steal a look without permission. But if you like what you see, is it so terrible to look? Is it really stealing to take what is presented, take it to heart and let it live inside you a while? There I lay, immensely world, flooded with experience and no one to stop it. I couldn't stop the world from filling me, either. Eventually, I found a way to get some of it out of me, to write some of it down.

ENTRY # ONE

February end. Spring's just around the corner. No let up to the cold just yet. I'm waiting. Nothing has happened for days here. There's a stillness about the place. There's this absolute quiet I'm listening to. I picture the quiet as isolation, as though a wall with no windows or doors surrounds this world, a defense mechanism of the wilderness or a defiance to let anything in or out. Yet I know that someone is coming today. I've been expecting the visit for a while. Maybe now's the time.

TWO

Just past four in the afternoon. I can read the time without a clock. It's mostly an internal light that lets me find the hour. I don't know where inside I see the time, but it's my talent to be able to tell. The clouds don't hinder me. It doesn't make much difference whether I see the sun or not. I believe with practice I could be an atomic clock. But I don't have much practice left in me. It doesn't matter about practice or clocks. I know he will come soon. I just don't know who.

THREE

I am getting old just waiting. I'm tired of this life. It's not fun any more. I'm losing grip of what is real and what is imagined. I lie about all day here. Alone. I've lived this way for long it seems, finding a way to get by. I barely see others except some shadowy locals who bring me food – mustard soup, mushroom stew, tahini, bread, mac and cheese, dried venison when I need some meat. I think I want to go vegetarian, though. Life's got a funny way of making you change. Anyone would have thought I'd've gone to the shore, that I'd've become like a bird, flown south. But I went north instead. I came this cold way, to shake off the clever authorities. They were followers and searchers after my life. I think I've done a pretty good job so far to distance myself. I've mastered things the way the sun masters the earth. With such mastery, I've stayed ahead of my fate.

FOUR

Ah, wilderness. It's been a while since I last wrote. Used to keep a journal, used to write poems when I was younger. Now I get by on survival skills alone. Ah, woods and wilds. I find water by digging. I deal with wind and cold. I avoid hypothermia at all costs. If a deer can do it, so can I. It is how I began this life. If an animal can fight every element that comes her way, so can I. It's how I continue here. Animals don't retire to the zoo if given the choice. They don't come crawling into houses, into comfort, into a person's bed. They live out their lives and die when they're good and ready. And I in my seventies, eighties, nineties, millions, am damn sure old enough to know how to live on my own. I'll do as the animals do. I won't seek comfort. I'll live unaided if I must.

FIVE

Occasionally, I excavate and find more than water. I discover my past. It's dirt and stones, mostly. Old loves, homemade bread, a name that makes me think, that sort of thing. It's an uncertain foundation I get to. There's not enough time for building any more. There's too much time for the nonsense of regret. But I can't give my thinking over to what I've lost: long-gone mother and father, two far-off brothers, friends and neighbors I can't even recall, some husbandly type who may've played games with me and had fun with his words, too. Whowashe once? Whoosh, he's gone. And some children like chicks among the grains and low grasses, those tiny clucks. Seems like I must've had chickens somewhere along the line. I mean children, of course. I suppose I loved them all, the way I love this world with a great deal of longing, all of it good. And did I have an affair as well? Some illicit love with a farmer boy, a painter with a talent for ultramarine on the canvas and cerulean blue of his eyes? How could it matter now? Where is that time, my lover-boy? What I've got is the blue of the sky where the clouds give way. What I've got is the natural world, tall trees and patches of light between. I've got the stream over there with stones. I've got the pond in front with lycopodium growing near. It's been this one place for years, I think. I've learned to recognize plants and other changing things. I think women, as they grow older, prefer to live alone. So be it. Always have been comfortable in my head and skin. My head is where I'm home until I look out even further and whoever comes will make his way into me, will make himself known. Who's it going to be, I wonder?

SIX

Ear to the earth, I hear footsteps. Who's it going to be? Will he carry me back to the shore, you think? To the place where I was born, you think? To die, you think, in a better world? Don't be so sure. I'm a fighter. I won't be carried off to die. I'll stay where I want for as long as I want, and move when I want to move on. The days of February have all toughened themselves as my opponent, but I'm still here. Every day it's been some different hour hacking at me, howling like a wolf. **Cut loose, move on,** the hours cry. But I will only do what I'm ready to do. There is no one strong enough to change me now. Just after four in this gray afternoon. Look – no one.

SEVEN

Then he appears. He's right beside me. I swear I did not hear his boots till they kicked snow right into my ears. My mind was entirely occupied composing this entry, I guess. And though he doesn't startle me, I act as if he does, and I let fly my notepad onto the frozen pond. I'm not sure if any words are released as it flies. Not sure if anything much has even made it to the pages. I have no pen or ink, and these woods are a mere idea coming to terms. There is a mystery to this world sometimes, working its own scenes, having its own say.

EIGHT

The sky is gray again today, but there's reason for hope. My guess is 4:14, even without the sun. As for causing my words to fly, he apologizes profusely, and runs to fetch the little book of me.

"Here," he says, handing the pad, as he returns from the pond.
"Dr. Livingston, I presume."
"I'm not a doctor," he tells me. "Do you need one?"
"Do I look injured?"
"A slight cut on your forehead. Are you alright?"
"Do I look ill?"
"No," he says.
"Do I look old?"
"I'd feel rude if I said yes."
"Say what's true, don't worry about rudeness."
"Well, you look sort of tired. Yeah, you do look old."
"That's rude to say. Imagine me younger. You should always say something pleasant to someone you first meet."
"I'm sorry. Okay. I see a nineteen, almost twenty year old girl, really young looking and healthy. Guys are lining up. Model agencies are doing what they can to contact her. Blood runs like crazy. No clogs, no stops, no holds barred. The sky's the limit."
"Okay, okay. You've got a good imagination. You win."
"Well, to be honest, you do seem very spry."
"Surprised? But I'm not surprised. I knew you were coming. I thought you'd be older, but it hardly matters. How old are you?"
"I'm fifteen, now," says the young man.

"Fifteen. Can't be. You're making it up. Stop playing games."

The young man's eyes laugh. The laughter falls on me like wind.

"What's so funny?" I ask.

"That I'd come out here to play games. I'm not like my sister with her fantasies. I've got a serious bent about me. I love to think and work."

"Got no humor, then?"

"Oh, I'm human," he tells me.

"Are you a hunter?"

"No."

"How did you find me?"

"I followed your tracks, your scats. The sounds you made were unhearable to most ears but not to me."

"To mine." I correct him.

"I don't mind," he says, and I hear the weird playfulness of our rapport. "The trees are to blame, too," he continues. "They let on to you. The breeze coming through the evergreen sis—"

"What sister is that? Me?"

"I didn't say sis. I said the breeze coming through the evergreens is different when it touches a person than, say, when it scrapes with a bear or coyote."

"How clever of you to have noticed I'm different. Are you some scout? A lost eagle or troupe leader?"

"I'm the plowman's first son."

"Piers Plowman, the poem?"

"I'm no dock or verse."

"Nordoc Orvis," I say. "Strange name. Hello, I'm Ave. Do you like it?"

"Like what?"

"Who you are?"

"Sure, why not. I can play along with it."

"I've noticed. But, before, you told me just the opposite, about your serious bent."

"I did?" says the young man. "I must've been crazy back then. I'm glad I've grown out of it. Some day it'll return."

He takes out a stick from his back pocket.

"What's that?" I ask.

"Banjo."

"Can you play?"

"I'm okay," he says. "My mother taught me creation, my father taught me to pluck. You can never go wrong with banjo music."

So Nordoc Orvis, the instrument boy, gets into position and I lay back on the accepting earth. He plays a lyrical song that lifts even birds. The bright of the music opens the sky to a whole bunch of blue, and warms away the chill winter. It's a real toe-tapping tune to wake tall trees and get the sap running. The notes melt the pond with the gentle force of sunlight, and they take on the snow like it's coming on spring. I feel young again. I feel good.

"Look at the earth," says Nordoc. "It's dripping."

NINE

Now that his playing is over, time has moved on. Yo, brother, it's nice out here at the edge of these woods. We sit in the stillness and listen to the melt and drip, noting the puddles and mud.

"What's today?" I ask.

"Just another day," he says. "But a good one."

"There's the ground again. I never would have imagined it here, under all that snow."

"Seasons come and go," he explains. "Fall, winter, flee-n-tick."

"Flee-n-tick. Who told you that?"

"Morgan."

"Who's she?"

"A friend," he says. "I'm just getting to know her."

"And she tells you such intimate things?"

"Lots of people tell me things. I tell myself things, too."

"What things do you tell yourself?"

"The earth holds onto our bodies, but our spirits soar free."

"You're a young philosopher," I suggest.

"Not really. My father would like to be one. He's got all these ideas in his head."

"What good are ideas if you keep them to yourself?" I wonder.

"My Pop's got people to share stuff with," says the young man. "So do I. But out here, there's no one. Do you like where you are?"

"What do you mean, where I am?"

"Out here," he says.

"For better or worse, it's okay. I'm decaying into the place. How can I ever leave?"

The young man does not answer. He looks everywhere but on me, not wanting to witness my rot, I guess. I like the boy, though. Don't want him to feel uncomfortable with me.

"You seem to have melted the ice," I say. "You've got some mighty thaw in that banjo stick. Who are you again? Nordoc, you said. What is that, Finnish?"

"Plowman's boy," he repeats. "I'm John's older brother. He had some problems when he was born, but he gets stronger every day. O Terra Firma is my name, even though I'm a Pisces."

"I'm sorry to have misheard. Hello, Oscar. I'm Miss Ave. Ave Anabel Something Whatever. Did I say that already?"

"Not all of it."

"Well, there's more," I tell him. "I live out here for some reason I haven't come to express."

"All by yourself?"

"Do you see anyone else?" I don't mean to be snappish. But he doesn't seem to mind, and asks:

"So, were you born in this place?"

"Far from it. I, too, was born by the water. In a marsh, as a matter of fact."

"You're out of your element," says Oscar.

"A bit," I say. "I love the smell of the woods, but warm winter bread and summer baked saltiness are more my passions, the way you like baked custard and baked beans with a fried egg on top."

"Beans with a poached egg on top," he corrects.

"Whatever. I don't care for eggs. I like to write. I like to move. I love the saltmarsh in all seasons, and what the water teaches."

"What does it teach?" asks Oscar.

"Transformation and adaptability. Water can adapt to any form."

"So, why aren't you more where you wish to be?" Oscar wonders.

"Easy for you to say. You're young, where wishes are roads and travel comes easy."

"No."

"What do you mean, No?"

"I mean you're making excuses for yourself. I think you're just refusing to do what it takes. You're being stubborn."

"Hold on, bub. Remember your manners when you're talking to me. I'm much older than you. I've lived a long life."

"I think you're making stuff up to explain your mood," says Oscar. "Why aren't you home where you're supposed to be? Why aren't you writing more and learning about the shore? Why aren't you out seeing the world? Why aren't you doing what you love? Why are you lying here like a lump?"

"A lump. That's cruel."

"Sorry," says the young man. "It's just I see potential."

"Everyone has potential – to go either way. Me, I'm still deciding."

"Do you have any sonnets or songs prepared?" asks Oscar.

"I told you I'm deciding whether or not."

"Which way are you leaning?"

"Toward the not, as in not any more coffee for me and not any more days at the beach. Feel it's healthier that way. Caffeine makes me jumpy. The sun dries me out. And too much poetry makes me obscure. I want to be secure, not obscure. I want to be real and knowable. The poetry I've written is in my blank journal I keep hidden."

"How much is in your bank?"

"Plenty of unpaid interest. Little activity."

"Not even one line?" he asks. "Come on. I won't laugh."

"This love I live in showers me with air."

"That's your line."

"It's one," I say.

"It's okay. How about another?"

"Tonight I round the world I owe / it answers, turns and lets me go."

"You see, that's sad," says Oscar. "When I think of you, I think of gulls. I see sunlight. I say sanguine."

I hear him. I hear him. I want to explain. It must be someone else who wrote those words.

TEN

We sit overlooking the sparkly pond. 4:51. Monotonous trees border the east, but the west is open meadow, long reaches of land and, thanks to the young man's temperate music, the melting snow. I see a hare. A pair of coyotes stand far off. I wonder how long we've been together.

"My father once told me of an Ave," says Oscar. "I was much younger, fifteen years back."

"I thought you said you were fifteen, now."

"That was a long time ago," he tells me. "I'm twenty-five. Engaged to be married."

"Who is she?"

"Morgan's her name."

"I think we've met," I say. "At least, I've heard the name. Is there more to her?"

"Merry May Morgan Maryland Morning She's The One Apples With Cheese."

"She's a mouthful."

"I'm really in love, this time," says Os.

"It's about time," I say.

"Why do you say that?"

"I don't know why. Everything is hard to explain. Don't pay attention to a word."

"Well," Oscar goes on, "Mama's happy for me. She takes one thing at a time. But Pop, he puts everything on his plate at once. If you ask him, I bet he'll tell you what's wrong."

"He with you, in the woods? Is he waiting for an invitation?"

"No. I'm on my own now," says Oscar. "I wanted to bring Some-John out, you know, to show him survival techniques and how to track. But he's got some youth orchestra thing coming up. Besides, Mama's still so protective, even though the boy's much stronger."

"Who is your mother again? Maybe I know her."

"Sophie Alexander is her maiden name. You might know her from **The Spartina Group**, it's a musical theater company under the umbrella of **Walking The Dog**."

"None of it rings a bell."

"Well, that's pretty much my family. But like I said a minute ago, thinking on your name, I remember Papa pinning a story on a woman he called Ave."

"What story did Papa spin?" I ask.

"How he found her once, trickle of blood coming down her cheek from a slight lacerations to the brow. At first he thought she'd been in an accident, but saw no tracks except his own and those of the trees scratching up the sky because of all the wind. Maybe it was a bobcat did her the injustice. A bit of gravel, or maybe a branch."

"Didn't he ask her?"

"He was about to, then he remembered the place was haunted. He thought she was a ghost, and it turns out she was."

"How did it turn out she was?"

"He closed his eyes against the snow. It blew heavy, and the flakes pricked his lids. When he opened his eyes, she was gone."

"Proves nothing," I say. "She could have been quicker. She could have run off when he wasn't looking."

"Maybe, but before it, as they stood together, he saw right through her as they spoke."

"It's a common way of describing a person," I say. "To see right through. She could have been shallow. Probably wanted to lounge about on the beaches like some babe. Was she pretty? Did she like to flirt?"

"He didn't really say, but I saw in his eyes that she was nice to look at."

"Is you father happily married?"

"Yes."

"You don't think he was looking for some action on the side?"

"I gave you no reason to believe that," says Oscar.

"The thing is, you think you know someone, but you'd be surprised what goes on in this world."

"I know my father," says Oscar. "He's faithful. I trust what he says."

"Good for him. And you," I say. "Still proves nothing about a ghost."

"Well, maybe the snow provides the proof."

"What makes the snow such a convincing witness?"

"Was snowing hard that afternoon," begins Oscar. "The flakes were big and wet. The friendly snow—"

"Objection."

"The snow that fell from heaven—"

"Objection, again."

Oscar takes a breath, and then he finds an acceptable way back into the story.

"The snow that fell from the clouds clung to only my father and trees. It fell upon him and collected on his jacket. Whereas it fell upon Ave and found no body. He took a picture with his cellphone, and no one was there."

"Circumstantial evidence," I tell the young fellow. "Your father may've wanted so much to see a ghost that he invented one on the spot. With a real ghost, you need some solid evidence, such as electromagnetic disturbances or a displacement of photons."

"We're talking about spirit," says Oscar. "It's immaterial."

"Of course, it's relevant," I say.

"I mean," says Oscar. "If it's not the material world, you've got to think differently."

"Was this Ave a none, someone chosen by God to serve emptiness?"

"I don't think so."

"Well, what did your father do when he saw no form and yet suspected her foundation? What did he do to increase his certainty that this Ave was real, if only in an otherworldly sense?"

"He called after her," said Oscar.

"For how long? How long did he call for her?"

"Every day. He was so sad that she was gone from this world. He thought it was something he'd done, something he'd said."

"But it wasn't," I say.

"I know that and you know that, but he spun out of control with grief."

"Did someone notify the police?"

"What can authorities do to return a loved one to life?"

"And his wife, your mother?" I ask.

"Her take on things is much more holistic. She was stricken in a different way."

"Which?"

"No. Just a regular mortal. No one in the family has magic, dark or bright. Macbeth was never a favorite of hers. She knows her herbs, though. Dandelion root. Pot of Basil, if that's what you mean. She reads Keats, now and then. Ode to a Nighten gown, or whatever it is."

"You seem a bit befuddled," I say.

"It's all these questions. Seems like you're accusing my family of so much uncaring. But Mama loves her children more than I can say. She's a woman of the world, but her connections are intimate. In regards to this Ave, she kept her sadness to herself. "

"Why such sorrow for a ghost?"

"My parents are way too sensitive," says Oscar. "I tell them so. I'm sensitive in a different way."

"How?"

"OOOOO-OOOOOOO-ooooooooo."

"What are you doing?"

"Howling. I could probably do it better, but I'm out of practice."

"That was fine. But I didn't want you to howl. In what way are you sensitive?"

"I'm sorry," says Oscar. "Words keep me guessing. I want to get to the truth of things, but sometimes it's a very intellectual experience. My brother, John, is more intuitive than I. He knows angels up close, and elementals have lunch with him in the glen out back. He pushes aside veils of the world. He hears sounds that are not yet sounds, and sees light before it can be seen.

"He should have been with your father when he spoke with this Ave."

"I said the same thing exactly. John hears the truth in music, not in language."

"You have an interesting family," I say. "I'm sorry if I made you think otherwise. You are very thoughtful yourself, and I thank you for sharing so much of your time."

"Thank you, Ave. But what's your story? You know so much about me. Do you have a husband? Children? Are they grown? Can I bring you back to town and help you find a place? You can have dinner at our house. Mama loves all people."

"It's difficult to answer so many questions at once. All the warmth you've brought, it confuses me. The sky is me looking up, but I'm not sure what to do next."

Together, we look at the clearing sky and become it. And our invisible companion, Silence, takes over the conversation, speaking his mind abundantly.

ELEVEN

Oscar kicks at the last bit of snow in front of him. After a while, he says, "It will be a nice day tomorrow."

"Is it too late?" I ask.

"Too late?"

"You know," I say.

"Not at all," says Oscar. "It's only five."

A fine young man, with a chiseled face, sun bright smile, and sky blue eyes like mine. His fiancé is a lucky woman. Morning. Merry. Lucky. Morgan. Apples and Cheese. I look this man in his gentle eyes. I try to be as fine as he.

"Is your father really a plowman?" I ask.

"He does it to be neighborly. I've seen him dig up a field, too."

"Why does he dig a field?"

"For rocks. He uses them. He likes to build walls. He chips away at them, too. Sometimes he plants his feet firmly in the ground."

"A farmer?"

"Sure, he likes to form things. He can use his hands. But his mind's his favorite thing."

Here we sit, looking over the rippling pond. There's a breeze from the south that shovels away the clouds. The nearby snow has melted to mere patchwork. If I were to walk upon the ground, I'd sink into mud. I'd dig my heels in. Then I'd be stuck.

"Yo, Ave. You see up there?" handsome Oscar asks. He's pointing to the highest ridge in the distance. Looks like Everest, Fuji, or Kilimanjaro. It is picture perfect in muted evening light. Calendar art.

"Yes."

"I'm going there someday."

"You are?"

"Not right now, but soon."

"Why?" I ask.

"The joy climbing. What else? Coming to know something I don't know already. It's the worst thing for me to think I'd stay put like some nail in an old barn."

"Are you making a comment on my life?"

"Not at all," he says. And I believe him. He goes on about all the places he's been, the people he's met on his travels, the work he's done in the world. It's an adrenaline rush.

"You're very ambitious," I say. "And wise for your age."

"I'm not afraid."

"Same with me," I say.

"Now, some people think a rock has no spirit, but I—" Oscar stops midstare at the imaginary mountains.

"You don't agree." I complete his thought.

"I have trouble limiting things."

"But there are limits," I say. "It's wishful thinking to say there are no limits in life."

"I didn't say there weren't boundaries," says Oscar.

"You didn't?"

"I said I have trouble with them."

"Like the borders between countries, where some guard stops you?" I ask.

"More like the borders between people where you stop yourself. I love looking at people, seeing to their soul, if I can, seeing to their deep undrinkable I."

He was looking at me when he said this, this young familiar man with his gentle eyes and piercing gaze. Looking. At. Me.

"Why undrinkable?"

"Doesn't belong to me. It's not mine. I can see to the true person, but I shouldn't sip unless she's offered to me." He's embarrassed, I sense. "Also the lines and faces of everything else."

"What about them?"

"I love looking at the lines of a mountain or the face of a rock."

"A rock has a face?" I ask.

"I don't see why not. Now a rock is something most interesting because it has greater endurance than most people. But where's the personality, you wonder. A rock just sits there, patiently. Sort of boring, if you get down to it. But if you really get down and intuit, it's interesting. A rock appears to be independent, appears to be free, but it can't think for itself. A rock knows nothing. Has such small consciousness, a rock on earth, but if it had just enough to let you know, you'd hear great music."

"Why music?"

"You'd hear songs like that lyre boy Apollo played."

"Orpheus is the one you mean," I tell him. "He played the lyre, and the earth heard his music and cried."

"Yeah, Orpheus. You know your myths."

"And you know the thoughts and dreams of rocks."

"I like to think about things," said Os.

"Fifteen, twenty-five. It all seems young for such large ideas."

"I see similarities between the periods of an individual life and the epochs of history. There's a relationship between how a single human being lives her life on earth and how the whole human species evolves over time. There is a pattern, a comparison between the two, and it reveals something about the spirit of life itself. As a fetus follows forms, so a person from birth to death follows the epochs of earth from its human beginnings."

This wakes my interest. I want him to go on.

"Tell me more of what you mean," I say.

"Some day, when I know it better."

"I might not be here," I worry.

"Sure you will," says Oscar. "We'll find one another. We'll talk."

"I'm so old," I say. "I'm dying."

"I don't mind death. It won't get in our way."

TWELVE

Oscar holds his banjo stick in his left hand, passing it between his fingers. His eyes scan the place.

> A raven by the wood edge
> upon a deer carcass,
> plucking at the meat.

He is eager to say something.

"What's on your mind?" I ask.

He shrugs and stares across the pond, toward spring. It's peculiar how he doesn't seem to respect my age, especially because he's such a nice young man. But I'm used to it. It's been so long since I've felt in harmony with my years. Feels to me now that I'm stuck at about nineteen, twenty. Of course, if I don't carry myself with wisdom and depth of experience, then I will be treated as if still a child.

"What if a person dies early," I say. "What if a person dies young in life?"

Oscar readjusts his body. He looks away.

"Nineteen, twenty," I suggest.

Is he even listening?

"You know," I go on, "like a tree that blossoms and the fruit is just beginning to develop, and then the tree's cut down."

He looks at me. Something else is on his mind, but I want to finish my idea first.

"Anyway, how might a person follow that unfolding evolution of yours if she is cut down too soon, called away from existence?"

Oscar doesn't hear my question, or it doesn't concern him.

"Wouldn't you mind that death?" I ask. "Would it bother you?"

He looks past my words and into me.

"What I like about you," he says, diverting his eyes to the trees beyond, "is that you will not be shut down. You take the breath of spirit that begins things, you build it up with your own wave, and you make your way to the earth, the shore."

His words bring to my soul the possibility of my life. I jot it down:

Like beach
ground boulder
irreducible grains of
music, love –
what place it is
where shorebirds
circle and waves
arrive aroar

"Yo, Ave. The ocean is full of waves. Not all of them reach land. Some die with the wind. Most ripple only so far, and then decide it's too difficult at the moment. But you've already made it. You're solidly ashore. And your song has no end."

Oscar puts down his banjo. I watch him turn a rock in his palm. I watch this man, his sunlit face, unkempt hair, simplicity and grace. He holds a rock. All things run together in my mind. People, times. I do not know who I'm talking to or if, in fact, it's real. Fleetingly, all of life burns me to understand it better.

"Why're you staring at me?" says the young man.

"I'm trying to figure you out," I say. It's an attempt at recognition, but it only results in a certain sadness. There's warmth in the air and the thought of shore. I rest my notebook in my lap and finger my necklace, which turns up every now and then when I least expect it.

"Remember when you first got it?" asks Oscar. It takes me a moment to understand what he means.

"Sometimes I forget I have it on," I say.

"Not the necklace," he clarifies. "Not your notebook, either. I mean understanding who you are and how you fit into a family, your mother and father, your two brothers. It probably started around three."

"Three o'clock?"

"Three years old," says Oscar. "Me me me me me. Later, you called yourself I. Things began to make sense – how you fit into a place and connect with the world around you. You are not a time traveling time killer, but someone whose feet are on the contemporary earth. Don't you get it? Don't you know me yet? The twilight's here now, and so are you. It will linger and go, and so will you. The shadows, then, will be erased, washed from you as from the earth. But that's not all there is. Not by a long shot. It's just the beginning, really. You're just getting started. What do you say?"

"Say?" I'm confused by his speech, that's what I want to say.

"People speak of Ave."

"People. What people?"

"Lay your heart on the earth," he says, in the first of three strange demands. "See with your eyes closed," he continues. "Listen as though your ears are clogged."

"I won't do any of that," I say. "Lay with my eyes closed and clog my ears. You can't be talking to me."

He doesn't hear my complaint, but it's true, I think. He talks as if to someone he doesn't see anymore.

"I hold you in my hand like this stone. The sky whispers shyly. The water ripples with the slightest breeze. And free to go. You are free to go. You are."

Oscar talks to the rock in his hand, which is a glowing rock in the heat of his hand. His are the eyes that are closed, not mine. His are the ears that are clogged. I cannot get through to him any more. He's lost in his words, which are spoken to the rock. The words obsess his mind and spill to the rock, which feels at this moment very much like me, cold and hard, with some hidden spirit. He says a few last words, very beautiful things that I don't write down. Then he throws me. And I travel far.

TWELVE

Arcing through air, up drafts cross skies down limbs to the ground. A gesture has brought me here. It was not my gesture, but it was conclusive, and I fell to where I am. One last roll of the stone. Loose wind through my hair. It is spring on the earth. It is autumn, too. It is being tossed about and trying to hold true. As I listen to the. As I lie with the. As I make light of the

WIND

Spring skies clear. Night clouds move off. Morning wind, born soft and round, remains innocent enough, even though it has grown each hour into a fast young woman. The wind has grown with confidence into a gale, that now, this evening, so harasses the limbs and trembles the skies, so hurls loose the whole world, that who wouldn't take it seriously?

That's one way to say it. Here's another:

Spring skies clear. The end of March, scantily dressed because she is hot, takes the day in hand and launches it with her blows. The wind sings mouthfuls in endless exhale. Trees tip their tops and empty bags sail across streets, over parking lots, pastures and moors. She's so fine, our wind. Is lion. She's free, loose, and easy. She jostles us all. But it is no vice, is it, to have a strong moving voice.

And a third:

Out of the way, clouds. The wind charges, sweeping the heavens blue. I'm coming with my fondles, my flings, my fierce gusts and gales, she announces. And the green clings to the grass, and birds grip their nests, cows hold to the ground, sheep to their fleece. A gaggle of children leaves the earth, rises inches it seems, returns unharmed. Tires lift slightly from the pavement, spin tread. Out of the way, says the wind. I'm feest, I'm spudding blaster, she garbles. As water that sprays from the tops of waves, mists the shore and nearby windowpanes.

A final try to get to the quick of it:

Spring in mind, clear skies above. Unstoppable March wind sacks the afternoon like a gang of teenagers cut loose for the genesis of it. When will the boister be done – this binge on earth with its relentless drunken noise?

Because:

Always the wind, never decease. What a bunch of lunatic rap, embracing the world this way and that. It's just wild enthusiasm, coming to what? A rush of adrenaline, a thrilling ride? No one's as lucky as I, says the funloving wind. So much swagger and sway I make of the world. Bringing blood to the face of the sky.

Blood. To the ringing. Face of the. Sky:

Evening unveils this delinquency as I watch. What's up with you wind, I'd like to know. Where are you taking yourself, talking lip to everyone, stealing across the open and rifling through pages, roughing up the hair of youngsters, adjusting the fur of kittens, and messing with the feathers of birds? You're so overdoing it. It's too much show and not enough subtlety. What's gotten into you?

No response from the blow. It's as if I don't exist. And the evening rolls on with hushing light, haish hish rushing earthward of the sun – to the falls the splurge the splash, ah the wetpaint radish sky, those wide brushed colors, a million primrose blooms, evening rosary, o ranging fleur. Ah, springtime flowers. I am vase. I am looking glass held to the world. The world is upon me, inside me, too. I see the slowing light. I see the dramatic tilt of trees. I see the changing sky. I see every move of the world on some interior canvas. The moves intrude upon my emotions. The wind swings with enough passion to wake the dead. I am not dead. I hear my place on earth. It is attempts at vibrato on every note.

It's a remarkable twilit March that has pounced like a cat, surprising me where I lie in my bed, coming on six o'clock. I have, you see, long since returned to a more fitting habitat. Not so grand or remote as my earlier wilderness. This is a simple room on the most depressing wing of the nursing home. **Whispering Pines At Sunset Cove** they call this place, or some other nonsense. Sometimes there's a smell of urine, but not today, which makes the day special. There's a window somewhere. No TV I C. People sit in the halls. The folk here are everywhere old. Most of them slump. But if I ever go past, which I do now and then, I try to walk upright and show them who I am. It isn't easy. I mean, it isn't easy to walk. I'd rather just lie still. I'm no better than Jana, who I met some days back and she told me while she was eating applesauce that if it was up to her she'd never leave her bed.

"Walking is way overrated," she said.

She looked at her applesauce and sighed.

"I hate this shit. It's cold sweet grainy soup."

Then she told me she hates visitors, too. In no uncertain terms, she swept me the hell out of her room, a place I didn't want to leave because, well, I'd just gotten there, and besides, she didn't know what she was saying. I've always liked applesauce myself, but I held my tongue. The gray woman was lonely and I thought she was just saying things to say them and not meaning to hurt, which sometimes a person does when something bothers her so much that she feels as if a thundercloud hangs over, ready to drench on her and her alone.

So I stayed with Jana then and held her hand, and we looked at the blue sky with sun. No thunderclouds. That was before all this wind came roaring from the west, trying to get us to flinch. Young people came rushing to shut all the windows. But not me. I mean, not mine. I wanted mine open. I told them not to close my window. I told them that I wouldn't be frightened. I told them that I would decide for myself the things in my life. I could deal with the wind no matter what, even if it tried to take my breath away.

Footsteps. A knock on my door. Who is it?

No one.

Some nurse's aid playing games.

I tell you, I'm not in the mood for games. I lie in my crumpled bed in this low lean L-shaped place. There're L's all over **The Whispering Pines**. A hall going long, then left. Sometimes there are T's, and sometimes just I's. No O's or P's or Y's. I'd like an O an N an A. There's no attic room, either, like the one where I used to sleep when I was young. No basement to this place, like the basement I remember where the washing machine would leak and I'd sit there sponging and complaining, *This machine's a piece of junk. Why don't we get another?* But no, we never did. And I would sponge the mess. And I'm sponging still, trying to absorb everything that leaks from my mind, that puddles and pools and damages the floor.

The problem is. Not the wind. It's never the wind. It's never something else. It's me. Can't calm my mind and make sense of things because details derail me. This room, for one. You'd think it'd be easy, but what's going on here? This bed the walls a table a window and, I guess, a door. How would I know there's a door if no one comes? People used to come. I can name some of them. A nurse, for example. Um, Hann. Hannum, I think was her name. Let's make it Hannah plain and simple, bright red cheeks and deep brown eyes. She had a brush in her hand and smelled like lemons and fried chicken, and when she spoke to me it sounded like bees in the springtime or geese in autumn. Once she came with bits of clover in her hair, as if she'd been lying in a field of it. Nice. But that was so long ago.

Now and then I listen to music in my room, the music of baroque masters – Bach, Corelli, Bravado, and Braggadocio. Papers blow off the table like. They float and spin to the. I watch the rise and fall of. I stare and stare at the remarkable. World at my eyes – that's what I'm saying. The beautiful bowing never breaking of trees outside my window, window with trees and sky and. Then, the music stops – Don't stop. I don't want it to stop, but it does anyway. The end of music doesn't mean to make me sad, but I am a bit sad and I know I shouldn't be. I shouldn't be sad because I've had a full life with lots of music, and I've smelled as many flowers as there are days. I've rolled in clover myself a few times like Hannah. And I've seen the surface of water reflect boats and birds and enough blue to impress the sky. I've seen faces. I've seen feelings be hurt. I've seen happiness regained. I've seen bees buzz by like fleeting thoughts. And that's just a few of the many things I've seen with my eyes.

What am I saying? It's been forever since someone's come through the door to bring me to life. Seems a person so old as myself would have a relative or two who could visit. Maybe they're all dead or have forgotten about me or just don't care. God, it'd be nice to see a fresh face, someone young and talented, so excited by the world like a Tom Sawyer or a Nick or Scout or someone. I'm telling you, it would be infectious and I'd be cured of all that's wrong. But no one pokes in his head, his hair disheveled, all smiles to see me, maybe tells me a joke: *Three fish and an oyster walk into a bar*. No one kisses me on the cheek so my heart can be at peace, at joy, at six o'clock this evening, which is really what's important in a relationship isn't it, not the time alone but the time together.

WHAT/EVER

I did not make it to the shore. Instead I came to this single storied building that houses others like me – um people, un people, old people. Just say it. We're at the end of the line. We're all on the brink, tired of breathing, not much to do but look out the window. I've been discarded here on the tassel of town. A fringe character. Easy to forget. I'm a reject on death row, an unfortunate fit. I'm separated from the weave of the world, and it makes me wonder if I ever was a part.

How I was convinced to leave my wilderness, I'll never know. At least there I had the natural world, which exhilarates me if I think about it. And wasn't there even a passer-by once, a Boy Scout or troupe leader lost from his group? He told me his story, and then he was gone and I got depressed. I don't often get depressed, but then I did. I suppose I was a difficult person to accept, living out in the wild, even though the foxes and bears put up so patiently with my intrusion, not to mention the deer. It's hard to believe that I could've survived there for years, for decades, for as long as it took until my whole body was brittle and nearly broke. It's inconceivable that not one fellow human made an effort to find me and bring me back in time. I lay in my wilderness, disintegrating until one day something changed, but by then it was too late. I was picked up as if by the wind and dropped here as an example of what happens when things go too far and all that you once had amounts to nothing. Now, nothing is left of me but this. I don't even have my journal, my worth, my words, or my work. Whatever will I do from here, I wonder?

All my money has been taken. My pockets contain only crumbs. My every worldly possession is gone, except my childhood necklace, which is a miracle that I still have it. I also have this uncomfortable watch on my wrist, and my same old clothes on my back. But not a phone in my hand or a friend beside. Not a book to be read to or a break to be had. No pencil, pen, or feather quill. My journal – who knows? My home – who can say? My family – what of them? My self – I'm at a loss. Whatever I've done with my life is over. Whoever I've loved is gone. And who knows why I've been treated this way? It's malicious and rude. They'll do anything to the elderly nowadays. They'll sell us encyclopedias published thirty years ago, and auto insurance even though we don't own cars. They'll give reduced tuition to the university, or mortgage our gold fillings just to get at our money. I'm amazed they didn't hack my hair and hock it, like in that Magi story. Call me lucky on that score, though who'd want my scraggly hair anyway?

Maybe I'm just being cynical, which really is not like me, but I heard people laughing, saw them pointing as I came up the road. Thinking about it now, it's like a movie I'm watching of myself. I'm in the car, passenger seat. Someone is driving me. I don't look over to see the driver. I'm leaning toward the door, looking out the window. I see my face, as if from the outside, as if I'm also the camera. Then there's a cut to what I'm seeing: Passing trees, blurry foliage, laughing people, the evening sky going red in the face, going black. That's the end of the shot, and it makes me think.

Sometimes what a person does can be very unlike herself, and she doesn't necessarily mean to do it, but there it is anyway. It's hard to figure. It's like the people I saw as I came to this place. They were making faces like the moon as I entered the gates. They were pointing at me like disinterested branches. Next thing I knew there was no more car, no more driver. Movie over. And I was alone here, making my way as best I could.

"Hey granny," someone said.

I looked up. What a gibbous face he had.

"What's that on your back old woman?" he said.

I thought about this for a moment, and then I decided on a particular tree.

"Sassafras," I said, because I liked the word.

"Out of gas?" said the loon.

"Sassafras," I repeated.

"Whatever," said the guy.

I should've explained how a Sassafras tree reminds me of where I was born. But I didn't tell that clown a thing.

It is a nice word, though, isn't it? Sassafras. The fact is, however, I wasn't carrying the tree. The tree was carrying me. How had the Whatever Man not seen that? It was like how Aeneas carried his father on his shoulders, out of the burning Troy. The duffer who asked probably wouldn't even have known who I meant had I said Aeneas. He would've pictured Troy, Michigan or Troy, New York. I'm glad I didn't extend the conversation. I held my head high and listened to my tree. I heard a redwing sing on the branch. I heard a song to the marsh. I heard the tidal world alive in my heart.

And when the tree put me down, that's when I took it up. I planted the Sassafras out back, behind the building in the dirty lot near the dumpster.

"What'd you do that for, granny?" some new jack said, from his perch high above the hedgerow, tossing back sunlight like it was his hair.

"Memorial," was my only word, as if maybe that jay would understand about a Sassafras tree and what it meant to someone like me. Which he didn't. The watcher sat there just as dumb, no sign he recognized either me or my longing.

But I don't mean to suggest that everyone was rude. There is one person who sticks in my mind as being different during my last hours here. I feel it only fair to mention him. His name is Junny or Johnny Boy or something, and he's a thin, quiet kid, somewhat uneven in his eyes, but only because one eye is somewhat more special than the other. When the youngster comes calling, his one eye sees right through me. That's how the saying goes, but I mean that his eye sees *to* me, behind my mess to where I actually am. I'm not sure, however, that he knows his gift. He is, I said, a kid, a mere suggestion of a man. Not more than twelve, thirteen.

If memory serves me, John-Eye has come my way almost every day since I've been here. I first saw him peddling his bike, and I waved for him to join me before he found something better to do. First time, if I'm remembering right, it was late afternoon. I wasn't in my room but kneeling in the dirt out back, thinking about sunflowers, which is a poem by Blake. This boy I'm talking about came wheeling up with a cello rigged to his back. He placed the instrument down to the side and spun in the drive, kicking up gold like an alchemist. Hello, he said, not with a word but with a smart, happy face. I've got no complaints about Johnny Bright. His bike went in circles, then he stopped and handed me a green apple. I didn't take it at first. What could I do with an apple? But he held it and held it until I had to take the biblical thing.

So this boy came often, sometimes with a cello, sometimes not, I don't know why, but I began feeling him out. Story unfolded, the cub has a brother, Oscar, and a sister, too, but I never could figure out where they all lived, even though I thought daily of asking him. Of course, thinking about something doesn't make it happen. Then one evening, being extra brave and sociable, I just spit it out and asked about his life. It was a most remarkable evening, just like now, with a delinquent wind and the sky all blushed with colors. I was sitting at my writing desk, propped with pillows, half looking out the window. The boy sat on a stool nearby, moving his fingers and arms as though the wind lived inside him and he couldn't stop blowing.

Bowing.

Growing.

He couldn't stop growing. I knew he was summing toward something big.

"Now tell me, Ho-John Hum-jo. I need to know where you reside."

"Huh?"

He was no simpleton. I'd just interrupted his playing.

"I'm sorry," I said, when I realized my faux pas.

He lay down his cello, loosened his bow.

"What'd you say?"

"Tell me, good bowboy, son of what man whoso once ploughed the seas and shot the stars before your time, son of what gypsy-eyed mother who's the strongest woman ever to hit high C, hair singing down her back, singeing the eyes of men, tell me where is your home?"

He stared at me like I was crazy.

"I thought you liked Bach."

"You know I do," I said. "Just Bach off with the music and tell me with words."

"I thought it sounded good," he said. "I've almost got the first prelude down."

"You do," I agreed. "It's just you're way too inward. You're only a boy and should be outside playing soccer with your spring buds. What's keeping you inside on a day like today?"

We looked out the window, I from my slump, and he from his stool.

"It's a beautiful March evening," I said.

"Did you say March?"

"No," I said. "I don't want you to go. I don't want this day to be over."

"Can't stop it from ending," he said.

And he was right. The sun had one drip remaining. Who's leaving us now? Listen, he's almost. Last drop of him. Done. No more, no less. The very last of, the very last day. We were officially sunless, then. I watched the trees wave good-bye. Every tree, I loved them all. I saw my Sassafras quiver in a violent push of wind. How my marsh tree had grown. Its leaves were mitts and its bark, I once was told, tasted of licorice.

"You know that tree of yours is no good," said Johnny. "All the other Maples are sugar."

"It's not a Maple, my boy. Sassafras."

"Whatever," he said. "It's dead."

"Give it time," I said.

He packed his instrument into its soft case, made it disappear.

"Well, I guess I have to go. Mama's picking me up."

"So soon. You only just got here."

"What are you talking about?"

"Talking about time. Talking about you. Talking about being. Talking about here."

"I'm hungry," he said, ignoring my talk. "You got anything good?"

"Not a thing."

"What time's it, anyway?" he asked.

"There's a clock somewhere," I said. He looked until he found it on my wrist.

"Since when do you wear a watch?"

"Since I was given it to hold for a few days."

"Who gave it?"

"Who knows," I said. "Now, don't ask any more personal questions. Okay?"

Young John rolled his eyes. "Tomorrow, I'm going with Nick to find a piece of wood to make a bow and arrow. Oscar might be coming home soon. But just for a day."

I watched him with the cello.

"How do you carry such a large instrument?"

"It's easy. Haven't you seen pictures of people from like China and Hong Kong? They've got to carry things tied to them. And they all ride bikes. I've got a book, nothing but pictures."

I nodded.

"It's balance," he said.

"Do you have far to go?" I asked.

"What d'you mean?"

I saw my chance.

"When your mother comes by, where will she take you?" I asked. "With what sort of family do you live? How many dogs, and was there ever one named Homer? How many cats who drink milk? And are there any snakes in your basement, any bats in the belfry, any prints on the wall like Picasso's *Lady Weeping* like *Christ Preaching* by Rembrandt like Sunflower's *Van Gogh*, any pepper on the table, salt spills on the floor, any spices like basil or mustard, cayenne in the top drawer? And do you love your mother Sophie, your father Christopher, your family first and formative, your town and the country, too? Do you do well in school? Alpha beta socialize well? Or do you spend all your time watching movies, playing games, and counting the jellyfish you see from the end of the town dock? What skills have you learned to help you in life? Do you know Fibonacci, limulus, and the whelk? Can you add what's important and subtract what's impostor? And tell me about the books you read. Do you read about social injustice? Or Middle Earth? Or Master Pip? Read any about mollusks, stars, or dowsing for ghosts? Did you know the Dutch put the *H* in ghost just for the hell of it? Or was it the Danes? But really, what craved voyages do you wish to make? To what places strange and far? Spain, Egypt, Patagonia? Do you know the seven seas, the wonders of the world? Do you know eight times nine is nine times eight, yet neither answer is exactly alike because they each have their own address in time and space? 72. 72. They're like twins. They look the same and all but you've got to love them separately. Numbers are pretty cool. People, too. And what do you know of the planet you live on? It's got a core and crinkly mountain ranges. Everyone knows that. There's gold in them there hills and in the sea, as well. And how about the marshy places like Enosh, The Preserve, and Slaughter Creek? You ever heard of Jonesy Island? Ever seen it when the sun first comes up and tinges its trees? That's the best time. And what about Hemming Island where the moon one night and I one night... Let me tell you, I was young, then, and met a guy in the light of the moon and fell in love. I don't mean to bore you, but he and I, we talked forever but it wasn't ever enough. I remember it because for me it's still a fire in my heart that won't go out. Course, that's just how I am, and I don't want to talk about it anymore. So, what about you? What do you say when you catch a glimpse of a snake or follow a thought through the day? Do you move like the tides, never much keeping still? Or do you sit like a shell on the mudflat, holding your tongue? I'm just curious. I don't mean to pry. Do you rock with the waves when you see them? Do you watch speedboats go by and follow the spread of their wakes? You don't need to answer. I'm just asking. Do you fall with the wind when it's up? Spring with the season into light? You ever well up like tears in the eyes, or while away your time listening to music? I only wish to get a sense of you. You seem like a boy who holds to life with ease, and I like that about you. You've got a place to live and a good sense of others. Come on, John. Tell me how it is for you. Tell me where is your home and how."

"My Roman cow?" It was all he had culled from my massive inquiry. He went on, "Some people think of Rome too much and cows too much."

"I'm not asking about those people," I said. "I'm asking about you."

"Ot says he'll take me to the woods in the October somewhere far from here and we'll sleep out under the stars and track foxes and see owls and stuff. It's going—"

John looked out the window, thinking he heard a car.

"Going where?" I asked.

"Going to be fun," he said.

"Did you say trap foxes?" I asked.

"No traps. Traps are torture. Can you imagine what it'd be like to die like that?"

I decided to change the subject.

"Nick. You mentioned him earlier."

"What about him?"

This is important, I wanted to say. This is real. Bring me to life again. Don't leave me now. I'm starving to live. Starting. Like a bird. Starling. Stark raven. Raving mad. Swallowing hope. Coming to nothing. It goes so quick.

He reached my way, handing me an apple from out of thin air, like it was magic. A green one again. It was always green apples with him. Green is my hand in my hand is green, I thought. My whole inside was grim. Gray my growing color as the sun ran off and the light followed in pursuit.

"Granny Smith?" I asked. "Because I'm like your old gram?"

"You like them, right?"

"You're a good kid. Keep picking."

"I didn't pick it. I found it in a bowl."

"Picking, bowling. You've got a knack with that cello."

"It's picking on a guitar. Bowling in an alley. You mean bow."

"Yes, that's what I'm thinking." The bow of a ship. When the bough breaks. Bow tie. Beau regards. About to go. A Canadian boat.

After a moment, John went on.

"Nick's good on the guitar," he said.

"He is."

"Mama's okay, too," said John.

"I wish I could play," I said.

"You know when she sings," began John.

"Who?"

"Mama."

"What about it?"

"Even the saddest songs make you happy," said John.

"That's unbelievable to me," I said. "You know why. It's because I'm inconsolable. When a person gets like this, nothing matters. Nothing helps. Nothing can hurt any more than it already does. And nothing can make me happy. Nothing."

"I think it's weird," said John, ignoring my rant.

"What's weird?"

"To feel sad and happy at the same time."

"It's impossible," I said.

But John insisted that nothing's impossible.

"Something always works out. You just have to want it to happen enough, and then it does."

"Whatever you say," I said.

"Like I like to play. I just do. I want to be in a symphony orchestra, a soloist."

"Well, practice hard," I advised.

"I do."

"And don't take anything for granted."

"What's that mean?"

"Don't take rides from strangers."

"What strangers?"

"And wash behind your ears."

"Why would I do that?"

"Because of crust."

"I don't eat crusts. And I don't put them behind my ears."

"The crust is the worst," I agreed.

"Nuts are okay, but not acorns," he said.

"Well, eat all your broccoli."

"Mama says E coli comes from chickens that are mistreated. She likes free range."

"Freedom takes a lot of work."

"Free range, I said," said John.

"Don't refrain from work," I told him. "And brush your teeth at night," I added. "Rinse and floss. And make some real good friends. Be social, you know. Don't lock yourself in. See the best in people. Don't go swimming alone at night with no one but the moon. Don't drive during a snowstorm or get saddled with death."

"You worry too much."

"I know," I said. "Did I say *death*? I meant *debt*."

"What's debt?"

"It's owing people."

"Like slavery?"

"Owing, not owning."

"Oh," he said.

"Okay," I said. "So, we're good?"

Young John was looking out the window. Or was it the world that looked in at him?

"I hate eating chicken," he said. "Don't you? You ever seen where they have to live? It's a million in a room? I saw a truck once with all the cages piled high, and Ave said they were going to be slaughtered? They were going off to die that day."

"Who?"

"The chickens."

"No, who said it?"

"My sister. She hates to see things die. Can't even kill a fly buzzing around her head. Once she stepped on a spider by accident and it took her all day to get over it. She wrote it a poem."

"What did you say her name was?"

"I don't know. She didn't name it."

"I mean, who wrote the poem?"

"You know the one I mean," he went on. "It's on the fridge."

"Maybe I do," I said to him. "She should have named it Arachne."

"The fridge?"

"No. The spider."

"Oh," said John. He was nodding.

And I wanted to tell him other things, too. Thousands of things. Things that would keep him talking, because I liked how he spoke. His voice hadn't changed yet, it was simple and pure. I wanted to tell him to approach the world in exactly that way, pure and simple, a little each day. I wanted to tell him to always be creative, to find his foundation and build from it, to make great music that fills the skies and flows from the heart and says the things the way words say things to unhide life. Life doesn't want to be hid anymore, it wants to be out in the open. It wants to be useful on earth and spoken of in optimal terms.

But what if the boy had asked me about those terms? Well, I would've told him that they are the words that roots say to the rain and leaves say to the sun. They are the words of the moth who's in love with the lamplight and of the bee in love with the clover. Those are the terms of life I mean. I would've told him these words, too: A stone in your hand, a small dead bug, and a wave that reaches the shore, if you listen. But don't let me tell you what to listen to, I would've said. You've got to do the listening yourself. You've got to know for yourself the goodness and wisdom of life. I wanted to tell him to listen for life in everything, and not to think it isn't there. Don't think for a minute that life isn't there. It is, and you can know it.

I wanted to tell him to listen for me, too, because I was somewhere even if I wasn't. I wanted to be somewhere, just like everybody wants to be somewhere, and I was sad to be missing and sad to have missed out, and in my overwhelming sadness I couldn't find much happiness. I'd missed most everything, really. Even the things that happened in my life, I'd let slip by unnoticed. I'd missed the feeling behind each color, even though I saw those colors. And I'd missed the soft sureness of skin, even though I'd touched it. I'd missed knowing my own family, and enjoying each moment with an unmitigating heart. I'd missed the boat once, and few days of work when I was sick. I had missed the chance to give people hugs and to have a husband and children and playful love. Instead, there was the whole inside-me full of wind blowing through. And I hated the barrenness and didn't want any of that for John. Didn't want him to be unproductive and to miss out on things, on anything. I knew he would get where he wanted to go. I knew he was alive on the earth and would be okay. I knew this, yet could not tell him because I couldn't find the words to secure the fact. I looked and looked and waited and hoped and maybe I saw them, the words, one or two, in the sky with the evening star. Maybe out there with that star. And then...

S CAR

John, the young clue, went from my room before I had a chance to speak. I'd been staring a long while, allowing time to settle without taking it in hand. Then, the moment I turned with some small bit of love to give, the boy was already out the door, walking toward his mother who'd come in her car but did not come in.

From my window I watched the kid approach his mother's car. Someone's car. Mama's car. Standing near the trunk, she was all smiles, like him. Beautiful hair, long down her back in a braid, just like I'd imagined. She fixed his hair. She cupped his shoulder with her palm. They spoke, but I couldn't make out the words, I was so far away. Those words had a mothering touch, though. Their texture was mother, which was 100 percent cotton, 100 percent organic, 100 percent support. I could hear the firmness, the smoothness, the warmth and good. I rubbed my mind over the sounds, back and forth, trying to make heat, practicing the soothe. I liked the feel of what she was saying. It made me question myself – whether or not I'd ever had such a relaxed and accepting quality about me. Whether or not I'd been as comfortable in the world as she.

I had no answer for that, only hope. She was a wonderful mother, I could tell. And it wasn't because she swung by in that old silver car to pick up her boy even though he wasn't down, he wasn't blue, wasn't crimson blush, wasn't rose madder, wasn't cowardly yellow. She was a wonderful mother because she took the apple he offered her and smiled at the gift as if it was the most perfect thing ever. She then bit the apple open, and the flesh sweetened even her mouth, and the juice eased down her throat. It was good. So good, she nodded, her hand on his back. And she loaded his bike and he carried his cello to the front seat, buckled it in like a passenger. And East to the lowlands, they went, as I watched, away from what light remained in the day, away till I hardly knew them. I hardly knew them in my gray hour that day, but I wanted to know. And I didn't know why it mattered, but it did.

A LINGERING BEAT/ONE SEARING THOUGHT

Music of the car, the world, the ride. It was the last time I saw either the boy or his mother. Death seemed so near as to be clapped upon my back, but it was life that kept a hand on me like a residue of light in the darkening air. My enduring candle had been carried away, yet I still knew the flame. There were bright touches that came with wind, and I rode the idea of life as if I still had a chance. If I could rise I would, I thought. If I could change I would. If I could do it all again and find a better way to be...

I did wonder, however, as anyone might, how much better it would be not to draw this out like taffy. Just to die and be done. Or, how much better if time is simply smashed when you least expect it – a massive attack when you're sleeping or a blow to the head when you're lying on the earth looking up at the marvelous sky. How much better, one quick end to the light, one knock to the skull and your candle is snuffed. No insufferable waning of the moon into dark. Rather to be cut off at your fullest and most seen, before you've had a chance to mess up your life. It's got to be better that way, I thought. Only I. I would never accept the shock, the sudden end. I would not go easy. I am meant for this earth.

After John left, I continued to look. Does it matter, I debated, if my life comes to nothing, is nothing? Should I be content with the happiness of others – Boy Johnny, for example, and his Mama? Should I be content that others alone will make something of themselves and not I? Should I think of my life as a path laid out for others as they purposely stride? Walk on me, I am your way, mere stepping-stones for all who can use me. Or is my life like the life of a cripple, a poor woman who is pitied, whose purpose it is to bring forth the goodwill of others? Isn't her role as noble and necessary as the good deed doer? Or the woman, say, with her chronic illness. She suffers for the sake of doctors who might some day, gaining insight through her pain, find a cure. Or think of the baby who dies – why does that baby have to die? She does so not for herself but for all of life, to add her unsullied goodness and her potency to the spiritual stew so others birthed upon the earth may be better nourished. Thus does life gain by loss, by the death of an infant. But what if death comes at nineteen, say? There is no longer that innocence, and the power of life is no longer a gift but a responsibility of the girl herself, something to be taken up with her days. What is to be gained by losing a *nineteen* – that prime number? Wouldn't it be better for her to keep going?

So I continued in my existential way. To be or not to be is not the question to ask. Granted life, the thing is to commit yourself to the unreturnable gift. You've got to do what it takes to live on the earth. And in doing, seek love. Easy to say, isn't it. The difficulty is all the things that come up each day, from a choice between breakfast cereals to a chance to get to know someone. There's no end to the list. And the difficulty also is all the stuff that gets in the way, as if each obstacle isn't exactly what you need.

Something's always in the way, doesn't it seem? How could you need so many impediments? Sometimes it's a slow car in front of you that keeps you from getting a ticket. Sometimes it's a father with his principled ideas. But it's not often death, is it, that puts up a wall and laughs at your inability to get passed? Anyway, how could death be what you need? If death gets in the way of your personal life before you've had time to finish, then the question is: What do you do? Do you roll over and succumb? Do you fight for your self? Do you find some way around the roadblock with your clever mind? Do you make your way through death as if there's nothing wrong, and the circle of life remains unbroken? Do you...

Too many questions. I'm just asking, and I keep asking myself. But I am not ready for any of it. Are you?

A POEM I PROCLAIM

Just beyond, the road reveals no
clarity. I'm disappearing. I am
unable to see who I've been. There is
nowhere for me to go. I'm living
this moment on a world
I'm losing. You, my body,
used to be someone and now
you're lying on the earth hardly
listening. What are the waves saying
to the shore? And people in houses
and cars in drive – the roar of this
world, soaring mountains, rising birds?
No one appears as an encouraging
word. Come again. Come. All
is silence and the air stings
vanishingly, sings one last note
for as long as might be forever

II

And I float like the tremble of sun
light upon the rippled nap of the creek.
How happy the shakiness

makes me – a beautiful persuasion
compelling enough to pull me
through, sparkling to let me be, saying
my name in waves. Roll call, Ave.
I ride the water. I glean the marsh
grass at last. And arrive like a swan,
driftwood, a boat. I land and listen: You
last only a lifetime, says the shore. Then
back to sea in peace and calm, the palm
of night your transport, the quiet lift
of stars

III

What sweetness, what good
is any of that? I don't want to be
at peace in eternal life
that has no sway. What use a voice
that has no say on earth? What purpose
am I if I am not?
Let the wind
blow blows, I'll strike back trees. I'll
shake the shore and shift like sands
to untried forms. I'll reform my time
and undermine the shape of truth
if that is what it takes to say I'm here.
For what good is will, what world
to be, what untilled ground might I
prepare, if I let go my life?

A MONTAGE I MAKE OF ME

It's a remarkable twilit March that has pounced like a cat, surprising me where I lie in my bed, coming on six o'clock.

> **The dead** in the woods lie unknown.
> Tree limbs have no need of names. The owls
> watch for life, then fly away silent.

I open the door of the truck and get out, holding the door for safety. I look at the road where my car has gone off. See the hint of tracks through the furious snow. See no sign of the dead animal. Get back in the cab, snow in my hair. We sit for a quiet stretch, no cars, and no let up to the world around. On account of the weather, the world presses close.

Maybe if I knock on the door a woman will come my way and survey the situation. She'll look at my sneakers, look at my bare hands, look up to my face, and ask me in, ask me what's wrong. And I'll tell her. She'll understand everything.

I sit for the loneliest while and wait. It's like I'm in my grave. I must've done the worst thing in the world to be so deserted. I wait for the twilight to come and go, for the night to begin and end. I wait for the dawn. There's analogy in the dawn.

The straight way has been lost, so I take what curves. I descend unquestioningly. Everything spirals. I know somewhere inside that I'll never make it back to where things are familiar. I'll never get home, even though a curve by degrees becomes a circle. Though that's on one plane, isn't it? The world is different now. Things aren't what they used to be, or, suddenly I've become a stranger.

It really is a welcoming world that awaits her. It really is her joy that sates things, that mates with things and brings them to life. There's no doubt that she's a young, living person. And though to her, her mind may seem small, like the flecks of white asters at the edge of the woods, it is in truth growing larger and burning to sing.

The young woman emerges from the trees, walking on the pathless hill. She hurries down the steep terrain and stumbles toward her house. She's coming from a party, still in her mask. Who is she, really? She might be a Carthage queen, a dogcatcher, or a young farmer with her loose button shirt and heavy shoes.

Outside, the sun mounts the sky. The conversation no longer enters her mind. She stands at the window. The ground is dry and hard. There's been no rain for weeks. She laces her shoes and takes her pack. She carries a chunk of bread and a canteen, hears the kitchen say something about sausage, as out the door into the warm morning air she goes. Stands smelling the heat rise from the ground as the sunlight settles on her.

The girl stares at the marsh and the creek below. "I wish I was somewhere else than home. You know, on some adventure."

Days pass without regret. The light comes forth and subsides. And the whole sky she suckles for years just floating. She suckles the sun, the stars, Venus, the moon. She suckles the rain clouds, the gray clouds, the cumulus and the nimbus. There's plenty of food, plenty of drink. And as the air carries her onward, it leaves upon her brow such a gentle breath that the growing girl smiles as though she is kissed by God.

There is one voice inside many voices, arms around the tiny baby. What words sound as birdsong every now and then, as insect hum and shifting bodies? What words spin winds, sprung of the world? What are these words that jump red and engulf blue, that hone as heat and then coo coo cool? What wetnesses are they and what dry? The words are everywhere. There is no end to the curiosity.

April, she is born. Stars gone early on, larva of day – the dawn.

E PIT O ME

I'm shrinking crazy, more unable each minute. Unstandable, I suffer collapse. What's with this life? My motionless body makes no sense, and the hour does not tick but attacks, as if time is my enemy. Pieces of six strike from the face of my watch, whose broken hands appear as swords. Unattributable music plays in my ears. The notes of wind string me out, cast me in such disbelief from which I cannot return, and the unsympathetic evening knocks me to sleep, dazzlingly slow, beautiful glow, all of it melding, fading, ending. No— Soon I'll see specters who'll whisk me far. Soon I'll hear voices from what unworldly beyond. But I hold my ground, my bedsheets. I hold this place.

I do not like the scene, my inaction. I do not like the play I'm in. I want a different part. There are still words to be said on this side. But the whelm of another, the Angel director in my ears – it does not cease. Silence, silence, he commands my silence. Me I Ave, what good is my adamancy against this foe? What good is defiance? What's my defense?

The months and days, the hours I've lived. The minutes of my story. Nothing makes sense to me. I hold to the world, securing my path, which has been one breath from birth till now. I see no end to my breathing. I brave the vanishing forms. I brave the folding of the light. What good my defeat, what loss my life, what better witness than I to decide my route, my right of passage, my way?

EPIPHANY SPEAKS

It's nothing new, I say.

It's news to me, Ave. I'm intrigued by how you've told your story.

When did you get back?

I've never been away.

Here all this time? I ask.

Time – there's mysteriousness to it, says my guest. Am I your guest? he adds, and then continues: Three minutes after six, the last night of September.

September? How's it September? I could've sworn it was spring.

The minutes keep watch over you, Ave. Here you lie, beside the woods, just outside. You've taken us around the zodiac. You've spun hours and months, but here we are, back together, twelve minutes away from where we started.

So much for my life, then, I say. Still, I won't go.

You left home early, not long after Nicolas. Where was he going again?

Again and again with your questions.

You spent the day out walking. You packed a lunch. You went into the wind. You lifted from the earth like a bird. You took such delight. You gave back joy. You couldn't believe how lucky you were. You returned to this spot not far from home. Your mind was bright, your body warm. You lay on this hill just outside the woods. Just for a moment, you said to yourself, till it was time to go back down.

When was that? I ask. I don't have the feel of it anymore.

The autumn olives, the goldenrod around. Ah, sunflowers. And treetops still hold sway, fighting for freedom against their stubborn trunks. What do you think of this wind, now?

I feel nothing good or new. Didn't I just say that? Weren't you listening? All I can say is that my eyes are stupid blind. Blindness comes from the greatest stupidity. It wasn't always this way. What's happened? Don't answer that. I won't let anyone speak for me. You say I'm outside. You say I'm out in the wind, dying light. It's the last day of September and I'm, you tell me, on my back. Tree limbs above me. Trees, you say. Windswept trees above. I don't need you to tell me things. I know what's going on.

I know you do, Ave.

I see in my mind a beautiful place. I see in my heart where I wish to be. I know where I am.

Ah, Sweetie. You are my spring. I am your soul. We can walk from here together.

Ah, nothing. I know where I am, and I'm not ready to leave.

So, You've got nothing to say to that. Why don't you have something to say?

The story won't end here, Ave.

I know it won't end. As long as I stay, there's hope.

What I mean is, there are so many places for you to go with life. They wait to greet you.

So many, you say. You can't take me away.

I would never do that. But I can't give you more time here, either.

There's plenty of time, I say. The whole world is time. There's a sky shaped by wind and orbit and all that moves. There's a house at my back, some home lit by the sun. And the shore plays like children somewhere near. Voices of children. Salt spray nips my nostrils and rough waters rip at my mind. And look – a blue person flies over grass, loose and free, grace and easy living. Look at her. She's light as a feather and sanguine as an elf. Who is it, this fairy, this blue sprite? Is she coming to play with me like I'm nine and she's my best friend? Is she coming to talk about snakes and stuff, to deliver a message about some boy or news from across the water? Will she talk blue to me, like her dress? There are orange words of sunset. Yeah, I like what she's doing. Do I even know her, though? So I look again. It's a sham. What a shame. She's no one, really. A blue dress flipping out on the clothesline. Flapping hard to get – nowhere. And it's not even a clothesline in this room where I'm now. Not even. But in my memory is all. And I don't even remember when or where or even if it happened. A wavery blue dress is what I see of a person and it brings to mind nothing really, maybe a thought of wrinkled water. What is it, some irony – this? Needs ironing. Needs substance. What? The point is, it's no life at all. That girl is no one, just a dress I must have seen drying on the line outside some house. Call it mine, if you want. Thirty-three Livet Lane, Island View, Enosh by the marsh, by the bay, in the beginning – Bang. A world I used to know, I guess. Trees, fields, snakes, and squirrels. They exist as shadows, and fading ones at that, in my head my soul my view – whatever. I feel used up, or maybe just used. All I want is shore, this earth, a place to be, but it's nowhere near me now. I'd walk there if I had the energy, but it's no life now. There is no life to me, only stupid pictures. My mind playing games. And it isn't funny. Not a fun game.

You've got a good imagination, Ave.

What's that supposed to mean?

Where are you, Ave?

In this room. On this bed. Old lonely loony blind me. Fighting for my life.

And the girl who lies dead outside these woods? The one we were talking about only a moment ago? The one who saw Nicolas this morning? The one who left after breakfast? The one who walked here?

Whose life is hers – I cannot know – was last seen in this world, though.

I thought you were waking out of this dream.

Think again, my friend.

I see you better than you see yourself, Ave.

Puff of air is what you see. Venting words.

Preventing, yes.

Preventing what?

You, mostly. I should tell you more directly.

No one wants to hear more nonsense. It's sentimental crap. Just leave it alone.

We're trying to get somewhere, Ave.

I don't want to go.

Just like this girl. She won't get up.

I'm not interested in her.

She's nothing but a child, Ave. You might think she's done nothing with her life. Nothing worth saying. You might think—

I don't want to listen to what you've got to say about her. I've said it already. I've said it with feeling the way it's meant to be known. Why are you bothering me with more words? There's no welcome for them. You pester, you poke and prod and press. It's like my body is covered with you. You hover everywhere. Why? To fill my space with your own until I'm gone. I'd rather make my way, figure things for myself. Study that girl, you say. I don't know her. I don't know why she won't get up. Maybe you've put her to sleep. Maybe you've dulled her senses. I seem to remember a happy girl, once. She was like a gull by day, a cygnet hugging the shore. Nobody shot her. Nobody would. Mud between her toes. Smell of the marsh baking in the sun. Then I was not her any more. I had breasts and adult thoughts. I couldn't fly, but nothing was lost, don't you get it. There was an even better world that I could live with and love. I began to insist on being a grateful member of that world. And why not? I figured I could master it. But no chance at that, was there. It all came to ruin, and there was no one to tell me why, no one to explain the collapse. And now I'm old like a horseshoe crab, an ancient shark tooth, a snapping turtle, a...

I should make up my mind. Stop this chatter. Be strong and say what I want. Do what I want. Be what I— One strong move to counter the darkness. Two minutes more. Don't give up on me, yet. Three minutes, three is all I need. A little time to say what I'm trying to say. Stay near till I've finished. You've got nowhere to go, do you?

No, sweetie. I don't.

You don't have to rip me with your words, do you?

I wouldn't say *rip*.

You scare me hovering over. Your giant hand. A crush of. I'm afraid to listen to anything you might say. Where can it lead? It can't go well. Keep your thoughts to yourself. They'll kill me. I'd rather just die on my own of natural causes. Of old age, like that Chinese man who told the emperor how he wished to die. You know the story?

I think so.

You can have my necklace, if you want. You can have it when I'm gone. Take it right off my neck. Give the watch back to Nicolas. I wish you could give him my love, but I don't know what it is. I don't know where I am any longer. Just leave me in peace and I'll think it out. I...

I had a family once. Mother, father, dogs, cats, house. All of it. I've lost them. Two brothers. I can't picture them when I think. Thinking does nothing for me. And what does it matter? Friends, animals, asters, oysters, oars in the water, stars in the night sky. O, I was happy somewhere in my life. I sat in trees. I walked in mud. Stood around. I was in love, too. And he was in love with me. Wind, you asked me before. When his hair blew on his face, he'd brush it off. And his hand would be empty, so he'd brush it again. Beautiful person. I liked how he brushed against my life. I liked his body. I liked my body, too. I liked my being with him. He'd touch my breasts and I'd wake in his touch like a flower in the sun. And the Seraphim in Heaven did not covet our love but were happy for us. They took in our love as though it were breathing to them. They fed upon it and were filled. Our love made them radiant with marks of light. I saw the light every-where I looked: the gleaming rim of a puddle, the spark on an oyster shell, and sheen on a leaf. You know.

Who are these Seraphim, Ave?

I felt it inside me. This life. Love. I remember it now: I was standing in a storm, in a barn once, in the blue eyes of another, in love with a man. His face never startled me to look at it, so I looked again and was rooted and at the same time released like a sigh. I looked again – small hairs on his arms, and my blood went wild. Did I only want him and nothing more? I was happy and rocked like a boat in the harbor when the wind comes gentle up your back and up your shirt and you feel it on your skin, maybe goose bumps. You are in hands and the hands are in love with you. So I drove his car with the windows down, to let in the wind, to let my mind discover things by blows. When we were out together, we looked at shadow geometry on the walls of old barns and at purple clover where fence pickets grew from the ground. We looked at geese in their Vees and listened to the arc talk of gulls. I don't know what we ourselves talked about, but we must've talked. I know we talked. And walked hot in fields with the ruts and cows. Sweated in town, went for a drink of water or beer or, took the boat to the point and swam real cool. We real cool. And what we did we only did some. Do you know what I'm saying? Only did it some. There is this earth and it's a lot more to know. And we did what we did to get only where? Coordinate geometry. X Y. To shape ourselves how? To curve somewhere round? To link? Together? To...

But I. I went out alone, didn't I? Left the house in the morning, green apples on the table from my brother, John. Nick's canvas half finished of me. I think it was blues. I think it was browns. I think it was greens. I walked east toward the home where I grew up. I went by myself after breakfast and thought of Van Gogh because Nico because he gave me a book and because the wind in the sky whirled ideas, and I thought of his skin under what he was wearing, which was a ripped shirt, which was his favorite shirt. And where I walked was back roads, off roads, green paths, fields and branches and roots. The country was mine. The rural I roamed. I was endless that day just following my heart. I was so lucky, the luckiest I. And saw over trees toward the marsh and creeks. Saw beyond trees to the water I hoped for. Headed the direction where I was born, no reason really, but it was a long way off and I had all day. I didn't need to get there. I didn't really need anything. I had it all inside me. Beside me. Alive. How the branches blew and the leaves tore at the sky. Howl, hiss of leaves against the blue beautiful sky. There it was. This earth, you know. And I'd had it so often that you'd think the earth was nothing special, and the sun just an ordinary star. But nothing is ordinary that you begin to see with your heart. The world and I rode and spun and we were mapped in what some might say is a forgettable corner of a casual galaxy. Yet, I was centered, at home in the universe, sun above, fast feasting wind, and earth under me. It was all, all and also not enough. And I ran I walked I stopped to take it in. My home is humble. My home is here and now. My home is growing, I thought. No stopping it. I sat in the field and light fed me, thoughts flooded over like a slow tide that did not sweep me off but gave me lift. I could have drowned in thoughts, but I sailed, ballasted with wonder, ready for outrageous fortune and all the more world yet to come. Arms around me, hands I'd give my own hands to. I'd give my shoes, my shirt, my thoughts, my praise. I loved the flow of my mind, the ease, and my open eyes. I loved the wind on my face. I loved the waving trees and the audacity of myself that was not a breakable thing, but a bend-able, workable, sayable thing.

I was in love – and wasn't it someone? Did I make up that love? I don't remember making. He was shy and reflective like the still creek, speaking both on the surface and deep in me. My blood was excited just to hear his voice. I was a body circulating his word and mine – a dream of the future in ever increasing rounds.

Then there I stood at the edge of the woods. A lure of light. I must have been leaning on lure. Everything, everything brought me closer. Then I lay on the ground for a minute, just looking. I looked where the tall maples danced. Their green leaves rolled with wind and called my name, churning and hissing on my mind, as though my mind was a shore for the waves for the day for the loose and the lay of the wind. I never saw any water the whole of the day, but dew and then acres of blue sky, acres to sail upon. To explore again. Never to cease exploring. It will never be enough. This earth, this universe. To find out and fill it infinitely till I know where I am. Till I am where I know.

> How came this marshling
> From God's love to
> Acres of mud and green
> From the mystery to the cove
> From unseen to seen

Ave Isolde Anabel Me. That this is who I am. I've been on shady ground, shaded on the ground ever since the sun went behind the low clouds. I'm in trouble or troubled, trembling like the leaves. I don't know what's right with the world or what's going to be left of me. I don't know what is Ave, and what is not, but that the feeling I pin to the name is sadness. And the days having passed are dark inside me, the hours, I mean years, amount to no fulfilled life, no sense but separation, a detachment from being. And though I know it's not true, it also is.

And who cares how much I cry? No angel. No one. Who cares, now, as though everything has left me that helped me here? It helps me now no more. I have a misbegotten heavenly forgotten yes forsaken so I cannot waken it place in my soul. As though life spat me out, cut me loose and left me lonely, on my own. Why, I'm so confused, so wrinkled now in my soul, as though I've been sworn down by time. Damn her stubbornness, says the clock. Why won't she quit? But I don't, not yet. My clock is in, it's eternal. I will not die. I will decide. And I count slow like this:

One

Two

Thr...

I don't want to finish the last word. I want to regain what's been lost to me. I want to reclaim my body and regale myself with life. I want to rev up my time and take it to the world again. I get nothing out of what I'm not, cannot get where I'm wishing to be. I want to see myself wide creek creation, bay, beginning sea. I want to see myself vast as a wetland sanctuary, with air that tramples grasses, the crisis of wind sidling by. Give me storm, me driving rain. I am unafraid of any scene.

Even I who am unsure know that God would not so swiftly dissever a person from her life, banish her from the self she's grown like a plant that hasn't yet gone to seed. It is not likely. It is not possible. I can't believe that she will not rise like the moon from the bed of earth, bloom like a night owl, walk for me home along the road, talk to Nicolas soon, body and soul, speak of this world in wide and wider circles of self.

Ave, wake up. Who are you lying around like that this last evening of September? Don't be so lazy, so heavy and grave on the ground, so grim. Get up and be heard. You'll stand strong as red oak. You'll go home cross the field, braving the wind. You'll find Nico waiting for you there, curve your hand over his arm, straighten your eyes into his. I know this. And you're only a child, nineteen and a half. Sweet gum. I see you now. Red maple. I see you there on the tufts of grass, the autumn ground. Thoughts will stir you. You'll make for the ocean as though there're still other shores to be had, so much of the earth to be found, to be made firm in your soul, and molded inside you – what life itself may be. Do you have any idea? Some day, who knows, you may even return here, come to be lying on your back this very spot, much like today, maybe come springtime, some March, winter December, smooth June, looking at the evening star, one hand on the earth, one hand on your leg. And what will you say then, looking at the world? I wish I could know it. The things you will say. And I wish I could foresee that day enough to make it so. What far-reaching benevolence will stream from you that all leaves and birds and human souls will be still for a moment? I look forward to leaning upon your words and learning from you. I wish I could hear the words now. But even so I know the gist. I know what you'll say. It'll be a symphony of existence, each word an instrument, and all that you play will be in the direction of love. You'll say what's always been in you to say, only more pronounced. And I will listen better then. My patience will have doubled. My thinking will have sharpened. How I look forward to that time when my heart will be a fearless receptacle. I'll listen to the lines of you. Light by light, together we'll understand what before we did not.

Do you see it now? I'm not willing to die. Too many people and too much hope. There is loads of love that I've never said. Let me have my say with you. You are captain, you are the eye of my soul, my seeking life. Eyes on me, I am audible. Hear it that I may have a body to be. Hear me that I am not lost in the dark.

Hear anyone hear what I say, that I may live on in Ave live on as Ave, as wave after wave upon the shore until all my saying is this life on earth and there is no more here to do. Do not turn it off just yet.

> God I am not you
> There is no woven
> There is no unity
> My words go nowhere
> Still strong the sound I
> Wings beat on for
> Love of life and have
> No end to wishing
> I am unweakened
> Let each word work me
> One that sings me and I
> Will unfold my being
> That love brings life to
> The world, the world of
> Abode a body – how
>   may I
>
> Fulfill it

LIGHT ON THE WALL

With dancing shadows. The morning sun shines through the windblown branches. It streams into the room and visibly sings.

Wake up, Ave.

She's still asleep. Her mother enters the attic and leans over the bed. Ave is a child, twelve years old. No end to her wishes that fortell who she'll be, no end to her future. Her mother looks at Ave's sweet, round face and the covers of the bed in the shape of her body. Why wake her, she thinks, but the girl needs to get up. It's bright and early. There's breakfast, there's school, there are things to get done. If not right now, then soon enough.

Sophie her mother moves her hand near Ave's shoulder to give her a gentle shove. Shadows dance on the wall where there is no light. Where there is light, there are no shadows. The thing about the shadows and light is how beautifully they work together. The earth is no place for aloneness. Day and night. Shadow with light. One moment without the next, one person without another, just isn't as good.

Sophie's hand comes near. The morning keeps pace, but doesn't interrupt. A gentle love, and words again.

Did you just say something? asks Ave, her eyes still closed.

Good morning, sweetie, says her mother.

What time is it?

It's time to wake up.

www.ingramcontent.com/pod-product-compliance
Lightning Source LLC
Chambersburg PA
CBHW062132170626
46813CB00002B/668